OUTDOORLAND

R. W. CHAMBERS

CHAPTER I

HIS OWN PEOPLE

"You never met Selwyn, did you?"

"No, sir."

"Never heard anything definite about his trouble?" insisted Gerard.

"Oh, yes, sir!" replied young Erroll, "I've heard a good deal about it. Everybody has, you know."

"Well, I *don't* know," retorted Austin Gerard irritably, "what 'everybody' has heard, but I suppose it's the usual garbled version made up of distorted fact and malicious gossip. That's why I sent for you. Sit down."

Gerald Erroll seated himself on the edge of the big, polished table in Austin's private office, one leg swinging, an unlighted cigarette between his lips.

Austin Gerard, his late guardian, big, florid, with that peculiar blue eye which seems to characterise hasty temper, stood by the window, tossing up and catching the glittering gold piece—souvenir of the directors' meeting which he had just left.

"What has happened," he said, "is this. Captain Selwyn is back in town—sent up his card to me, but they told him I was attending a directors' meeting. When the meeting was over I found his card and a message scribbled, saying he'd recently landed and was going uptown to call on Nina. She'll keep him there, of course, until I get home, so I shall see him this evening. Now, before you meet him, I want you to plainly understand the truth about this unfortunate affair; and that's why I telephoned your gimlet-eyed friend Neergard just now to let you come around here for half an hour."

The boy nodded and, drawing a gold matchbox from his waistcoat pocket, lighted his cigarette.

"Why the devil don't you smoke cigars?" growled Austin, more to himself than to Gerald; then, pocketing the gold piece, seated himself heavily in his big leather desk-chair.

"In the first place," he said, "Captain Selwyn is my brother-in-law—which wouldn't make an atom of difference to me in my judgment of what has happened if he had been at fault. But the facts of the case are these." He held up an impressive forefinger and laid it flat across the large, ruddy palm of the other hand. "First of all, he married a cat! C-a-t, cat. Is that clear, Gerald?"

"Yes, sir."

"Good! What sort of a dance she led him out there in Manila, I've heard. Never mind that, now. What I want you to know is how he behaved— with what quiet dignity, steady patience, and sweet temper under constant provocation and mortification, he conductedhimself. Then that fellow Ruthven turned up—and—Selwyn is above that sort of suspicion. Besides, his scouts took the field within a week."

He dropped a heavy, highly coloured fist on his desk with a bang.

"After that hike, Selwyn came back, to find that Alixe had sailed with Jack Ruthven. And what did he do; take legal measures to free himself, as you or I or anybody with an ounce of temper in 'em would have done? No; he didn't. That infernal Selwyn conscience began to get busy, making him believe that if a woman kicks over the traces it must be because of some occult shortcoming on his part. In some way or other that man persuaded himself of his responsibility for her misbehaviour. He knew what it meant if he didn't ask the law to aid him to get rid of her; he knew perfectly well that his silence meant acknowledgment of culpability; that he couldn't remain in the service under such suspicion.

"And now, Gerald," continued Austin, striking his broad palm with extended forefinger and leaning heavily forward, "I'll tell you what sort of a man Philip Selwyn is. He permitted Alixe to sue him for absolute divorce—and, to give her every chance to marry Ruthven, he refused to defend the suit. That sort of chivalry is very picturesque, no doubt, but it cost him his career—set him adrift at thirty-five, a man branded as having been divorced from his wife for cause, with no profession left him, no business, not much money—a man in the prime of life and hope and ambition, clean in thought and deed; an upright, just, generous, sensitive man, whose whole career has been blasted because he was too merciful, too generous to throw the blame where it belonged. And it belongs on the shoulders of that Mrs. Jack Ruthven—Alixe Ruthven—whose name you may see in the columns of any paper that truckles to the sort of society she figures in."

Austin stood up, thrust his big hands into his pockets, paced the room for a few moments, and halted before Gerald.

"If any woman ever played me a dirty trick," he said, "I'd see that the public made no mistake in placing the blame. I'm that sort"—he shrugged—"Phil Selwyn isn't; that's the difference—and it may be in his favour from an ethical and sentimental point of view. All right; let it go at that. But all I meant you to understand is that he is every inch a man; and when you have the honour to meet him, keep that fact in the back of your head, among the few brains with which Providence has equipped you."

"Thanks!" said Gerald, colouring up. He cast his cigarette into the empty fireplace, slid off the edge of the table, and picked up his hat. Austin eyed him without particular approval.

"You buy too many clothes," he observed. "That's a new suit, isn't it?"

"Certainly," said Gerald; "I needed it."

"Oh! if you can afford it, all right. . . . How's the nimble Mr. Neergard?"

"Neergard is flourishing. We put through that Rose Valley deal. I tell you what, Austin, I wish you could see your way clear to finance one or two—"

Austin's frown cut him short.

"Oh, all right! You know your own business, of course," said the boy, a little resentfully. "Only as Fane, Harmon & Co. have thought it worth while—"

"I don't care what Fane, Harmon think," growled Austin, touching a button over his desk. His stenographer entered; he nodded a curt dismissal to Gerald, adding, as the boy reached the door:

"Your sister expects you to be on hand to-night—and so do we."

Gerald halted.

"I'd clean forgotten," he began; "I made another—a rather important engagement—"

But Austin was not listening; in fact, he had already begun to dictate to his demure stenographer, and Gerald stood a moment, hesitating, then turned on his heel and went away down the resounding marble corridor.

"They never let me alone," he muttered; "they're always at me—following me up as though I were a schoolboy. . . . Austin's the worst—never satisfied. . . . What do I care for all these functions—sitting around with the younger set and keeping the cradle of conversation rocking? I won't go to that infernal baby-show!"

He entered the elevator and shot down to the great rotunda, still scowling over his grievance. For he had made arrangements to join a card-party at Julius Neergard's rooms that night, and he had no intention of foregoing that pleasure just because his sister's first grown-up dinner-party was fixed for the same date.

As for this man Selwyn, whom he had never met, he saw no reason why he should drop business and scuttle uptown in order to welcome him. No doubt he was a good fellow; no doubt he had behaved very decently in a matter which, until a few moments before, he had heard little about. He meant to be civil; he'd look up Selwyn when he had a chance, and ask him to dine at the club. But this afternoon he couldn't do it; and, as for the evening, he had made his arrangements, and he had no intention of disturbing them on Austin's account.

4

When he reached his office he picked up the telephone and called up Gerard's house; but neither his sister nor anybody else was there except the children and servants, and Captain Selwyn had not yet called. So he left no message, merely saying that he'd call up again. Which he forgot to do.

Meanwhile Captain Selwyn was sauntering along Fifth Avenue under the leafless trees, scanning the houses of the rich and great across the way; and these new houses of the rich and great stared back at him out of a thousand casements as polished and expressionless as the monocles of the mighty.

And, strolling at leisure in the pleasant winter weather, he came presently to a street, stretching eastward in all the cold impressiveness of very new limestone and plate-glass.

Could this be the street where his sister now lived?

As usual when perplexed he slowly raised his hand to his moustache; and his pleasant gray eyes, still slightly blood-shot from the glare of the tropics, narrowed as he inspected this unfamiliar house.

The house was a big elaborate limestone affair, evidently new. Winter sunshine sparkled on lace-hung casement, on glass marquise, and the burnished bronze foliations of grille and door.

It was flood-tide along Fifth Avenue; motor, brougham, and victoria swept by on the glittering current; pretty women glanced out from limousine and tonneau; young men of his own type, silk-hatted, frock-coated, the crooks of their walking sticks tucked up under their left arms, passed on the Park side.

But the nods of recognition, lifted hats, the mellow warnings of motor horns, clattering hoofs, the sun flashing on carriage wheels and polished panels, on liveries, harness, on the satin coats of horses—a gem like a spark of fire smothered by the sables at a woman's throat, and the bright indifference of her beauty—all this had long since lost any meaning for him. For him the pageant passed as the west wind passes in Samar over the glimmering valley grasses; and he saw it through sun-dazzled eyes—all this, and the leafless trees beyond against the sky, and the trees mirrored in a little wintry lake as brown as the brown of the eyes which were closed to him now forever.

As he stood there, again he seemed to hear the whistle signal, clear, distant, rippling across the wind-blown grasses where the brown constabulary lay firing in the sunshine; but the rifle shots were the crack of whips, and it was only a fat policeman of the traffic squad whistling to clear the swarming jungle trails of the great metropolis.

5

Again Selwyn turned to the house, hesitating, unreconciled. Every sun-lit window stared back at him.

He had not been prepared for so much limestone and marquise magnificence where there was more renaissance than architecture and more bay-window than both; but the number was the number of his sister's house; and, as the street and the avenue corroborated the numbered information, he mounted the doorstep, rang, and leisurely examined four stiff box-trees flanking the ornate portal—meagre vegetation compared to what he had been accustomed to for so many years.

Nobody came; once or twice he fancied he heard sounds proceeding from inside the house. He rang again and fumbled for his card case. Somebody was coming.

The moment that the door opened he was aware of a distant and curious uproar—far away echoes of cheering, and the faint barking of dogs. These seemed to cease as the man in waiting admitted him; but before he could make an inquiry or produce a card, bedlam itself apparently broke loose somewhere in the immediate upper landing—noise in its crudest elemental definition—through which the mortified man at the door strove to make himself heard: "Beg pardon, sir, it's the children broke loose an' runnin' wild-like—"

"The *what?*"

"Only the children, sir—fox-huntin' the cat, sir—"

His voice was lost in the yelling dissonance descending crescendo from floor to floor. Then an avalanche of children and dogs poured down the hall-stairs in pursuit of a rumpled and bored cat, tumbling with yelps and cheers and thuds among the thick rugs on the floor.

Here the cat turned and soundly cuffed a pair of fat beagle puppies, who shrieked and fled, burrowing for safety into the yelling heap of children and dogs on the floor. Above this heap legs, arms, and the tails of dogs waved wildly for a moment, then a small boy, blond hair in disorder, staggered to his knees, and, setting hollowed hand to cheek, shouted: "Hi! for'rard! Harkaway for'rard! Take him, Rags! Now, Tatters! After him, Owney! Get on, there, Schnitzel! Worry him, Stinger! Tally-ho-o!"

At which encouraging invitation the two fat beagle pups, a waddling dachshund, a cocker, and an Irish terrier flew at Selwyn's nicely creased trousers; and the small boy, rising to his feet, became aware of that astonished gentleman for the first time.

"Steady, there!" exclaimed Selwyn, bringing his walking stick to a brisk bayonet defence; "steady, men! Prepare to receive infantry—and doggery, too!" he added, backing away. "No quarter! Remember the Alamo!"

6

The man at the door had been too horrified to speak, but he found his voice now.

"Oh, you hush up, Dawson!" said the boy; and to Selwyn he added tentatively, "Hello!"

"Hello yourself," replied Selwyn, keeping off the circling pups with the point of his stick. "What is this, anyway—a Walpurgis hunt?—or Eliza and the bloodhounds?"

Several children, disentangling themselves from the heap, rose to confront the visitor; the shocked man, Dawson, attempted to speak again, but Selwyn's raised hand quieted him.

The small boy with the blond hair stepped forward and dragged several dogs from the vicinity of Selwyn's shins.

"This is the Shallowbrook hunt," he explained; "I am Master of Hounds; my sister Drina, there, is one of the whips. Part of the game is to all fall down together and pretend we've come croppers. You see, don't you?"

"I see," nodded Selwyn; "it's a pretty stiff hunting country, isn't it?"

"Yes, it is. There's wire, you know," volunteered the girl, Drina, rubbing the bruises on her plump shins.

"Exactly," agreed Selwyn; "bad thing, wire. Your whips should warn you."

The big black cat, horribly bored by the proceedings, had settled down on a hall seat, keeping one disdainful yellow eye on the dogs.

"All the same, we had a pretty good run," said Drina, taking the cat into her arms and seating herself on the cushions; "didn't we, Kit-Ki?" And, turning to Selwyn, "Kit-Ki makes a pretty good fox—only she isn't enough afraid of us to run away very fast. Won't you sit down? Our mother is not at home, but we are."

"Would you really like to have me stay?" asked Selwyn.

"Well," admitted Drina frankly, "of course we can't tell yet how interesting you are because we don't know you. We are trying to be polite—" and, in a fierce whisper, turning on the smaller of the boys— "Winthrop! take your finger out of your mouth and stop staring at guests! Billy, you make him behave himself."

The blond-haired M.F.H. reached for his younger brother; the infant culprit avoided him and sullenly withdrew the sucked finger but not his fascinated gaze.

"I want to know who he ith," he lisped in a loud aside.

"So do I," admitted a tiny maid in stickout skirts.

7

Drina dropped the cat, swept the curly hair from her eyes, and stood up very straight in her kilts and bare knees.

"They don't really mean to be rude," she explained; "they're only children." Then, detecting the glimmering smile in Selwyn's eyes, "But perhaps you wouldn't mind telling us who you are because we all would like to know, but we are not going to be ill-bred enough to ask."

Their direct expectant gaze slightly embarrassed him; he laughed a little, but there was no response from them.

"Well," he said, "as a matter of fact and record, I am a sort of relative of yours—a species of avuncular relation."

"What is that?" asked Drina coldly.

"That," said Selwyn, "means that I'm more or less of an uncle to you. Hope you don't mind. You don't have to entertain me, you know."

"An uncle!" repeated Drina.

"Our uncle?" echoed Billy. "You are not our soldier uncle, are you? You are not our Uncle Philip, are you?"

"It amounts to that," admitted Selwyn. "Is it all right?"

There was a dead silence, broken abruptly by Billy; "Where is your sword, then?"

"At the hotel. Would you like to see it, Billy?"

The five children drew a step nearer, inspecting him with merciless candour.

"Is it all right?" asked Selwyn again, smilingly uneasy under the concentrated scrutiny. "How about it, Drina? Shall we shake hands?"

Drina spoke at last: "Ye-es," she said slowly, "I think it is all right to shake hands." She took a step forward, stretching out her hand.

Selwyn stooped; she laid her right hand across his, hesitated, looked up fearlessly, and then, raising herself on tiptoe, placed both arms upon his shoulders, offering her lips.

One by one the other children came forward to greet this promising new uncle whom the younger among them had never before seen, and whom Drina, the oldest, had forgotten except as that fabled warrior of legendary exploits whose name and fame had become cherished classics of their nursery.

And now children and dogs clustered amicably around him; under foot tails wagged, noses sniffed; playful puppy teeth tweaked at his coat-skirts; and in front and at either hand eager flushed little faces were upturned to his, shy hands sought his and nestled confidently into the hollow of his palms or took firm proprietary hold of sleeve and coat.

"I infer," observed Selwyn blandly, "that your father and mother are not at home. Perhaps I'd better stop in later."

"But you are going to stay here, aren't you?" exclaimed Drina in dismay. "Don't you expect to tell us stories? Don't you expect to stay here and live with us and put on your uniform for us and show us your swords and pistols? *Don't* you?"

"We have waited such a very long time for you to do this," added Billy.

"If you'll come up to the nursery we'll have a drag-hunt for you," pleaded Drina. "Everybody is out of the house and we can make as much noise as we please! Will you?"

"Haven't you any governesses or nurses or something?" asked Selwyn, finding himself already on the stairway, and still being dragged upward.

"Our governess is away," said Billy triumphantly, "and our nurses can do nothing with us."

"I don't doubt it," murmured Selwyn; "but where are they?"

"Somebody must have locked them in the schoolroom," observed Billy carelessly. "Come on, Uncle Philip; we'll have a first-class drag-hunt before we unlock the schoolroom and let them out."

"Anyway, they can brew tea there if they are lonely," added Drina, ushering Selwyn into the big sunny nursery, where he stood, irresolute, looking about him, aware that he was conniving at open mutiny. From somewhere on the floor above persistent hammering and muffled appeals satisfied him as to the location and indignation of the schoolroom prisoners.

"You ought to let them out," he said. "You'll surely be punished."

"We will let them out after we've made noise enough," said Billy calmly. "We'll probably be punished anyway, so we may as well make a noise."

"Yes," added Drina, "we are going to make all the noise we can while we have the opportunity. Billy, is everything ready?"

And before Selwyn understood precisely what was happening, he found himself the centre of a circle of madly racing children and dogs. Round and round him they tore. Billy yelled for the hurdles and Josephine knocked over some chairs and dragged them across the course of the route; and over them leaped and scrambled children and puppies, splitting the air with that same quality of din which had greeted him upon his entrance to his sister's house.

When there was no more breath left in the children, and when the dogs lay about, grinning and lolling, Drina approached him, bland and dishevelled.

9

"That circus," she explained, "was for your entertainment. Now will you please do something for ours?"

"Certainly," said Selwyn, looking about him vaguely; "shall we—er—build blocks, or shall I read to you—er—out of that big picture-book—"

"*Picture*-book!" repeated Billy with scorn; "that's good enough for nurses to read. You're a soldier, you know. Soldiers have real stories to tell."

"I see," he said meekly. "What am I to tell you about—our missionaries in Sulu?"

"In the first place," began Drina, "you are to lie down flat on the floor and creep about and show us how the Moros wriggle through the grass to bolo our sentinels."

"Why, it's—it's this way," began Selwyn, leaning back in his rocking-chair and comfortably crossing one knee over the other; "for instance, suppose—"

"Oh, but you must *show* us!" interrupted Billy. "Get down on the floor please, uncle."

"I can tell it better!" protested Selwyn; "I can show you just the—"

"Please lie down and show us how they wriggle?" begged Drina.

"I don't want to get down on the floor," he said feebly; "is it necessary?"

But they had already discovered that he could be bullied, and they had it their own way; and presently Selwyn lay prone upon the nursery floor, impersonating a ladrone while pleasant shivers chased themselves over Drina, whom he was stalking.

And it was while all were passionately intent upon the pleasing and snake-like progress of their uncle that a young girl in furs, ascending the stairs two at a time, peeped perfunctorily into the nursery as she passed the hallway—and halted amazed.

Selwyn, sitting up rumpled and cross-legged on the floor, after having boloed Drina to everybody's exquisite satisfaction, looked around at the sudden rustle of skirts to catch a glimpse of a vanishing figure—a glimmer of ruddy hair and the white curve of a youthful face, half-buried in a muff.

Mortified, he got to his feet, glanced out into the hallway, and began adjusting his attire.

"No, you don't!" he said mildly, "I decline to perform again. If you want any more wriggling you must accomplish it yourselves. Drina, has your governess—by any unfortunate chance—er—red hair?"

"No," said the child; "and won't you *please* crawl across the floor and bolo me—just *once* more?"

"Bolo me!" insisted Billy. "I haven't been mangled yet!"

"Let Billy assassinate somebody himself. And, by the way, Drina, are there any maids or nurses or servants in this remarkable house who occasionally wear copper-tinted hair and black fox furs?"

"No. Eileen does. Won't you please wriggle—"

"Who is Eileen?"

"Eileen? Why—don't you know who Eileen is?"

"No, I don't," began Captain Selwyn, when a delighted shout from the children swung him toward the door again. His sister, Mrs. Gerard, stood there in carriage gown and sables, radiant with surprise.

"Phil! *You!* Exactly like you, Philip, to come strolling in from the antipodes—dear fellow!" recovering from the fraternal embrace and holding both lapels of his coat in her gloved hands. "Six years!" she said again and again, tenderly reproachful; "Alexandrine was a baby of six— Drina, child, do you remember my brother—do you remember your Uncle Philip? She doesn't remember; you can't expect her to recollect; she is only twelve, Phil—"

"I remember *one* thing," observed Drina serenely.

Brother and sister turned toward her in pride and delight; and the child went on: "My Aunt Alixe; I remember her. She was *so* pretty," concluded Drina, nodding thoughtfully in the effort to remember more; "Uncle Philip, where is she now?"

But her uncle seemed to have lost his voice as well as his colour, and Mrs. Gerard's gloved fingers tightened on the lapels of his coat.

"Drina—child—" she faltered; but Drina, immersed in reflection, smiled dreamily; "So pretty," she murmured; "I remember my Aunt Alixe—"

"Drina!" repeated her mother sharply, "go and find Bridget this minute!"

Selwyn's hesitating hand sought his moustache; he lifted his eyes—the steady gray eyes, slightly bloodshot—to his sister's distressed face.

"I never dreamed—" she began—"the child has never spoken of—of her from that time to this! I never dreamed she could remember—"

"I don't understand what you are talking about, mother," said Drina; but her pretty mother caught her by the shoulders, striving to speak lightly; "Where in the world is Bridget, child? Where is Katie? And what is all this I hear from Dawson? It can't be possible that you have been fox-hunting all over the house again! Your nurses know perfectly well that you are not to hunt anywhere except in your own nursery."

"I know it," said Drina, "but Kit-Ki got out and ran downstairs. We had to follow her, you know, until she went to earth."

11

Selwyn quietly bent over toward Billy: "'Ware wire, my friend," he said under his breath; "_you'd_ better cut upstairs and unlock that schoolroom."

And while Mrs. Gerard turned her attention to the cluster of clamouring younger children, the boy vanished only to reappear a moment later, retreating before the vengeful exclamations of the lately imprisoned nurses who pursued him, caps and aprons flying, bewailing aloud their ignominious incarceration.

"Billy!" exclaimed his mother, "_did_ you do that? Bridget, Master William is to take supper by himself in the schoolroom—and _no_ marmalade!—No, Billy, not one drop!"

"We all saw him lock the door," said Drina honestly.

"And you let him? Oh, Drina!—And Ellen! Katie! No marmalade for Miss Drina—none for any of the children. Josie, mother feels dreadfully because you all have been so naughty. Winthrop!—your finger! Instantly! Clemence, baby, where on earth did you acquire all that grime on your face and fists?" And to her brother: "Such a household, Phil! Everybody incompetent—including me; everything topsy-turvy; and all five dogs perfectly possessed to lie on that pink rug in the music room.—_Have_ they been there to-day, Drina?—while you were practising?"

"Yes, and there are some new spots, mother. I'm _very_sorry."

"Take the children away!" said Mrs. Gerard. But she bent over, kissing each culprit as the file passed out, convoyed by the amply revenged nurses. "No marmalade, remember; and mother has a great mind _not_ to come up at bedtime and lean over you. Mother has no desire to lean over her babies to-night."

To "lean over" the children was always expected of this mother; the direst punishment on the rather brief list was to omit this intimate evening ceremony.

"M-mother," stammered the Master of Fox Hounds, "you _will_ lean over us, won't you?"

"Mother hasn't decided—"

"Oh, muvver!" wailed Josie; and a howl of grief and dismay rose from Winthrop, modified to a gurgle by the forbidden finger.

"You _will_, won't you?" begged Drina. "We've been pretty bad, but not bad enough for that!"

"I—Oh, yes, I will. Stop that noise, Winthrop! Josie, I'm going to lean over you—and you, too, Clemence, baby. Katie, take those dogs away immediately; and remember about the marmalade."

Reassured, smiling through tears, the children trooped off, it being the bathing hour; and Mrs. Gerard threw her fur stole over one shoulder and linked her slender arm in her brother's.

"You see, I'm not much of a mother," she said; "if I was I'd stay here all day and every day, week in and year out, and try to make these poor infants happy. I have no business to leave them for one second!"

"Wouldn't they get too much of you?" suggested Selwyn.

"Thanks. I suppose that even a mother had better practise an artistic absence occasionally. Are they not sweet? *What* do you think of them? You never before saw the three youngest; you saw Drina when you went east—and Billy was a few months old—what do you think of them? Honestly, Phil?"

"All to the good, Ninette; very ornamental. Drina—and that Josephine kid are real beauties. I—er—take to Billy tremendously. He told me that he'd locked up his nurses. I ought to have interfered. It was really my fault, you see."

"And you didn't make him let them out? You are not going to be very good morally for my young. Tell me, Phil, have you seen Austin?"

"I went to the Trust Company, but he was attending a directors' confab. How is he? He's prosperous anyhow, I observe," with a humorous glance around the elaborate hallway which they were traversing.

"Don't dare laugh at us!" smiled his sister. "I wish we were back in Tenth Street. But so many children came—Billy, Josephine, Winthrop, and Tina—and the Tenth Street house wasn't half big enough; and a dreadful speculative builder built this house and persuaded Austin to buy it. Oh, dear, and here we are among the rich and great; and the steel kings and copper kings and oil kings and their heirs and dauphins. *Do* you like the house?"

"It's—ah—roomy," he said cheerfully.

"Oh! It isn't so bad from the outside. And we have just had it redecorated inside. Mizner did it. Look, dear, isn't that a cunning bedroom?" drawing him toward a partly open door. "Don't be so horridly critical. Austin is becoming used to it now, so don't stir him up and make fun of things. Anyway you're going to stay here."

"No, I'm at the Holland."

"Of *course* you're to live with us. You've resigned from the service, haven't you?"

He looked at her sharply, but did not reply.

A curious flash of telepathy passed between them; she hesitated, then:

"You once promised Austin and me that you would stay with us."

13

"But, Nina—"

"No, no, no! Wait," pressing an electric button; "Watson, Captain Selwyn's luggage is to be brought here immediately from the Holland! Immediately!" And to Selwyn: "Austin will not be at home before half-past six. Come up with me now and see your quarters—a perfectly charming place for you, with your own smoking-room and dressing-closet and bath. Wait, we'll take the elevator—as long as we have one."

Smilingly protesting, yet touched by the undisguised sincerity of his welcome, he suffered himself to be led into the elevator—a dainty white and rose rococo affair. His sister adjusted a tiny lever; the car moved smoothly upward and, presently stopped; and they emerged upon a wide landing.

"Here," said Nina, throwing open a door. "Isn't this comfortable? Is there anything you don't fancy about it? If there is, tell me frankly."

"Little sister," he said, imprisoning both her hands, "it is a paradise—but I don't intend to come here and squat on my relatives, and I won't!"

"Philip! You are common!"

"Oh, I know you and Austin *think* you want me."

"Phil!"

"All right, dear. I'll—it's awfully generous of you—so I'll pay you a visit—for a little while."

"You'll live here, that's what you'll do—though I suppose you are dreaming and scheming to have all sorts of secret caves and queer places to yourself—horrid, grimy, smoky bachelor quarters where you can behave *sans-façon*."

"I've had enough of *sans-façon*" he said grimly. "After shacks and bungalows and gun-boats and troopships, do you suppose this doesn't look rather heavenly?"

"Dear fellow!" she said, looking tenderly at him; and then under her breath: "What a ghastly life you have led!"

But he knew she did not refer to the military portion of his life.

He threw back his coat, dug both hands into his pockets, and began to wander about the rooms, halting sometimes to examine nondescript articles of ornament or bits of furniture as though politely interested. But she knew his thoughts were steadily elsewhere.

"'There is no reason,' she said, 'why you should not call this house home.'"

Sauntering about, aware at moments that her troubled eyes were following him, he came back, presently, to where she sat perched upon his bed.

"It all looks most inviting, Nina," he said cheerfully, seating himself beside her. "I—well, you can scarcely be expected to understand how this idea of a home takes hold of a man who has none."

"Yes, I do," she said.

"All this—" he paused, leisurely, to select his words—"all this—you—the children—that jolly nursery—" he stopped again, looking out of the window; and his sister looked at him through eyes grown misty.

"There is no reason," she said, "why you should not call this house home."

"N-no reason. Thank you. I will—for a few days."

"*No reason*, dear," she insisted. "We are your own people; we are all you have, Phil!—the children adore you already; Austin—you know what he thinks of you; and—and I—"

"You are very kind, Ninette." He sat partly turned from her, staring at the sunny window. Presently he slid his hand back along the bed-covers until it touched and tightened over hers. And in silence she raised it to her lips.

They remained so for a while, he still partly turned from her, his perplexed and narrowing gaze fixed on the window, she pressing his clenched hand to her lips, thoughtful and silent.

"Before Austin comes," he said at length, "let's get the thing over—and buried—as long as it will stay buried."

"Yes, dear."

"Well, then—then—" but his throat closed tight with the effort.

"Alixe is here," she said gently; "did you know it?"

He nodded.

"You know, of course, that she's married Jack Ruthven?"

He nodded again.

"Are you on leave, Phil, or have you really resigned?"

"Resigned."

"I knew it," she sighed.

He said: "As I did not defend the suit I couldn't remain in the service. There's too much said about us, anyway—about us who are appointed from civil life. And then—to have *that*happen!"

"Phil?"

"What?"

"Will you answer me one thing?"

"Yes, I guess so."

"Do you still care for—her?"

"I am sorry for her."

After a painful silence his sister said: "Could you tell me how it began, Phil?"

"How it began? I don't know that, either. When Bannard's command took the field I went with the scouts. Alixe remained in Manila. Ruthven

16

was there for Fane, Harmon & Co. That's how it began, I suppose; and it's a rotten climate for morals; and that's how it began."

"Only that?"

"We had had differences. It's been one misunderstanding after another. If you mean was I mixed up with another woman—no! She knew that."

"She was very young, Phil."

He nodded: "I don't blame her."

"Couldn't anything have been done?"

"If it could, neither she nor I did it—or knew how to do it, I suppose. It went wrong from the beginning; it was founded on froth—she had been engaged to Harmon, and she threw him over for 'Boots' Lansing. Then I came along—Boots behaved like a thoroughbred—that is all there is to it—inexperience, romance, trouble—a quick beginning, a quick parting, and two more fools to give the lie to civilization, and justify the West Pointers in their opinions of civil appointees."

"Try not to be so bitter, Phil; did you know she was going before she left Manila?"

"I hadn't the remotest idea of the affair. I thought that we were trying to learn something about life and about each other. . . . Then that climax came."

He turned and stared out of the window, dropping his sister's hand. "She couldn't stand me, she couldn't stand the life, the climate, the inconveniences, the absence of what she was accustomed to. She was dead tired of it all. I can understand that. And I—I didn't know what to do about it. . . . So we drifted; and the catastrophe came very quickly. Let me tell you something; a West Pointer, an Annapolis man, knows what sort of life he's going into and what he is to expect when he marries. Usually, too, he marries into the Army or Navy set; and the girl knows, too, what kind of a married life that means.

"But I didn't. Neither did Alixe. And we went under; that's all—fighting each other heart and soul to the end. . . . Is she happy with Ruthven? I never knew him—and never cared to. I suppose they go about in town among the yellow set. Do they?"

"Yes. I've met Alixe once or twice. She was perfectly composed—formal but unembarrassed. She has shifted her milieu somewhat—it began with the influx of Ruthven's friends from the 'yellow' section of the younger married set—the Orchils, Fanes, Minsters, and Delmour-Carnes. Which is all right if she'd stay there. But in town you're likely to encounter anybody where the somebodies of one set merge into the somebodies of another. And we're always looking over our fences, you know. . . . By the way," she added cheerfully, "I'm dipping into the younger set myself to-night—on Eileen's account. I brought her out Thursday and I'm giving a dinner for her to-night."

"Who's Eileen?" he asked.

"Eileen? Why, don't you—why, of *course*, you don't know yet that I've taken Eileen for my own. I didn't want to write you; I wanted first to see how it would turn out; and when I saw that it was turning out perfectly, I thought it better to wait until you could return and hear all about it from me, because one can't write that sort of thing—"

"Nina!"

"What, dear?" she said, startled.

"Who the dickens *is* Eileen?"

"Philip! You are precisely like Austin; you grow impatient of preliminary details when I'm doing my very best attempting to explain just as clearly as I can. Now I will go on and say that Eileen is Molly Erroll's daughter, and the courts appointed Austin and me guardians for her and for her brother Gerald."

"Oh!"

"Now is it clear to you?"

"Yes," he said, thinking of the tragedy which had left the child so utterly alone in the world, save for her brother and a distant kinship by marriage with the Gerards.

For a while he sat brooding, arms loosely folded, immersed once more in his own troubles.

"It seems a shame," he said, "that a family like ours, whose name has always spelled decency, should find themselves entangled in the very things their race has always hated and managed to avoid. And through me, too."

"It was not your fault, Phil."

"No, not the divorce part. Do you suppose I wouldn't have taken any kind of medicine before resorting to that! But what's the use; for you can try as you may to keep your name clean, and then you can fold your arms and wait to see what a hopeless fool fate makes of you."

"But no disgrace touches you, dear," she said tremulously.

"I've been all over that, too," he said with quiet bitterness. "You are partly right; nobody cares in this town. Even though I did not defend the suit, nobody cares. And there's no disgrace, I suppose, if nobody cares enough even to condone. Divorce is no longer noticed; it is a matter of ordinary occurrence—a matter of routine in some sets. Who cares?—except decent folk? And they only think it's a pity—and wouldn't do it themselves. The horrified clamour comes from outside the

18

social registers and blue books; we know they're right, but it doesn't affect us. What does affect us is that we *were* the decent folk who permitted ourselves the luxury of being sorry for others who resorted to divorce as a remedy but wouldn't do it ourselves! . . . Now we've done it and—"

"Phil! I will not have you feel that way."

"What way?"

"The way you feel. We are older than we were—everybody is older—the world is, too. What we were brought up to consider impossible—"

"What we were brought up to consider impossible was what kept me up to the mark out there, Nina." He made a gesture toward the East. "Now, I come back here and learn that we've all outgrown those ideas—"

"Phil! I never meant that."

He said: "If Alixe found that she cared for Ruthven, I don't blame her. Laws and statutes can't govern such matters. If she found she no longer cared for me, I could not blame her. But two people, mismated, have only one chance in this world—to live their tragedy through with dignity. That is absolutely all life holds for them. Beyond that, outside of that dead line—treachery to self and race and civilisation! That is my conclusion after a year's experience in hell." He rose and began to pace the floor, fingers worrying his moustache. "Law? Can a law, which I do not accept, let me loose to risk it all again with another woman?"

She said slowly, her hands folded in her lap: "It is well you've come to me at last. You've been turning round and round in that wheeled cage until you think you've made enormous progress; and you haven't. Dear, listen to me; what you honestly believe to be unselfish and high-minded adherence to principle, is nothing but the circling reasoning of a hurt mind—an intelligence still numbed from shock, a mental and physical life forced by sheer courage into mechanical routine. . . . Wait a moment; there is nobody else to say this to you; and if I did not love you I would not interfere with this great mistake you are so honestly making of your life, and which, perhaps, is the only comfort left you. I say, 'perhaps,' for I do not believe that life holds nothing happier for you than the sullen content of martyrdom."

"Nina!"

"I am right!" she said, almost fiercely; "I've been married thirteen years and I've lost that fear of men's portentous judgments which all girls outgrow one day. And do you think I am going to acquiesce in this attitude of yours toward life? Do you think I can't distinguish between a tragical mistake and a mistaken tragedy? I tell you your life is not finished; it is not yet begun!"

He looked at her, incensed; but she sprang to the floor, her face bright with colour, her eyes clear, determined: "I thought, when you took the

19

oath of military service, you swore to obey the laws of the land? And the very first law that interferes with your preconceived notions—crack!—you say it's not for you! Look at me—you great, big, wise brother of mine—who knows enough to march a hundred and three men into battle, but not enough to know where pride begins and conscience ends. You're badly hurt; you are deeply humiliated over your resignation; you believe that ambition for a career, for happiness, for marriage, and for children is ended for you. You need fresh air—and I'm going to see you have it. You need new duties, new faces, new scenes, new problems. You shall have them. Dear, believe me, few men as young as you—as attractive, as human, as lovable, as affectionate as you, wilfully ruin their lives because of a hurt pride which they mistake for conscience. You will understand that when you become convalescent. Now kiss me and tell me you're much obliged—for I hear Austin's voice on the stairs."

He held her at arms' length, gazing at her, half amused, half indignant; then, unbidden, a second flash of the old telepathy passed between them—a pale glimmer lighted his own dark heart in sympathy; and for a moment he seemed to have a brief glimpse of the truth; and the truth was not as he had imagined it. But it was a glimpse only—a fleeting suspicion of his own fallibility; then it vanished into the old, dull, aching, obstinate humiliation. For truth would not be truth if it were so easily discovered.

"Well, we've buried it now," breathed Selwyn. "You're all right, Nina—from your own standpoint—and I'm not going to make a stalking nuisance of myself; no fear, little sister. Hello!"—turning swiftly—"here's that preposterous husband of yours."

They exchanged a firm hand clasp; Austin Gerard, big, smooth shaven, humorously inclined toward the ruddy heaviness of successful middle age; Selwyn, lean, bronzed, erect, and direct in all the powerful symmetry and perfect health of a man within sight of maturity.

"Hail to the chief—et cetera," said Austin, in his large, bantering voice. "Glad to see you home, my bolo-punctured soldier boy. Welcome to our city! I suppose you've both pockets stuffed with loot, now haven't you?—pearls and sarongs and dattos—yes? Have you inspected the kids? What's your opinion of the Gerard batallion? Pretty fit? Nina's commanding, so it's up to her if we don't pass dress parade. By the way, your enormous luggage is here—consisting of one dinky trunk and a sword done up in chamois skin."

"Nina's good enough to want me for a few days—" began Selwyn, but his big brother-in-law laughed scornfully:

"A few days! We've got you now!" And to his wife: "Nina, I suppose I'm due to lean over those infernal kids before I can have a minute with your brother. Are they in bed yet? All right, Phil; we'll be down in a minute; there's tea and things in the library. Make Eileen give you some."

He turned, unaffectedly taking his pretty wife's hand in his large florid paw, and Selwyn, intensely amused, saw them making for the nursery absorbed in conjugal confab. He lingered to watch them go their way, until they disappeared; and he stood a moment longer alone there in the hallway; then the humour faded from his sun-burnt face; he swung wearily on his heel, and descended the stairway, his hand heavy on the velvet rail.

The library was large and comfortable, full of agreeably wadded corners and fat, helpless chairs—a big, inviting place, solidly satisfying in dull reds and mahogany. The porcelain of tea paraphernalia caught the glow of the fire; a reading lamp burned on a centre table, shedding subdued lustre over ceiling, walls, books, and over the floor where lay a few ancient rugs of Beloochistan, themselves full of mysterious, sombre fire.

Hands clasped behind his back, he stood in the centre of the room, considering his environment with the grave, absent air habitual to him when brooding. And, as he stood there, a sound at the door aroused him, and he turned to confront a young girl in hat, veil, and furs, who was leisurely advancing toward him, stripping the gloves from a pair of very white hands.

"How do you do, Captain Selwyn," she said. "I am Eileen Erroll and I am commissioned to give you some tea. Nina and Austin are in the nursery telling bedtime stories and hearing assorted prayers. The children seem to be quite crazy about you—" She unfastened her veil, threw back stole and coat, and, rolling up her gloves on her wrists, seated herself by the table. "—*Quite* crazy about you," she continued, "and you're to be included in bedtime prayers, I believe—No sugar? Lemon?—Drina's mad about you and threatens to give you her new maltese puppy. I congratulate you on your popularity."

"Did you see me in the nursery on all fours?" inquired Selwyn, recognising her bronze-red hair.

Unfeigned laughter was his answer. He laughed, too, not very heartily.

"My first glimpse of our legendary nursery warrior was certainly astonishing," she said, looking around at him with frank malice. Then, quickly: "But you don't mind, do you? It's all in the family, of course."

"Of course," he agreed with good grace; "no use to pretend dignity here; you all see through me in a few moments."

She had given him his tea. Now she sat upright in her chair, smiling, *distraite*, her hat casting a luminous shadow across her eyes; the fluffy furs, fallen from throat and shoulder, settled loosely around her waist.

Glancing up from her short reverie she encountered his curious gaze.

"To-night is to be my first dinner dance, you know," she said. Faint tints of excitement stained her white skin; the vivid scarlet contrast of her mouth was almost startling. "On Thursday I was introduced—" she explained, "and now I'm to have the gayest winter I ever dreamed of. . . . And I'm going to leave you in a moment if Nina doesn't hurry and come. Do you mind?"

"Of course I mind," he protested amiably, "but I suppose you wish to devote several hours to dressing."

She nodded. "Such a dream of a gown! Nina's present! You'll see it. I hope Gerald will be here to see it. He promised. You'll say you like it if you do like it, won't you?"

"I'll say it, anyway."

"Oh, well—if you are contented to be commonplace like other men—"

"I've no ambition to be different at my age."

"Your age?" she repeated, looking up quickly. "You are as young as Nina, aren't you? Half the men in the younger set are no younger than you—and you know it," she concluded—"you are only trying to make me say so—and you've succeeded. I'm not very experienced yet. Does tea bring wisdom, Captain Selwyn?" pouring herself a cup. "I'd better arm myself immediately." She sank back into the depths of the chair, looking gaily at him over her lifted cup. "To my rapid education in worldly wisdom!" She nodded, and sipped the tea almost pensively.

He certainly did seem young there in the firelight, his narrow, thoroughbred head turned toward the fire. Youth, too, sat lightly on his shoulders; and it was scarcely a noticeably mature hand that touched the short sun-burnt moustache at intervals. From head to waist, from his loosely coupled, well-made limbs to his strong, slim foot, strength seemed to be the keynote to a physical harmony most agreeable to look at.

The idea entered her head that he might appear to advantage on horseback.

"We must ride together," she said, returning her teacup to the tray; "if you don't mind riding with me? Do you? Gerald never has time, so I go with a groom. But if you would care to go—" she laughed. "Oh, you see I am already beginning a selfish family claim on you. I foresee that you'll be very busy with us all persistently tugging at your coat-sleeves; and what with being civil to me and a martyr to Drina, you'll have very little time to yourself. And—I hope you'll like my brother Gerald when you meet him. Now I *must* go."

Then, rising and partly turning to collect her furs:

"It's quite exciting to have you here. We will be good friends, won't we? . . . and I think I had better stop my chatter and go, because my cunning little Alsatian maid is not very clever yet. . . . Good-bye."

She stretched out one of her amazingly white hands across the table, giving him a friendly leave-taking and welcome all in one frank handshake; and left him standing there, the fresh contact still cool in his palm.

Nina came in presently to find him seated before the fire, one hand shading his eyes; and, as he prepared to rise, she rested both arms on his shoulders, forcing him into his chair again.

"So you've bewitched Eileen, too, have you?" she said tenderly. "Isn't she the sweetest little thing?"

"She's—ah—as tall as I am," he said, blinking at the fire.

"She's only nineteen; pathetically unspoiled—a perfect dear. Men are going to rave over her and—*not* spoil her. Did you ever see such hair?— that thick, ruddy, lustrous, copper tint?—and sometimes it's like gold afire. And a skin like snow and peaches!—she's sound to the core. I've had her exercised and groomed and hardened and trained from the very beginning—every inch of her minutely cared for exactly like my own babies. I've done my best," she concluded with a satisfied sigh, and dropped into a chair beside her brother.

"Thoroughbred," commented Selwyn, "to be turned out to-night. Is she bridle-wise and intelligent?"

"More than sufficiently. That's one trouble—she's had, at times, a depressing, sponge-like desire for absorbing all sorts of irrelevant things that no girl ought to concern herself with. I—to tell the truth—if I had not rigorously drilled her—she might have become a trifle tiresome; I don't mean precisely frumpy—but one of those earnest young things whose intellectual conversation becomes a visitation—one of the wants-to-know-for-the-sake-of-knowledge sort—a dreadful human blotter! Oh, dear; show me a girl with her mind soaking up 'isms' and I'll show you a social failure with a wisp of hair on her cheek, who looks the dowdier the more expensively she's gowned."

"So you believe you've got that wisp of copper-tinted hair tucked up snugly?" asked Selwyn, amused.

"I—it's still a worry to me; at intervals she's inclined to let it slop. Thank Heaven, I've made her spine permanently straight and her head is screwed properly to her neck. There's not a slump to her from crown to heel—*I* know, you know. She's had specialists to forestall every blemish. I made up my mind to do it; I'm doing it for my own babies. That's what a mother is for—to turn out her offspring to the world as flawless and wholesome as when they came into it!—physically and mentally sound—or a woman betrays her stewardship. They must be as healthy

23

of body and limb as they are innocent and wholesome minded. The happiest of all creatures are drilled thoroughbreds. Show me a young girl, unspoiled mentally and spiritually untroubled, with a superb physique, and I'll show you a girl equipped for the happiness of this world. And that is what Eileen is."

"I should say," observed Selwyn, "that she's equipped for the slaughter of man."

"Yes, but *I* am selecting the victim," replied his sister demurely.

"Oh! Have you? Already?"

"Tentatively."

"Who?"

"Sudbury Gray, I think—with Scott Innis for an understudy—perhaps the Draymore man as alternate—I don't know; there's time."

"Plenty," he said vaguely, staring into the fire where a log had collapsed into incandescent ashes.

She continued to talk about Eileen until she noticed that his mind was on other matters—his preoccupied stare enlightened her. She said nothing for a while.

But he woke up when Austin came in and settled his big body in a chair.

"Drina, the little minx, called me back on some flimsy pretext," he said, relighting his cigar; "I forgot that time was going—and she was wily enough to keep me talking until Miss Paisely caught me at it and showed me out. I tell you," turning on Selwyn—"children are what make life worth wh—" He ceased abruptly at a gentle tap from his wife's foot, and Selwyn looked up.

Whether or not he divined the interference he said very quietly: "I'd rather have had children than anything in the world. They're about the best there is in life; I agree with you, Austin."

His sister, watching him askance, was relieved to see his troubled face become serene, though she divined the effort.

"Kids are the best," he repeated, smiling at her. "Failing them, for second choice, I've taken to the laboratory. Some day I'll invent something and astonish you, Nina."

"We'll fit you up a corking laboratory," began Austin cordially; "there is—"

"You're very good; perhaps you'll all be civil enough to move out of the house if I need more room for bottles and retorts—"

24

"Of *course*, Phil must have his laboratory," insisted Nina. "There's loads of unused room in this big barn—only you don't mind being at the top of the house, do you, Phil?"

"Yes, I do; I want to be in the drawing-room—or somewhere so that you all may enjoy the odours and get the benefit of premature explosions. Oh, come now, Austin, if you think I'm going to plant myself here on you—"

"Don't notice him, Austin," said Nina, "he only wishes to be implored. And, by the same token, you'd both better let me implore you to dress!" She rose and bent forward in the firelight to peer at the clock. "Goodness! Do you creatures think I'm going to give Eileen half an hour's start with her maid?—and I carrying my twelve years' handicap, too. No, indeed! I'm decrepit but I'm going to die fighting. Austin, get up! You're horribly slow, anyhow. Phil, Austin's man—such as he is—will be at your disposal, and your luggage is unpacked."

"Am I really expected to grace this festival of babes?" inquired Selwyn. "Can't you send me a tray of toast or a bowl of gruel and let me hide my old bones in a dressing-gown somewhere?"

"Oh, come on," said Austin, smothering the yawn in his voice and casting his cigar into the ashes. "You're about ripe for the younger set— one of them, anyhow. If you can't stand the intellectual strain we'll side-step the show later and play a little—what do you call it in the army?— pontoons?"

They strolled toward the door, Nina's arms linked in theirs, her slim fingers interlocked on her breast.

"We are certainly going to be happy—we three—in this innocent *ménage à trois*," she said. "I don't know what more you two men could ask for— or I, either—or the children or Eileen. Only one thing; I think it is perfectly horrid of Gerald not to be here."

Traversing the hall she said: "It always frightens me to be perfectly happy—and remember all the ghastly things that could happen. . . . I'm going to take a glance at the children before I dress. . . . Austin, did you remember your tonic?"

She looked up surprised when her husband laughed.

"I've taken my tonic and nobody's kidnapped the kids," he said. She hesitated, then picking up her skirts she ran upstairs for one more look at her slumbering progeny.

The two men glanced at one another; their silence was the tolerant, amused silence of the wiser sex, posing as such for each other's benefit; but deep under the surface stirred the tremors of the same instinctive solicitude that had sent Nina to the nursery.

25

"I used to think," said Gerard, "that the more kids you had the less anxiety per kid. The contrary is true; you're more nervous over half a dozen than you are over one, and your wife is always going to the nursery to see that the cat hasn't got in or the place isn't afire or spots haven't come out all over the children."

They laughed tolerantly, lingering on the sill of Selwyn's bedroom.

"Come in and smoke a cigarette," suggested the latter. "I have nothing to do except to write some letters and dress."

But Gerard said: "There seems to be a draught through this hallway; I'll just step upstairs to be sure that the nursery windows are not too wide open. See you later, Phil. If there's anything you need just dingle that bell."

And he went away upstairs, only to return in a few minutes, laughing under his breath: "I say, Phil, don't you want to see the kids asleep? Billy's flat on his back with a white 'Teddy bear' in either arm; and Drina and Josephine are rolled up like two kittens in pajamas; and you should see Winthrop's legs—"

"Certainly," said Selwyn gravely, "I'll be with you in a second."

And turning to his dresser he laid away the letters and the small photograph which he had been examining under the drop-light, locking them securely in the worn despatch box until he should have time to decide whether to burn them all or only the picture. Then he slipped on his smoking jacket.

"—Ah, about Winthrop's legs—" he repeated vaguely, "certainly; I should be very glad to examine them, Austin."

"I don't want you to examine them," retorted Gerard resentfully, "I want you to see them. There's nothing the matter with them, you understand."

"Exactly," nodded Selwyn, following his big brother-in-law into the hall, where, from beside a lamp-lit sewing table a trim maid rose smiling:

"Miss Erroll desires to know whether Captain Selwyn would care to see her gown when she is ready to go down?"

"By all means," said Selwyn, "I should like to see that, too. Will you let me know when Miss Erroll is ready? Thank you."

Austin said as they reached the nursery door: "Funny thing, feminine vanity—almost pathetic, isn't it? . . . Don't make too much noise! . . . What do you think of that pair of legs, Phil?—and he's not yet five. . . . And I want you to speak frankly; *did* you ever see anything to beat that bunch of infants? Not because they're ours and we happen to be your own people—" he checked himself and the smile faded as he laid his big ruddy hand on Selwyn's shoulder;—"*your own people*, Phil. Do you understand? . . . And if I have not ventured to say anything about—

26

what has happened—you understand that, too, don't you? You know I'm just as loyal to you as Nina is—as it is natural and fitting that your own people should be. Only a man finds it difficult to convey his—his—"

"Don't say 'sympathies'!" cut in Selwyn nervously.

"I wasn't going to, confound you! I was going to say 'sentiments.' I'm sorry I said anything. Go to the deuce!"

Selwyn did not even deign to glance around at him. "You big red-pepper box," he muttered affectionately, "you'll wake up Drina. Look at her in her cunning pajamas! Oh, but she is a darling, Austin. And look at that boy with his two white bears! He's a corker! He's a wonder—honestly, Austin. As for that Josephine kid she can have me on demand; I'll answer to voice, whistle, or hand. . . . I say, ought we to go away and leave Winthrop's thumb in his mouth?"

"I guess I can get it out without waking him," whispered Gerard. A moment later he accomplished the office, leaned down and drew the bed-covers closer to Tina's dimpled chin, then grasped Selwyn above the elbow in sudden alarm: "If that trained terror, Miss Paisely, finds us in here when she comes from dinner, we'll both catch it! Come on; I'll turn off the light. Anyway, we ought to have been dressed long ago; but you insisted on butting in here."

In the hallway below they encountered a radiant and bewildering vision awaiting them: Eileen, in all her glory.

"Wonderful!" said Gerard, patting the vision's rounded bare arm as he hurried past—"fine gown! fine girl!—but I've got to dress and so has Philip—" He meant well.

"*Do* you like it, Captain Selwyn?" asked the girl, turning to confront him, where he had halted. "Gerald isn't coming and—I thought perhaps you'd be interested—"

The formal, half-patronising compliment on his tongue's tip remained there, unsaid. He stood silent, touched by the faint under-ringing wistfulness in the laughing voice that challenged his opinion; and something within him responded in time:

"Your gown is a beauty; such wonderful lace. Of course, anybody would know it came straight from Paris or from some other celestial region—"

"But it didn't!" cried the girl, delighted. "It looks it, doesn't it? But it was made by Letellier! Is there anything you don't like about it, Captain Selwyn? *Anything?*"

"Nothing," he said solemnly; "it is as adorable as the girl inside it, who makes it look like a Parisian importation from Paradise!"

She colored enchantingly, and with pretty, frank impulse held out both her hands to him:

"You *are* a dear, Captain Selwyn! It is my first real dinner gown and I'm quite mad about it; and—somehow I wanted the family to share my madness with me. Nina will—she gave it to me, the darling. Austin admires it, too, of course, but he doesn't notice such things very closely; and Gerald isn't here. . . . Thank you for letting me show it to you before I go down."

She gave both his hands a friendly little shake and, glancing down at her skirt in blissful consciousness of its perfection, stepped backward into her own room.

Later, while he stood at his dresser constructing an immaculate knot in his white tie, Nina knocked.

"Hurry, Phil! Oh, may I come in? . . . You ought to be downstairs with us, you know. . . . And it was very sweet of you to be so nice to Eileen. The child had tears in her eyes when I went in. Oh, just a single diamond drop in each eye; your sympathy and interest did it. . . . I think the child misses her father on an occasion such as this—the beginning of life—the first step out into the world. Men do not understand what it means to us; Gerald doesn't, I'm sure. I've been watching her, and I know the shadow of that dreadful tragedy falls on her more often than Austin and I are aware of. . . . Shall I fix that tie for you, dear? . . . Certainly I can; Austin won't let a man touch him. . . . There, Phil. . . . Wait! . . . Now if you are decently grateful you'll tell me I look well. Do I? Really? Nonsense, I *don't* look twenty; but—say it, Phil. Ah, that clever maid of mine knows some secrets—never mind!—but Drina thinks I'm a beauty. . . . Come, dear; and thank you for being kind to Eileen. One's own kin counts so much in this world. And when a girl has none, except a useless brother, little things like that mean a lot to her." She turned, her hand falling on his sleeve. "*You* are among your own people, anyhow!"

His own people! The impatient tenderness of his sister's words had been sounding in his ears all through the evening. They rang out clear and insistent amid the gay tumult of the dinner; he heard them in the laughing confusion of youthful voices; they stole into the delicate undertones of the music to mock him; the rustling of silk and lace repeated them; the high heels of satin slippers echoed them in irony.

His own people!

The scent of overheated flowers, the sudden warm breeze eddying from a capricious fan, the mourning thrill of the violins emphasised the emphasis of the words.

And they sounded sadder and more meaningless now to him, here in his own room, until the monotony of their recurrent mockery began to unnerve him.

He turned on the electricity, shrank from it, extinguished it. And for a long time he sat there in the darkness of early morning, his unfilled pipe clutched in his nerveless hand.

CHAPTER II

A DREAM ENDS

To pick up once more and tighten and knot together the loosened threads which represented the unfinished record that his race had woven into the social fabric of the metropolis was merely an automatic matter for Selwyn.

His own people had always been among the makers of that fabric. Into part of its vast and intricate pattern they had woven an inconspicuously honourable record—chronicles of births and deaths and marriages, a plain memorandum of plain living, and upright dealing with their fellow men.

Some public service of modest nature they had performed, not seeking it, not shirking; accomplishing it cleanly when it was intrusted to them.

His forefathers had been, as a rule, professional men—physicians and lawyers; his grandfather died under the walls of Chapultepec Castle while twisting a tourniquet for a cursing dragoon; an uncle remained indefinitely at Malvern Hill; an only brother at Montauk Point having sickened in the trenches before Santiago.

His father's services as division medical officer in Sheridan's cavalry had been, perhaps, no more devoted, no more loyal than the services of thousands of officers and troopers; and his reward was a pension offer, declined. He practised until his wife died, then retired to his country home, from which house his daughter Nina was married to Austin Gerard.

Mr. Selwyn, senior, continued to pay his taxes on his father's house in Tenth Street, voted in that district, spent a month every year with the Gerards, read a Republican morning newspaper, and judiciously enlarged the family reservation in Greenwood—whither he retired, in due time, without other ostentation than half a column in the *Evening Post*, which paper he had, in life, avoided.

The first gun off the Florida Keys sent Selwyn's only brother from his law office in hot haste to San Antonio—the first*étape* on his first and last campaign with Wood's cavalry.

That same gun interrupted Selwyn's connection with Neergard& Co., operators in Long Island real estate; and, a year later, the captaincy offered him in a Western volunteer regiment operating on the Island of Leyte, completed the rupture.

And now he was back again, a chance career ended, with option of picking up the severed threads—his inheritance at the loom—and of retying them, warp and weft, and continuing the pattern according to the designs of the tufted, tinted pile-yarn, knotted in by his ancestors before him.

There was nothing else to do; so he did it. Civil and certain social obligations were mechanically reassumed; he appeared in his sister's pew for worship, he reënrolled in his clubs as a resident member once more; the directors of such charities as he meddled with he notified of his return; he remitted his dues to the various museums and municipal or private organisations which had always expected support from his family; he subscribed to the *Sun*.

He was more conservative, however, in mending the purely social strands so long relaxed or severed. The various registers and blue-books recorded his residence under "dilatory domiciles"; he did not subscribe to the opera, preferring to chance it in case harmony-hunger attacked him; pre-Yuletide functions he dodged, considering that his sister's days in January and attendance at other family formalities were sufficient.

Meanwhile he was looking for two things—an apartment and a job—the first energetically combated by his immediate family.

It was rather odd—the scarcity of jobs. Of course Austin offered him one which Selwyn declined at once, comfortably enraging his brother-in-law for nearly ten minutes.

"But what do I know about the investment of trust funds?" demanded Selwyn; "you wouldn't take me if I were not your wife's brother—and that's nepotism."

Austin's harmless fury raged for nearly ten minutes, after which he cheered up, relighted his cigar, and resumed his discussion with Selwyn concerning the merits of various boys' schools—the victim in prospective being Billy.

A little later, reverting to the subject of his own enforced idleness, Selwyn said: "I've been on the point of going to see Neergard—but somehow I can't quite bring myself to it—slinking into his office as a rank failure in one profession, to ask him if he has any use for me again."

"Stuff and fancy!" growled Gerard; "it's all stuff and fancy about your being any kind of a failure. If you want to resume with that Dutchman, go to him and say so. If you want to invest anything in his Long Island schemes he'll take you in fast enough. He took in Gerald and some twenty thousand."

"Isn't he very prosperous, Austin?"

"Very—on paper. Long Island farm lands and mortgages on Hampton hen-coops are not fragrant propositions to me. But there's always one more way of making a living after you counted 'em all up on your fingers. If you've any capital to offer Neergard, he won't shriek for help."

"But isn't suburban property—"

"On the jump? Yes—both ways. Oh, I suppose that Neergard is all right—if he wasn't I wouldn't have permitted Gerald to go into it. Neergard sticks to his commissions and doesn't back his fancy in certified checks. I don't know exactly how he operates; I only know that we find nothing in that sort of thing for our own account. But Fane, Harmon & Co. do. That's their affair, too; it's all a matter of taste, I tell you."

Selwyn reflected: "I believe I'd go and see Neergard if I were perfectly sure of my personal sentiments toward him. . . . He's been civil enough to me, of course, but I have always had a curious feeling about Neergard—that he's for ever on the edge of doing something—doubtful—"

"His business reputation is all right. He shaves the dead line like a safety razor, but he's never yet cut through it. On principle, however, look out for an apple-faced Dutchman with a thin nose and no lips. Neither Jew, Yankee, nor American stands any chance in a deal with that type of financier. Personally my feeling is this: if I've got to play games with Julius Neergard, I'd prefer to be his partner. And so I told Gerald. By the way—"

Austin checked himself, looked down at his cigar, turned it over and over several times, then continued quietly:

—"By the way, I suppose Gerald is like other young men of his age and times—immersed in his own affairs—thoughtless perhaps, perhaps a trifle selfish in the cross-country gallop after pleasure. . . . I was rather severe with him about his neglect of his sister. He ought to have come here to pay his respects to you, too—"

"Oh, don't put such notions into his head—"

31

"Yes, I will!" insisted Austin; "however indifferent and thoughtless and selfish he is to other people, he's got to be considerate toward his own family. And I told him so. Have you seen him lately?"

"N-o," admitted Selwyn.

"Not since that first time when he came to do the civil by you?"

"No; but don't—"

"Yes, I will," repeated his brother-in-law; "and I'm going to have a thorough explanation with him and learn what he's up to. He's got to be decent to his sister; he ought to report to me occasionally; that's all there is to it. He has entirely too much liberty with his bachelor quarters and his junior whipper-snapper club, and his house parties and his cruises on Neergard's boat!"

He got up, casting his cigar from him, and moved about bulkily, muttering of matters to be regulated, and firmly, too. But Selwyn, looking out of the window across the Park, knew perfectly well that young Erroll, now of age, with a small portion of his handsome income at his mercy, was past the regulating stage and beyond the authority of Austin. There was no harm in him; he was simply a joyous, pleasure-loving cub, chock full of energetic instincts, good and bad, right and wrong, out of which, formed from the acts which become habits, character matures. This was his estimate of Gerald.

The next morning, riding in the Park with Eileen, he found a chance to speak cordially of her brother.

"I've meant to look up Gerald," he said, as though the neglect were his own fault, "but every time something happens to switch me on to another track."

"I'm afraid that I do a great deal of the switching," she said; "don't I? But you've been so nice to me and to the children that—"

Miss Erroll's horse was behaving badly, and for a few moments she became too thoroughly occupied with her mount to finish her sentence.

The belted groom galloped up, prepared for emergencies, and he and Selwyn sat their saddles watching a pretty battle for mastery between a beautiful horse determined to be bad and a very determined young girl who had decided he was going to be good.

Once or twice the excitement of solicitude sent the colour flying into Selwyn's temples; the bridle-path was narrow and stiff with freezing sand, and the trees were too near for such lively manoeuvres; but Miss Erroll had made up her mind—and Selwyn already had a humorous idea that this was no light matter. The horse found it serious enough, too, and suddenly concluded to be good. And the pretty scene ended so abruptly that Selwyn laughed aloud as he rejoined her:

"There was a man—'Boots' Lansing—in Bannard's command. One night on Samar the bolo-men rushed us, and Lansing got into the six-foot major's boots by mistake—seven-leaguers, you know—and his horse bucked him clean out of them."

"Hence his Christian name, I suppose," said the girl; "but why such a story, Captain Selwyn? I believe I stuck to my saddle?"

"With both hands," he said cordially, always alert to plague her. For she was adorable when teased—especially in the beginning of their acquaintance, before she had found out that it was a habit of his—and her bright confusion always delighted him into further mischief.

"But I wasn't a bit worried," he continued; "you had him so firmly around the neck. Besides, what horse or man could resist such a pleading pair of arms around the neck?"

"What you saw," she said, flushing up, "is exactly the way I shall do any pleading with the two animals you mention."

"Spur and curb and thrash us? Oh, my!"

"Not if you're bridle-wise, Captain Selwyn," she returned sweetly. "And you know you always are. And sometimes"—she crossed her crop and looked around at him reflectively—"*sometimes*, do you know, I am almost afraid that you are so very, very good, that perhaps you are becoming almost goody-good."

"*What!*" he exclaimed indignantly; but his only answer was her head thrown back and a ripple of enchanting laughter.

Later she remarked: "It's just as Nina says, after all, isn't it?"

"I suppose so," he replied suspiciously; "what?"

"That Gerald isn't really very wicked, but he likes to have us think so. It's a sign of extreme self-consciousness, isn't it," she added innocently, "when a man is afraid that a woman thinks he is very, very good?"

"That," he said, "is the limit. I'm going to ride by myself."

Her pleasure in Selwyn's society had gradually become such genuine pleasure, her confidence in his kindness so unaffectedly sincere, that, insensibly, she had fallen into something of his manner of badinage— especially since she realised how much amusement he found in her own smiling confusion when unexpectedly assailed. Also, to her surprise, she found that he could be plagued very easily, though she did not quite dare to at first, in view of his impressive years and experience.

But once goaded to it, she was astonished to find how suddenly it seemed to readjust their personal relations—years and experience falling from his shoulders like a cloak which had concealed a man very nearly her own age; years and experience adding themselves to her, and at least an inch to her stature to redress the balance between them.

It had amused him immensely as he realised the subtle change; and it pleased him, too, because no man of thirty-five cares to be treated *en grandpère* by a girl of nineteen, even if she has not yet worn the polish from her first pair of high-heeled shoes.

"It's astonishing," he said, "how little respect infirmity and age command in these days."

"I do respect you," she insisted, "especially your infirmity of purpose. You said you were going to ride by yourself. But, do you know, I don't believe you are of a particularly solitary disposition; are you?"

He laughed at first, then suddenly his face fell.

"Not from choice," he said, under his breath. Her quick ear heard, and she turned, semi-serious, questioning him with raised eyebrows.

"Nothing; I was just muttering. I've a villainous habit of muttering mushy nothings—"

"You *did* say something!"

"No; only ghoulish gabble; the mere murky mouthings of a meagre mind."

"You *did*. It's rude not to repeat it when I ask you."

"I didn't mean to be rude."

"Then repeat what you said to yourself."

"Do you wish me to?" he asked, raising his eyes so gravely that the smile faded from lip and voice when she answered: "I beg your pardon, Captain Selwyn. I did not know you were serious."

"Oh, I'm not," he returned lightly, "I'm never serious. No man who soliloquises can be taken seriously. Don't you know, Miss Erroll, that the crowning absurdity of all tragedy is the soliloquy?"

Her smile became delightfully uncertain; she did not quite understand him—though her instinct warned her that, for a second, something had menaced their understanding.

Riding forward with him through the crisp sunshine of mid-December, the word "tragedy" still sounding in her ears, her thoughts reverted naturally to the only tragedy besides her own which had ever come very near to her—his own.

Could he have meant *that?* Did people mention such things after they had happened? Did they not rather conceal them, hide them deeper and deeper with the aid of time and the kindly years for a burial past all recollection?

Troubled, uncomfortably intent on evading every thought or train of ideas evoked, she put her mount to a gallop. But thought kept pace with her.

She was, of course, aware of the situation regarding Selwyn's domestic affairs; she could not very well have been kept long in ignorance of the facts; so Nina had told her carefully, leaving in the young girl's mind only a bewildered sympathy for man and wife whom a dreadful and incomprehensible catastrophe had overtaken; only an impression of something new and fearsome which she had hitherto been unaware of in the world, and which was to be added to her small but, unhappily, growing list of sad and incredible things.

The finality of the affair, according to Nina, was what had seemed to her the most distressing—as though those two were already dead people. She was unable to understand it. Could no glimmer of hope remain that, in that magic "some day" of all young minds, the evil mystery might dissolve? Could there be no living "happily ever after" in the wake of such a storm? She had managed to hope for that, and believe in it.

Then, in some way, the news of Alixe's marriage to Ruthven filtered through the family silence. She had gone straight to Nina, horrified, unbelieving. And, when the long, tender, intimate interview was over, another unhappy truth, very gently revealed, was added to the growing list already learned by this young girl.

Then Selwyn came. She had already learned something of the world's customs and manners before his advent; she had learned more since his advent; and she was learning something else, too—to understand how happily ignorant of many matters she had been, had better be, and had best remain. And she harboured no malsane desire to know more than was necessary, and every innocent instinct to preserve her ignorance intact as long as the world permitted.

As for the man riding there at her side, his problem was simple enough as he summed it up: to face the world, however it might chance to spin, that small, ridiculous, haphazard world rattling like a rickety roulette ball among the numbered nights and days where he had no longer any vital stake at hazard—no longer any chance to win or lose.

This was an unstable state of mind, particularly as he had not yet destroyed the photograph which he kept locked in his despatch box. He had not returned it, either; it was too late by several months to do that, but he was still fool enough to consider the idea at moments— sometimes after a nursery romp with the children, or after a good-night kiss from Drina on the lamp-lit landing, or when some commonplace episode of the domesticity around him hurt him, cutting him to the

35

quick with its very simplicity, as when Nina's hand fell naturally into Austin's on their way to "lean over" the children at bedtime, or their frank absorption in conjugal discussion to his own exclusion as he sat brooding by the embers in the library.

"I'm like a dead man at times," he said to himself; "nothing to expect of a man who is done for; and worst of all, I no longer expect anything of myself."

This was sufficiently morbid, and he usually proved it by going early to his own quarters, where dawn sometimes surprised him asleep in his chair, white and worn, all the youth in his hollow face extinct, his wife's picture fallen face downward on the floor.

But he always picked it up again when he awoke, and carefully dusted it, too, even when half stupefied with sleep.

Returning from their gallop, Miss Erroll had very little to say. Selwyn, too, was silent and absent-minded. The girl glanced furtively at him from time to time, not at all enlightened. Man, naturally, was to her an unknown quantity. In fact she had no reason to suspect him of being anything more intricate than the platitudinous dance or dinner partner in black and white, or any frock-coated entity in the afternoon, or any flannelled individual at the nets or on the links or cantering about the veranda of club, casino, or cottage, in evident anxiety to be considerate and agreeable.

This one, however, appeared to have individual peculiarities; he differed from his brother Caucasians, who should all resemble one another to any normal girl. For one thing he was subject to illogical moods— apparently not caring whether she noticed them or not. For another, he permitted himself the liberty of long and unreasonable silences whenever he pleased. This she had accepted unquestioningly in the early days when she was a little in awe of him, when the discrepancy of their ages and experiences had not been dissipated by her first presumptuous laughter at his expense.

Now it puzzled her, appearing as a specific trait differentiating him from Man in the abstract.

He had another trick, too, of retiring within himself, even when smiling at her sallies or banteringly evading her challenge to a duel of wits. At such times he no longer looked very young; she had noticed that more than once. He looked old, and ill-tempered.

Perhaps some sorrow—the actuality being vague in her mind; perhaps some hidden suffering—but she learned that he had never been wounded in battle and had never even had measles.

The sudden sullen pallor, the capricious fits of silent reserve, the smiling aloofness, she never attributed to the real source. How could she? The Incomprehensible Thing was a Finality accomplished according to law. And the woman concerned was now another man's wife. Which conclusively proved that there could be no regret arising from the Incomprehensible Finality, and that nobody involved cared, much less suffered. Hence *that* was certainly not the cause of any erratic or specific phenomena exhibited by this sample of man who differed, as she had noticed, somewhat from the rank and file of his neutral-tinted brothers.

"It's this particular specimen, *per se*," she concluded; "it's himself, *sui generis*—just as I happen to have red hair. That is all."

And she rode on quite happily, content, confident of his interest and kindness. For she had never forgotten his warm response to her when she stood on the threshold of her first real dinner party, in her first real dinner gown—a trivial incident, trivial words! But they had meant more to her than any man specimen could understand—including the man who had uttered them; and the violets, which she found later with his card, must remain for her ever after the delicately fragrant symbol of all he had done for her in a solitude, the completeness of which she herself was only vaguely beginning to realise.

Thinking of this now, she thought of her brother—and the old hurt at his absence on that night throbbed again. Forgive? Yes. But how could she forget it?

"I wish you knew Gerald well," she said impulsively; "he is such a dear fellow; and I think you'd be good for him—and besides," she hastened to add, with instinctive loyalty, lest he misconstrue, "Gerald would be good for you. We were a great deal together—at one time."

He nodded, smilingly attentive.

"Of course when he went away to school it was different," she added. "And then he went to Yale; that was four more years, you see."

"I was a Yale man," remarked Selwyn; "did he—" but he broke off abruptly, for he knew quite well that young Erroll could have made no senior society without his hearing of it. And he had not heard of it—not in the cane-brakes of Leyte where, on his sweat-soaked shirt, a small pin of heavy gold had clung through many a hike and many a scout and by many a camp-fire where the talk was of home and of the chances of crews and of quarter-backs.

"What were you going to ask me, Captain Selwyn?"

"Did he row—your brother Gerald?"

"No," she said. She did not add that he had broken training; that was her own sorrow, to be concealed even from Gerald. "No; he played polo sometimes. He rides beautifully, Captain Selwyn, and he is so clever when he cares to be—at the traps, for example—and—oh—anything. He once swam—oh, dear, I forget; was it five or fifteen or fifty miles? Is that *too* far? Do people swim those distances?"

"Some of those distances," replied Selwyn.

"Well, then, Gerald swam some of those distances—and everybody was amazed. . . . I do wish you knew him well."

"I mean to," he said. "I must look him up at his rooms or his club or—perhaps—at Neergard & Co."

"*Will* you do this?" she asked, so earnestly that he glanced up surprised.

"Yes," he said; and after a moment: "I'll do it to-day, I think; this afternoon."

"Have you time? You mustn't let me—"

"Time?" he repeated; "I have nothing else, except a watch to help me get rid of it."

"I'm afraid I help you get rid of it, too. I heard Nina warning the children to let you alone occasionally—and I suppose she meant that for me, too. But I only take your mornings, don't I? Nina is unreasonable; I never bother you in the afternoons or evenings; do you know I have not dined at home for nearly a month—except when we've asked people?"

"Are you having a good time?" he asked condescendingly, but without intention.

"Heavenly. How can you ask that?—with every day filled and a chance to decline something every day. If you'd only go to one—just one of the dances and teas and dinners, you'd be able to see for yourself what a good time I am having. . . . I don't know why I should be so delightfully lucky, but everybody asks me to dance, and every man I meet is particularly nice, and nobody has been very horrid to me; perhaps because I like everybody—"

She rode on beside him; they were walking their horses now; and as her silken-coated mount paced forward through the sunshine she sat at ease, straight as a slender Amazon in her habit, ruddy hair glistening at the nape of her neck, the scarlet of her lips always a vivid contrast to that wonderful unblemished skin of snow.

He thought to himself, quite impersonally: "She's a real beauty, that youngster. No wonder they ask her to dance and nobody is horrid. Men are likely enough to go quite mad about her as Nina predicts: probably some of 'em have already—that chuckle-headed youth who was there Tuesday, gulping up the tea—" And, "What was his name?" he asked aloud.

"Whose name?" she inquired, roused by his voice from smiling retrospection.

38

"That chuckle head—the young man who continued to haunt you so persistently when you poured tea for Nina on Tuesday. Of course they *all* haunted you," he explained politely, as she shook her head in sign of non-comprehension; "but there was one who—ah—gulped at his cup."

"Please—you are rather dreadful, aren't you?"

"Yes. So was he; I mean the infatuated chinless gentleman whose facial ensemble remotely resembled the features of a pleased and placid lizard of the Reptilian period."

"Oh, George Fane! That is particularly disagreeable of you, Captain Selwyn, because his wife has been very nice to me—Rosamund Fane— and she spoke most cordially of you—"

"Which one was she?"

"The Dresden china one. She looks—she simply cannot look as though she were married. It's most amusing—for people always take her for somebody's youngest sister who will be out next winter. . . . Don't you remember seeing her?"

"No, I don't. But there were dozens coming and going every minute whom I didn't know. Still, I behaved well, didn't I?"

"Pretty badly—to Kathleen Lawn, whom you cornered so that she couldn't escape until her mother made her go without any tea."

"Was *that* the reason that old lady looked at me so queerly?"

"Probably. I did, too, but you were taking chances, not hints. . . . She *is* attractive, isn't she?"

"Very fetching," he said, leaning down to examine his stirrup leathers which he had already lengthened twice. "I've got to have Cummins punch these again," he muttered; "or am I growing queer-legged in my old age?"

As he straightened up, Miss Erroll said: "Here comes Mr. Fane now— with a strikingly pretty girl. How beautifully they are mounted"— smilingly returning Fane's salute—"and she—oh! so you *do* know her, Captain Selwyn? Who is she?"

Crop raised mechanically in dazed salute, Selwyn's light touch on the bridle had tightened to a nervous clutch which brought his horse up sharply.

"What is it?" she asked, drawing bridle in her turn and looking back into his white, stupefied face.

"Pain," he said, unconscious that he spoke. At the same instant the stunned eyes found their focus—and found her beside his stirrup, leaning wide from her seat in sweet concern, one gloved hand resting on the pommel of his saddle.

"Are you ill?" she asked; "shall we dismount? If you feel dizzy, please lean against me."

"I am all right," he said coolly; and as she recovered her seat he set his horse in motion. His face had become very red now; he looked at her, then beyond her, with all the deliberate concentration of aloof indifference.

Confused, conscious that something had happened which she did not comprehend, and sensitively aware of the preoccupation which, if it did not ignore her, accepted her presence as of no consequence, she permitted her horse to set his own pace.

Neither self-command nor self-control was lacking now in Selwyn; he simply was too self-absorbed to care what she thought—whether she thought at all. And into his consciousness, throbbing heavily under the rushing reaction from shock, crowded the crude fact that Alixe was no longer an apparition evoked in sleeplessness, in sun-lit brooding; in the solitude of crowded avenues and swarming streets; she was an actual presence again in his life—she was here, bodily, unchanged— unchanged!—for he had conceived a strange idea that she must have changed physically, that her appearance had altered. He knew it was a grotesquely senseless idea, but it clung to him, and he had nursed it unconsciously.

He had, truly enough, expected to encounter her in life again— somewhere; though what he had been preparing to see, Heaven alone knew; but certainly not the supple, laughing girl he had known—that smooth, slender, dark-eyed, dainty visitor who had played at marriage with him through a troubled and unreal dream; and was gone when he awoke—so swift the brief two years had passed, as swift in sorrow as in happiness.

Two vision-tinted years!—ended as an hour ends with the muffled chimes of a clock, leaving the air of an empty room vibrant. Two years!—a swift, restless dream aglow with exotic colour, echoing with laughter and bugle-call and the noise of the surf on Samar rocks—a dream through which stirred the rustle of strange brocades and the whisper of breezes blowing over the grasses of Leyte; and the light, dry report of rifles, and the shuffle of bare feet in darkened bungalows, and the whisper of dawn in Manila town.

Two years!—wherever they came from, wherever they had gone. And now, out of the ghostly, shadowy memory, behold her stepping into the world again!—living, breathing, quickening with the fire of life undimmed in her. And he had seen the bright colour spreading to her eyes, and the dark eyes widen to his stare; he had seen the vivid blush, the forced smile, the nod, the voiceless parting of her stiffened lips. Then she was gone, leaving the whole world peopled with her living presence and the very sky ringing with the words her lips had never uttered, never would utter while sun and moon and stars endured.

Shrinking from the clamouring tumult of his thoughts he looked around, hard-eyed and drawn of mouth, to find Miss Erroll riding a length in advance, her gaze fixed resolutely between her horse's ears.

How much had she noticed? How much had she divined?—this straight, white-throated young girl, with her self-possession and her rounded, firm young figure, this child with the pure, curved cheek, the clear, fearless eyes, untainted, ignorant, incredulous of shame, of evil.

Severe, confident, untroubled in the freshness of adolescence, she rode on, straight before her, symbolic innocence leading the disillusioned. And he followed, hard, dry eyes narrowing, ever narrowing and flinching under the smiling gaze of the dark-eyed, red-mouthed ghost that sat there on his saddle bow, facing him, almost in his very arms.

Luncheon had not been served when they returned. Without lingering on the landing as usual, they exchanged a formal word or two, then Eileen mounted to her own quarters and Selwyn walked nervously through the library, where he saw Nina evidently prepared for some mid-day festivity, for she wore hat and furs, and the brougham was outside.

"Oh, Phil," she said, "Eileen probably forgot that I was going out; it's a directors' luncheon at the exchange. Please tell Eileen that I can't wait for her; where is she?"

"Dressing, I suppose. Nina, I—"

"One moment, dear. I promised the children that you would lunch with them in the nursery. Do you mind? I did it to keep them quiet; I was weak enough to compromise between a fox hunt or fudge; so I said you'd lunch with them.. Will you?"

"Certainly. . . . And, Nina—what sort of a man is this George Fane?"

"Fane?"

"Yes—the chinless gentleman with gentle brown and protruding eyes and the expression of a tame brontosaurus."

"Why—how do you mean, Phil? What sort of man? He's a banker. He isn't very pretty, but he's popular."

"Oh, popular!" he nodded, as close to a sneer as he could ever get.

"He has a very popular wife, too; haven't you met Rosamund? People like him; he's about everywhere—very useful, very devoted to pretty women; but I'm really in a hurry, Phil. Won't you please explain to Eileen that I couldn't wait? You and she were almost an hour late. Now I must pick up my skirts and fly, or there'll be some indignant dowagers downtown. . . . Good-bye, dear. . . . And *don't* let the children eat too fast! Make Drina take thirty-six chews to every bite; and Winthrop is to have no bread if he has potatoes—" Her voice dwindled and died, away through the hall; the front door clanged.

He went to his quarters, drove out Austin's man, arranged his own fresh linen, took a sulky plunge; and, an unlighted cigarette between his teeth, completed his dressing in sullen introspection.

When he had tied his scarf and bitten his cigarette to pieces, he paced the room once or twice, squared his shoulders, breathed deeply, and, unbending his eyebrows, walked off to the nursery.

"Hello, you kids!" he said, with an effort. "I've come to luncheon. Very nice of you to want me, Drina."

"I wanted you, too!" said Billy; "I'm to sit beside you—"

"So am I," observed Drina, pushing Winthrop out of the chair and sliding in close to Selwyn. She had the cat, Kit-Ki, in her arms. Kit-Ki, divining nourishment, was purring loudly.

Josephine and Clemence, in pinafores and stickout skirts, sat wriggling, with Winthrop between them; the five dogs sat in a row behind; Katie and Bridget assumed the functions of Hibernian Hebes; and luncheon began with a clatter of spoons.

It being also the children's dinner—supper and bed occurring from five to six—meat figured on the card, and Kit-Ki's purring increased to an ecstatic and wheezy squeal, and her rigid tail, as she stood up on Drina's lap, was constantly brushing Selwyn's features.

"The cat is shedding, too," he remarked, as he dodged her caudal appendage for the twentieth time; "it will go in with the next spoonful, Drina, if you're not careful about opening your mouth."

"I love Kit-Ki," said Drina placidly. "I have written a poem to her—where is it?—hand it to me, Bridget."

And, laying down her fork and crossing her bare legs under the table, Drina took breath and read rapidly:

"LINES	TO		MY		CAT
"Why					
Do	I		love		Kit-Ki
And		run			after
Her		with			laughter
And	rub		her		fur
So	she		will		purr?
Why	do		I		know
That	Kit-Ki	loves		me	so?
I	know		it		if

42

Her	tail	stands	up	stiff
And		she		beguiles
Me with smiles—"				

"Huh!" said Billy, "cats don't smile!"

"They do. When they look pleasant they smile," said Drina, and continued reading from her own works:

"Be	kind	in	all
You	say	and	do
For	God	made	Kit-Ki
The	same	as	you.
"Yours			truly,

"ALEXANDRINA GERARD.

She looked doubtfully at Selwyn. "Is it all right to sign a poem? I believe that poets sign their works, don't they, Uncle Philip?"

"Certainly. Drina, I'll give you a dollar for that poem."

"You may have it, anyway," said Drina, generously; and, as an after-thought: "My birthday is next Wednesday."

"What a hint!" jeered Billy, casting a morsel at the dogs.

"It isn't a hint. It had nothing to do with my poem, and I'll write you several more, Uncle Philip," protested the child, cuddling against him, spoon in hand, and inadvertently decorating his sleeve with cranberry sauce.

Cat hairs and cranberry are a great deal for a man to endure, but he gave Drina a reassuring hug and a whisper, and leaned back to remove traces of the affectionate encounter just as Miss Erroll entered.

"Oh, Eileen! Eileen!" cried the children; "are you coming to luncheon with us?"

As Selwyn rose, she nodded, amused.

"I am rather hurt," she said. "I went down to luncheon, but as soon as I heard where you all were I marched straight up here to demand the reason of my ostracism."

"We thought you had gone with mother," explained Drina, looking about for a chair.

Selwyn brought it. "I was commissioned to say that Nina couldn't wait—dowagers and cakes and all that, you know. Won't you sit down? It's rather messy and the cat is the guest of honour."

"We have three guests of honour," said Drina; "you, Eileen, and Kit-Ki. Uncle Philip, mother has forbidden me to speak of it, so I shall tell her and be punished—but *wouldn't* it be splendid if Aunt Alixe were only here with us?"

43

Selwyn turned sharply, every atom of colour gone; and the child smiled up at him. "*Wouldn't* it?" she pleaded.

"Yes," he said, so quietly that something silenced the child. And Eileen, giving ostentatious and undivided attention to the dogs, was now enveloped by snooping, eager muzzles and frantically wagging tails.

"My lap is full of paws!" she exclaimed; "take them away, Katie! And oh!—my gown, my gown!—Billy, stop waving your tumbler around my face! If you spill that milk on me I shall ask your Uncle Philip to put you in the guard-house!"

"You're going to bolo us, aren't you, Uncle Philip?" inquired Billy. "It's my turn to be killed, you remember—"

"I have an idea," said Selwyn, "that Miss Erroll is going to play for you to sing."

They liked that. The infant Gerards were musically inclined, and nothing pleased them better than to lift their voices in unison. Besides, it always distressed Kit-Ki, and they never tired laughing to see the unhappy cat retreat before the first minor chord struck on the piano. More than that, the dogs always protested, noses pointed heavenward. It meant noise, which was always welcome in any form.

"Will you play, Miss Erroll?" inquired Selwyn.

Miss Erroll would play.

"Why do you always call her 'Miss Erroll'?" asked Billy. "Why don't you say 'Eileen'?"

Selwyn laughed. "I don't know, Billy; ask her; perhaps she knows."

Eileen laughed, too, delicately embarrassed and aware of his teasing smile. But Drina, always impressed by formality, said: "Uncle Philip isn't Eileen's uncle. People who are not relations say *Miss and Mrs.*"

"Are faver and muvver relations?" asked Josephine timidly.

"Y-es—no!—I don't know," admitted Drina; "*are* they, Eileen?"

"Why, yes—that is—that is to say—" And turning to Selwyn: "What dreadful questions. *Are* they relations, Captain Selwyn? Of course they are!"

"They were not before they were married," he said, laughing.

"If you married Eileen," began Billy, "you'd call her Eileen, I suppose."

"Certainly," said Selwyn.

"Why don't you?"

"That is another thing you must ask her, my son."

"Well, then, Eileen—"

But Miss Erroll was already seated at the nursery piano, and his demands were drowned in a decisive chord which brought the children clustering around her, while their nurses ran among them untying bibs and scrubbing faces and fingers in fresh water.

They sang like seraphs, grouped around the piano, fingers linked behind their backs. First it was "The Vicar of Bray." Then—and the cat fled at the first chord—"Lochleven Castle":

"Put	off,	put	off,
And	row	with	speed

For now is the time and the hour of need."

Miss Erroll sang, too; her voice leading—a charmingly trained, but childlike voice, of no pretensions, as fresh and unspoiled as the girl herself.

There was an interval after "Castles in the Air"; Eileen sat, with her marvellously white hands resting on the keys, awaiting further suggestion.

"Sing that funny song, Uncle Philip!" pleaded Billy; "you know—the one about:

"She	hit	him	with	a	shingle
Which	made	his	breeches		tingle
Because	he	pinched	his	little	baby	brother;
And	he	ran	down	the	lane
With	his	pants	full	of	pain.

Oh, a boy's best friend is his mother!"

"*Billy!*" gasped Miss Erroll.

Selwyn, mortified, said severely: "That is a very dreadful song, Billy—"

"But *you* taught it to me—"

Eileen swung around on the piano stool, but Selwyn had seized Billy and was promising to bolo him as soon as he wished.

And Eileen, surveying the scene from her perch, thought that Selwyn's years seemed to depend entirely upon his occupation, for he looked very boyish down there on his knees among the children; and she had not yet forgotten the sunken pallor of his features in the Park—no, nor her own question to him, still unanswered. For she had asked him who that woman was who had been so direct in her smiling salute. And he had not yet replied; probably never would; for she did not expect to ask him again.

Meanwhile the bolo-men were rushing the outposts to the outposts' intense satisfaction.

"Bang-bang!" repeated Winthrop; "I hit you, Uncle Philip. You are dead, you know!"

"Yes, but here comes another! Fire!" shouted Billy. "Save the flag! Hurrah! Pound on the piano, Eileen, and pretend it's cannon."

Chord after chord reverberated through the big sunny room, punctuated by all the cavalry music she had picked up from West Point and her friends in the squadron.

"We	can't	get	'em	up!
We	can't	get	'em	up!
We	can't	get	'em	up

In the morning!"

she sang, calmly watching the progress of the battle, until Selwyn disengaged himself from the _mêlée_ and sank breathlessly into a chair.

"All over," he said, declining further combat. "Play the 'Star-spangled Banner,' Miss Erroll."

"Boom!" crashed the chord for the sunset gun; then she played the anthem; Selwyn rose, and the children stood up at salute.

The party was over.

Selwyn and Miss Erroll, strolling together out of the nursery and down the stairs, fell unconsciously into the amiable exchange of badinage again; she taunting him with his undignified behaviour, he retorting in kind.

"Anyway that was a perfectly dreadful verse you taught Billy," she concluded.

"Not as dreadful as the chorus," he remarked, wincing.

"You're exactly like a bad small boy, Captain Selwyn; you look like one now—so sheepish! I've seen Gerald attempt to avoid admonition in exactly that fashion."

"How about a jolly brisk walk?" he inquired blandly; "unless you've something on. I suppose you have."

"Yes, I have; a tea at the Fanes, a function at the Grays. . . . Do you know Sudbury Gray? It's his mother."

They had strolled into the living room—a big, square, sunny place, in golden greens and browns, where a bay-window overlooked the Park.

Kneeling on the cushions of the deep window seat she flattened her delicate nose against the glass, peering out through the lace hangings.

"Everybody and his family are driving," she said over her shoulder. "The rich and great are cornering the fresh-air supply. It's interesting, isn't it, merely to sit here and count coteries! There is Mrs. Vendenning and

46

Gladys Orchil of the Black Fells set; there is that pretty Mrs. Delmour-Carnes; Newport! Here come some Cedarhurst people—the Fleetwoods. It always surprises one to see them out of the saddle. There is Evelyn Cardwell; she came out when I did; and there comes Sandon Craig with a very old lady—there, in that old-fashioned coach—oh, it is Mrs. Jan Van Elten, senior. What a very, very quaint old lady! I have been presented at court," she added, with a little laugh, "and now all the law has been fulfilled."

For a while she kneeled there, silently intent on the passing pageant with all the unconscious curiosity of a child. Presently, without turning: "They speak of the younger set—but what is its limit? So many, so many people! The hunting crowd—the silly crowd—the wealthy sets—the dreadful yellow set—then all those others made out of metals—copper and coal and iron and—" She shrugged her youthful shoulders, still intent on the passing show.

"Then there are the intellectuals—the artistic, the illuminated, the musical sorts. I—I wish I knew more of them. They were my father's friends—some of them." She looked over her shoulder to see where Selwyn was, and whether he was listening; smiled at him, and turned, resting one hand on the window seat. "So many kinds of people," she said, with a shrug.

"Yes," said Selwyn lazily, "there are all kinds of kinds. You remember that beautiful nature-poem:

```
'"The                                          sea-gull
And                        the                 eagul
And            the                 dipper-dapper-duck
And                        the                 Jew-fish
And                        the                 blue-fish
And      the          turtle      in    the    muck;
And                        the                 squir'l
And                        the                 girl
And      the          flippy      floppy       bat
Are                                            differ-ent
As              gent           from            gent.
So let it go at that!'"
```

"What hideous nonsense," she laughed, in open encouragement; but he could recall nothing more—or pretended he couldn't.

"You asked me," he said, "whether I know Sudbury Gray. I do, slightly. What about him?" And he waited, remembering Nina's suggestion as to that wealthy young man's eligibility.

"He's one of the nicest men I know," she replied frankly.

"Yes, but you don't know 'Boots' Lansing."

"The gentleman who was bucked out of his footwear? Is he attractive?"

47

"Rather. Shrieks rent the air when 'Boots' left Manila."

"Feminine shrieks?"

"Exclusively. The men were glad enough. He has three months' leave this winter, so you'll see him soon."

She thanked him mockingly for the promise, watching him from amused eyes. After a moment she said:

"I ought to arise and go forth with timbrels and with dances; but, do you know, I am not inclined to revels? There has been a little—just a very little bit too much festivity so far. . . . Not that I don't adore dinners and gossip and dances; not that I do not love to pervade bright and glittering places. Oh, no. Only—I—"

She looked shyly a moment at Selwyn: "I sometimes feel a curious desire for other things. I have been feeling it all day."

"What things?"

"I—don't know—exactly; substantial things. I'd like to learn about things. My father was the head of the American School of Archæology in Crete. My mother was his intellectual equal, I believe—"

Her voice had fallen as she spoke. "Do you wonder that physical pleasure palls a little at times? I inherit something besides a capacity for dancing."

He nodded, watching her with an interest and curiosity totally new.

"When I was ten years old I was taken abroad for the winter. I saw the excavations in Crete for the buried city which father discovered near Præsos. We lived for a while with Professor Flanders in the Fayum district; I saw the ruins of Kahun, built nearly three thousand years before the coming of Christ; I myself picked up a scarab as old as the ruins! . . . Captain Selwyn—I was only a child of ten; I could understand very little of what I saw and heard, but I have never, never forgotten the happiness of that winter! . . . And that is why, at times, pleasures tire me a little; and a little discontent creeps in. It is ungrateful and ungracious of me to say so, but I did wish so much to go to college—to have something to care for—as mother cared for father's work. Why, do you know that my mother accidentally discovered the thirty-seventh sign in the Karian Signary?"

"No," said Selwyn, "I did not know that." He forbore to add that he did not know what a Signary resembled or where Karia might be.

Miss Erroll's elbow was on her knee, her chin resting within her open palm.

"Do you know about my parents?" she asked. "They were lost in the *Argolis* off Cyprus. You have heard. I think they meant that I should go to college—as well as Gerald; I don't know. Perhaps after all it is better for me to do what other young girls do. Besides, I enjoy it; and my mother did, too, when she was my age, they say. She was very much gayer than I am; my mother was a beauty and a brilliant woman. . . . But there were other qualities. I—have her letters to father when Gerald and I were very little; and her letters to us from London. . . . I have missed her more, this winter, it seems to me, than even in that dreadful time—"

She sat silent, chin in hand, delicate fingers restlessly worrying her red lips; then, in quick impulse:

"You will not mistake me, Captain Selwyn! Nina and Austin have been perfectly sweet to me and to Gerald."

"I am not mistaking a word you utter," he said.

"No, of course not. . . . Only there are times . . . moments . . ."

Her voice died; her clear eyes looked out into space while the silent seconds lengthened into minutes. One slender finger had slipped between her lips and teeth; the burnished strand of hair which Nina dreaded lay neglected against her cheek.

"I should like to know," she began, as though to herself, "something about everything. That being out of the question, I should like to know everything about something. That also being out of the question, for third choice I should like to know something about something. I am not too ambitious, am I?"

Selwyn did not offer to answer.

"*Am* I?" she repeated, looking directly at him.

"I thought you were asking yourself."

"But you need not reply; there is no sense in my question."

She stood up, indifferent, absent-eyed, half turning toward the window; and, raising her hand, she carelessly brought the rebel strand of hair under discipline.

"You *said* you were going to look up Gerald," she observed.

"I am; now. What are you going to do?"

"I? Oh, dress, I suppose. Nina ought to be back now, and she expects me to go out with her."

She nodded a smiling termination of their duet, and moved toward the door. Then, on impulse, she turned, a question on her lips—left unuttered through instinct. It had to do with the identity of the pretty woman who had so directly saluted him in the Park—a perfectly friendly, simple, and natural question. Yet it remained unuttered.

She turned again to the doorway; a maid stood there holding a note on a salver.

"For Captain Selwyn, please," murmured the maid.

Miss Erroll passed out.

Selwyn took the note and broke the seal:

"MY DEAR SELWYN: I'm in a beastly fix—an I.O.U. due to-night and *pas de quoi*! Obviously I don't want Neergard to know, being associated as I am with him in business. As for Austin, he's a peppery old boy, bless his heart, and I'm not very secure in his good graces at present. Fact is I got into a rather stiff game last night—and it's a matter of honour. So can you help me to tide it over? I'll square it on the first of the month.

"Yours sincerely,

"GERALD ERROLL.

"P.S.—I've meant to look you up for ever so long, and will the first moment I have free."

Below this was pencilled the amount due; and Selwyn's face grew very serious.

The letter he wrote in return ran:

"DEAR GERALD: Check enclosed to your order. By the way, can't you lunch with me at the Lenox Club some day this week? Write, wire, or telephone when.

"Yours,

"SELWYN."

When he had sent the note away by the messenger he walked back to the bay-window, hands in his pockets, a worried expression in his gray eyes. This sort of thing must not be repeated; the boy must halt in his tracks and face sharply the other way. Besides, his own income was limited—much too limited to admit of many more loans of that sort.

He ought to see Gerald at once, but somehow he could not in decency appear personally on the heels of his loan. A certain interval must elapse between the loan and the lecture; in fact he didn't see very well how he could admonish and instruct until the loan had been cancelled—that is, until the first of the New Year.

Pacing the floor, disturbed, uncertain as to the course he should pursue, he looked up presently to see Miss Erroll descending the stairs, fresh and sweet in her radiant plumage. As she caught his eye she waved a silvery chinchilla muff at him—a marching salute—and passed on, calling back to him: "Don't forget Gerald!"

"No," he said, "I won't forget Gerald." He stood a moment at the window watching the brougham below where Nina awaited Miss Erroll. Then, abruptly, he turned back into the room and picked up the telephone receiver, muttering: "This is no time to mince matters for the sake of appearances." And he called up Gerald at the offices of Neergard & Co.

"Is it you, Gerald?" he asked pleasantly. "It's all right about that matter; I've sent you a note by your messenger. But I want to talk to you about another matter—something concerning myself—I want to ask your advice, in a way. Can you be at the Lenox by six? . . . You have an engagement at eight? Oh, that's all right; I won't keep you. . . . It's understood, then; the Lenox at six. . . . Good-bye."

There was the usual early evening influx of men at the Lenox who dropped in for a glance at the ticker, or for a cocktail or a game of billiards or a bit of gossip before going home to dress.

Selwyn sauntered over to the basket, inspected a yard or two of tape, then strolled toward the window, nodding to Bradley Harmon and Sandon Craig.

As he turned his face to the window and his back to the room, Harmon came up rather effusively, offering an unusually thin flat hand and further hospitality, pleasantly declined by Selwyn.

"Horrible thing, a cocktail," observed Harmon, after giving his own order and seating himself opposite Selwyn. "I don't usually do it. Here comes the man who persuades me!—my own partner—"

Selwyn looked up to see Fane approaching; and instantly a dark flush overspread his face.

"You know George Fane, don't you?" continued Harmon easily; "well, that's odd; I thought, of course—Captain Selwyn, Mr. Fane. It's not usual—but it's done."

They exchanged formalities—dry and brief on Selwyn's part, gracefully urbane on Fane's.

"I've heard so pleasantly of you from Gerald Erroll," he said, "and of course our people have always been on cordial terms. Neither Mrs. Fane nor I was fortunate enough to meet you last Tuesday at the Gerards— such a crush, you know. Are you not joining us, Captain Selwyn?" as the servant appeared to take orders.

Selwyn declined again, glancing at Harmon—a large-framed, bony young man with blond, closely trimmed and pointed beard, and the fair colour of a Swede. He had the high, flat cheek-bones of one, too; and a thicket of corn-tinted hair, which was usually damp at the ends, and curled flat against his forehead. He seemed to be always in a slight perspiration—he had been, anyway, every time Selwyn met him anywhere.

51

Sandon Craig and Billy Fleetwood came wandering up and joined them; one or two other men, drifting by, adhered to the group.

Selwyn, involved in small talk, glanced sideways at the great clock, and gathered himself together for departure.

Fleetwood was saying to Craig: "Certainly it was a stiff game—Bradley, myself, Gerald Erroll, Mrs. Delmour-Carnes, and the Ruthvens."

"Were you hit?" asked Craig, interested.

"No; about even. Gerald got it good and plenty, though. The Ruthvens were ahead as usual—"

Selwyn, apparently hearing nothing, quietly rose and stepped out of the circle, paused to set fire to a cigarette, and then strolled off toward the visitors' room, where Gerald was now due.

Fane stretched his neck, looking curiously after him. Then he said to Fleetwood: "Why begin to talk about Mrs. Ruthven when our friend yonder is about? Rotten judgment you show, Billy."

"Well, I clean forgot," said Fleetwood; "what did I say, anyway? A man can't always remember who's divorced from who in this town."

Harmon, whose civility to Selwyn had possibly been based on his desire for pleasant relations with Austin Gerard and the Arickaree Loan and Trust Company, looked at Fleetwood thoroughly vexed. But nobody could have suspected vexation in that high-boned smile which showed such very red lips through the blond beard.

Fane, too, smiled; his prominent soft brown eyes expressed gentlest good-humour, and he passed his hand reflectively over his unusually small and retreating chin. Perhaps he was thinking of the meeting in the Park that morning. It was amusing; but men do not speak of such things at their clubs, no matter how amusing. Besides, if the story were aired and were traced to him, Ruthven might turn ugly. There was no counting on Ruthven.

Meanwhile Selwyn, perplexed and worried, found young Erroll just entering the visitors' room, and greeted him with nervous cordiality.

"If you can't stay and dine with me," he said, "I won't put you down. You know, of course, I can only ask you once in a year, so we'll stay here and chat a bit."

"Right you are," said young Erroll, flinging off his very new and very fashionable overcoat—a wonderfully handsome boy, with all the attraction that a quick, warm, impulsive manner carries. "And I say, Selwyn, it was awfully decent of you to—"

"Bosh! Friends are for that sort of thing, Gerald. Sit here—" He looked at the young man hesitatingly; but Gerald calmly took the matter out of his jurisdiction by nodding his order to the club attendant.

52

"Lord, but I'm tired," he said, sinking back into a big arm-chair; "I was up till daylight, and then I had to be in the office by nine, and to-night Billy Fleetwood is giving—oh, something or other. By the way, the market isn't doing a thing to the shorts! You're not in, are you, Selwyn?"

"No, not that way. I hope you are not, either; are you, Gerald?"

"Oh, it's all right," replied the young fellow confidently; and raising his glass, he nodded at Selwyn with a smile.

"You were mighty nice to me, anyhow," he said, setting his glass aside and lighting a cigar. "You see, I went to a dance, and after a while some of us cleared out, and Jack Ruthven offered us trouble; so half a dozen of us went there. I had the worst cards a man ever drew to a kicker. That was all about it."

The boy was utterly unconscious that he was treading on delicate ground as he rattled on in his warmhearted, frank, and generous way. Totally oblivious that the very name of Ruthven must be unwelcome if not offensive to his listener, he laughed through a description of the affair, its thrilling episodes, and Mrs. Jack Ruthven's blind luck in the draw.

"One moment," interrupted Selwyn, very gently; "do you mind saying whether you banked my check and drew against it?"

"Why, no; I just endorsed it over."

"To—to whom?—if I may venture—"

"Certainly," he said, with a laugh; "to Mrs. Jack—" Then, in a flash, for the first time the boy realised what he was saying, and stopped aghast, scarlet to his hair.

Selwyn's face had little colour remaining in it, but he said very kindly: "It's all right, Gerald; don't worry—"

"I'm a beast!" broke out the boy; "I beg your pardon a thousand times."

"Granted, old chap. But, Gerald, may I say one thing—or perhaps two?"

"Go ahead! Give it to me good and plenty!"

"It's only this: couldn't you and I see one another a little oftener? Don't be afraid of me; I'm no wet blanket. I'm not so very aged, either; I know something of the world—I understand something of men. I'm pretty good company, Gerald. What do you say?"

"I say, *sure!*" cried the boy warmly.

"It's a go, then. And one thing more: couldn't you manage to come up to the house a little oftener? Everybody misses you, of course; I think your sister is a trifle sensitive—"

"I will!" said Gerald, blushing. "Somehow I've had such a lot on hand—all day at the office, and something on every evening. I know perfectly well I've neglected Eily—and everybody. But the first moment I can find free—"

Selwyn nodded. "And last of all," he said, "there's something about my own affairs that I thought you might advise me on."

Gerald, proud, enchanted, stood very straight; the older man continued gravely:

"I've a little capital to invest—not very much. Suppose—and this, I need not add, is in confidence between us—suppose I suggested to Mr. Neergard—"

"Oh," cried young Erroll, delighted, "that is fine! Neergard would be glad enough. Why, we've got that Valleydale tract in shape now, and there are scores of schemes in the air—scores of them—important moves which may mean—anything!" he ended, excitedly.

"Then you think it would be all right—in case Neergard likes the idea?"

Gerald was enthusiastic. After a while they shook hands, it being time to separate. And for a long time Selwyn sat there alone in the visitors' room, absent-eyed, facing the blazing fire of cannel coal.

How to be friends with this boy without openly playing the mentor; how to gain his confidence without appearing to seek it; how to influence him without alarming him! No; there was no great harm in him yet; only the impulse of inconsiderate youth; only an enthusiastic capacity for pleasure.

One thing was imperative—the boy must cut out his card-playing for stakes at once; and there was a way to accomplish that by impressing Gerald with the idea that to do anything behind Neergard's back which he would not care to tell him about was a sort of treachery.

Who were these people, anyway, who would permit a boy of that age, and in a responsible position, to play for such stakes? Who were they to encourage such—?

Selwyn's tightening grasp on his chair suddenly relaxed; he sank back, staring at the brilliant coals. He, too, had forgotten.

Now he remembered, in humiliation unspeakable, in bitterness past all belief.

Time sped, and he sat there, motionless; and gradually the bitterness became less perceptible as he drifted, intent on drifting, back through the exotic sorcery of dead years—back into the sun again, where honour was bright and life was young—where all the world awaited happy conquest—where there was no curfew in the red evening glow; no end to day, because the golden light had turned to silver; but where the earliest hint of dawn was a challenge, and where every yellow star whispered "Awake!"

And out of the magic *she* had come into his world again!

Sooner or later he would meet her now. That was sure. When? Where? And of what significance was it, after all?

Whom did it concern? Him? Her? And what had he to say to her, after all? Or she to him?

Not one word.

About midnight he roused himself and picked up his hat and coat.

"Do you wish a cab, please?" whispered the club servant who held his coat; "it is snowing very hard, sir."

CHAPTER III

UNDER THE ASHES

He had neither burned nor returned the photograph to Mrs. Ruthven. The prospect perplexed and depressed Selwyn.

He was sullenly aware that in a town where the divorced must ever be reckoned with when dance and dinner lists are made out, there is always some thoughtless hostess—and sometimes a mischievous one; and the chances were that he and Mrs. Jack Ruthven would collide, either through the forgetfulness or malice of somebody or, through sheer hazard, at some large affair where Destiny and Fate work busily together in criminal copartnership.

And he encountered her first at a masque and revel given by Mrs. Delmour-Carnes where Fate contrived that he should dance in the same set with his *ci-devant* wife before the unmasking, and where, unaware, they gaily exchanged salute and hand-clasp before the jolly *mêlée* of unmasking revealed how close together two people could come after parting for ever and a night at the uttermost ends of the earth.

When masks at last were off there was neither necessity nor occasion for the two surprised and rather pallid young people to renew civilities; but later, Destiny, the saturnine partner in the business, interfered; and some fool in the smoking room tried to introduce Selwyn to

Ruthven. The slightest mistake on their parts would have rendered the incident ridiculous; and Ruthven made that mistake.

That was Selwyn's first encounter with the Ruthvens. A short time afterward at the opera Gerald dragged him into a parterre to say something amiable to one of the débutante Craig girls—and Selwyn found himself again facing Alixe.

If there was any awkwardness it was not apparent, although they both knew that they were in full view of the house.

A cool bow and its cooler acknowledgment, a formal word and more formal reply; and Selwyn made his way to the corridor, hot with vexation, unaware of where he was going, and oblivious of the distressed and apologetic young man, who so contritely kept step with him through the brilliantly crowded promenade.

That was the second time—not counting distant glimpses in crowded avenues, in the Park, at Sherry's, or across the hazy glitter of thronged theatres. But the third encounter was different.

It was all a mistake, born of the haste of a heedless and elderly matron, celebrated for managing to do the wrong thing, but who had been excessively nice to him that winter, and whose position in Manhattan was not to be assailed.

"Dear Captain Selwyn," she wheezed over the telephone, "I'm short one man; and we dine at eight and it's that now. *Could* you help me? It's the rich and yellow, this time, but you won't mind, will you?"

Selwyn, standing at the lower telephone in the hall, asked her to hold the wire a moment, and glanced up at his sister who was descending the stairs with Eileen, dinner having at that instant been announced.

"Mrs. T. West Minster—flying signals of distress," he said, carefully covering the transmitter as he spoke; "man overboard, and will I kindly take a turn at the wheel?"

"What a shame!" said Eileen; "you are going to spoil the first home dinner we have had together in weeks!"

"Tell her to get some yellow pup!" growled Austin, from above.

"As though anybody could get a yellow pup when they whistle," said Nina hopelessly.

"That's true," nodded Selwyn; "I'm the original old dog Tray. Whistle, and I come padding up. Ever faithful, you see."

And he uncovered the transmitter and explained to Mrs. T. West Minster his absurd delight at being whistled at. Then he sent for a cab and sauntered into the dining-room, where he was received with undisguised hostility.

"She's been civil to me," he said; "*jeunesse oblige*, you know. And that's why I—"

"There'll be a lot of débutantes there! What do you want to go for, you cradle robber!" protested Austin—"a lot of water-bibbing, olive-eating, talcum-powdered débutantes—"

Eileen straightened up stiffly, and Selwyn's teasing smile and his offered hand in adieu completed her indignation.

"Oh, good-bye! No, I won't shake hands. There's your cab, now. I wish you'd take Austin, too; Nina and I are tired of dining with the prematurely aged."

"Indeed, we are," said Mrs. Gerard; "go to your club, Austin, and give me a chance to telephone to somebody under the anesthetic age."

Selwyn departed, laughing, but he yawned in his cab all the way to Fifty-third Street, where he entered in the wake of the usual laggards and, surrendering hat and coat in the cloak room, picked up the small slim envelope bearing his name.

The card within disclosed the information that he was to take in Mrs. Somebody-or-Other; he made his way through a great many people, found his hostess, backed off, stood on one leg for a moment like a reflective water-fowl, then found Mrs. Somebody-or-Other and was absently good to her through a great deal of noise and some Spanish music, which seemed to squirt through a thicket of palms and bespatter everybody.

"Wonderful music," observed his dinner partner, with singular originality; "*so* like Carmen."

"Is it?" he replied, and took her away at a nod from his hostess, whose daughter Dorothy leaned forward from her partner's arm at the same moment, and whispered: "I *must* speak to you, mamma! You *can't* put Captain Selwyn there because—"

But her mother was deaf and smilingly sensitive about it, so she merely guessed what reply her child expected: "It's all settled, dear; Captain Selwyn arrived a moment ago." And she closed the file.

It was already too late, anyhow; and presently, turning to see who was seated on his left, Selwyn found himself gazing into the calm, flushed face of Alixe Ruthven. It was their third encounter.

They exchanged a dazed nod of recognition, a meaningless murmur, and turned again, apparently undisturbed, to their respective dinner partners.

A great many curious eyes, lingering on them, shifted elsewhere, in reluctant disappointment.

As for the hostess, she had, for one instant, come as near to passing heavenward as she could without doing it when she discovered the situation. Then she accepted it with true humour. She could afford to. But her daughters, Sheila and Dorothy, suffered acutely, being of this year's output and martyrs to responsibility.

Meanwhile, Selwyn, grimly aware of an accident somewhere, and perfectly conscious of the feelings which must by this time dominate his hostess, was wondering how best to avoid anything that might resemble a situation.

Instead of two or three dozen small tables, scattered among the palms of the winter garden, their hostess had preferred to construct a great oval board around the aquarium. The arrangement made it a little easier for Selwyn and Mrs. Ruthven. He talked to his dinner partner until she began to respond in monosyllables, which closed each subject that he opened and wearied him as much as he was boring her. But Bradley Harmon, the man on her right, evidently had better fortune; and presently Selwyn found himself with nobody to talk to, which came as near to embarrassing him as anything could, and which so enraged his hostess that she struck his partner's name from her lists for ever. People were already glancing at him askance in sly amusement or cold curiosity.

Then he did a thing which endeared him to Mrs. T. West Minster and to her two disconsolate children.

"Mrs. Ruthven," he said, very naturally and pleasantly, "I think perhaps we had better talk for a moment or two—if you don't mind."

She said quietly, "I don't mind," and turned with charming composure. Every eye shifted to them, then obeyed decency or training; and the slightest break in the gay tumult was closed up with chatter and laughter.

"Plucky," said Sandon Craig to his fair neighbour; "but by what chance did our unfortunate hostess do it?"

"She's usually doing it, isn't she? What occupies me," returned his partner, "is how on earth Alixe could have thrown away that adorable man for Jack Ruthven. Why, he is already trying to scramble into Rosamund Fane's lap—the horrid little poodle!—always curled up on the edge of your skirt!"

She stared at Mrs. Ruthven across the crystal reservoir brimming with rose and ivory-tinted water-lilies.

"That girl is marked for destruction," she said slowly; "the gods have done their work already."

But whatever Alixe had been, whatever she now was, she showed to her little world only a pale brunette symmetry—a strange and changeless lustre, varying as little as the moon's phases; and like that burnt-out planet, reflecting any flame that flared until her clear, young beauty seemed pulsating with the promise of hidden fire.

Selwyn, outwardly amiable and formal, was saying in a low voice: "My dinner partner is quite impossible, you see; and I happen to be here as a filler in—commanded to the presence only a few minutes ago. It's a pardonable error; I bear no malice. But I'm sorry for you."

There was a silence; Alixe straightened her slim figure, and turned; but young Innis, who had taken her in, had become confidential with Mrs. Fane. As for Selwyn's partner, she probably divined his conversational designs on her, but she merely turned her bare shoulder a trifle more unmistakably and continued her gossip with Bradley Harmon.

Alixe broke a tiny morsel from her bread, sensible of the tension.

"I suppose," she said, as though reciting to some new acquaintance an amusing bit of gossip—"that we are destined to this sort of thing occasionally and had better get used to it."

"I suppose so."

"Please," she added, after a pause, "aid me a little."

"I will if I can. What am I to say?"

"Have you nothing to say?" she asked, smiling; "it need not be very civil, you know—as long as nobody hears you."

To school his features for the deception of others, to school his voice and manner and at the same time look smilingly into the grave of his youth and hope called for the sort of self-command foreign to his character. Glancing at him under her smoothly fitted mask of amiability, she slowly grew afraid of the situation—but not of her ability to sustain her own part.

They exchanged a few meaningless phrases, then she resolutely took young Innis away from Rosamund Fane, leaving Selwyn to count the bubbles in his wine-glass.

But in a few moments, whether by accident or deliberate design, Rosamund interfered again, and Mrs. Ruthven was confronted with the choice of a squabble for possession of young Innis, of conspicuous silence, or of resuming once more with Selwyn. And she chose the last resort.

"You are living in town?" she asked pleasantly.

"Yes."

"Of course; I forgot. I met a man last night who said you had entered the firm of Neergard & Co."

"I have. Who was the man?"

"You can never guess, Captain Selwyn."

"I don't want to. Who was he?"

"Please don't terminate so abruptly the few subjects we have in reserve. We may be obliged to talk to each other for a number of minutes if Rosamund doesn't let us alone. . . . The man was 'Boots' Lansing."

"'Boots!' Here!"

"Arrived from Manila Sunday. *Sans gêne* as usual he introduced you as the subject, and told me—oh, dozens of things about you. I suppose he began inquiring for you before he crossed the troopers' gangplank; and somebody sent him to Neergard& Co. Haven't you seen him?"

"No," he said, staring at the brilliant fish, which glided along the crystal tank, goggling their eyes at the lights.

"You—you are living with the Gerards, I believe," she said carelessly.

"For a while."

"Oh, 'Boots' says that he is expecting to take an apartment with you somewhere."

"What! Has 'Boots' resigned?"

"So he says. He told me that you had resigned. I did not understand that; I imagined you were here on leave until I heard about Neergard & Co."

"Do you suppose I could have remained in the service?" he demanded. His voice was dry and almost accentless.

"Why not?" she returned, paling.

"You may answer that question more pleasantly than I can."

She usually avoided champagne; but she had to do something for herself now. As for him, he took what was offered without noticing what he took, and grew whiter and whiter; but a fixed glow gradually appeared and remained on her cheeks; courage, impatience, a sudden anger at the forced conditions steadied her nerves.

"Will you please prove equal to the situation?" she said under her breath, but with a charming smile. "Do you know you are scowling? These people here are ready to laugh; and I'd much prefer that they tear us to rags on suspicion of our over-friendliness."

"Who is that fool woman who is monopolising your partner?"

"Rosamund Fane; she's doing it on purpose. You must try to smile now and then."

"My face is stiff with grinning," he said, "but I'll do what I can for you—"

"Please include yourself, too."

"Oh, I can stand their opinions," he said; "I only meet the yellow sort occasionally; I don't herd with them."

"I do, thank you."

"How do you like them? What is your opinion of the yellow set? Here they sit all about you—the Phoenix Mottlys, Mrs. Delmour-Carnes yonder, the Draymores, the Orchils, the Vendenning lady, the Lawns of Westlawn—" he paused, then deliberately—"and the 'Jack' Ruthvens. I forgot, Alixe, that you are now perfectly equipped to carry aloft the golden hod."

"Go on," she said, drawing a deep breath, but the fixed smile never altered.

"No," he said; "I can't talk. I thought I could, but I can't. Take that boy away from Mrs. Fane as soon as you can."

"I can't yet. You must go on. I ask your aid to carry this thing through. I—I am afraid of their ridicule. Could you try to help me a little?"

"If you put it that way, of course." And, after a silence, "What am I to say? What in God's name shall I say to you, Alixe?"

"Anything bitter—as long as you control your voice and features. Try to smile at me when you speak, Philip."

"All right. I have no reason to be bitter, anyway," he said; "and every reason to be otherwise."

"That is not true. You tell me that I have ruined your career in the army. I did not know I was doing it. Can you believe me?"

And, as he made no response: "I did not dream you would have to resign. Do you believe me?"

"There is no choice," he said coldly. "Drop the subject!"

"That is brutal. I never thought—" She forced a smile and drew her glass toward her. The straw-tinted wine slopped over and frothed on the white skin of her arm.

"Well," she breathed, "this ghastly dinner is nearly ended."

He nodded pleasantly.

"And—Phil?"—a bit tremulous.

"What?"

"Was it all my fault? I mean in the beginning? I've wanted to ask you that—to know your view of it. Was it?"

"No. It was mine, most of it."

"Not all—not half! We did not know how; that is the wretched explanation of it all."

"And we could never have learned; that's the rest of the answer. But the fault is not there."

"I know; 'better to bear the ills we have.'"

"Yes; more respectable to bear them. Let us drop this in decency's name, Alixe!"

After a silence, she began: "One more thing—I must know it; and I am going to ask you—if I may. Shall I?"

He smiled cordially, and she laughed as though confiding a delightful bit of news to him:

"Do you regard me as sufficiently important to dislike me?"

"I do not—dislike you."

"Is it stronger than dislike, Phil?"

"Y-es."

"Contempt?"

"No."

"What is it?"

"It is that—I have not yet—become—reconciled."

"To my—folly?"

"To mine."

She strove to laugh lightly, and failing, raised her glass to her lips again.

"Now you know," he said, pitching his tones still lower. "I am glad after all that we have had this plain understanding. I have never felt unkindly toward you. I can't. What you did I might have prevented had I known enough; but I cannot help it now; nor can you if you would."

"If I would," she repeated gaily—for the people opposite were staring.

"We are done for," he said, nodding carelessly to a servant to refill his glass; "and I abide by conditions because I choose to; not," he added contemptuously, "because a complacent law has tethered you to—to the thing that has crawled up on your knees to have its ears rubbed."

The level insult to her husband stunned her; she sat there, upright, the white smile stamped on her stiffened lips, fingers tightening about the stem of her wine-glass.

62

He began to toss bread crumbs to the scarlet fish, laughing to himself in an ugly way. "*I* wish to punish you? Why, Alixe, only look at *him!*—Look at his gold wristlets; listen to his simper, his lisp. Little girl—oh, little girl, what have you done to yourself?—for you have done nothing to me, child, that can match it in sheer atrocity!"

Her colour was long in returning.

"Philip," she said unsteadily, "I don't think I can stand this—"

"Yes, you can."

"I am too close to the wall. I—"

"Talk to Scott Innis. Take him away from Rosamund Fane; that will tide you over. Or feed those fool fish; like this! Look how they rush and flap and spatter! That's amusing, isn't it—for people with the intellects of canaries. . . . Will you please try to say something? Mrs. T. West is exhibiting the restless symptoms of a hen turkey at sundown and we'll all go to roost in another minute. . . . Don't shiver that way!"

"I c-can't control it; I will in a moment. . . . Give me a chance; talk to me, Phil."

"Certainly. The season has been unusually gay and the opera most stupidly brilliant; stocks continue to fluctuate; another old woman was tossed and gored by a mad motor this morning. . . . More time, Alixe? . . . With pleasure; Mrs. Vendenning has bought a third-rate castle in Wales; a man was found dead with a copy of the *Tribune* in his pocket— the verdict being in accordance with fact; the Panama Canal—"

But it was over at last; a flurry of sweeping skirts; ranks of black and white in escort to the passage of the fluttering silken procession.

"Good-bye," she said; "I am not staying for the dance."

"Good-bye," he said pleasantly; "I wish you better fortune for the future. I'm sorry I was rough."

He was not staying, either. A dull excitement possessed him, resembling suspense—as though he were awaiting a dénouement; as though there was yet some crisis to come.

Several men leaned forward to talk to him; he heard without heeding, replied at hazard, lighted his cigar with the others, and leaned back, his coffee before him—a smiling, attractive young fellow, apparently in lazy enjoyment of the time and place and without one care in the world he found so pleasant.

For a while his mind seemed to be absolutely blank; voices were voices only; he saw lights, and figures moving through a void. Then reality took shape sharply; and his pulses began again hammering out the irregular measure of suspense, though what it was that he was awaiting, what expecting, Heaven alone knew.

And after a while he found himself in the ballroom.

The younger set was arriving; he recognised several youthful people, friends of Eileen Erroll; and taking his bearings among these bright, fresh faces—amid this animated throng, constantly increased by the arrival of others, he started to find his hostess, now lost to sight in the breezy circle of silk and lace setting in from the stairs.

He heard names announced which meant nothing to him, which stirred no memory; names which sounded vaguely familiar; names which caused him to turn quickly—but seldom were the faces as familiar as the names.

He said to a girl, behind whose chair he was standing: "All the younger brothers and sisters are coming here to confound me; I hear a Miss Innis announced, but it turns out to be her younger sister—"

"By the way, do you know my name?" she asked.

"No," he said frankly, "do you know mine?"

"Of course, I do; I listened breathlessly when somebody presented you wholesale at your sister's the other day. I'm Rosamund Fane. You might as well be instructed because you're to take me in at the Orchils' next Thursday night, I believe."

"Rosamund Fane," he repeated coolly. "I wonder how we've avoided each other so consistently this winter? I never before had a good view of you, though I heard you talking to young Innis at dinner. And yet," he added, smiling, "if I had been instructed to look around and select somebody named Rosamund, I certainly should have decided on you."

"A compliment?" she asked, raising her delicate eyebrows.

"Ask yourself," he said.

"I do; and I get snubbed."

And, smiling still, he said: "Do you know the most mischievous air that Schubert ever worried us with?"

"'Rosamund,'" she said; "and—thank you, Captain Selwyn." She had coloured to the hair.

"'Rosamund,'" he nodded carelessly—"the most mischievous of melodies—" He stopped short, then coolly resumed: "That mischievous quality is largely a matter of accident, I fancy. Schubert never meant that 'Rosamund' should interfere with anybody's business."

"And—when did you first encounter the malice in 'Rosamund,' Captain Selwyn?" she asked with perfect self-possession.

He did not answer immediately; his smile had died out. Then: "The first time I really understood 'Rosamund' was when I heard Rosamund during a very delightful dinner."

She said: "If a woman keeps at a man long enough she'll extract compliments or yawns." And looking up at a chinless young man who had halted near her: "George, Captain Selwyn has acquired such a charmingly Oriental fluency during his residence in the East that I thought—if you ever desired to travel again—" She shrugged, and, glancing at Selwyn: "Have you met my husband? Oh, of course."

They exchanged a commonplace or two, then other people separated them without resistance on their part. And Selwyn found himself drifting, mildly interested in the vapid exchange of civilities which cost nobody a mental effort.

His sister, he had once thought, was certainly the most delightfully youthful matron in New York. But now he made an exception of Mrs. Fane; Rosamund Fane was much younger—must have been younger, for she still had something of that volatile freshness—that vague atmosphere of immaturity clinging to her like a perfume almost too delicate to detect. And under that the most profound capacity for mischief he had ever known of. Sauntering amiably amid the glittering groups continually forming and disintegrating under the clustered lights, he finally succeeded in reaching his hostess.

And Mrs. T. West Minster disengaged herself from the throng with intention as he approached.

No—and he was so sorry; and it was very amiable of his hostess to want him, but he was not remaining for the dance.

So much for the hostess, who stood there massive and gem-laden, her kindly and painted features tinted now with genuine emotion.

"*Je m'accuse, mon fils!*—but you acted like a perfect dear," she said. "*Mea culpa, mea culpa*; and *can* you forgive a very much mortified old lady who is really and truly fond of you?"

He laughed, holding her fat, ringed hands in both of his with all the attractive deference that explained his popularity. Rising excitement had sent the colour into his face and cleared his pleasant gray eyes; and he looked very young and handsome, his broad shoulders bent a trifle before the enamelled and bejewelled matron.

"Forgive you?" he repeated with a laugh of protest; "on the contrary, I thank you. Mrs. Ruthven is one of the most charming women I know, if that is what you mean?"

Looking after him as he made his way toward the cloak room: "The boy is thoroughbred," she reflected cynically; "and the only amusement anybody can get out of it will be at my expense! Rosamund is a perfect cat!"

He had sent for his cab, which, no doubt, was in line somewhere, wedged among the ranks of carriages stretching east and west along the snowy street; and he stood on the thick crimson carpet under the awning while it was being summoned. A few people like himself were not staying for the dance; others who had dined by prearrangement with other hostesses, had now begun to arrive, and the confusion grew as coach and brougham and motor came swaying up through the falling snow to deposit their jewelled cargoes of silks and laces under the vast awning picketed by policemen and lined with fur-swathed grooms and spindle-legged chauffeurs in coats of pony-skin.

The Cornelius Suydams, emerging from the house, offered Selwyn tonneau room, but he smilingly declined, having a mind for solitude and the Lenox Club. A phalanx of débutantes, opera bound, also left. Then the tide set heavily the other way, and there seemed no end to the line of arriving vehicles and guests, until he heard a name pronounced; a policeman warned back an approaching Fiat; and Selwyn saw Mrs. Ruthven, enveloped in white furs, step from the portal.

She saw him as he moved back, nodded, passed directly to her brougham, and set foot on the step. Pausing here, she looked about her, right and left, then over her shoulder straight back at Selwyn; and as she stood in silence evidently awaiting him, it became impossible for him any longer to misunderstand without a public affront to her.

When he started toward her she spoke to her maid, and the latter moved aside with a word to the groom in waiting.

"My maid will dismiss your carriage," she said pleasantly when he halted beside her. "There is one thing more which I must say to you."

Was this what he had expected hazard might bring to him?—was this the prophecy of his hammering pulses?

"Please hurry before people come out," she added, and entered the brougham.

"I can't do this," he muttered.

"I've sent away my maid," she said. "Nobody has noticed; those are servants out there. Will you please come before anybody arriving or departing does notice?"

And, as he did not move: "Are you going to make me conspicuous by this humiliation before servants?"

He said something between his set teeth and entered the brougham.

"Do you know what you've done?" he demanded harshly.

"Yes; nothing yet. But you would have done enough to stir this borough if you had delayed another second."

"Your maid saw—"

"My maid is *my* maid."

He leaned back in his corner, gray eyes narrowing.

"Naturally," he said, "you are the one to be considered, not the man in the case."

"Thank you. *Are* you the man in the case?"

"There is no case," he said coolly.

"Then why worry about me?"

He folded his arms, sullenly at bay; yet had no premonition of what to expect from her.

"You were very brutal to me," she said at length.

"I know it; and I did not intend to be. The words came."

"You had me at your mercy; and showed me little—a very little at first. Afterward, none."

"The words came," he repeated; "I'm sick with self-contempt, I tell you."

She set her white-gloved elbow on the window sill and rested her chin in her palm.

"That—money," she said with an effort. "You set—some—aside for me."

"Half," he nodded calmly.

"Why?"

He was silent.

"*Why?* I did not ask for it? There was nothing in the—the legal proceedings to lead you to believe that I desired it; was there?"

"No."

"Well, then," her breath came unsteadily, "what was there in *me* to make you think I would accept it?"

He did not reply.

"Answer me. This is the time to answer me."

"The answer is simple enough," he said in a low voice. "Together we had made a failure of partnership. When that partnership was dissolved, there remained the joint capital to be divided. And I divided it. Why not?"

"That capital was yours in the beginning; not mine. What I had of my own you never controlled; and I took it with me when I went."

"It was very little," he said.

"What of that? Did that concern you? Did you think I would have accepted anything from you? A thousand times I have been on the point of notifying you through attorney that the deposit now standing in my name is at your disposal."

"Why didn't you notify me then?" he asked, reddening to the temples.

"Because—I did not wish to hurt you—by doing it that way. . . . And I had not the courage to say it kindly over my own signature. That is why, Captain Selwyn."

And, as he remained silent: "That is what I had to say; not all—because—I wish to—to thank you for offering it. . . . You did not have very much, either; and you divided what you had. So I thank you—and I return it.". . . The tension forced her to attempt a laugh. "So we stand once more on equal terms; unless you have anything of mine to return—"

"I have your photograph," he said.

The silence lasted until he straightened up and, rubbing the fog from the window glass, looked out.

"We are in the Park," he remarked, turning toward her.

"Yes; I did not know how long it might take to explain matters. You are free of me now whenever you wish."

He picked up the telephone, hesitated: "Home?" he inquired with an effort. And at the forgotten word they looked at one another in stricken silence.

"Y-yes; to *your* home first, if you will let me drop you there—"

"Thank you; that might be imprudent."

"No, I think not. You say you are living at the Gerards?"

"Yes, temporarily. But I've already taken another place."

"Where?"

"Oh, it's only a bachelor's kennel—a couple of rooms—"

"Where, please?"

"Near Lexington and Sixty-sixth. I could go there; it's only partly furnished yet—"

"Then tell Hudson to drive there."

"Thank you, but it is not necessary—"

"Please let me; tell Hudson, or I will."

"You are very kind," he said; and gave the order.

Silence grew between them like a wall. She lay back in her corner, swathed to the eyes in her white furs; he in his corner sat upright, arms loosely folded, staring ahead at nothing. After a while he rubbed the moisture from the pane again.

"Still in the Park! He must have driven us nearly to Harlem Mere. It *is* the Mere! See the café lights yonder. It all looks rather gay through the snow."

"Very gay," she said, without moving. And, a moment later: "Will you tell me something? . . . You see"—with a forced laugh—"I can't keep my mind—from it."

"From what?" he asked.

"The—tragedy; ours."

"It has ceased to be that; hasn't it?"

"Has it? You said—you said that w-what I did to you was n-not as terrible as what I d-did to myself."

"That is true," he admitted grimly.

"Well, then, may I ask my question?"

"Ask it, child."

"Then—are you happy?"

He did not answer.

"—Because I desire it, Philip. I want you to be. You will be, won't you? I did not dream that I was ruining your army career when I—went mad—"

"How did it happen, Alixe?" he asked, with a cold curiosity that chilled her. "How did it come about?—wretched as we seemed to be together— unhappy, incapable of understanding each other—"

"Phil! There *were* days—"

He raised his eyes.

"You speak only of the unhappy ones," she said; "but there were moments—"

"Yes; I know it. And so I ask you, *why?*"

"Phil, I don't know. There was that last bitter quarrel—the night you left for Leyte after the dance. . . . I—it all grew suddenly intolerable. *You* seemed so horribly unreal—everything seemed unreal in that ghastly city—you, I, our marriage of crazy impulse—the people, the sunlight, the deathly odours, the torturing, endless creak of the punkha. . . . It was not a question of—of love, of anger, of hate. I tell you I was stunned—I had no emotions concerning you or myself—after that last scene—only a stupefied, blind necessity to get away; a groping instinct to move toward home—to make my way home and be rid for ever of the dream that drugged me! . . . And then—and then—"

"*He* came," said Selwyn very quietly. "Go on."

But she had nothing more to say.

"Alixe!"

She shook her head, closing her eyes.

"Little girl!—oh, little girl!" he said softly, the old familiar phrase finding its own way to his lips—and she trembled slightly; "was there no other way but that? Had marriage made the world such a living hell for you that there was no other way but *that?*"

"Phil, I helped to make it a hell."

"Yes—because I was pitiably inadequate to design anything better for us. I didn't know how. I didn't understand. I, the architect of our future—failed."

"It was worse than that, Phil; we"—she looked blindly at him—"we had yet to learn what love might be. We did not know. . . . If we could have waited—only waited!—perhaps—because there *were* moments—" She flushed crimson.

"I could not make you love me," he repeated; "I did not know how."

"Because you yourself had not learned how. But—at times—now looking back to it—I think—I think we were very near to it—at moments. . . . And then that dreadful dream closed down on us again. . . . And then— the end."

"If you could have held out," he breathed; "if I could have helped! It was I who failed you after all!"

For a long while they sat in silence; Mrs. Ruthven's white furs now covered her face. At last the carriage stopped.

As he sprang to the curb he became aware of another vehicle standing in front of the house—a cab—from which Mrs. Ruthven's maid descended.

"What is she doing here?" he asked, turning in astonishment to Mrs. Ruthven.

"Phil," she said in a low voice, "I knew you had taken this place. Gerald told me. Forgive me—but when I saw you under the awning it came to me in a flash what to do. And I've done it. . . . Are you sorry?"

"No. . . . Did Gerald tell you that I had taken this place?"

"Yes; I asked him."

Selwyn looked at her gravely; and she looked him very steadily in the eyes.

"Before I go—may I say one more word?" he asked gently.

"Yes—if you please. Is it about Gerald?"

"Yes. Don't let him gamble. . . . You saw the signature on that check?"

"Yes, Phil."

"Then you understand. Don't let him do it again."

"No. And—Phil?"

"What?"

"That check is—is deposited to your credit—with the rest. I have never dreamed of using it." Her cheeks were afire again, but with shame this time.

"You will have to accept it, Alixe."

"I cannot."

"You must! Don't you see you will affront Gerald? He has repaid me; that check is not mine, nor is it his."

"I can't take it," she said with a shudder. "What shall I do with it?"

"There are ways—hospitals, if you care to. . . . Good-night, child."

She stretched out her gloved arm to him; he took her hand very gently and retained it while he spoke.

"I wish you happiness," he said; "I ask your forgiveness."

"Give me mine, then."

"Yes—if there is anything to forgive. Good-night."

"Good-night—boy," she gasped.

He turned sharply, quivering under the familiar name. Her maid, standing in the snow, moved forward, and he motioned her to enter the brougham.

"Home," he said unsteadily; and stood there very still for a minute or two, even after the carriage had whirled away into the storm. Then, looking up at the house, he felt for his keys; but a sudden horror of being alone arrested him, and he stepped back, calling out to his cabman, who was already turning his horse's head, "Wait a moment; I think I'll drive back to Mrs. Gerard's. . . . And take your time."

It was still early—lacking a quarter of an hour to midnight—when he arrived. Nina had retired, but Austin sat in the library, obstinately plodding through the last chapters of a brand-new novel.

"This is a wretched excuse for sitting up," he yawned, laying the book flat on the table, but still open. "I ought never to be trusted alone with any book." Then he removed his reading glasses, yawned again, and surveyed Selwyn from head to foot.

"Very pretty," he said. "Well, how are the yellow ones, Phil? Or was it all débutante and slop-twaddle?"

"Few from the cradle, but bunches were arriving for the dance as I left."

"Eileen went at half-past eleven."

"I didn't know she was going," said Selwyn, surprised.

"She didn't want you to. The Playful Kitten business, you know—frisks apropos of nothing to frisk about. But we all fancied you'd stay for the dance." He yawned mightily, and gazed at Selwyn with ruddy gravity.

"Whisk?" he inquired.

"No."

"Cigar?"—mildly urgent.

"No, thanks."

"Bed?"

"I think so. But don't wait for me, Austin. . . . Is that the evening paper? Where is St. Paul?"

Austin passed it across the table and sat for a moment, alternately yawning and skimming the last chapter of his novel.

"Stuff and rubbish, mush and piffle!" he muttered, closing the book and pushing it from him across the table; "love, as usual, grossly out of proportion to the ensemble. That theory of the earth's rotation, you know; all these absurd books are built on it. Why do men read 'em? They grin when they do it! Love is only the sixth sense—just one-sixth of a man's existence. The other five-sixths of his time he's using his other senses working for a living."

Selwyn looked up over his newspaper, then lowered and folded it.

"In these novels," continued Gerard, irritably, "five-sixths of the pages are devoted to love; everything else is subordinated to it; it controls all motives, it initiates all action, it drugs reason, it prolongs the tuppenny suspense, sustains cheap situations, and produces agonisingly profitable climaxes for the authors. . . . Does it act that way in real life?"

"Not usually," said Selwyn.

72

"Nobody else thinks so, either. Why doesn't somebody tell the truth? Why doesn't somebody tell us how a man sees a nice girl and gradually begins to tag after her when business hours are over? A respectable man is busy from eight or nine until five or six. In the evening he's usually at the club, or dining out, or asleep; isn't he? Well, then, how much time does it leave for love? Do the problem yourself in any way you wish; the result is a fraction every time; and that fraction represents the proper importance of the love interest in its proper ratio to a man's entire life."

He sat up, greatly pleased with himself at having reduced sentiment to a fixed proportion in the ingredients of life.

"If I had time," he said, "I could tell them how to write a book—" He paused, musing, while the confident smile spread. Selwyn stared at space.

"What does a young man know about love, anyway?" demanded his brother-in-law.

"Nothing," replied Selwyn listlessly.

"Of course not. Look at Gerald. He sits on the stairs with a pink and white ninny; and at the next party he does it with another. That's wholesome and natural; and that's the way things really are. Look at Eileen. Do you suppose she has the slightest suspicion of what love is?"

"Naturally not," said Selwyn.

"Correct. Only a fool novelist would attribute the deeper emotions to a child like that. What does she know about anything? Love isn't a mere emotion, either—that is all fol-de-rol and fizzle!—it's the false basis of modern romance. Love is reason—not a nervous phenomenon. Love is a sane passion, founded on a basic knowledge of good and evil. That's what love is; the rest!"—he lifted the book, waved it contemptuously, and pushed it farther away—"the rest is neuritis; the remedy a pill. I'm going to bed; are you?"

But Selwyn had lighted a cigar, and was again unfolding his evening paper; so his brother-in-law moved ponderously away, yawning frightfully at every heavy stride, and the younger man settled back in his chair, a fragrant cigar balanced between his strong, slim fingers, one leg dropped loosely over the other. After a while the newspaper fell to the floor.

He sat there without moving for a long time; his cigar, burning close, had gone out. The reading-lamp spread a circle of soft light over the floor; on the edge of it lay Kit-Ki, placid, staring at him. After a while he noticed her. "You?" he said absently; "you hid so they couldn't put you out."

At the sound of his voice she began to purr.

"Oh, it's all very well," he nodded; "but it's against the law. However," he added, "I'm rather tired of rules and regulations myself. Besides, the world outside is very cold to-night. Purr away, old lady; I'm going to bed."

But he did not stir.

A little later, the fire having burned low, he rose, laid a pair of heavy logs across the coals, dragged his chair to the hearth, and settled down in it deeply. Then he lifted the cat to his knees. Kit-Ki sang blissfully, spreading and relaxing her claws at intervals as she gazed at the mounting blaze.

"I'm going to bed, Kit-Ki," he repeated absently, "because that's a pretty good place for me . . . far better than sitting up here with you—and conscience."

But he only lay back deeper in the velvet chair and lighted another cigar.

"Kit-Ki," he said, "the words men utter count in the reckoning; but not as heavily as the words men leave unuttered; and what a man does scores deeply; but—alas for the scars of the deeds he has left undone."

The logs were now wrapped in flame, and their low mellow roaring mingled to a monotone with the droning of the cat on his knees.

Long after his cigar burnt bitter, he sat with eyes fixed on the blaze. When the flames at last began to flicker and subside, his lids fluttered, then drooped; but he had lost all reckoning of time when he opened them again to find Miss Erroll in furs and ball-gown kneeling on the hearth and heaping kindling on the coals, and her pretty little Alsatian maid beside her, laying a log across the andirons.

"Upon my word!" he murmured, confused; then rising quickly, "Is that you, Miss Erroll? What time is it?"

"Four o'clock in the morning, Captain Selwyn," she said, straightening up to her full height. "This room is icy; are you frozen?"

Chilled through, he stood looking about in a dazed way, incredulous of the hour and of his own slumber.

"I was conversing with Kit-Ki a moment ago," he protested, in such a tone of deep reproach that Eileen laughed while her maid relieved her of furs and scarf.

"Susanne, just unhook those two that I can't manage; light the fire in my bedroom; *et merci bien, ma petite!*"

The little maid vanished; Kit-Ki, who had been unceremoniously spilled from Selwyn's knees, sat yawning, then rose and walked noiselessly to the hearth.

"I don't know how I happened to do it," he muttered, still abashed by his plight.

"We rekindled the fire for your benefit," she said; "you had better use it before you retire." And she seated herself in the arm-chair, stretching out her ungloved hands to the blaze—smooth, innocent hands, so soft, so amazingly fresh and white.

He moved a step forward into the warmth, stood a moment, then reached forward for a chair and drew it up beside hers.

"Do you mean to say you are not sleepy?" he asked.

"I? No, not in the least. I will be to-morrow, though."

"Did you have a good time?"

"Yes—rather."

"Wasn't it gay?"

"Gay? Oh, very."

Her replies were unusually short—almost preoccupied. She was generally more communicative.

"You danced a lot, I dare say," he ventured.

"Yes—a lot," studying the floor.

"Decent partners?"

"Oh, yes."

"Who was there?"

She looked up at him. "*You* were not there," she said, smiling.

"No; I cut it. But I did not know you were going; you said nothing about it."

"Of course, you would have stayed if you had known, Captain Selwyn?" She was still smiling.

"Of course," he replied.

"Would you really?"

"Why, yes."

There was something not perfectly familiar to him in the girl's bright brevity, in her direct personal inquiry; for between them, hitherto, the gaily impersonal had ruled except in moments of lightest badinage.

"Was it an amusing dinner?" she asked, in her turn.

"Rather." Then he looked up at her, but she had stretched her slim silk-shod feet to the fender, and her head was bent aside, so that he could

75

see only the curve of the cheek and the little close-set ear under its ruddy mass of gold.

"Who was there?" she asked, too, carelessly.

For a moment he did not speak; under his bronzed cheek the flat muscles stirred. Had some meddling, malicious fool ventured to whisper an unfit jest to this young girl? Had a word—or a smile and a phrase cut in two—awakened her to a sorry wisdom at his expense? Something had happened; and the idea stirred him to wrath—as when a child is wantonly frightened or a dumb creature misused.

"What did you ask me?" he inquired gently.

"I asked you who was there, Captain Selwyn."

He recalled some names, and laughingly mentioned his dinner partner's preference for Harmon. She listened absently, her chin nestling in her palm, only the close-set, perfect ear turned toward him.

"Who led the cotillion?" he asked.

"Jack Ruthven—dancing with Rosamund Fane."

She drew her feet from the fender and crossed them, still turned away from him; and so they remained in silence until again she shifted her position, almost impatiently.

"You are very tired," he said.

"No; wide awake."

"Don't you think it best for you to go to bed?"

"No. But you may go."

And, as he did not stir: "I mean that you are not to sit here because I do." And she looked around at him.

"What has gone wrong, Eileen?" he said quietly.

He had never before used her given name, and she flushed up.

"There is nothing the matter, Captain Selwyn. Why do you ask?"

"Yes, there is," he said.

"There is not, I tell you—"

"—And, if it is something you cannot understand," he continued pleasantly, "perhaps it might be well to ask Nina to explain it to you."

"There is nothing to explain."

"—Because," he went on, very gently, "one is sometimes led by malicious suggestion to draw false and unpleasant inferences from harmless facts—"

"Captain Selwyn—"

"Yes, Eileen."

But she could not go on; speech and thought itself remained sealed; only a confused consciousness of being hurt remained—somehow to be remedied by something he might say—might deny. Yet how could it help her for him to deny what she herself refused to believe?—refused through sheer instinct while ignorant of its meaning.

Even if he had done what she heard Rosamund Fane say he had done, it had remained meaningless to her save for the manner of the telling. But now—but now! Why had they laughed—why had their attitudes and manner and the disconnected phrases in French left her flushed and rigid among the idle group at supper? Why had they suddenly seemed to remember her presence—and express their abrupt consciousness of it in such furtive signals and silence?

It was false, anyway—whatever it meant. And, anyway, it was false that he had driven away in Mrs. Ruthven's brougham. But, oh, if he had only stayed—if he had only remained!—this friend of hers who had been so nice to her from the moment he came into her life—so generous, so considerate, so lovely to her—and to Gerald!

For a moment the glow remained, then a chill doubt crept in; would he have remained had he known she was to be there? *Where* did he go after the dinner? As for what they said, it was absurd. And yet—and yet—

He sat, savagely intent upon the waning fire; she turned restlessly again, elbows close together on her knees, face framed in her hands.

"You ask me if I am tired," she said. "I am—of the froth of life."

His face changed instantly. "What?" he exclaimed, laughing.

But she, very young and seriously intent, was now wrestling with the mighty platitudes of youth. First of all she desired to know what meaning life held for humanity. Then she expressed a doubt as to the necessity for human happiness; duty being her discovery as sufficient substitute.

But he heard in her childish babble the minor murmur of an undercurrent quickening for the first time; and he listened patiently and answered gravely, touched by her irremediable loneliness.

For Nina must remain but a substitute at best; what was wanting must remain wanting; and race and blood must interpret for itself the subtler and unasked questions of an innocence slowly awaking to a wisdom which makes us all less wise.

So when she said that she was tired of gaiety, that she would like to study, he said that he would take up anything she chose with her. And when she spoke vaguely of a life devoted to good works—of the wiser charity, of being morally equipped to aid those who required material

77

aid, he was very serious, but ventured to suggest that she dance her first season through as a sort of flesh-mortifying penance preliminary to her spiritual novitiate.

"Yes," she admitted thoughtfully; "you are right. Nina would feel dreadfully if I did not go on—or if she imagined I cared so little for it all. But one season is enough to waste. Don't you think so?"

"Quite enough," he assured her.

"—And—why should I ever marry?" she demanded, lifting her clear, sweet eyes to his.

"Why indeed?" he repeated with conviction. "I can see no reason."

"I am glad you understand me," she said. "I am not a marrying woman."

"Not at all," he assured her.

"No, I am not; and Nina—the darling—doesn't understand. Why, what do you suppose!—but *would* it be a breach of confidence to anybody if I told you?"

"I doubt it," he said; "what is it you have to tell me?"

"Only—it's very, very silly—only several men—and one nice enough to know better—Sudbury Gray—"

"Asked you to marry them?" he finished, nodding his head at the cat.

"Yes," she admitted, frankly astonished; "but how did you know?"

"Inferred it. Go on."

"There is nothing more," she said, without embarrassment. "I told Nina each time; but she confused me by asking for details; and the details were too foolish and too annoying to repeat. . . . I do not wish to marry anybody. I think I made that very plain to—everybody."

"Right as usual," he said cheerfully; "you are too intelligent to consider that sort of thing just now."

"You *do* understand me, don't you?" she said gratefully. "There are so many serious things in life to learn and to think of, and that is the very last thing I should ever consider. . . . I am very, very glad I had this talk with you. Now I am rested and I shall retire for a good long sleep."

With which paradox she stood up, stifling a tiny yawn, and looked smilingly at him, all the old sweet confidence in her eyes. Then, suddenly mocking:

"Who suggested that you call me by my first name?" she asked.

"Some good angel or other. May I?"

78

"If you please; I rather like it. But I couldn't very well call you anything except 'Captain Selwyn.'"

"On account of my age?"

"Your *age!*"—contemptuous in her confident equality.

"Oh, my wisdom, then? You probably reverence me too deeply."

"Probably not. I don't know; I couldn't do it—somehow—"

"Try it—unless you're afraid."

"I'm not afraid!"

"Yes, you are, if you don't take a dare."

"You dare me?"

"I do."

"Philip," she said, hesitating, adorable in her embarrassment. "No! No! No! I can't do it that way in cold blood. It's got to be 'Captain Selwyn'. . . for a while, anyway. . . . Good-night."

He took her outstretched hand, laughing; the usual little friendly shake followed; then she turned gaily away, leaving him standing before the whitening ashes.

He thought the fire was dead; but when he turned out the lamp an hour later, under the ashes embers glowed in the darkness of the winter morning.

CHAPTER IV

MID-LENT

"Mid-Lent, and the Enemy grins," remarked Selwyn as he started for church with Nina and the children. Austin, knee-deep in a dozen Sunday supplements, refused to stir; poor little Eileen was now convalescent from grippe, but still unsteady on her legs; her maid had taken the grippe, and now moaned all day: "*Mon dieu! Mon dieu! Che fais mourir!*"

Boots Lansing called to see Eileen, but she wouldn't come down, saying her nose was too pink. Drina entertained Boots, and then Selwyn returned and talked army talk with him until tea was served. Drina poured tea very prettily; Nina had driven Austin to vespers. The family dined at seven so Drina could sit up; special treat on account of Boots's presence at table. Gerald was expected, but did not come.

The next morning, Selwyn went downtown at the usual hour and found Gerald, pale and shaky, hanging over his desk and trying to dictate letters to an uncomfortable stenographer.

So he dismissed the abashed girl for the moment, closed the door, and sat down beside the young man.

"Go home, Gerald" he said with decision; "when Neergard comes in I'll tell him you are not well. And, old fellow, don't ever come near the office again when you're in this condition."

"I'm a perfect fool," faltered the boy, his voice trembling; "I don't really care for that sort of thing, either; but you know how it is in that set—"

"What set?"

"Oh, the Fanes—the Ruthv—" He stammered himself into silence.

"I see. What happened last night?"

"The usual; two tables full of it. There was a wheel, too. . . . I had no intention—but you know yourself how it parches your throat—the jollying and laughing and excitement. . . . I forgot all about what you—what we talked over. . . . I'm ashamed and sorry; but I can stay here and attend to things, of course—"

"I don't want Neergard to see you," repeated Selwyn.

"W-why," stammered the boy, "do I look as rocky as that?"

"Yes. See here, you are not afraid of me, are you?"

"No—"

"You don't think I'm one of those long-faced, blue-nosed butters-in, do you? You have confidence in me, haven't you? You know I'm an average and normally sinful man who has made plenty of mistakes and who understands how others make them—you know that, don't you, old chap?"

"Y-es."

"Then you *will* listen, won't you, Gerald?"

The boy laid his arms on the desk and hid his face in them. Then he nodded.

For ten minutes Selwyn talked to him with all the terse and colloquial confidence of a comradeship founded upon respect for mutual fallibility. No instruction, no admonition, no blame, no reproach—only an affectionately logical review of matters as they stood—and as they threatened to stand.

The boy, fortunately, was still pliable and susceptible, still unalarmed and frank. It seemed that he had lost money again—this time to Jack

Ruthven; and Selwyn's teeth remained sternly interlocked as, bit by bit, the story came out. But in the telling the boy was not quite as frank as he might have been; and Selwyn supposed he was able to stand his loss without seeking aid.

"Anyway," said Gerald in a muffled voice, "I've learned one lesson—that a business man can't acquire the habits and keep the infernal hours that suit people who can take all day to sleep it off."

"Right," said Selwyn.

"Besides, my income can't stand it," added Gerald naïvely.

"Neither could mine, old fellow. And, Gerald, cut out this card business; it's the final refuge of the feebleminded. . . . You like it? Oh, well, if you've got to play—if you've no better resource for leisure, and if non-participation isolates you too completely from other idiots—play the imbecile gentleman's game; which means a game where nobody need worry over the stakes."

"But—they'd laugh at me!"

"I know; but Boots Lansing wouldn't—and you have considerable respect for him."

Gerald nodded; he had immediately succumbed to Lansing like everybody else.

"And one thing more," said Selwyn; "don't play for stakes—no matter how insignificant—where women sit in the game. Fashionable or not, it is rotten sport—whatever the ethics may be. And, Gerald, tainted sport and a clean record can't take the same fence together."

The boy looked up, flushed and perplexed. "Why, every woman in town—"

"Oh, no. How about your sister and mine?"

"Of course not; they are different. Only—well, you approve of Rosamund Fane and—Gladys Orchil—don't you?"

"Gerald, men don't ask each other such questions—except as you ask, without expecting or desiring an answer from me, and merely to be saying something nice about two pretty women."

The reproof went home, deeply, but without a pang; and the boy sat silent, studying the blotter between his elbows.

A little later he started for home at Selwyn's advice. But the memory of his card losses frightened him, and he stopped on the way to see what money Austin would advance him.

Julius Neergard came up from Long Island, arriving at the office about noon. The weather was evidently cold on Long Island; he had the complexion of a raw ham, but the thick, fat hand, with its bitten nails, which he offered Selwyn as he entered his office, was unpleasantly hot, and, on the thin nose which split the broad expanse of face, a bead or two of sweat usually glistened, winter and summer.

"Where's Gerald?" he asked as an office-boy relieved him of his heavy box coat and brought his mail to him.

"I advised Gerald to go home," observed Selwyn carelessly; "he is not perfectly well."

Neergard's tiny mouse-like eyes, set close together, stole brightly in Selwyn's direction; but they usually looked just a little past a man, seldom at him.

"Grippe?" he asked.

"I don't think so," said Selwyn.

"Lots of grippe 'round town," observed Neergard, as though satisfied that Gerald had it. Then he sat down and rubbed his large, membranous ears.

"Captain Selwyn," he began, "I'm satisfied that it's a devilish good thing."

"Are you?"

"Emphatically. I've mastered the details—virtually all of 'em. Here's the situation in a grain of wheat!—the Siowitha Club owns a thousand or so acres of oak scrub, pine scrub, sand and weeds, and controls four thousand more; that is to say—the club pays the farmers' rents and fixes their fences and awards them odd jobs and prizes for the farm sustaining the biggest number of bevies. Also the club pays them to maintain the millet and buckwheat patches and to act as wardens. In return the farmers post their four thousand acres for the exclusive benefit of the club. Is that plain?"

"Perfectly."

"Very well, then. Now the Siowitha is largely composed of very rich men—among them Bradley Harmon, Jack Ruthven, George Fane, Sanxon Orchil, the Hon. Delmour-Carnes—*that*crowd—rich and stingy. That's why they are contented with a yearly agreement with the farmers instead of buying the four thousand acres. Why put a lot of good money out of commission when they can draw interest on it and toss an insignificant fraction of that interest as a sop to the farmers? Do you see? That's your millionaire method—and it's what makes 'em in the first place."

He drew a large fancy handkerchief from his pistol-pocket and wiped the beads from the bridge of his limber nose. But they reappeared again.

"Now," he said, "I am satisfied that, working very carefully, we can secure options on every acre of the four thousand. There is money in it either way and any way we work it; we get it coming and going. First of all, if the Siowitha people find that they really cannot get on without controlling these acres—why"—and he snickered so that his nose curved into a thin, ruddy beak—"why, Captain, I suppose we *could* let them have the land. Eh? Oh, yes—if they *must* have it!"

Selwyn frowned slightly.

"But the point is," continued Neergard, "that it borders the railroad on the north; and where the land is not wavy it's flat as a pancake, and"—he sank his husky voice—"it's fairly riddled with water. I paid a thousand dollars for six tests."

"Water!" repeated Selwyn wonderingly; "why, it's dry as a desert!"

"*Underground water!*—only about forty feet on the average. Why, man, I can hit a well flowing three thousand gallons almost anywhere. It's a gold mine. I don't care what you do with the acreage—split it up into lots and advertise, or club the Siowitha people into submission—it's all the same; it's a gold mine—to be swiped and developed. Now there remains the title searching and the damnable job of financing it—because we've got to move cautiously, and knock softly at the doors of the money vaults, or we'll be waking up some Wall Street relatives or secret business associates of the yellow crowd; and if anybody bawls for help we'll be up in the air next New Year's, and still hiking skyward."

He stood up, gathering together the mail matter which his secretary had already opened for his attention. "There's plenty of time yet; their leases were renewed the first of this year, and they'll run the year out. But it's something to think about. Will you talk to Gerald, or shall I?"

"You," said Selwyn. "I'll think the matter over and give you my opinion. May I speak to my brother-in-law about it?"

Neergard turned in his tracks and looked almost at him.

"Do you think there's any chance of his financing the thing?"

"I haven't the slightest idea of what he might do. Especially"—he hesitated—"as you never have had any loans from his people—I understand—"

"No," said Neergard; "I haven't."

"It's rather out of their usual, I believe—"

"So they say. But Long Island acreage needn't beg favours now. That's all over, Captain Selwyn. Fane, Harmon & Co. know that; Mr. Gerard ought to know it, too."

Selwyn looked troubled. "Shall I consult Mr. Gerard?" he repeated. "I should like to if you have no objection."

Neergard's small, close-set eyes were focused on a spot just beyond Selwyn's left shoulder.

"Suppose you sound him," he suggested, "in strictest—"

"Naturally," cut in Selwyn dryly; and turning to his littered desk, opened the first letter his hand encountered. Now that his head was turned, Neergard looked full at the back of his neck for a long minute, then went out silently.

That night Selwyn stopped at his sister's house before going to his own rooms, and, finding Austin alone in the library, laid the matter before him exactly as Neergard had put it.

"You see," he added, "that I'm a sort of an ass about business methods. What I like—what I understand, is to use good judgment, go in and boldly buy a piece of property, wait until it becomes more valuable, either through improvements or the natural enhancement of good value, then take a legitimate profit, and repeat the process. That, in outline, is what I understand. But, Austin, this furtive pouncing on a thing and clubbing other people's money out of them with it—this slyly acquiring land that is necessary to an unsuspecting neighbour and then holding him up—I don't like. There's always something of this sort that prevents my cordial co-operation with Neergard—always something in the schemes which hints of—of squeezing—of something underground—"

"Like the water which he's going to squeeze out of the wells?"

Selwyn laughed.

"Phil," said his brother-in-law, "if you think anybody can do a profitable business except at other people's expense, you are an ass."

"Am I?" asked Selwyn, still laughing frankly.

"Certainly. The land is there, plain enough for anybody to see. It's always been there; it's likely to remain for a few æons, I fancy.

"Now, along comes Meynheer Julius Neergard—the only man who seems to have brains enough to see the present value of that parcel to the Siowitha people. Everybody else had the same chance; nobody except Neergard knew enough to take it. Why shouldn't he profit by it?"

"Yes—but if he'd be satisfied to cut it up into lots and do what is fair—"

"Cut it up into nothing! Man alive, do you suppose the Siowitha people would let him? They've only a few thousand acres; they've *got* to control that land. What good is their club without it? Do you imagine they'd let a town grow up on three sides of their precious game-preserve? And, besides, I'll bet you that half of their streams and lakes take rise on other people's property—and that Neergard knows it—the Dutch fox!"

"That sort of—of business—that kind of coercion, does not appeal to me," said Selwyn gravely.

"Then you'd better go into something besides business in this town," observed Austin, turning red. "Good Lord, man, where would my Loan and Trust Company be if we never foreclosed, never swallowed a good thing when we see it?"

"But you don't threaten people."

Austin turned redder. "If people or corporations stand in our way and block progress, of course we threaten. Threaten? Isn't the threat of punishment the very basis of law and order itself? What are laws for? And we have laws, too—laws, under the law—"

"Of the State of New Jersey," said Selwyn, laughing. "Don't flare up, Austin; I'm probably not cut out for a business career, as you point out—otherwise I would not have consulted you. I know some laws—including 'The Survival of the Fittest,' and the 'Chain-of-Destruction'; and I have read the poem beginning

"'Big bugs have little bugs to bite 'em.'

"That's all right, too; but speaking of laws, I'm always trying to formulate one for my particular self-government; and you don't mind, do you?"

"No," said Gerard, much amused, "I don't mind. Only when you talk ethics—talk sense at the same time."

"I wish I knew how," he said.

They discussed Neergard's scheme for a little while longer; Austin, shrewd and cautious, declined any personal part in the financing of the deal, although he admitted the probability of prospective profits.

"Our investments and our loans are of a different character," he explained, "but I have no doubt that Fane, Harmon & Co.—"

"Why, both Fane and Harmon are members of the club!" laughed Selwyn. "You don't expect Neergard to go to them?"

A peculiar expression flickered in Gerard's heavy features; perhaps he thought that Fane and Harmon and Jack Ruthven were not above exploiting their own club under certain circumstances. But whatever his opinion, he said nothing further; and, suggesting that Selwyn remain to dine, went off to dress.

A few moments later he returned, crestfallen and conciliatory:

"I forgot, Nina and I are dining at the Orchils. Come up a moment; she wants to speak to you."

So they took the rose-tinted rococo elevator; Austin went away to his own quarters, and Selwyn tapped at Nina's boudoir.

"Is that you, Phil? One minute; Watson is finishing my hair. . . . Come in, now; and kindly keep your distance, my friend. Do you suppose I want Rosamund to know what brand of war-paint I use?"

"Rosamund," he repeated, with a good-humoured shrug; "it's likely— isn't it?"

"Certainly it's likely. You'd never know you were telling her anything— but she'd extract every detail in ten seconds. . . . I understand she adores you, Phil. What have you done to her?"

"That's likely, too," he remarked, remembering his savagely polite rebuke to that young matron after the Minster dinner.

"Well, she does; you've probably piqued her; that's the sort of man she likes. . . . Look at my hair—how bright and wavy it is, Phil. Tell me, *do* I appear fairly pretty to-night?"

"You're all right, Nina; I mean it," he said. "How are the kids? How is Eileen?"

"That's why I sent for you. Eileen is furious at being left here all alone; she's practically well and she's to dine with Drina in the library. Would you be good enough to dine there with them? Eileen, poor child, is heartily sick of her imprisonment; it would be a mercy, Phil."

"Why, yes, I'll do it, of course; only I've some matters at home—"

"Home! You call those stuffy, smoky, impossible, half-furnished rooms *home*! Phil, when are you ever going to get some pretty furniture and art things? Eileen and I have been talking it over, and we've decided to go there and see what you need and then order it, whether you like it or not."

"Thanks," he said, laughing; "it's just what I've tried to avoid. I've got things where I want them now—but I knew it was too comfortable to last. Boots said that some woman would be sure to be good to me with an art-nouveau rocking-chair."

"A perfect sample of man's gratitude," said Nina, exasperated; "for I've ordered two beautiful art-nouveau rocking-chairs, one for you and one for Mr. Lansing. Now you can go and humiliate poor little Eileen, who took so much pleasure in planning with me for your comfort. As for your friend Boots, he's unspeakable—with my compliments."

Selwyn stayed until he made peace with his sister, then he mounted to the nursery to "lean over" the younger children and preside at prayers. This being accomplished, he descended to the library, where Eileen Erroll in a filmy, lace-clouded gown, full of turquoise tints, reclined with her arm around Drina amid heaps of cushions, watching the waitress prepare a table for two.

He took the fresh, cool hand she extended and sat down on the edge of her couch.

"All O.K. again?" he inquired, retaining Eileen's hand in his.

"Thank you—quite. Are you really going to dine with us? Are you sure you want to? Oh, I know you've given up some very gay dinner somewhere—"

"I was going to dine with Boots when Nina rescued me. Poor Boots!—I think I'll telephone—"

"Telephone him to come here!" begged Drina. "Would he come? Oh, please—I'd love to have him."

"I wish you would ask him," said Eileen; "it's been so lonely and stupid to lie in bed with a red nose and fishy eyes and pains in one's back and limbs. Please do let us have a party."

"'Two pillows,' said Drina sweetly."

So Selwyn went to the telephone, and presently returned, saying that Boots was overwhelmed and would be present at the festivities; and Drina, enraptured, ordered flowers to be brought from the dining-room and a large table set for four, with particular pomp and circumstance.

Mr. Archibald Lansing arrived very promptly—a short, stocky young man of clean and powerful build, with dark, keen eyes always alert, and humorous lips ever on the edge of laughter under his dark moustache.

His manner with Drina was always delightful—a mixture of self-repressed idolatry and busily naïve belief in a thorough understanding between them to exclude Selwyn from their company.

"This Selwyn fellow here!" he exclaimed. "I warned him over the 'phone we'd not tolerate him, Drina. I explained to him very carefully that you and I were dining together in strictest privacy—"

"He begged so hard," said Eileen. "Will somebody place an extra pillow for Drina?"

They seized the same pillow fiercely, confronting each other; massacre appeared imminent.

"*Two* pillows," said Drina sweetly; and extermination was averted. The child laughed happily, covering one of Boots's hands with both of hers.

"So you've left the service, Mr. Lansing?" began Eileen, lying back and looking smilingly at Boots.

"Had to, Miss Erroll. Seven millionaires ran into my quarters and chased me out and down Broadway into the offices of the Westchester Air Line Company. Then these seven merciless multi-millionaires in buckram bound and gagged me, stuffed my pockets full of salary, and forced me to typewrite a fearful and secret oath to serve them for five long, weary years. That's a sample of how the wealthy grind the noses of the poor, isn't it, Drina?"

The child slipped her hand from his, smiling uncertainly.

"You don't mean all that, do you?"

"Indeed I do, sweetheart."

"Are you not a soldier lieutenant any more, then?" she inquired, horribly disappointed.

"Only a private in the workman's battalion, Drina."

"I don't care," retorted the child obstinately; "I like you just as much."

"Have you really done it?" asked Selwyn as the first course was served.

"*I?* No. *They?* Yes. We'll probably lose the Philippines now," he added gloomily; "but it's my thankless country's fault; you all had a chance to make me dictator, you know. Miss Erroll, do you want a second-hand sword? Of course there are great dents in it—"

"I'd rather have those celebrated boots," she replied demurely; and Mr. Lansing groaned.

"How tall you're growing, Drina," remarked Selwyn.

"Probably the early spring weather," added Boots. "You're twelve, aren't you?"

"Thirteen," said Drina gravely.

"Almost time to elope with me," nodded Boots.

"I'll do it now," she said—"as soon as my new gowns are made—if you'll take me to Manila. Will you? I believe my Aunt Alixe is there—"

She caught Eileen's eye and stopped short. "I forgot," she murmured; "I beg your pardon, Uncle Philip—"

Boots was talking very fast and laughing a great deal; Eileen's plate claimed her undivided attention; Selwyn quietly finished his claret; the child looked at them all.

"By the way," said Boots abruptly, "what's the matter with Gerald? He came in before noon looking very seedy—" Selwyn glanced up quietly.

"Wasn't he at the office?" asked Eileen anxiously.

"Oh, yes," replied Selwyn; "he felt a trifle under the weather, so I sent him home."

"Is it the grippe?"

"N-no, I believe not—"

"Do you think he had better have a doctor? Where is he?"

"He was here," observed Drina composedly, "and father was angry with him."

"What?" exclaimed Eileen. "When?"

"This morning, before father went downtown."

Both Selwyn and Lansing cut in coolly, dismissing the matter with a careless word or two; and coffee was served—cambric tea in Drina's case.

"Come on," said Boots, slipping a bride-rose into Drina's curls; "I'm ready for confidences."

"Confidences" had become an established custom with Drina and Boots; it meant that every time they saw one another they were pledged to tell each other everything that had occurred in their lives since their last meeting.

So Drina, excitedly requesting to be excused, jumped up and, taking Lansing's hand in hers, led him to a sofa in a distant corner, where they immediately installed themselves and began an earnest and whispered exchange of confidences, punctuated by little whirlwinds of laughter from the child.

Eileen settled deeper among her pillows as the table was removed, and Selwyn drew his chair forward.

"Suppose," she said, looking thoughtfully at him, "that you and I make a vow to exchange confidences? Shall we, Captain Selwyn?"

"Good heavens," he protested; "I—confess to *you*! You'd faint dead away, Eileen."

"Perhaps. . . . But will you?"

He gaily evaded an answer, and after a while he fancied she had forgotten. They spoke of other things, of her convalescence, of the engagements she had been obliged to cancel, of the stupid hours in her room—doubly stupid, as the doctor had not permitted her to read or sew.

"And every day violets from you," she said; "it was certainly nice of you. And—do you know that somehow—just because you have never yet failed me—I thought perhaps—when I asked your confidence a moment ago—"

He looked up quickly.

"*What* is the matter with Gerald?" she asked. "Could you tell me?"

"Nothing serious is the matter, Eileen."

"Is he not ill?"

"Not very."

She lay still a moment, then with the slightest gesture: "Come here."

He seated himself near her; she laid her hand fearlessly on his arm.

"Tell me," she demanded. And, as he remained silent: "Once," she said, "I came suddenly into the library. Austin and Gerald were there; Austin seemed to be very angry with my brother. I heard him say something that worried me; and I slipped out before they saw me."

Selwyn remained silent.

"Was *that* it?"

"I—don't know what you heard."

"*Don't* you understand me?"

"Not exactly."

"Well, then"—she crimsoned—"has Gerald m-misbehaved again?"

"What did you hear Austin say?" he demanded.

"I heard—something about dissipation. He was very angry with Gerald. It is not the best way, I think, to become angry with either of us—either me or Gerald—because then we are usually inclined to do it again— whatever it is. . . . I do not mean for one moment to be disloyal to Austin; you know that. . . . But I am so thankful that Gerald is fond of you. . . . You like him, too, don't you?"

"I am very fond of him."

"Well, then," she said, "you will talk to him pleasantly—won't you? He is *such* a boy; and he adores you. It is easy to influence a boy like that, you know—easy to shame him out of the silly things he does. . . . That is all the confidence I wanted, Captain Selwyn. And you haven't told me a word, you see—and I have not fainted—have I?"

They laughed a little; her fingers, which had tightened on his arm, relaxed; her hand fell away, and she straightened up, sitting Turk fashion, and smoothing her hair which contact with the pillows had disarranged so that it threatened to come tumbling over eyes and cheeks.

"Oh, hair, hair!" she murmured, "you're Nina's despair and my endless punishment. I'd twist and pin you tight if I dared—some day I will, too. . . . What are you looking at so curiously, Captain Selwyn? My mop?"

"It's about the most stunningly beautiful thing I ever saw," he said, still curious.

She nodded gaily, both hands still busy with the lustrous strands. "It *is* nice; but I never supposed you noticed it. It falls to my waist; I'll show it to you some time. . . . But I had no idea *you* noticed such things," she repeated, as though to herself.

"Oh, I'm apt to notice all sorts of things," he said, looking so provokingly wise that she dropped her hair and clapped both hands over her eyes.

"Now," she said, "if you are so observing, you'll know the colour of my eyes. What are they?"

"Blue—with a sort of violet tint," he said promptly.

She laughed and lowered her hands.

"All that personal attention paid to me!" she exclaimed. "You are turning my head, Captain Selwyn. Besides, you are astonishing me, because you never seem to know what women wear or what they resemble when

91

I ask you to describe the girls with whom you have been dining or dancing."

It was a new note in their cordial intimacy—this nascent intrusion of the personal. To her it merely meant his very charming recognition of her maturity—she was fast becoming a woman like other women, to be looked at and remembered as an individual, and no longer classed vaguely as one among hundreds of the newly emerged whose soft, unexpanded personalities all resembled one another.

For some time, now, she had cherished this tiny grudge in her heart—that he had never seemed to notice anything in particular about her except when he tried to be agreeable concerning some new gown. The contrast had become the sharper, too, since she had awakened to the admiration of other men. And the awakening was only a half-convinced happiness mingled with shy surprise that the wise world should really deem her so lovely.

"A red-headed girl," she said teasingly; "I thought you had better taste than—than—"

"Than to think you a raving beauty?"

"Oh," she said, "you don't think that!"

As a matter of fact he himself had become aware of it so suddenly that he had no time to think very much about it. It was rather strange, too, that he had not always been aware of it; or was it partly the mellow light from the lamp tinting her till she glowed and shimmered like a young sorceress, sitting so straight there in her turquoise silk and misty lace?

Delicate luminous shadow banded her eyes; her hair, partly in shadow, too, became a sombre mystery in rose-gold.

"Whatever *are* you staring at?" she laughed. "Me? I don't believe it! Never have you so honoured me with your fixed attention, Captain Selwyn. You really glare at me as though I were interesting. And I know you don't consider me that; do you?"

"How old are you, anyway?" he asked curiously.

"Thank you, I'll be delighted to inform you when I'm twenty."

"You look like a mixture of fifteen and twenty-five to-night," he said deliberately; "and the answer is more and less than nineteen."

"And you," she said, "talk like a frivolous sage, and your wisdom is as weighty as the years you carry. And what is the answer to that? Do you know, Captain Selwyn, that when you talk to me this way you look about as inexperienced as Gerald?"

"And do *you* know," he said, "that I feel as inexperienced—when I talk to you this way?"

92

She nodded. "It's probably good for us both; I age, you renew the frivolous days of youth when you were young enough to notice the colour of a girl's hair and eyes. Besides, I'm very grateful to you. Hereafter you won't dare sit about and cross your knees and look like the picture of an inattentive young man by Gibson. You've admitted that you like two of my features, and I shall expect you to notice and *admit* that you notice the rest."

"I admit it now," he said, laughing.

"You mustn't; I won't let you. Two kinds of dessert are sufficient at a time. But to-morrow—or perhaps the day after, you may confess to me your approbation of one more feature—only one, remember!—just one more agreeable feature. In that way I shall be able to hold out for quite a while, you see—counting my fingers as separate features! Oh, you've given me a taste of it; it's your own fault, Captain Selwyn, and now I desire more if you please—in semi-weekly lingering doses—"

A perfect gale of laughter from the sofa cut her short.

"Drina!" she exclaimed; "it's after eight!—and I completely forgot."

"Oh, dear!" protested the child, "he's being so funny about the war in Samar. Couldn't I stay up—just five more minutes, Eileen? Besides, I haven't told him about Jessie Orchil's party—"

"Drina, dear, you *know* I can't let you. Say good-night, now—if you want Mr. Lansing and your Uncle Philip to come to another party."

"I'll just whisper one more confidence very fast," she said to Boots. He inclined his head; she placed both hands on his shoulders, and, kneeling on the sofa, laid her lips close to his ear. Eileen and Selwyn waited.

When the child had ended and had taken leave of all, Boots also took his leave; and Selwyn rose, too, a troubled, careworn expression replacing the careless gaiety which had made him seem so young in Miss Erroll's youthful eyes.

"Wait, Boots," he said; "I'm going home with you." And, to Eileen, almost absently: "Good-night; I'm so very glad you are well again."

"Good-night," she said, looking up at him. The faintest sense of disappointment came over her—at what, she did not know. Was it because, in his completely altered face she realised the instant and easy detachment from herself, and what concerned her?—was it because other people, like Mr. Lansing—other interests—like those which so plainly, in his face, betrayed his preoccupation—had so easily replaced an intimacy which had seemed to grow newer and more delightful with every meeting?

What was it, then, that he found more interesting, more important, than their friendship, their companionship? Was she never to grow old enough, or wise enough, or experienced enough to exact—without exacting—his paramount consideration and interest? Was there no common level of mental equality where they could meet?—where termination of interviews might be mutual—might be fairer to her?

Now he went away, utterly detached from her and what concerned her—to seek other interests of which she knew nothing; absorbed in them to her utter exclusion, leaving her here with the long evening before her and nothing to do—because her eyes were not yet strong enough to use for reading.

Lansing was saying: "I'll drive as far as the club with you, and then you can drop me and come back later."

"Right, my son; I'll finish a letter and then come back—"

"Can't you write it at the club?"

"Not that letter," he replied in a low voice; and, turning to Eileen, smiled his absent, detached smile, offering his hand.

But she lay back, looking straight up at him.

"Are you going?"

"Yes; I have several—"

"Stay with me," she said in a low voice.

For a moment the words meant nothing; then blank surprise silenced him, followed by curiosity.

"Is there something you wished to tell me?" he asked.

"N-no."

His perplexity and surprise grew. "Wait a second, Boots," he said; and Mr. Lansing, being a fairly intelligent young man, went out and down the stairway.

"Now," he said, too kindly, too soothingly, "what is it, Eileen?"

"Nothing. I thought—but I don't care. Please go, Captain Selwyn."

"No, I shall not until you tell me what troubles you."

"I can't."

"Try, Eileen."

"Why, it is nothing; truly it is nothing. . . . Only I was—it is so early—only a quarter past eight—"

He stood there looking down at her, striving to understand.

"That is all," she said, flushing a trifle; "I can't read and I can't sew and there's nobody here. . . . I don't mean to bother you—"

"Child," he exclaimed, "do you *want* me to stay?"

"Yes," she said; "will you?"

He walked swiftly to the landing outside and looked down.

"Boots!" he called in a low voice, "I'm not going home yet. Don't wait for me at the Lenox."

"All right," returned Mr. Lansing cheerfully. A moment later the front door closed below. Then Selwyn came back into the library.

For an hour he sat there telling her the gayest stories and talking the most delightful nonsense, alternating with interesting incisions into serious subjects: which it enchanted her to dissect under his confident guidance.

Alert, intelligent, all aquiver between laughter and absorption, she had sat up among her silken pillows, resting her weight on one rounded arm, her splendid young eyes fixed on him to detect and follow and interpret every change in his expression personal to the subject and to her share in it.

His old self again! What could be more welcome? Not one shadow in his pleasant eyes, not a trace of pallor, of care, of that gray aloofness. How jolly, how young he was after all!

They discussed, or laughed at, or mentioned and dismissed with a gesture a thousand matters of common interest in that swift hour—incredibly swift, unless the hall clock's deadened chimes were mocking Time itself with mischievous effrontery.

She heard them, the enchantment still in her eyes; he nodded, listening, meeting her gaze with his smile undisturbed. When the last chime had sounded she lay back among her cushions.

"Thank you for staying," she said quite happily.

"Am I to go?"

Smilingly thoughtful she considered him from her pillows:

"Where were you going when I—spoiled it all? For you were going somewhere—out there"—with a gesture toward the darkness outside—"somewhere where men go to have the good times they always seem to have. . . . Was it to your club? What do men do there? Is it very gay at men's clubs? . . . It must be interesting to go where men have such jolly times—where men gather to talk that mysterious man-talk which we so often wonder at—and pretend we are indifferent. But we are very curious, nevertheless—even about the boys of Gerald's age—whom we laugh at and torment; and we can't help wondering how they talk to each other—what they say that is so interesting; for they somehow manage to convey that impression to us—even against our will. . . . If you stay, I shall never have done with chattering. When you sit there with one lazy knee so leisurely draped over the other, and your eyes laughing at me through your cigar-smoke, about a million ideas flash up in me which I desire to discuss with you. . . . So you had better go."

"I am happier here," he said, watching her.

"Really?"

"Really."

"Then—then—am *I*, also, one of the 'good times' a man can have?—when he is at liberty to reflect and choose as he idles over his coffee?"

"A man is fortunate if you permit that choice."

"Are you serious? I mean a man, not a boy—not a dance or dinner partner, or one of the men one meets about—everywhere from pillar to post. Do you think me interesting to real men?—like you and Boots?"

"Yes," he said deliberately, "I do. I don't know how interesting, because—I never quite realised how—how you had matured. . . . That was my stupidity."

"Captain Selwyn!" in confused triumph; "you never gave me a chance; I mean, you always were nice in—in the same way you are to Drina. . . . I liked it—don't please misunderstand—only I knew there was something else to me—something more nearly your own age. It was jolly to know you were really fond of me—but youthful sisters grow faster than you imagine. . . . And now, when you come, I shall venture to believe it is not wholly to do me a kindness—but—a little—to do yourself one, too. Is that not the basis of friendship?"

"Yes."

"Community and equality of interests?—isn't it?"

"Yes."

"—And—in which the—the charity of superior experience and the inattention of intellectual preoccupation and the amused concession to ignorance must steadily, if gradually, disappear? Is that it, too?"

Astonishment and chagrin at his misconception of her gave place to outright laughter at his own expense.

"Where on earth did you—I mean that I am quite overwhelmed under your cutting indictment of me. Old duffers of my age—"

"Don't say that," she said; "that is pleading guilty to the indictment, and reverting to the old footing. I shall not permit you to go back."

"I don't want to, Eileen—"

"I am wondering," she said airily, "about that 'Eileen.' I'm not sure but that easy and fluent 'Eileen' is part of the indictment. What do you call Gladys Orchil, for example?"

"What do I care what I call anybody?" he retorted, laughing, "as long as they

"'Answer   to   "Hi!"
Or to any loud cry'?"

"But *I* won't answer to 'Hi!'" she retorted very promptly; "and now that you admit that I am a 'good time,' a mature individual with distinguishing characteristics, and your intellectual equal if not your peer in experience, I'm not sure that I shall answer at all whenever you begin 'Eileen.' Or I shall take my time about it—or I may even reflect and look straight through you before I reply—or," she added, "I may be so profoundly preoccupied with important matters which do not concern you, that I might not even hear you speak at all."

Their light-hearted laughter mingled delightfully—fresh, free, uncontrolled, peal after peal. She sat huddled up like a schoolgirl, lovely head thrown back, her white hands clasping her knees; he, both feet squarely on the floor, leaned forward, his laughter echoing hers.

"What nonsense! What blessed nonsense you and I are talking!" she said, "but it has made me quite happy. Now you may go to your club and your mysterious man-talk—"

"I don't want to—"

"Oh, but you must!"—*she* was now dismissing*him*—"because, although I am convalescent, I am a little tired, and Nina's maid is waiting to tuck me in."

"So you send me away?"

"*Send* you—" She hesitated, delightfully confused in the reversal of roles—not quite convinced of this new power which, of itself, had seemed to invest her with authority over man. "Yes," she said, "I must send you away." And her heart beat a little faster in her uncertainty as to his obedience—then leaped in triumph as he rose with a reluctance perfectly visible.

"To-morrow," she said, "I am to drive for the first time. In the evening I may be permitted to go to the Grays' mid-Lent dance—but not to dance much. Will you be there? Didn't they ask you? I shall tell Suddy Gray what I think of him—I don't care whether it's for the younger set or not! Goodness me, aren't you as young as anybody! . . . Well, then! . . . So we won't see each other to-morrow. And the day after that—oh, I wish I had my engagement list. Never mind, I will telephone you when I'm to be at home—or wherever I'm going to be. But it won't be anywhere in particular because it's Lent, of course. . . . Good-night, Captain Selwyn; you've been very sweet to me, and I've enjoyed every single instant."

When he had gone she rose, a trifle excited in the glow of abstract happiness, and walked erratically about, smiling to herself, touching and rearranging objects that caught her attention. Then an innocent instinct led her to the mirror, where she stood a moment looking back into the lovely reflected face with its disordered hair.

"After all," she said, "I'm not as aged as I pretended. . . . I wonder if he is laughing at me now. . . . But he was very, very nice to me—wherever he has gone in quest of that 'good time' and to talk his man-talk to other men—"

In a reverie she stood at the mirror considering her own flushed cheeks and brilliant eyes.

"What a curiously interesting man he is," she murmured naïvely. "I shall telephone him that I am not going to that *mi-carême* dance. . . . Besides, Suddy Gray is a bore with the martyred smile he's been cultivating. . . . As though a happy girl would dream of marrying anybody with all life before her to learn important things in! . . . And that dreadful, downy Scott Innis—trying to make me listen to *him*! . . . until I was ashamed to be alive! And Bradley Harmon—ugh!—and oh, that mushy widower, Percy Draymore, who got hold of my arm before I dreamed—"

She shuddered and turned back into the room, frowning and counting her slow steps across the floor.

"After all," she said, "their silliness may be their greatest mystery—but I don't include Captain Selwyn," she added loyally; "he is far too intelligent to be like other men."

Yet, like other men, at that very moment Captain Selwyn was playing the fizzing contents of a siphon upon the iced ingredients of a tall, thin glass which stood on a table in the Lenox Club.

The governor's room being deserted except by himself and Mr. Lansing, he continued the animated explanation of his delay in arriving.

"So I stayed," he said to Boots with an enthusiasm quite boyish, "and I had a perfectly bully time. She's just as clever as she can be—startling at moments. I never half appreciated her—she formerly appealed to me in a different way—a young girl knocking at the door of the world, and no mother or father to open for her and show her the gimcracks and the freaks and the side-shows. Do you know, Boots, that some day that girl is going to marry somebody, and it worries me, knowing men as I do—unless you should think of—"

"Great James!" faltered Mr. Lansing, "are you turning into a schatschen? Are you planning to waddle through the world making matches for your friends? If you are I'm quitting you right here."

"It's only because you are the decentest man I happen to know," said Selwyn resentfully. "Probably she'd turn you down, anyway. But—" and he brightened up, "I dare say she'll choose the best to be had; it's a pity though—"

"What's a pity?"

"That a charming, intellectual, sensitive, innocent girl like that should be turned over to a plain lump of a man."

"When you've finished your eulogy on our sex," said Lansing, "I'll walk home with you."

"Come on, then; I can talk while I walk; did you think I couldn't?"

And as they struck through the first cross street toward Lexington Avenue: "It's a privilege for a fellow to know that sort of a girl—so many surprises in her—the charmingly unexpected and unsuspected!—the pretty flashes of wit, the naïve egotism which is as amusing as it is harmless. . . . I had no idea how complex she is. . . . If you think you have the simple feminine on your hands—forget it, Boots!—for she's as evanescent as a helio-flash and as stunningly luminous as a searchlight. . . . And here I've been doing the benevolent prig, bestowing society upon her as a man doles out indigestible stuff to a kid, using a sort of guilty discrimination in the distribution—"

"What on earth is all this?" demanded Lansing; "are you perhaps *non compos*, dear friend?"

"I'm trying to tell you and explain to myself that little Miss Erroll is a rare and profoundly interesting specimen of a genus not usually too amusing," he replied with growing enthusiasm. "Of course, Holly Erroll was her father, and that accounts for something; and her mother seems to have been a wit as well as a beauty—which helps you to understand; but the brilliancy of the result—aged nineteen, mind you—is out of all proportion; cause and effect do not balance. . . . Why, Boots, an ordinary man—I mean an everyday fellow who dines and dances and does the harmlessly usual about town, dwindles to anæmic insignificance when compared to that young girl—even now when she's practically undeveloped—when her intelligence is like an uncut gem still in the matrix of inexperience—"

"Help!" said Boots feebly, attempting to bolt; but Selwyn hooked arms with him, laughing excitedly. In fact Lansing had not seen his friend in such excellent spirits for many, many months; and it made him exceedingly light-hearted, so that he presently began to chant the old service canticle:

"I   have   another,   he's   just   as   bad,
He almost drives me crazy—"

And arm in arm they swung into the dark avenue, singing "Barney
Riley" in resonant undertones, while overhead the chilly little Western
stars looked down through pallid convolutions of moving clouds, and
the wind in the gas-lit avenue grew keener on the street-corners.

"Cooler followed by clearing," observed Boots in disgust. "Ugh; it's the
limit, this nipping, howling hemisphere." And he turned up his overcoat
collar.

"I prefer it to a hemisphere that smells like a cheap joss-stick," said
Selwyn.

"After all, they're about alike," retorted Boots—"even to the ladrones of
Broad Street and the dattos of Wall. . . . And here's our bally bungalow
now," he added, fumbling for his keys and whistling "taps" under his
breath.

As the two men entered and started to ascend the stairs, a door on the
parlour floor opened and their landlady appeared, enveloped in a soiled
crimson kimona and a false front which had slipped sideways.

"There's the Sultana," whispered Lansing, "and she's making sign-
language at you. Wig-wag her, Phil. Oh . . . good-evening, Mrs. Greeve;
did you wish to speak to me? Oh!—to Captain Selwyn. Of course."

"If *you* please," said Mrs. Greeve ominously, so Lansing continued
upward; Selwyn descended; Mrs. Greeve waved him into the icy parlour,
where he presently found her straightening her "front" with work-worn
fingers.

"Captain Selwyn, I deemed it my duty to set up in order to inform you of
certain special doin's," she said haughtily.

"What 'doings'?" he inquired.

"Mr. Erroll's, sir. Last night he evidentially found difficulty with the
stairs and I seen him asleep on the parlour sofa when I come down to
answer the milkman, a-smokin' a cigar that wasn't lit, with his feet on
the angelus."

"I'm very, very sorry, Mrs. Greeve," he said—"and so is Mr. Erroll. He
and I had a little talk to-day, and I am sure that he will be more careful
hereafter."

"There is cigar-holes burned into the carpet," insisted Mrs. Greeve, "and
a mercy we wasn't all insinuated in our beds, one window-pane broken
and the gas a blue an' whistlin' streak with the curtains blowin' into it
an' a strange cat on to that satin dozy-do; the proof being the repugnant
perfume."

"All of which," said Selwyn, "Mr. Erroll will make every possible amends for. He is very young, Mrs. Greeve, and very much ashamed, I am sure. So please don't make it too hard for him."

She stood, little slippered feet planted sturdily in the first position in dancing, fat, bare arms protruding from the kimona, her work-stained fingers linked together in front of her. With a soiled thumb she turned a ring on her third finger.

"I ain't a-goin' to be mean to nobody," she said; "my gentlemen is always refined, even if they do sometimes forget theirselves when young and sporty. Mr. Erroll is now a-bed, sir, and asleep like a cherub, ice havin' been served three times with towels, extra. Would you be good enough to mention the bill to him in the morning?—the grocer bein' sniffy." And she handed the wadded and inky memorandum of damages to Selwyn, who pocketed it with a nod of assurance.

"There was," she added, following him to the door, "a lady here to see you twice, leavin' no name or intentions otherwise than business affairs of a pressin' nature."

"A—lady?" he repeated, halting short on the stairs.

"Young an' refined, allowin' for a automobile veil."

"She—she asked for me?" he repeated, astonished.

"Yes, sir. She wanted to see your rooms. But havin' no orders, Captain Selwyn—although I must say she was that polite and ladylike and," added Mrs. Greeve irrelevantly, "a art rocker come for you, too, and another for Mr. Lansing, which I placed in your respective settin'-rooms."

"Oh," said Selwyn, laughing in relief, "it's all right, Mrs. Greeve. The lady who came is my sister, Mrs. Gerard; and whenever she comes you are to admit her whether or not I am here."

"She said she might come again," nodded Mrs. Greeve as he mounted the stairs; "am I to show her up any time she comes?"

"Certainly—thank you," he called back—"and Mr. Gerard, too, if he calls."

He looked into Boots's room as he passed; that gentleman, in bedroom costume of peculiar exotic gorgeousness, sat stuffing a pipe with shag, and poring over a mass of papers pertaining to the Westchester Air Line's property and prospective developments.

"Come in, Phil," he called out; "and look at the dinky chair somebody sent me!" But Selwyn shook his head.

"Come into my rooms when you're ready," he said, and closed the door again, smiling and turning away toward his own quarters.

101

Before he entered, however, he walked the length of the hall and cautiously tried the handle of Gerald's door. It yielded; he lighted a match and gazed at the sleeping boy where he lay very peacefully among his pillows. Then, without a sound, he reclosed the door and withdrew to his apartment.

As he emerged from the bedroom in his dressing-gown he heard the front door-bell below peal twice, but paid no heed, his attention being concentrated on the chair which Nina had sent him. First he walked gingerly all around it, then he ventured nearer to examine it in detail, and presently he tried it.

"Of course," he sighed—"bless her heart!—it's a perfectly impossible chair. It squeaks, too." But he was mistaken; the creak came from the old stairway outside his door, weighted with the tread of Mrs. Greeve. The tread and the creaking ceased; there came a knock, then heavy descending footsteps on the aged stairway, every separate step protesting until the incubus had sunk once more into the depths from which it had emerged.

As this happened to be the night for his laundry, he merely called out, "All right!" and remained incurious, seated in the new chair and striving to adjust its stiff and narrow architecture to his own broad shoulders. Finally he got up and filled his pipe, intending to try the chair once more under the most favourable circumstances.

As he lighted his pipe there came a hesitating knock at the door; he jerked his head sharply; the knock was repeated.

Something—a faintest premonition—the vaguest stirring of foreboding committed him to silence—and left him there motionless. The match burned close to his fingers; he dropped it and set his heel upon the sparks.

Then he walked swiftly to the door, flung it open full width—and stood stock still.

And Mrs. Ruthven entered the room, partly closing the door behind, her gloved hand still resting on the knob.

For a moment they confronted one another, he tall, rigid, astounded; she pale, supple, relaxing a trifle against the half-closed door behind her, which yielded and closed with a low click.

At the sound of the closing door he found his voice; it did not resemble his own voice either to himself or to her; but she answered his bewildered question:

"I don't know why I came. Is it so very dreadful? Have I offended you? . . . I did not suppose that men cared about conventions."

"But—why on earth—did you come?" he repeated. "Are you in trouble?"

"I seem to be now," she said with a tremulous laugh; "you are frightening me to death, Captain Selwyn."

Still dazed, he found the first chair at hand and dragged it toward her.

She hesitated at the offer; then: "Thank you," she said, passing before him. She laid her hand on the chair, looked a moment at him, and sank into it.

Resting there, her pale cheek against her muff, she smiled at him, and every nerve in him quivered with pity.

"World without end; amen," she said. "Let the judgment of man pass."

"The judgment of this man passes very gently," he said, looking down at her. "What brings you here, Mrs. Ruthven?"

"Will you believe me?"

"Yes."

"Then—it is simply the desire of the friendless for a friend. Nothing else—nothing more subtle, nothing of effrontery; n-nothing worse. Do you believe me?"

"I don't understand—"

"Try to."

"Do you mean that you have differed with—"

"Him?" She laughed. "Oh, no; I was talking of real people, not of myths. And real people are not very friendly to me, always—not that they are disagreeable, you understand, only a trifle overcordial; and my most intimate friend kisses me a little too frequently. By the way, she has quite succumbed to you, I hear."

"Who do you mean?"

"Why, Rosamund."

He said something under his breath and looked at her impatiently.

"Didn't you know it?" she asked, smiling.

"Know what?"

"That Rosamund is quite crazy about you?"

"Good Lord! Do you suppose that any of the monkey set are interested in me or I in them?" he said, disgusted. "Do I ever go near them or meet them at all except by accident in the routine of the machinery which sometimes sews us in tangent patches on this crazy-quilt called society?"

"'I don't know why I came.'"

"But Rosamund," she said, laughing, "is now cultivating Mrs. Gerard."

"What of it?" he demanded.

"Because," she replied, still laughing, "I tell you, she is perfectly mad about you. There's no use scowling and squaring your chin. Oh, I ought to know what that indicates! I've watched you do it often enough; but the fact is that the handsomest and smartest woman in town is for ever dinning your perfections into my ears—"

"I know," he said, "that this sort of stuff passes in your set for wit; but let me tell you that any man who cares for that brand of humour can have it any time he chooses. However, he goes outside the residence district to find it."

She flushed scarlet at his brutality; he drew up a chair, seated himself very deliberately, and spoke, his unlighted pipe in his left hand:

"The girl I left—the girl who left me—was a modest, clean-thinking, clean-minded girl, who also had a brain to use, and employed it. Whatever conclusion that girl arrived at concerning the importance of marriage-vows is no longer my business; but the moment she confronts me again, offering friendship, then I may use a friend's privilege, as I do. And so I tell you that loosely fashionable badinage bores me. And another matter—privileged by the friendship you acknowledge—forces me to ask you a question, and I ask it, point-blank: Why have you again permitted Gerald to play cards for stakes at your house, after promising you would not do so?"

The colour receded from her face and her gloved fingers tightened on the arms of her chair.

"That is one reason I came," she said; "to explain—"

"You could have written."

"I say it was *one* reason; the other I have already given you—because I— I felt that you were friendly."

"I am. Go on."

"I don't know whether you are friendly to me; I thought you were—that night. . . . I did not sleep a wink after it . . . because I was quite happy. . . . But now—I don't know—"

"Whether I am still friendly? Well, I am. So please explain about Gerald."

"Are you sure?" raising her dark eyes, "that you mean to be kind?"

"Yes, sure," he said harshly. "Go on."

"You are a little rough with me; a-almost insolent—"

"I—I have to be. Good God! Alixe, do you think this is nothing to me?— this wretched mess we have made of life! Do you think my roughness and abruptness comes from anything but pity?—pity for us both, I tell you. Do you think I can remain unmoved looking on the atrocious punishment you have inflicted on yourself?—tethered to—to *that*!—for life!—the poison of the contact showing in your altered voice and manner!—in the things you laugh at, in the things you live for—in the twisted, misshapen ideals that your friends set up on a heap of nuggets for you to worship? Even if we've passed through the sea of mire, can't

105

we at least clear the filth from our eyes and see straight and steer straight to the anchorage?"

She had covered her pallid face with her muff; he bent forward, his hand on the arm of her chair.

"Alixe, was there nothing to you, after all? Was it only a tinted ghost that was blown into my bungalow that night—only a twist of shredded marsh mist without substance, without being, without soul?—to be blown away into the shadows with the next and stronger wind—and again to drift out across the waste places of the world? I thought I knew a sweet, impulsive comrade of flesh and blood; warm, quick, generous, intelligent—and very, very young—too young and spirited, perhaps, to endure the harness which coupled her with a man who failed her—and failed himself.

"That she has made another—and perhaps more heart-breaking mistake, is bitter for me, too—because—because—I have not yet forgotten. And even if I ceased to remember, the sadness of it must touch me. But I have not forgotten, and because I have not, I say to you, anchor! and hold fast. Whatever *he* does, whatever you suffer, whatever happens, steer straight on to the anchorage. Do you understand me?"

Her gloved hand, moving at random, encountered his and closed on it convulsively.

"Do you understand?" he repeated.

"Y-es, Phil."

Head still sinking, face covered with the silvery fur, the tremors from her body set her hand quivering on his.

Heart-sick, he forbore to ask for the explanation; he knew the real answer, anyway—whatever she might say—and he understood that any game in that house was Ruthven's game, and the guests his guests; and that Gerald was only one of the younger men who had been wrung dry in that house.

No doubt at all that Ruthven needed the money; he was only a male geisha for the set that harboured him, anyway—picked up by a big, hard-eyed woman, who had almost forgotten how to laugh, until she found him furtively muzzling her diamond-laden fingers. So, when she discovered that he could sit up and beg and roll over at a nod, she let him follow her; and since then he had become indispensable and had curled up on many a soft and silken knee, and had sought and fetched and carried for many a pretty woman what she herself did not care to touch, even with white-gloved fingers.

What had she expected when she married him? Only innocent ignorance of the set he ornamented could account for the horror of her disillusion. What splendours had she dreamed of from the outside?

What flashing and infernal signal had beckoned her to enter? What mute eyes had promised? What silent smile invited? All skulls seem to grin; but the world has yet to hear them laugh.

"Philip?"

"Yes, Alixe."

"I did my best, w-without offending Gerald. Can you believe me?"

"I know you did. . . . Don't mind what I said—"

"N-no, not now. . . . You do believe me, don't you?"

"Yes, I do."

"Thank you. . . . And, Phil, I will try to s-steer straight—because you ask me."

"You must."

"I will. . . . It is good to be here. . . . I must not come again, must I?"

"Not again, Alixe."

"On your account?"

"On your own. . . . What do *I* care?"

"I didn't know. They say—"

"What?" he asked sharply.

"A rumour—I heard it—others speak of it—perhaps to be disagreeable to me—"

"What have you heard?"

"That—that you might marry again—"

"Well, you can nail that lie," he said hotly.

"Then it is not true?"

"True! Do you think I'd take that chance again even if I felt free to do it?"

"Free?" she faltered; "but you *are* free, Phil!"

"I am not," he said fiercely; "no man is free to marry twice under such conditions. It's a jest at decency and a slap in the face of civilisation! I'm done for—finished; I had my chance and I failed. Do you think I consider myself free to try again with the chance of further bespattering my family?"

"Wait until you really love," she said tremulously.

He laughed incredulously.

"I am glad that it is not true. . . . I am glad," she said. "Oh, Phil! Phil!—for a single one of the chances we had again and again and again!—and we did not know—we did not know! And yet—there were moments—"

Dry-lipped he looked at her, and dry of eye and lip she raised her head and stared at him—through him—far beyond at the twin ghosts floating under the tropic stars locked fast in their first embrace.

Then she rose, blindly, covering her face with her hands, and he stumbled to his feet, shrinking back from her—because dead fires were flickering again, and the ashes of dead roses stirred above the scented embers—and the magic of all the East was descending like a veil upon them, and the Phantom of the Past drew nearer, smiling, wide-armed, crowned with living blossoms.

The tide rose, swaying her where she stood; her hands fell from her face. Between them the grave they had dug seemed almost filled with flowers now—was filling fast. And across it they looked at one another as though stunned. Then his face paled and he stepped back, staring at her from stern eyes.

"Phil," she faltered, bewildered by the mirage, "is it only a bad dream, after all?" And as the false magic glowed into blinding splendour to engulf them: "Oh, boy! boy!—is it hell or heaven where we've fallen—?"

There came a loud rapping at the door.

CHAPTER V

AFTERGLOW

"Phil," she wrote, "I am a little frightened. Do you suppose Boots suspected who it was? I must have been perfectly mad to go to your rooms that night; and we both were—to leave the door unlocked with the chance of somebody walking in. But, Phil, how could I know it was the fashion for your friends to bang like that and then come in without the excuse of a response from you?

"I have been so worried, so anxious, hoping from day to day that you would write to reassure me that Boots did not recognise me with my back turned to him and my muff across my eyes.

"But scared and humiliated as I am I realise that it was well that he knocked. Even as I write to you here in my own room, behind locked doors, I am burning with the shame of it.

"But I am *not* that kind of woman, Phil; truly, truly, I am not. When the foolish impulse seized me I had no clear idea of what I wanted except to see you and learn for myself what you thought about Gerald's playing at my house after I had promised not to let him.

"Of course, I understood what I risked in going; I realised what common interpretation might be put upon what I was doing. But ugly as it might appear to anybody except you, my motive, you see, must have been quite innocent—else I should have gone about it in a very different manner.

"I wanted to see you, that is absolutely all; I was lonely for a word—even a harsh one—from the sort of man you are. I wanted you to believe it was in spite of me that Gerald came and played that night.

"He came without my knowledge. I did not know he was invited. And when he appeared I did everything to prevent him from playing; *you* will never know what took place—what I submitted to—

"I am trying to be truthful, Phil; I want to lay my heart bare for you— but there are things a woman cannot wholly confess. Believe me, I did what I could. . . . And *that* is all I can say. Oh, I know what it costs you to be mixed up in such contemptible complications. I, for my part, can scarcely bear to have you know so much about me—and what I am come to. That is my real punishment, Phil—not what you said it was.

"I do not think it is well for me that you know so much about me. It is not too difficult to face the outer world with a bold front—or to deceive any man in it. But our own little world is being rapidly undeceived; and now the only real man remaining in it has seen my gay mask stripped off—which is not well for a woman, Phil.

"I remember what you said about an anchorage; I am trying to clear these haunted eyes of mine and steer clear of phantoms—for the honour of what we once were to each other before the world. But steering a ghost-ship through endless tempests is hard labour, Phil; so be a little kind—a little more than patient, if my hand grows tired at the wheel.

"And now—with all these madly inked pages scattered across my desk, I draw toward me another sheet—the last I have still unstained; to ask at last the question which I have shrunk from through all these pages— and for which these pages alone were written:

"*What* do you think of me? Asking you, shows how much I care; dread of your opinion has turned me coward until this last page. *What* do you think of me? I am perfectly miserable about Boots, but that is partly fright—though I know I am safe enough with such a man. But what sets my cheeks blazing so that I cannot bear to face my own eyes in the mirror, is the fear of what *you* must think of me in the still, secret places of that heart of yours, which I never, never understood. ALIXE."

It was a week before he sent his reply—although he wrote many answers, each in turn revised, corrected, copied, and recopied, only to be destroyed in the end. But at last he forced himself to meet truth with truth, cutting what crudity he could from his letter:

"You ask me what I think of you; but that question should properly come from me. What do *you* think of a man who exhorts and warns a woman to stand fast, and then stands dumb at the first impact of temptation?

"A sight for gods and men—that man! Is there any use for me to stammer out trite phrases of self-contempt? The fact remains that I am unfit to advise, criticise, or condemn anybody for anything; and it's high time I realised it.

"If words of commendation, of courage, of kindly counsel, are needed by anybody in this world, I am not the man to utter them. What a hypocrite must I seem to you! I who sat there beside you preaching platitudes in strong self-complacency, instructing you how morally edifying it is to be good and unhappy.

"Then, what happened? I don't know exactly; but I'm trying to be honest, and I'll tell you what I think happened:

"You are—you; I am—I; and we are still those same two people who understood neither the impulse that once swept us together, nor the forces that tore us apart—ah, more than that! we never understood each other! And we do not now.

"That is what happened. We were too near together again; the same spark leaped, the same blindness struck us, the same impulse swayed us—call it what we will!—and it quickened out of chaos, grew from nothing into unreasoning existence. It was the terrific menace of emotion, stunning us both—simply because you are you and I am I. And that is what happened.

"We cannot deny it; we may not have believed it possible—or in fact considered it at all. I did not; I am sure you did not. Yet it occurred, and we cannot deny it, and we can no more explain or understand it than we can understand each other.

"But one thing we do know—not through reason but through sheer instinct: We cannot venture to meet again—that way. For I, it seems, am a man like other men except that I lack character; and you are— *you*! still unchanged—with all the mystery of attraction, all the magic force of vitality, all the esoteric subtlety with which you enveloped me the first moment my eyes met yours.

110

"There was no more reason for it then than there is now; and, as you admit, it was not love—though, as you also admit, there were moments approaching it. But nothing can have real being without a basis of reason; and so, whatever it was, it vanished. This, perhaps, is only the infernal afterglow.

"As for me, I am, as you are, all at sea, self-confidence gone, self-faith lost—a very humble person, without conceit, dazed, perplexed, but still attempting to steer through toward that safe anchorage which I dared lately to recommend to you.

"And it is really there, Alixe, despite the fool who recites his creed so tritely.

"All this in attempt to bring order into my own mental confusion; and the result is that I have formulated nothing.

"So now I end where I began with that question which answers yours without the faintest suspicion of reproach: What can you think of such a man as I am? And in the presence of my *second* failure your answer must be that you now think what you once thought of him when you first realised that he had failed you, PHILIP SELWYN."

That very night brought him her reply:

"Phil, dear, I do not blame you for one instant. Why do you say you ever failed in anything? It was entirely my fault. But I am so happy that you wrote as you did, taking all the blame, which is like you. I can look into my mirror now—for a moment or two.

"It is brave of you to be so frank about what you think came over us. I can discuss nothing, admit nothing; but you always did reason more clearly than I. Still, whatever spell it was that menaced us I know very well could not have threatened you seriously; I know it because you reason about it so logically. So it could have been nothing serious. Love alone is serious; and it sometimes comes slowly, sometimes goes slowly; but if you desire it to come quickly, close your eyes! And if you wish it to vanish, *reason about it!*

"We are on very safe ground again, Phil; you see we are making little epigrams about love.

"Rosamund is impatient—it's a symphony concert, and I must go—the horrid little cynic!—I half believe she suspects that I'm writing to you and tearing off yards of sentiment. It is likely I'd do that, isn't it!—but I don't care what she thinks. Besides, it behooves her to be agreeable, and she knows that I know it does! *Voilà!*

"By the way, I saw Mrs. Gerard's pretty ward at the theatre last night— Miss Erroll. She certainly is stunning—"

Selwyn flattened out the letter and deliberately tore out the last paragraph. Then he set it afire with a match.

"At least," he said with an ugly look, "I can keep her out of this"; and he dropped the brittle blackened paper and set his heel on it. Then he resumed his perusal of the mutilated letter, reread it, and finally destroyed it.

"Alixe," he wrote in reply, "we had better stop this letter-writing before somebody stops us. Anybody desiring to make mischief might very easily misinterpret what we are doing. I, of course, could not close the correspondence, so I ask you to do so without any fear that you will fail to understand why I ask it. Will you?"

To which she replied:

"Yes, Phil. Good-bye.

"ALIXE."

A box of roses left her his debtor; she was too intelligent to acknowledge them. Besides, matters were going better with her.

And that was all for a while.

Meanwhile Lent had gone, and with it the last soiled snow of winter. It was an unusually early spring; tulips in Union Square appeared coincident with crocus and snow-drop; high above the city's haze wavering wedges of wild-fowl drifted toward the Canadas; a golden perfumed bloom clotted the naked branches of the park shrubs; Japanese quince burst into crimson splendour; tender chestnut leaves unfolded; the willows along the Fifty-ninth Street wall waved banners of gilded green; and through the sunshine battered butterflies floated, and the wild bees reappeared, scrambling frantically, powdered to the thighs in the pollen of a million dandelions.

"Spring, with that nameless fragrance in the air
Which breathes of all things fair,"

sang a young girl riding in the Park. And she smiled to herself as she guided her mare through the flowering labyrinths. Other notes of the Southern poet's haunting song stole soundless from her lips; for it was only her heart that was singing there in the sun, while her silent, smiling mouth mocked the rushing melody of the birds.

Behind her, powerfully mounted, ambled the belted groom; she was riding alone in the golden weather because her good friend Selwyn was very busy in his office downtown, and Gerald, who now rode with her occasionally, was downtown also, and there remained nobody else to ride with. Also the horses were to be sent to Silverside soon, and she wanted to use them as much as possible while the Park was at its loveliest.

She, therefore, galloped conscientiously every morning, sometimes with Nina, but usually alone. And every afternoon she and Nina drove there, drinking the freshness of the young year—the most beautiful year of her life, she told herself, in all the exquisite maturity of her adolescence.

So she rode on, straight before her, head high, the sun striking face and firm, white throat; and in her heart laughed spring eternal, whose voiceless melody parted her lips.

Breezes blowing from beds of iris quickened her breath with their perfume; she saw the tufted lilacs sway in the wind, and the streamers of mauve-tinted wistaria swinging, all a-glisten with golden bees; she saw a crimson cardinal winging through the foliage, and amorous tanagers flashing like scarlet flames athwart the pines.

From rock and bridge and mouldy archway tender tendrils of living green fluttered, brushing her cheeks. Beneath the thickets the under-wood world was very busy, where squirrels squatted or prowled and cunning fox-sparrows avoided the starlings and blackbirds; and the big cinnamon-tinted, speckle-breasted thrashers scuffled among last year's leaves or, balanced on some leafy spray, carolled ecstatically of this earthly paradise.

It was near Eighty-sixth Street that a girl, splendidly mounted, saluted her, and wheeling, joined her—a blond, cool-skinned, rosy-tinted, smoothly groomed girl, almost too perfectly seated, almost too flawless and supple in the perfect symmetry of face and figure.

"Upon my word," she said gaily, "you are certainly spring incarnate, Miss Erroll—the living embodiment of all this!" She swung her riding-crop in a circle and laughed, showing her perfect teeth. "But where is that faithful attendant cavalier of yours this morning? Is he so grossly material that he prefers Wall Street, as does my good lord and master?"

"Do you mean Gerald?" asked Eileen innocently, "or Captain Selwyn?"

"Oh, either," returned Rosamund airily; "a girl should have something masculine to talk to on a morning like this. Failing that she should have some pleasant memories of indiscretions past and others to come, D.V.; at least one little souvenir to repent—smilingly. Oh, la! Oh, me! All these wretched birds a-courting and I bumping along on Dobbin, lacking even my own Gilpin! Shall we gallop?"

Eileen nodded.

When at length they pulled up along the reservoir, Eileen's hair had rebelled as usual and one bright strand eurled like a circle of ruddy light across her cheek; but Rosamund drew bridle as immaculate as ever and coolly inspected her companion.

"What gorgeous hair," she said, staring. "It's worth a coronet, you know—if you ever desire one."

"I don't," said the girl, laughing and attempting to bring the insurgent curl under discipline.

"I dare say you're right; coronets are out of vogue among us now. It's the fashion to marry our own good people. By the way, you are continuing to astonish the town, I hear."

"What do you mean, Mrs. Fane?"

"Why, first it was Sudbury, then Draymore, and how everybody says that Boots—"

"Boots!" repeated Miss Erroll blankly, then laughed deliciously.

"Poor, poor Boots! Did they say *that* about him? Oh, it really is too bad, Mrs. Fane; it is certainly horridly impertinent of people to say such things. My only consolation is that Boots won't care; and if he doesn't, why should I?"

Rosamund nodded, crossing her crop.

"At first, though, I did care," continued the girl. "I was so ashamed that people should gossip whenever a man was trying to be nice to me—"

"Pooh! It's always the men's own faults. Don't you suppose the martyr's silence is noisier than a shriek of pain from the house-tops? I know—a little about men," added Rosamund modestly, "and they invariably say to themselves after a final rebuff: 'Now, I'll be patient and brave and I'll bear with noble dignity this cataclysm which has knocked the world galley-west for me and loosened the moon in its socket and spoiled the symmetry of the sun.' And they go about being so conspicuously brave that any débutante can tell what hurts them."

Eileen was still laughing, but not quite at her ease—the theme being too personal to suit her. In fact, there usually seemed to be too much personality in Rosamund's conversation—a certain artificial indifference to convention, which she, Eileen, did not feel any desire to disregard. For the elements of reticence and of delicacy were inherent in her; the training of a young girl had formalised them into rules. But since her début she had witnessed and heard so many violations of convention that now she philosophically accepted such, when they came from her elders, merely reserving her own convictions in matters of personal taste and conduct.

For a while, as they rode, Rosamund was characteristically amusing, sailing blandly over the shoals of scandal, though Eileen never suspected it—wittily gay at her own expense, as well as at others, flitting airily from topic to topic on the wings of a self-assurance that becomes some women if they know when to stop. But presently the mischievous perversity in her bubbled up again; she was tired of being good; she had often meant to try the effect of a gentle shock on Miss Erroll; and, besides, she wondered just how much truth there might be in the unpleasantly persistent rumour of the girl's unannounced engagement to Selwyn.

114

"It *would* be amusing, wouldn't it?" she asked with guileless frankness; "but, of course, it is not true—this report of their reconciliation."

"Whose reconciliation?" asked Miss Erroll innocently.

"Why, Alixe Ruthven and Captain Selwyn. Everybody is discussing it, you know."

"Reconciled? I don't understand," said Eileen, astonished. "They can't be; how can—"

"But it *would* be amusing, wouldn't it? and she could very easily get rid of Jack Ruthven—any woman could. So if they really mean to remarry—"

The girl stared, breathless, astounded, bolt upright in her saddle.

"Oh!" she protested, while the hot blood mantled throat and cheek, "it is wickedly untrue. How could such a thing be true, Mrs. Fane! It is—is so senseless—"

"That is what I say," nodded Rosamund; "it's so perfectly senseless that it's amusing—even if they have become such amazingly good friends again. *I* never believed there was anything seriously sentimental in the situation; and their renewed interest in each other is quite the most frankly sensible way out of any awkwardness," she added cordially.

Miserably uncomfortable, utterly unable to comprehend, the girl rode on in silence, her ears ringing with Rosamund's words. And Rosamund, riding beside her, cool, blond, and cynically amused, continued the theme with admirable pretence of indifference:

"It's a pity that ill-natured people are for ever discussing them; and it makes me indignant, because I've always been very fond of Alixe Ruthven, and I am positive that she does *not*correspond with Captain Selwyn. A girl in her position would be crazy to invite suspicion by doing the things they say she is doing—"

"Don't, Mrs. Fane, please, don't!" stammered Eileen; "I—I really can't listen. I simply will not!" Then bewildered, hurt, and blindly confused as she was, the instinct to defend flashed up—though from what she was defending him she did not realise: "It is utterly untrue!" she exclaimed hotly—"all that yo—all that *they* say!—whoever they are—whatever they mean. I cannot understand it—I don't understand, and I will not! Nor will *he*!" she added with a scornful conviction that disconcerted Rosamund; "for if you knew him as I do, Mrs. Fane, you would never, never have spoken as you have."

Mrs. Fane relished neither the naïve rebuke nor the intimation that her own acquaintance with Selwyn was so limited; and least of all did she relish the implied intimacy between this red-haired young girl and Captain Selwyn.

"Dear Miss Erroll," she said blandly, "I spoke as I did only to assure you that I, also, disregard such malicious gossip—"

"But if you disregard it, Mrs. Fane, why do you repeat it?"

"Merely to emphasise to you my disbelief in it, child," returned Rosamund. "Do you understand?"

"Y-es; thank you. Yet, I should never have heard of it at all if you had not told me."

Rosamund's colour rose one degree:

"It is better to hear such things from a friend, is it not?"

"I didn't know that one's friends said such things; but perhaps it is better that way, as you say, only, I cannot understand the necessity of my knowing—of my hearing—because it is Captain Selwyn's affair, after all."

"And that," said Rosamund deliberately, "is why I told *you*."

"Told *me*? Oh—because he and I are such close friends?"

"Yes—such very close friends that I"—she laughed—"I am informed that your interests are soon to be identical."

The girl swung round, self-possessed, but dreadfully pale.

"If you believed that," she said, "it was vile of you to say what you said, Mrs. Fane."

"But I did *not* believe it, child!" stammered Rosamund, several degrees redder than became her, and now convinced that it was true. "I n-never dreamed of offending you, Miss Erroll—"

"Do you suppose I am too ignorant to take offence?" said the girl unsteadily. "I told you very plainly that I did not understand the matters you chose for discussion; but I do understand impertinence when I am driven to it."

"I am very, very sorry that you believe I meant it that way," said Rosamund, biting her lips.

"What did you mean? You are older than I, you are certainly experienced; besides, you are married. If you can give it a gentler name than insolence I would be glad—for your sake, Mrs. Fane. I only know that you have spoiled my ride, spoiled the day for me, hurt me, humiliated me, and awakened, not curiosity, not suspicion, but the horror of it, in me. You did it once before—at the Minsters' dance; not, perhaps, that you deliberately meant to; but you did it. And your subject was then, as it is now, Captain Selwyn—my friend—"

Her voice became unsteady again and her mouth curved; but she held her head high and her eyes were as fearlessly direct as a child's.

116

"And now," she said calmly, "you know where I stand and what I will not stand. Natural deference to an older woman, the natural self-distrust of a girl in the presence of social experience—and under its protection as she had a right to suppose—prevented me from checking you when your conversation became distasteful. You, perhaps, mistook my reticence for acquiescence; and you were mistaken. I am still quite willing to remain on agreeable terms with you, if you wish, and to forget what you have done to me this morning."

If Rosamund had anything left to say, or any breath to say it, there were no indications of it. Never in her flippant existence had she been so absolutely flattened by any woman. As for this recent graduate from fudge and olives, she could scarcely realise how utterly and finally she had been silenced by her. Incredulity, exasperation, amazement had succeeded each other while Miss Erroll was speaking; chagrin, shame, helplessness followed as bitter residue. But, in the end, the very incongruity of the situation came to her aid; for Rosamund very easily fell a prey to the absurd—even when the amusement was furnished at her own expense; and a keen sense of the ridiculous had more than once saved her dainty skirts from a rumpling that her modesty perhaps might have forgiven.

"I'm certainly a little beast," she said impulsively, "but I really do like you. Will you forgive?"

No genuine appeal to the young girl's generosity had ever been in vain; she forgave almost as easily as she breathed. Even now in the flush of just resentment it was not hard for her to forgive; she hesitated only in order to adjust matters in her own mind.

Mrs. Fane swung her horse and held out her right hand:

"Is it *pax*, Miss Erroll? I'm really ashamed of myself. Won't you forgive me?"

"Yes," said the young girl, laying her gloved hand on Rosamund's very lightly; "I've often thought," she added naïvely, "that I could like you, Mrs. Fane, if you would only give me a chance."

"I'll try—you blessed innocent! You've torn me into rags and tatters, and you did it adorably. What I said was idle, half-witted, gossiping nonsense. So forget every atom of it as soon as you can, my dear, and let me prove that I'm not an utter idiot, if *I* can."

"That will be delightful," said Eileen with a demure smile; and Rosamund laughed, too, with full-hearted laughter; for trouble sat very lightly on her perfect shoulders in the noontide of her strength and youth. Sin and repentance were rapid matters with Rosamund; cause, effect, and remorse a quick sequence to be quickly reckoned up, checked off, and cancelled; and the next blank page turned over to be ruled and filled with the next impeachment.

There was, in her, more of mischief than of real malice; and if she did pinch people to see them wiggle it was partly because she supposed that the pain would be as momentary as the pinch; for nothing lasted with her, not even the wiggle. So why should the pain produced by a furtive tweak interfere with the amusement she experienced in the victim's jump?

But what had often saved her from a social lynching was her ability to laugh at her own discomfiture, and her unfeigned liking and respect for the turning worm.

"And, my dear," she said, concluding the account of the adventure to Mrs. Ruthven that afternoon at Sherry's, "I've never been so roundly abused and so soundly trounced in my life as I was this blessed morning by that red-headed novice! Oh, my! Oh, la! I could have screamed with laughter at my own undoing."

"It's what you deserved," said Alixe, intensely annoyed, although Rosamund had not told her all that she had so kindly and gratuitously denied concerning her relations with Selwyn. "It was sheer effrontery of you, Rosamund, to put such notions into the head of a child and stir her up into taking a fictitious interest in Philip Selwyn which I know— which is perfectly plain to m—to anybody never existed!"

"Of course it existed!" retorted Rosamund, delighted now to worry Alixe. "She didn't know it; that is all. It really was simple charity to wake her up. It's a good match, too, and so obviously and naturally inevitable that there's no harm in playing prophetess. . . . Anyway, what do *we* care, dear? Unless you—"

"Rosamund!" said Mrs. Ruthven exasperated, "will you ever acquire the elements of reticence? I don't know why people endure you; I don't, indeed! And they won't much longer—"

"Yes, they will, dear; that's what society is for—a protective association for the purpose of enduring impossible people. . . . I wish," she added, "that it included husbands, because in some sets it's getting to be one dreadful case of who's whose. Don't you think so?"

Alixe, externally calm but raging inwardly, sat pulling on her gloves, heartily sorry she had lunched with Rosamund.

The latter, already gloved, had risen and was coolly surveying the room.

"*Tiens!*" she said, "there is the youthful brother of our red-haired novice, now. He sees us and he's coming to inflict himself—with another moon-faced creature. Shall we bolt?"

Alixe turned and stared at Gerald, who came up boyishly red and impetuous:

"How d'ye do, Mrs. Ruthven; did you get my note? How d'ye do, Mrs. Fane; awf'fly jolly to collide this way. Would you mind if—"

"You," interrupted Rosamund, "ought to be *downtown*—unless you've concluded to retire and let Wall Street go to smash. What are you pretending to do in Sherry's at this hour, you very dreadful infant?"

"I've been lunching with Mr. Neergard—and *would* you mind—"

"Yes, I would," began Rosamund, promptly, but Alixe interrupted: "Bring him over, Gerald." And as the boy thanked her and turned back:

"I've a word to administer to that boy, Rosamund, so attack the Neergard creature with moderation, please. You owe me *that* at least."

"No, I don't!" said Rosamund, disgusted; "I *won't* be afflicted with a—"

"Nobody wants you to be too civil to him, silly! But Gerald is in his office, and I want Gerald to do something for me. Please, Rosamund."

"Oh, well, if you—"

"Yes, I do. Here he is now; and *don't* be impossible and frighten him, Rosamund."

The presentation of Neergard was accomplished without disaster to anybody. On his thin nose the dew glistened, and his thick fat hands were hot; but Rosamund was too bored to be rude to him, and Alixe turned immediately to Gerald:

"Yes, I did get your note, but I'm not at home on Tuesday. Can't you come—wait a moment!—what are you doing this afternoon?"

"Why, I'm going back to the office with Mr. Neergard—"

"Nonsense! Oh, Mr. Neergard, *would* you mind"—very sweetly—"if Mr. Erroll did not go to the office this afternoon?"

Neergard looked at her—almost—a fixed and uncomfortable smirk on his round, red face: "Not at all, Mrs. Ruthven, if you have anything better for him—"

"I have—an allopathic dose of it. Thank you, Mr. Neergard. Rosamund, we ought to start, you know: Gerald!"—with quiet significance—"*good*-bye, Mr. Neergard. Please do not buy up the rest of Long Island, because we need a new kitchen-garden very badly."

Rosamund scarcely nodded his dismissal. And the next moment Neergard found himself quite alone, standing with the smirk still stamped on his stiffened features, his hat-brim and gloves crushed in his rigid fingers, his little black mousy eyes fixed on nothing, as usual.

A wandering head-waiter thought they were fixed on him and sidled up hopeful of favours, but Neergard suddenly snarled in his face and moved toward the door, wiping the perspiration from his nose with the most splendid handkerchief ever displayed east of Sixth Avenue and west of Third.

Mrs. Ruthven's motor moved up from its waiting station; Rosamund was quite ready to enter when Alixe said cordially: "Where can we drop you, dear? *Do* let us take you to the exchange if you are going there—"

Now Rosamund had meant to go wherever they were going, merely because they evidently wished to be alone. The abruptness of the check both irritated and amused her.

"If I knew anybody in the Bronx I'd make you take me there," she said vindictively; "but as I don't you may drop me at the Orchils'—you uncivil creatures. Gerald, I know *you*want me, anyway, because you've promised to adore, honour, and obey me. . . . If you'll come with me now I'll play double dummy with you. No? Well, of all ingratitude! . . . Thank you, dear, I perceive that this is Fifth Avenue, and furthermore that this ramshackle chassis of yours has apparently broken down at the Orchils' curb. . . . Good-bye, Gerald; it never did run smooth, you know. I mean the course of T.L. as well as this motor. Try to be a good boy and keep moving; a rolling stone acquires a polish, and you are not in the moss-growing business, I'm sure—"

"Rosamund! For goodness' sake!" protested Alixe, her gloved hands at her ears.

"Dear!" said Rosamund cheerfully, "take your horrid little boy!"

And she smiled dazzlingly upon Gerald, then turned up her pretty nose at him, but permitted him to attend her to the door.

When he returned to Alixe, and the car was speeding Parkward, he began again, eagerly:

"Jack asked me to come up and, of course, I let you know, as I promised I would. But it's all right, Mrs. Ruthven, because Jack said the stakes will not be high this time—"

"You accepted!" demanded Alixe, in quick displeasure.

"Why, yes—as the stakes are not to amount to anything—"

"Gerald!"

"What?" he said uneasily.

"You promised me that you would not play again in my house!"

"I—I said, for more than I could afford—"

"No, you said you would not play; that is what you promised, Gerald."

"Well, I meant for high stakes; I—well, you don't want to drive me out altogether—even from the perfectly harmless pleasure of playing for nominal stakes—"

"Yes, I do!"

"W-why?" asked the boy in hurt surprise.

"Because it is dangerous sport, Gerald—"

"What! To play for a few cents a point—"

"Yes, to play for anything. And as far as that goes there will be no such play as you imagine."

"Yes, there will—I beg your pardon—but Jack Ruthven said so—"

"Gerald, listen to me. A bo—a man like yourself has no business playing with people whose losses never interfere with their appetites next day. A business man has no right to play such a game, anyway. I wonder what Mr. Neergard would say if he knew you—"

"Neergard! Why, he does know."

"You confessed to him?"

"Y-es; I had to. I was obliged to—to ask somebody for an advance—"

"You went to him? Why didn't you go to Captain Selwyn?—or to Mr. Gerard?"

"I did!—not to Captain Selwyn—I was ashamed to. But I went to Austin and he fired up and lit into me—and we had a muss-up—and I've stayed away since."

"Oh, Gerald! And it simply proves me right."

"No, it doesn't; I did go to Neergard and made a clean breast of it. And he let me have what I wanted like a good fellow—"

"And made you promise not to do it again!"

"No, he didn't; he only laughed. Besides, he said that he wished he had been in the game—"

"What!" exclaimed Alixe.

"He's a first-rate fellow," insisted Gerald, reddening; "and it was very nice of you to let me bring him over to-day. . . . And he knows everybody downtown, too. He comes from a very old Dutch family, but he had to work pretty hard and do without college. . . . I'd like it awfully if you'd let me—if you wouldn't mind being civil to him—once or twice, you know—"

Mrs. Ruthven lay back in her seat, thoroughly annoyed.

"My theory," insisted the boy with generous conviction, "is that a man is what he makes himself. People talk about climbers and butters-in, but where would anybody be in this town if nobody had ever butted in? It's all rot, this aping the caste rules of established aristocracies; a decent fellow ought to be encouraged. Anyway, I'm going to propose, him for the Stuyvesant and the Proscenium. Why not?"

"I see. And now you propose to bring him to my house?"

"If you'll let me. I asked Jack and he seemed to think it might be all right if you cared to ask him to play—"

"I won't!" cried Alixe, revolted. "I will not turn my drawing-rooms into a clearing-house for every money-laden social derelict in town! I've had enough of that; I've endured the accumulated wreckage too long!—weird treasure-craft full of steel and oil and coal and wheat and Heaven knows what!—I won't do it, Gerald; I'm sick of it all—sick! sick!"

The sudden, flushed outburst stunned the boy. Bewildered, he stared round-eyed at the excited young matron who was growing more incensed and more careless of what she exposed every second:

"I will not make a public gambling-hell out of my own house!" she repeated, dark eyes very bright and cheeks afire; "I will not continue to stand sponsor for a lot of queer people simply because they don't care what they lose in Mrs. Ruthven's house! You babble to me of limits, Gerald; this is the limit! Do you—or does anybody else suppose that I don't know what is being said about us?—that play is too high in our house?—that we are not too difficile in our choice of intimates as long as they can stand the pace!"

"I—I never believed that," insisted the boy, miserable to see the tears flash in her eyes and her mouth quiver.

"You may as well believe it for it's true!" she said, exasperated.

"T-true!—Mrs. Ruthven!"

"Yes, true, Gerald! I—I don't care whether you know it; I don't care, as long as you stay away. I'm sick of it all, I tell you. Do you think I was educated for this?—for the wife of a chevalier of industry—"

"M-Mrs. Ruthven!" he gasped; but she was absolutely reckless now—and beneath it all, perhaps, lay a certainty of the boy's honour. She knew he was to be trusted—was the safest receptacle for wrath so long repressed. She let prudence go with a parting and vindictive slap, and opened her heart to the astounded boy. The tempest lasted a few seconds; then she ended as abruptly as she began.

To him she had always been what a pretty young matron usually is to a well-bred but hare-brained youth just untethered. Their acquaintance had been for him a combination of charming experiences diluted with gratitude for her interest and a harmless*soupçon* of sentimentality. In her particular case, however, there was a little something more—a hint of the forbidden—a troubled enjoyment, because he knew, of course, that Mrs. Ruthven was on no footing at all with the Gerards. So in her friendship he savoured a piquancy not at all distasteful to a very young man's palate.

But now!—he had never, never seen her like this—nor any woman, for that matter—and he did not know where to look or what to do.

She was sitting back in the limousine, very limp and flushed; and the quiver of her under lip and the slightest dimness of her averted brown eyes distressed him dreadfully.

"Dear Mrs. Ruthven," he blurted out with clumsy sympathy, "you mustn't think such things, b-because they're all rot, you see; and if any fellow ever said those things to me I'd jolly soon—"

"Do you mean to say you've never heard us criticised?"

"I—well—everybody is—criticised, of course—"

"But not as we are! Do you read the papers? Well, then, do you understand how a woman must feel to have her husband continually made the butt of foolish, absurd, untrue stories—as though he were a performing poodle! I—I'm sick of that, too, for another thing. Week after week, month by month, unpleasant things have been accumulating; and they're getting too heavy, Gerald—too crushing for my shoulders. . . . Men call me restless. What wonder! Women link my name with any man who is k-kind to me! Is there no excuse then for what they call my restlessness? . . . What woman would not be restless whose private affairs are the gossip of everybody? Was it not enough that I endured terrific publicity when—when trouble overtook me two years ago? . . . I suppose I'm a fool to talk like this; but a girl must do it some time or burst!—and to whom am I to go? . . . There was only one person; and I can't talk to—that one; he—that person knows too much about me, anyway; which is not good for a woman, Gerald, not good for a good woman. . . . I mean a pretty good woman; the kind people's sisters can still talk to, you know. . . . For I'm nothing more interesting than a divorcée, Gerald; nothing more dangerous than an unhappy little fool. . . . I wish I were. . . . But I'm still at the wheel! . . . A man I know calls it hard steering but assures me that there's anchorage ahead. . . . He's a splendid fellow, Gerald; you ought to know him—well—some day; he's just a clean-cut, human, blundering, erring, unreasonable, lovable man whom any woman, who is not a fool herself, could manage. . . . Some day I should like to have you know him—intimately. He's good for people of your sort—even good for a restless, purposeless woman of my sort. Peace to him!—if there's any in the world. . . . Turn your back; I'm sniveling."

A moment afterward she had calmed completely; and now she stole a curious side glance at the boy and blushed a little when he looked back at her earnestly. Then she smiled and quietly withdrew the hand he had been holding so tightly in both of his.

"So there we are, my poor friend," she concluded with a shrug; "the old penny shocker, you know, 'Alone in a great city!'—I've dropped my handkerchief."

"I want you to believe me your friend," said Gerald, in the low, resolute voice of unintentional melodrama.

"Why, thank you; are you so sure you want that, Gerald?"

"Yes, as long as I live!" he declared, generous emotion in the ascendant. A pretty woman upset him very easily even under normal circumstances. But beauty in distress knocked him flat—as it does every wholesome boy who is worth his salt.

And he said so in his own naïve fashion; and the more eloquent he grew the more excited he grew and the deeper and blacker appeared her wrongs to him.

At first she humoured him, and rather enjoyed his fresh, eager sympathy; after a little his increasing ardour inclined her to laugh; but it was very splendid and chivalrous and genuine ardour, and the inclination to laugh died out, for emotion is contagious, and his earnestness not only flattered her legitimately but stirred the slackened tension of her heart-strings until, tightening again, they responded very faintly.

"I had no idea that *you* were lonely," he declared.

"Sometimes I am, a little, Gerald." She ought to have known better. Perhaps she did.

"Well," he began, "couldn't I come and—"

"No, Gerald."

"I mean just to see you sometimes and have another of these jolly talks—"

"Do you call this a jolly talk?"—with deep reproach.

"Why—not exactly; but I'm awfully interested, Mrs. Ruthven, and we understand each other so well—"

"I don't understand *you*", she was imprudent enough to say.

This was delightful! Certainly he must be a particularly sad and subtle dog if this clever but misunderstood young matron found him what in romance is known as an "enigma."

So he protested with smiling humility that he was quite transparent; she insisted on doubting him and contrived to look disturbed in her mind concerning the probable darkness of that past so dear to any young man who has had none.

As for Alixe, she also was mildly flattered—a trifle disdainfully perhaps, but still genuinely pleased at the honesty of this crude devotion. She was touched, too; and, besides, she trusted him; for he was clearly as transparent as the spring air. Also most women lugged a boy about with them; she had had several, but none as nice as Gerald. To tie him up and tack his license on was therefore natural to her; and if she hesitated to conclude his subjection in short order it was that, far in a corner of her restless soul, there hid an ever-latent fear of Selwyn; of his opinions concerning her fitness to act mentor to the boy of whom he was fond, and whose devotion to him was unquestioned.

Yet now, in spite of that—perhaps even partly because of it, she decided on the summary taming of Gerald; so she let her hand fall, by accident, close to his on the cushioned seat, to see what he'd do about it.

It took him some time to make up his mind; but when he did he held it so gingerly, so respectfully, that she was obliged to look out of the window. Clearly he was quite the safest and nicest of all the unfledged she had ever possessed.

"Please, don't," she said sadly.

And by that token she took him for her own.

She was very light-hearted that evening when she dropped him at the Stuyvesant Club and whizzed away to her own house, for he had promised not to play again on her premises, and she had promised to be nice to him and take him about when she was shy of an escort. She also repeated that he was truly an "enigma" and that she was beginning to be a little afraid of him, which was an economical way of making him very proud and happy. Being his first case of beauty in distress, and his first harmless love-affair with a married woman, he looked about him as he entered the club and felt truly that he had already outgrown the young and callow innocents who haunted it.

On her way home Alixe smilingly reviewed the episode until doubt of Selwyn's approval crept in again; and her amused smile had faded when she reached her home.

The house of Ruthven was a small but ultra-modern limestone affair, between Madison and Fifth; a pocket-edition of the larger mansions of their friends, but with less excuse for the overelaboration since the

125

dimensions were only twenty by a hundred. As a matter of fact its narrow ornate facade presented not a single quiet space the eyes might rest on after a tiring attempt to follow and codify the arabesques, foliations, and intricate vermiculations of what some disrespectfully dubbed as "near-aissance."

However, into this limestone bonbon-box tripped Mrs. Ruthven, mounted the miniature stairs with a whirl of her scented skirts, peeped into the drawing-room, but continued mounting until she whipped into her own apartments, separated from those of her lord and master by a locked door.

That is, the door had been locked for a long, long time; but presently, to her intense surprise and annoyance, it slowly opened, and a little man appeared in slippered feet.

He was a little man, and plump, and at first glance his face appeared boyish and round and quite guiltless of hair or of any hope of it.

But, as he came into the electric light, the hardness of his features was apparent; he was no boy; a strange idea that he had never been assailed some people. His face was puffy and pallid and faint blue shadows hinted of closest shaving; and the line from the wing of the nostrils to the nerveless corners of his thin, hard mouth had been deeply bitten by the acid of unrest.

For the remainder he wore pale-rose pajamas under a silk-and-silver kimona, an obi pierced with a jewelled scarf-pin; and he was smoking a cigarette as thin as a straw.

"Well!" said his young wife in astonished displeasure, instinctively tucking her feet—from which her maid had just removed the shoes—under her own chamber-robe.

"Send her out a moment," he said, with a nod of his head toward the maid. His voice was agreeable and full—a trifle precise and overcultivated, perhaps.

When the maid retired, Alixe sat up on the lounge, drawing her skirts down over her small stockinged feet.

"What on earth is the matter?" she demanded.

"The matter is," he said, "that Gerald has just telephoned me from the Stuyvesant that he isn't coming."

"Well?"

"No, it isn't well. This is some of your meddling."

"What if it is?" she retorted; but her breath was coming quicker.

"I'll tell you; you can get up and ring him up and tell him you expect him to-night."

She shook her head, eyeing him all the while.

"I won't do it, Jack. What do you want him for? He can't play with the people who play here; he doesn't know the rudiments of play. He's only a boy; his money is so tied up that he has to borrow if he loses very much. There's no sport in playing with a boy like that—"

"So you've said before, I believe, but I'm better qualified to judge than you are. Are you going to call him up?"

"No, I am not."

He turned paler. "Get up and go to that telephone!"

"You little whippet," she said slowly, "I was once a soldier's wife—the only decent thing I ever have been. This bullying ends now—here, at this instant! If you've any dirty work to do, do it yourself. I've done my share and I've finished."

He was astonished; that was plain enough. But it was the sudden overwhelming access of fury that weakened him and made him turn, hand outstretched, blindly seeking for a chair. Rage, even real anger, were emotions he seldom had to reckon with, for he was a very tired and bored and burned-out gentleman, and vivid emotion was not good for his arteries, the doctors told him.

He found his chair, stood a moment with his back toward his wife, then very slowly let himself down into the chair and sat facing her. There was moisture on his soft, pallid skin, a nervous twitching of the under lip; he passed one heavily ringed hand across his closely shaven jaw, still staring at her.

"I want to tell you something," he said. "You've got to stop your interference with my affairs, and stop it now."

"I am not interested in your affairs," she said unsteadily, still shaken by her own revolt, still under the shock of her own arousing to a resistance that had been long, long overdue. "If you mean," she went on, "that the ruin of this boy is your affair, then I'll make it mine from this moment. I've told you that he shall not play; and he shall not. And while I'm about it I'll admit what you are preparing to accuse me of; I *did* make Sandon Craig promise to keep away; I *did* try to make that little fool Scott Innis promise, too; and when he wouldn't I informed his father. . . . And every time you try your dirty bucket-shop methods on boys like that, I'll do the same."

He swore at her quite calmly; she smiled, shrugged, and, imprisoning her knees in her clasped hands, leaned back and looked at him.

"What a ninny I have been," she said, "to be afraid of you so long!"

A gleam crossed his faded eyes, but he let her remark pass for the moment. Then, when he was quite sure that violent emotion had been exhausted within him:

127

"Do you want your bills paid?" he asked. "Because, if you do, Fane, Harmon & Co. are not going to pay them."

"We are living beyond our means?" she inquired disdainfully.

"Not if you will be good enough to mind your business, my friend. I've managed this establishment on our winnings for two years. It's a detail; but you might as well know it. My association with Fane, Harmon & Co. runs the Newport end of it, and nothing more."

"What did you marry me for?" she asked curiously.

A slight colour came into his face: "Because that damned Rosamund Fane lied about you."

"Oh! . . . You knew that in Manila? You'd heard about it, hadn't you— the Western timber-lands? Rosamund didn't mean to lie—only the titles were all wrong, you know. . . . And so you made a bad break, Jack; is that it?"

"Yes, that is it."

"And it cost you a fortune, and me a—husband. Is that it, my friend?"

"I can afford you if you will stop your meddling," he said coolly.

"I see; I am to stop my meddling and you are to continue your downtown gambling in your own house in the evenings."

"Precisely. It happens that I am sufficiently familiar with the stock-market to make a decent living out of the Exchange; and it also happens that I am sufficiently fortunate with cards to make the pleasure of playing fairly remunerative. Any man who can put up proper margin has a right to my services; any man whom I invite and who can take up his notes, has a right to play under my roof. If his note goes to protest, he forfeits that right. Now will you kindly explain to yourself exactly how this matter can be of any interest to you?"

"I have explained it," she said wearily. "Will you please go, now?"

He sat a moment, then rose:

"You make a point of excluding Gerald?"

"Yes."

"Very well; I'll telephone Draymore. And"—he looked back from the door of his own apartments—"I got Julius Neergard on the wire this afternoon and he'll dine with us."

He gathered up his shimmering kimona, hesitated, halted, and again looked back.

"When you're dressed," he drawled, "I've a word to say to you about the game to-night, and another about Gerald."

"I shall not play," she retorted scornfully, "nor will Gerald."

"Oh, yes, you will—and play your best, too. And I'll expect him next time."

"I shall not play!"

He said deliberately: "You will not only play, but play cleverly; and in the interim, while dressing, you will reflect how much more agreeable it is to play cards here than the fool at ten o'clock at night in the bachelor apartments of your late lamented."

And he entered his room; and his wife, getting blindly to her feet, every atom of colour gone from lip and cheek, stood rigid, both small hands clutching the foot-board of the gilded bed.

CHAPTER VI

THE UNEXPECTED

Differences of opinion between himself and Neergard concerning the ethics of good taste involved in forcing the Siowitha Club matter, Gerald's decreasing attention to business and increasing intimacy with the Fane-Ruthven coterie, began to make Selwyn very uncomfortable. The boy's close relations with Neergard worried him most of all; and though Neergard finally agreed to drop the Siowitha matter as a fixed policy in which Selwyn had been expected to participate at some indefinite date, the arrangement seemed only to cement the man's confidential companionship with Gerald.

This added to Selwyn's restlessness; and one day in early spring he had a long conference with Gerald—a most unsatisfactory one. Gerald, for the first time, remained reticent; and when Selwyn, presuming on the cordial understanding between them, pressed him a little, the boy turned sullen; and Selwyn let the matter drop very quickly.

But neither tact nor caution seemed to serve now; Gerald, more and more engrossed in occult social affairs of which he made no mention to Selwyn, was still amiable and friendly, even at times cordial and lovable; but he was no longer frank or even communicative; and Selwyn, fearing to arouse him again to sullenness or perhaps even to suspicious defiance, forbore to press him beyond the most tentative advances toward the regaining of his confidence.

This, very naturally, grieved and mortified the elder man; but what troubled him still more was that Gerald and Neergard were becoming so amazingly companionable; for it was easy to see that they had in common a number of personal interests which he did not share, and that their silence concerning these interests amounted to a secrecy almost offensive.

Again and again, coming unexpectedly upon them, he noticed that their confab ceased with his appearance. Often, too, glances of warning intelligence passed between them in his presence, which, no doubt, they supposed were unnoticed by him.

They left the office together frequently, now; they often lunched uptown. Whether they were in each other's company evenings, Selwyn did not know, for Gerald no longer volunteered information as to his whereabouts or doings. And all this hurt Selwyn, and alarmed him, too, for he was slowly coming to the conclusion that he did not like Neergard, that he would never sign articles of partnership with him, and that even his formal associateship with the company was too close a relation for his own peace of mind. But on Gerald's account he stayed on; he did not like to leave the boy alone for his sister's sake as well as for his own.

Matters drifted that way through early spring. He actually grew to dislike both Neergard and the business of Neergard & Co.—for no one particular reason, perhaps, but in general; though he did not yet care to ask himself to be more precise in his unuttered criticisms.

However, detail and routine, the simpler alphabet of the business, continued to occupy him. He consulted both Neergard and Gerald as usual; they often consulted him or pretended to do so. Land was bought and sold and resold, new projects discussed, new properties appraised, new mortgage loans negotiated; and solely because of his desire to remain near Gerald, this sort of thing might have continued indefinitely. But Neergard broke his word to him.

And one morning, before he left his rooms at Mrs. Greeve's lodgings to go downtown, Percy Draymore called him up on the telephone; and as that overfed young man's usual rising hour was notoriously nearer noon than eight o'clock, it surprised Selwyn to be asked to remain in his rooms for a little while until Draymore and one or two friends could call on him personally concerning a matter of importance.

He therefore breakfasted leisurely; and he was still scanning the real estate columns of a morning paper when Mrs. Greeve came panting to his door and ushered in a file of rather sleepy but important looking gentlemen, evidently unaccustomed to being abroad so early, and bored to death with their experience.

They were men he knew only formally, or, at best, merely as fellow club members; men whom he met when a dance or dinner took him out of the less pretentious sets he personally affected; men whom the newspapers and the public knew too well to speak of as "well known."

First there was Percy Draymore, overgroomed for a gentleman, fat, good-humoured, and fashionable—one of the famous Draymore family noted solely for their money and their tight grip on it; then came Sanxon Orchil, the famous banker and promoter, small, urbane, dark, with that rich almost oriental coloring which he may have inherited from his Cordova ancestors who found it necessary to dehumanise their names when Rome offered them the choice with immediate eternity as alternative.

Then came a fox-faced young man, Phoenix Mottly, elegant arbiter of all pertaining to polo and the hunt—slim-legged, hatchet-faced—and more presentable in the saddle than out of it. He was followed by Bradley Harmon, with his washed-out colouring of a consumptive Swede and his corn-coloured beard; and, looming in the rear like an amiable brontasaurus, George Fane, whose swaying neck carried his head as a camel carries his, nodding as he walks.

"Well!" said Selwyn, perplexed but cordial as he exchanged amenities with each gentleman who entered, "this is a killing combination of pleasure and mortification—because I haven't any more breakfast to offer you unless you'll wait until I ring for the Sultana—"

"Breakfast! Oh, damn! I've breakfasted on a pill and a glass of vichy for ten years," protested Draymore, "and the others either have swallowed their cocktails, or won't do it until luncheon. I say, Selwyn, you must think this a devilishly unusual proceeding."

"Pleasantly unusual, Draymore. Is this a delegation to tend me the nomination for the down-and-out club, perhaps?"

Fane spoke up languidly: "It rather looks as though we were the down-and-out delegation at present; doesn't it, Orchil?"

"I don't know," said Orchil; "it seems a trifle more promising to me since I've had the pleasure of seeing Captain Selwyn face to face. Go on, Percy; let the horrid facts be known."

"Well—er—oh, hang it all!" blurted out Draymore, "we heard last night how that fellow—how Neergard has been tampering with our farmers—what underhand tricks he has been playing us; and I frankly admit to you that we're a worried lot of near-sports. That's what this dismal matinee signifies; and we've come to ask you what it all really means."

"We lost no time, you see," added Orchil, caressing the long pomaded ends of his kinky moustache and trying to catch a glimpse of them out of his languid oriental eyes. He had been trying to catch this glimpse for thirty years; he was a persistent man with plenty of leisure.

"We lost no time," repeated Draymore, "because it's a devilish unsavoury situation for us. The Siowitha Club fully realises it, Captain Selwyn, and its members—some of 'em—thought that perhaps—er—you—ah—being the sort of man who can—ah—understand the sort of language we understand, it might not be amiss to—to—"

"Why did you not call on Mr. Neergard?" asked Selwyn coolly. Yet he was taken completely by surprise, for he did not know that Neergard had gone ahead and secured options on his own responsibility—which practically amounted to a violation of the truce between them.

Draymore hesitated, then with the brutality characteristic of the overfed: "I don't give a damn, Captain Selwyn, what Neergard thinks; but I do want to know what a gentleman like yourself, accidentally associated with that man, thinks of this questionable proceeding."

"Do you mean by 'questionable proceeding' your coming here?—or do you refer to the firm's position in this matter?" asked Selwyn sharply. "Because, Draymore, I am not very widely experienced in the customs and usages of commercial life, and I do not know whether it is usual for an associate member of a firm to express, unauthorised, his views on matters concerning the firm to any Tom, Dick, and Harry who questions him."

"But you know what is the policy of your own firm," suggested Harmon, wincing, and displaying his teeth under his bright red lips; "and all we wish to know is, what Neergard expects us to pay for this rascally lesson in the a-b-c of Long Island realty."

"I don't know," replied Selwyn, bitterly annoyed, "what Mr. Neergard proposes to do. And if I did I should refer you to him."

"May I ask," began Orchil, "whether the land will be ultimately for sale?"

"Oh, everything's always for sale," broke in Mottly impatiently; "what's the use of asking that? What you meant to inquire was the price we're expected to pay for this masterly squeeze in realty."

"And to that," replied Selwyn more sharply still, "I must answer again that I don't know. I know nothing about it; I did not know that Mr. Neergard had acquired control of the property; I don't know what he means to do with it. And, gentlemen, may I ask why you feel at liberty to come to me instead of to Mr. Neergard?"

"A desire to deal with one of our own kind, I suppose," returned Draymore bluntly. "And, for that matter," he said, turning to the others, "we might have known that Captain Selwyn could have had no hand in and no knowledge of such an underbred and dirty—"

Harmon plucked him by the sleeve, but Draymore shook him off, his little piggish eyes sparkling.

"What do I care!" he sneered, losing his temper; "we're in the clutches of a vulgar, skinflint Dutchman, and he'll wring us dry whether or not we curse *him* out. Didn't I tell you that Philip Selwyn had nothing to do with it? If he had, and I was wrong, our journey here might as well have been made to Neergard's office. For any man who will do such a filthy thing—"

132

"One moment, Draymore," cut in Selwyn; and his voice rang unpleasantly; "if you are simply complaining because you have been outwitted, go ahead; but if you think there has been any really dirty business in this matter, go to Mr. Neergard. Otherwise, being his associate, I shall not only decline to listen but also ask you to leave my apartments."

"Captain Selwyn is perfectly right," observed Orchil coolly. "Do you think, Draymore, that it is very good taste in you to come into a man's place and begin slanging and cursing a member of his firm for crooked work?"

"Besides," added Mottly, "it's not crooked; it's only contemptible. Anyway, we know with whom we have to deal, now; but some of you fellows must do the dealing—I'd rather pay and keep away than ask Neergard to go easy—and have him do it."

"I don't know," said Fane, grinning his saurian grin, "why you all assume that Neergard is such a social outcast. I played cards with him last week and he lost like a gentleman."

"I didn't say he was a social outcast," retorted Mottly—"because he's never been inside of anything to be cast out, you know."

"He seems to be inside this deal," ventured Orchil with his suave smile. And to Selwyn, who had been restlessly facing first one, then another: "We came—it was the idea of several among us—to put the matter up to you. Which was rather foolish, because you couldn't have engineered the thing and remained what we know you to be. So—"

"Wait!" said Selwyn brusquely; "I do not admit for one moment that there is anything dishonourable in this deal!—nor do I accept your right to question it from that standpoint. As far as I can see, it is one of those operations which is considered clever among business folk, and which is admired and laughed over in reputable business circles. And I have no doubt that hundreds of well-meaning business men do that sort of thing daily—yes, thousands!" He shrugged his broad shoulders. "Because I personally have not chosen to engage in matters of this— ah—description, is no reason for condemning the deal or its method—"

"Every reason!" said Orchil, laughing cordially—"*every* reason, Captain Selwyn. Thank you; we know now exactly where we stand. It was very good of you to let us come, and I'm sorry some of us had the bad taste to show any temper—"

"He means me," added Draymore, offering his hand; "good-bye, Captain Selwyn; I dare say we are up against it hard."

"Because we've got to buy in that property or close up the Siowitha," added Mottly, coming over to make his adieux. "By the way, Selwyn, you ought to be one of us in the Siowitha—"

"Thank you, but isn't this rather an awkward time to suggest it?" said Selwyn good-humouredly.

Fane burst into a sonorous laugh and wagged his neck, saying: "Not at all! Not at all! Your reward for having the decency to stay out of the deal is an invitation from us to come in and be squeezed into a jelly by Mr. Neergard. Haw! Haw!"

And so, one by one, with formal or informal but evidently friendly leave-taking, they went away. And Selwyn followed them presently, walking until he took the Subway at Forty-second Street for his office.

As he entered the elaborate suite of rooms he noticed some bright new placards dangling from the walls of the general office, and halted to read them:

"WHY PAY RENT!

What would you say if we built a house for you in Beautiful Siowitha Park and gave you ten years to pay for it!

If   anybody   says

YOU ARE A FOOL!

to expect this, refer him to us and we will answer him according to his folly.

TO PAY RENT

when you might own a home in Beautiful Siowitha Park, is not wise. We expect to furnish plans, or build after your own plans.

All	City			Improvements
Are				Contemplated!
Map	and		Plans	of
Beautiful		Siowitha		Park
Will	probably		be	ready
In	the		Near	Future.

Julius   Neergard   &   Co.
Long Island Real Estate."

Selwyn reddened with anger and beckoned to a clerk:

"Is Mr. Neergard in his office?"

"Yes, sir, with Mr. Erroll."

"Please say that I wish to see him."

He went into his own office, pocketed his mail, and still wearing hat and gloves came out again just as Gerald was leaving Neergard's office.

"Hello, Gerald!" he said pleasantly; "have you anything on for to-night?"

134

"Y-es," said the hoy, embarrassed—"but if there is anything I can do for you—"

"Not unless you are free for the evening," returned the other; "are you?"

"I'm awfully sorry—"

"Oh, all right. Let me know when you expect to be free—telephone me at my rooms—"

"I'll let you know when I see you here to-morrow," said the boy; but Selwyn shook his head: "I'm not coming here to-morrow, Gerald"; and he walked leisurely into Neergard's office and seated himself.

"So you have committed the firm to the Siowitha deal?" he inquired coolly.

Neergard looked up—and then past him: "No, not the firm. You did not seem to be interested in the scheme, so I went on without you. I'm swinging it for my personal account."

"Is Mr. Erroll in it?"

"I said that it was a private matter," replied Neergard, but his manner was affable.

"I thought so; it appears to me like a matter quite personal to you and characteristic of you, Mr. Neergard. And that being established, I am now ready to dissolve whatever very loose ties have ever bound me in any association with this company and yourself."

Neergard's close-set black eyes shifted a point nearer to Selwyn's; the sweat on his nose glistened.

"Why do you do this?" he asked slowly. "Has anybody offended you?"

"Do you *really* wish to know?"

"Yes, I certainly do, Captain Selwyn."

"Very well; it's because I don't like your business methods, I don't like— several other things that are happening in this office. It's purely a difference of views; and that is enough explanation, Mr. Neergard."

"I think our views may very easily coincide—"

"You are wrong; they could not. I ought to have known that when I came back here. And now I have only to thank you for receiving me, at my own request, for a six months' trial, and to admit that I am not qualified to co-operate with this kind of a firm."

"That," said Neergard angrily, "amounts to an indictment of the firm. If you express yourself in that manner outside, the firm will certainly resent it!"

"My personal taste will continue to govern my expressions, Mr. Neergard; and I believe will prevent any further business relations between us. And, as we never had any other kind of relations, I have merely to arrange the details through an attorney."

Neergard looked after him in silence; the tiny beads of sweat on his nose united and rolled down in a big shining drop, and the sneer etched on his broad and brightly mottled features deepened to a snarl when Selwyn had disappeared.

For the social prestige which Selwyn's name had brought the firm, he had patiently endured his personal dislike and contempt for the man after he found he could do nothing with him in any way.

He had accepted Selwyn purely in the hope of social advantage, and with the knowledge that Selwyn could have done much for him after business hours; if not from friendship, at least from interest, or a lively sense of benefits to come. For that reason he had invited him to participate in the valuable Siowitha deal, supposing a man as comparatively poor as Selwyn would not only jump at the opportunity, but also prove sufficiently grateful later. And he had been amazed and disgusted at Selwyn's attitude. But he had not supposed the man would sever his connection with the firm if he, Neergard, went ahead on his own responsibility. It astonished and irritated him; it meant, instead of selfish or snobbish indifference to his own social ambitions, an enemy to block his entrance into what he desired—the society of those made notorious in the columns of the daily press.

For Neergard cared only for the notorious in the social scheme; nothing else appealed to him. He had, all his life, read with avidity of the extravagances, the ostentation, the luxurious effrontery, the thinly veiled viciousness of what he believed to be society, and he craved it from the first, working his thick hands to the bone in dogged determination to one day participate in and satiate himself with the easy morality of what he read about in his penny morning paper—in the days when even a penny was to be carefully considered.

That was what he wanted from society—the best to be had in vice. That was why he had denied himself in better days. It was for that he hoarded every cent while actual want sharpened his wits and his thin nose; it was in that hope that he received Selwyn so cordially as a possible means of entrance into regions he could not attain unaided; it was for that reason he was now binding Gerald to him through remission of penalties for slackness, through loans and advances, through a companionship which had already landed him in the Ruthven's card-room, and promised even more from Mr. Fane, who had won his money very easily.

For Neergard did not care how he got in, front door or back door, through kitchen or card-room, as long as he got in somehow. All he desired was the chance to use opportunity in his own fashion, and wring from the forbidden circle all and more than they had unconsciously wrung from him in the squalid days of a poverty for which no equality he might now enjoy, no liberty of license, no fraternity in dissipation, could wholly compensate.

He was fairly on the outer boundary now, though still very far outside. But a needy gentleman inside was already compromised and practically pledged to support him; for his meeting with Jack Ruthven through Gerald had proven of greatest importance. He had lost gracefully to Ruthven; and in doing it had taken that gentleman's measure. And though Ruthven himself was a member of the Siowitha, Neergard had made no error in taking him secretly into the deal where together they were now in a position to exploit the club, from which Ruthven, of course, would resign in time to escape any assessment himself.

Neergard's progress had now reached this stage; his programme was simple—to wallow among the wealthy until satiated, then to marry into that agreeable community and found the house of Neergard. And to that end he had already bought a building site on Fifth Avenue, but held it in the name of the firm as though it had been acquired for purposes purely speculative.

About that time Boots Lansing very quietly bought a house on Manhattan Island. It was a small, narrow, three-storied house of brick, rather shabby on the outside, and situated on a modest block between Lexington and Park avenues, where the newly married of the younger set were arriving in increasing numbers, prepared to pay the penalty for all love matches.

It was an unexpected move to Selwyn; he had not been aware of Lansing's contemplated desertion; and that morning, returning from his final interview with Neergard, he was astonished to find his comrade's room bare of furniture, and a hasty and exclamatory note on his own table:

"Phil! I've bought a house! Come and see it! You'll find me in it! Carpetless floors and unpapered walls! It's the happiest day of my life!

"Boots!!!! House-owner!!!"

And Selwyn, horribly depressed, went down after a solitary luncheon and found Lansing sitting on a pile of dusty rugs, ecstatically inspecting the cracked ceiling.

"So this is the House that Boots built!" he said.

"Phil! It's a dream!"

"Yes—a bad one. What the devil do you mean by clearing out? What do you want with a house, anyhow?—you infernal idiot!"

"A house? Man, I've always wanted one! I've dreamed of a dinky little house like this—dreamed and ached for it there in Manila—on blistering hikes, on wibbly-wabbly gunboats—knee-deep in sprouting rice—I've dreamed of a house in New York like this! slopping through the steaming paddy-fields, sweating up the heights, floundering through smelly hemp, squatting by green fires at night! always, always I've longed for a home of my own. Now I've got it, and I'm the happiest man on Manhattan Island!"

"O Lord!" said Selwyn, staring, "if you feel that way! You never said anything about it—"

"Neither did you, Phil; but I bet you want one, too. Come now; don't you?"

"Yes, I do," nodded Selwyn; "but I can't afford one yet"—his face darkened—"not for a while; but," and his features cleared, "I'm delighted, old fellow, that *you* have one. This certainly is a jolly little kennel—you can fix it up in splendid shape—rugs and mahogany and what-nots and ding-dongs—and a couple of tabby cats and a good dog—"

"Isn't it fascinating!" cried Boots. "Phil, all this real estate is mine! And the idea makes me silly-headed. I've been sitting on this pile of rugs pretending that I'm in the midst of vast and expensive improvements and alterations; and estimating the cost of them has frightened me half to death. I tell you I never had such fun, Phil. Come on; we'll start at the cellar—there is some coal and wood and some wonderful cobwebs down there—and then we'll take in the back yard; I mean to have no end of a garden out there, and real clothes-dryers and some wistaria and sparrows—just like real back yards. I want to hear cats make harrowing music on my own back fence; I want to see a tidy laundress pinning up intimate and indescribable garments on my own clothes-lines; I want to have maddening trouble with plumbers and roofers; I want to—"

"Come on, then, for Heaven's sake!" said Selwyn, laughing; and the two men, arm in arm, began a minute tour of the house.

"Isn't it a corker! Isn't it fine!" repeated Lansing every few minutes. "I wouldn't exchange it for any mansion on Fifth Avenue!"

"You'd be a fool to," agreed Selwyn gravely.

"Certainly I would. Anyway, prices are going up like rockets in this section—not that I'd think of selling out at any price—but it's comfortable to know it. Why, a real-estate man told me—Hello! What was that? Something fell somewhere!"

"A section of the bath-room ceiling, I think," said Selwyn; "we mustn't step too heavily on the floors at first, you know."

138

"Oh, I'm going to have the entire thing done over—room by room—when I can afford it. Meanwhile *j'y suis, j'y reste.* . . . Look there, Phil! That's to be your room."

"Thanks, old fellow—not now."

"Why, yes! I expected you'd have your room here, Phil—"

"It's very good of you, Boots, but I can't do it."

Lansing faced him: "*Won't* you?"

Selwyn, smiling, shook his head; and the other knew it was final.

"Well, the room will be there—furnished the way you and I like it. When you want it, make smoke signals or wig-wag."

"I will; thank you, Boots."

Lansing said unaffectedly, "How soon do you think you can afford a house like this?"

"I don't know; you see, I've only my income now—"

"Plus what you make at the office—"

"I've left Neergard."

"What!"

"This morning; for good."

"The deuce!" he murmured, looking at Selwyn; but the latter volunteered no further information, and Lansing, having given him the chance, cheerfully switched to the other track:

"Shall I see whether the Air Line has anything in *your* line, Phil? No? Well, what are you going to do?"

"I don't exactly know what I shall do. . . . If I had capital—enough—I think I'd start in making bulk and dense powders—all sorts; gun-cotton, nitro-powders—"

"You mean you'd like to go on with your own invention—Chaosite?"

"I'd like to keep on experimenting with it if I could afford to. Perhaps I will. But it's not yet a commercial possibility—if it ever is to be. I wish I could control it; the ignition is simultaneous and absolutely complete, and there is not a trace of ash, not an unburned or partly burned particle. But it's not to be trusted, and I don't know what happens to it after a year's storage."

For a while they discussed the commercial possibilities of Chaosite, and how capital might be raised for a stock company; but Selwyn was not sanguine, and something of his mental depression returned as he sat there by the curtainless window, his head on his closed hand, looking out into the sunny street.

"Anyway," said Lansing, "you've nothing to worry over."

"No, nothing," assented Selwyn listlessly.

After a silence Lansing added: "But you do a lot of worrying all the same, Phil."

Selwyn flushed up and denied it.

"Yes, you do! I don't believe you realise how much of the time you are out of spirits."

"Does it impress you that way?" asked Selwyn, mortified; "because I'm really all right."

"Of course you are, Phil; I know it, but you don't seem to realise it. You're morbid, I'm afraid."

"You've been talking to my sister!"

"What of it? Besides, I knew there was something the matter—"

"You know what it is, too. And isn't it enough to subdue a man's spirits occasionally?"

"No," said Lansing—"if you mean your—mistake—two years ago. That isn't enough to spoil life for a man. I've wanted to tell you so for a long time."

And, as Selwyn said nothing: "For Heaven's sake make up your mind to enjoy your life! You are fitted to enjoy it. Get that absurd notion out of your head that you're done for—that you've no home life in prospect, no family life, no children—"

Selwyn turned sharply, but the other went on: "You can swear at me if you like, but you've no business to go through the world cuddling your own troubles closer and closer and squinting at everybody out of disenchanted eyes. It's selfish, for one thing; you're thinking altogether too much about yourself."

Selwyn, too annoyed to answer, glared at his friend.

"Oh, I know you don't like it, Phil, but what I'm saying may do you good. It's fine physic, to learn what others think about you; as for me, you can't mistake my friendship—or your sister's—or Miss Erroll's, or Mr. Gerard's. And one and all are of one opinion, that you have everything before you, including domestic happiness, which you care for more than anything. And there is no reason why you should not have it—no reason why you should not feel perfectly free to marry, and have a bunch of corking kids. It's not only your right, it's your business; and you're selfish if you don't!"

140

"Boots! I—I—"

"Go on!"

"I'm not going to swear; I'm only hurt, Boots—"

"Sure you are! Medicine's working, that's all. We strive to please, we kill to cure. Of course it hurts, man! But you know it will do you good; you know what I say is true. You've no right to club the natural and healthy inclinations out of yourself. The day for fanatics and dippy, dotty flagellants is past. Fox's martyrs are out of date. The man who grabs life in both fists and twists the essence out of it, counts. He is living as he ought to, he is doing the square thing by his country and his community—by every man, woman, and child in it! He's giving everybody, including himself, a square deal. But the man who has been upper-cut and floored, and who takes the count, and then goes and squats in a corner to brood over the fancy licks that Fate handed him— *he* isn't dealing fairly and squarely by his principles or by a decent and generous world that stands to back him for the next round. Is he, Phil?"

"Do you mean to say, Boots, that you think a man who has made the ghastly mess of his life that I have, ought to feel free to marry?"

"Think it! Man, I know it. Certainly you ought to marry if you wish—but, above all, you ought to feel free to marry. That is the essential equipment of a man; he isn't a man if he feels that he isn't free to marry. He may not want to do it, he may not be in love. That's neither here nor there; the main thing is that he is as free as a man should be to take any good opportunity—and marriage is included in the list of good opportunities. If you become a slave to morbid notions, no wonder you are depressed. Slaves usually are. Do you want to slink through life? Then shake yourself, I tell you; learn to understand that you're free to do what any decent man may do. That will take the morbidness out of you. That will colour life for you. I don't say go hunting for some one to love; I do say, don't avoid her when you meet her."

"You preach a very gay sermon, Boots," he said, folding his arms. "I've heard something similar from my sister. As a matter of fact I think you are partly right, too; but if the inclination for the freedom you insist I take is wanting, then what? I don't wish to marry, Boots; I am not in love, therefore the prospect of home and kids is premature and vague, isn't it?"

"As long as it's a prospect or a possibility I don't care how vague it is," said the other cordially. "Will you admit it's a possibility? That's all I ask."

"If it will please you, yes, I will admit it. I have altered certain ideas, Boots; I cannot, just now, conceive of any circumstances under which I should feel justified in marrying, but such circumstances might arise; I'll say that much."

Yet until that moment he had not dreamed of admitting as much to anybody, even to himself; but Lansing's logic, his own loneliness, his disappointment in Gerald, had combined to make him doubt his own methods of procedure. Too, the interview with Alixe Ruthven had not only knocked all complacency and conceit out of him, but had made him so self-distrustful that he was in a mood to listen respectfully to his peers on any question.

He was wondering now whether Boots had recognised Alixe when he had blundered into the room that night. He had never asked the question; he was very much inclined to, now. However, Boots's reply could be only the negative answer that any decent man must give.

Sitting there in the carpetless room piled high with dusty, linen-shrouded furniture, he looked around, an involuntary smile twitching his mouth. Somehow he had not felt so light-hearted for a long, long while—and whether it came from his comrade's sermon, or his own unexpected acknowledgment of its truth, or whether it was pure amusement at Boots in the rôle of householder and taxpayer, he could not decide. But he was curiously happy of a sudden; and he smiled broadly upon Mr. Lansing:

"What about *your* marrying," he said—"after all this talk about mine! What about it, Boots? Is this new house the first modest step toward the matrimony you laud so loudly?"

"Sure," said that gentleman airily; "that's what I'm here for."

"Really?"

"Well, of course, idiot. I've always been in love."

"You mean you actually have somebody in view—?"

"No, son. I've always been in love with—love. I'm a sentimental sentry on the ramparts of reason. I'm properly armed for trouble, now, so if I'm challenged I won't let my chance slip by me. Do you see? There are two kinds of sentimental warriors in this amorous world: the man and the nincompoop. The one brings in his prisoner, the other merely howls for her. So I'm all ready for the only girl in the world; and if she ever gets away from me I'll give you my house, cellar, and back yard, including the wistaria and both cats—"

"You have neither wistaria nor cats—yet."

"Neither am I specifically in love—yet. So that's all right—Philip. Come on; let's take another look at that fascinating cellar of mine!"

But Selwyn laughingly declined, and after a little while he went away, first to look up a book which he was having bound for Eileen, then to call on his sister who, with Eileen, had just returned from a week at Silverside with the children, preliminary to moving the entire establishment there for the coming summer; for the horses and dogs had already gone; also Kit-Ki, a pessimistic parrot, and the children's two Norwegian ponies.

"Silverside is too lovely for words!" exclaimed Nina as Selwyn entered the library. "The children almost went mad. You should have seen the dogs, too—tearing round and round the lawn in circles—poor things! They were crazy for the fresh, new turf. And Kit-Ki! she lay in the sun and rolled and rolled until her fur was perfectly filthy. Nobody wanted to come away; Eileen made straight for the surf; but it was an arctic sea, and as soon as I found out what she was doing I made her come out."

"I should think you would," he said; "nobody can do that and thrive."

"She seems to," said Nina; "she was simply glorious after the swim, and I hated to put a stop to it. And you should see her drying her hair and helping Plunket to roll the tennis-courts—that hair of hers blowing like gold flames, and her sleeves rolled to her arm-pits!—and you should see her down in the dirt playing marbles with Billy and Drina—shooting away excitedly and exclaiming 'fen-dubs!' and 'knuckle-down, Billy!'—like any gamin you ever heard of. Totally unspoiled, Phil!—in spite of all the success of her first winter!—and do you know that she had no end of men seriously entangled? I don't mind your knowing—but Sudbury Gray came to me, and I told him he'd better wait, but in he blundered and—he's done for, now; and so are my plans. He's an imbecile! And then, who on earth do you think came waddling into the arena? Percy Draymore! Phil, it was an anxious problem for me—and although I didn't really want Eileen to marry into that set—still—with the Draymores' position and tremendous influence—But she merely stared at him in cold astonishment. And there were others, too, callow for the most part. . . . Phil?"

"What?" he said, laughing.

His sister regarded him smilingly, then partly turned around and perched herself on the padded arm of a great chair.

"Phil, *am* I garrulous?"

"No, dear; you are far too reticent."

"Pooh! Suppose I do talk a great deal. I like to. Besides, I always have something interesting to say, don't I?"

"Always!"

"Well, then, why do you look at me so humorously out of those nice gray eyes? . . . Phil, you are growing handsome! Do you know it?"

"For Heaven's sake!" he protested, red and uncomfortable, "what utter nonsense you—"

"Of course it bores you to be told so; and you look so delightfully ashamed—like a reproved setter-puppy! Well, then, don't laugh at my loquacity again!—because I'm going to say something else. . . . Come

143

over here, Phil; no—close to me. I wish to put my hands on your shoulders; like that. Now look at me! Do you really love me?"

"Sure thing, Ninette."

"And you know I adore you; don't you?"

"Madly, dear, but I forgive you."

"No; I want you to be serious. Because I'm pretty serious. See, I'm not smiling now; I don't feel like it. Because it is a very, very important matter, Phil—this thing that has—has—almost happened. . . . It's about Eileen. . . . And it really has happened."

"What has she done?" he asked curiously.

His sister's eyes were searching his very diligently, as though in quest of something elusive; and he gazed serenely back, the most unsuspicious of smiles touching his mouth.

"Phil, dear, a young girl—a very young girl—is a vapid and uninteresting proposition to a man of thirty-five; isn't she?"

"Rather—in some ways."

"In what way is she not?"

"Well—to me, for example—she is acceptable as children are acceptable—a blessed, sweet, clean relief from the women of the Fanes' set, for example?"

"Like Rosamund?"

"Yes. And, Ninette, you and Austin seem to be drifting out of the old circles—the sort that you and I were accustomed to. You don't mind my saying it, do you?—but there were so many people in this town who had something besides millions—amusing, well-bred, jolly people who had no end of good times, but who didn't gamble and guzzle and stuff themselves and their friends—who were not eternally hanging around other people's wives. Where are they, dear?"

"If you are indicting all of my friends, Phil—"

"I don't mean all of your friends—only a small proportion—which, however, connects your circle with that deadly, idle, brainless bunch—the insolent chatterers at the opera, the gorged dowagers, the worn-out, passionless men, the enervated matrons of the summer capital, the chlorotic squatters on huge yachts, the speed-mad fugitives from the furies of ennui, the neurotic victims of mental cirrhosis, the jewelled animals whose moral code is the code of the barnyard—!"

"Philip!"

"Oh, I don't mean that they are any more vicious than the idle and mentally incompetent in any walk of life. East Side, West Side, Harlem,

Hell's Kitchen, Fifth Avenue, Avenue A, and Abingdon Square—the denizens are only locally different, not specifically—the species remains unchanged. But everywhere, in every quarter and class and set and circle there is always the depraved; and the logical links that connect them are unbroken from Fifth Avenue to Chinatown, from the half-crazed extravagances of the Orchils' Louis XIV ball to a New Year's reception at the Haymarket where Troy Lil's diamonds outshine the phony pearls of Hoboken Fanny, and Hatpin Molly leads the spiel with Clarence the Pig."

"Phil, you are too disgusting!"

"I'm sorry—it isn't very nice of me, I suppose. But, dear, I'm dead tired of moral squalor. I do like the brightness of things, too, but I don't care for the phosphorescence of social decay."

"What in the world is the matter?" she exclaimed in dismay. "You are talking like the wildest socialist."

He laughed. "We have become a nation of what you call 'socialists'—though there are other names for us which mean more. I am not discontented, if that is what you mean; I am only impatient; and there is a difference. . . . And you have just asked me whether a young girl is interesting to me. I answer, yes, thank God!—for the cleaner, saner, happier hours I have spent this winter among my own kind have been spent where the younger set dominated.

"They are good for us, Nina; they are the hope of our own kind—well-taught, well-drilled, wholesome even when negative in mind; and they come into our world so diffident yet so charmingly eager, so finished yet so unspoiled, that—how can they fail to touch a man and key him to his best? How can they fail to arouse in us the best of sympathy, of chivalry, of anxious solicitude lest they become some day as we are and stare at life out of the faded eyes of knowledge!"

He laid his hands in hers, smiling a little at his own earnestness.

"Alarmist? No! The younger set are better than those who bred them; and if, in time, they, too, fall short, they will not fall as far as their parents. And, in their turn, when they look around them at the younger set whom they have taught in the light and wisdom of their own shortcomings, they will see fresher, sweeter, lovelier young people than we see now. And it will continue so, dear, through the jolly generations. Life is all right, only, like art, it is very, very long sometimes."

"Good out of evil, Phil?" asked his sister, smiling; "innocence from the hotbeds of profligacy? purity out of vulgarity? sanity from hideous ostentation? Is that what you come preaching?"

"Yes; and isn't it curious! Look at that old harridan, Mrs. Sanxon Orchil! There are no more innocent and charming girls in Manhattan than her daughters. She *knew* enough to make them different; so does the

145

majority of that sort. Look at the Cardwell girl and the Innis girl and the Craig girl! Look at Mrs. Delmour-Carnes's children! And, Nina—even Molly Hatpin's wastrel waif shall never learn what her mother knows if Destiny will help Madame Molly ever so little. And I think that Destiny is often very kind—even to the Hatpin offspring."

Nina sat silent on the padded arm of her chair, looking up at her brother.

"Mad preacher! Mad Mullah!—dear, dear fellow!" she said tenderly; "all ills of the world canst thou discount, but not thine own."

"Those, too," he insisted, laughing; "I had a talk with Boots—but, anyway, I'd already arrived at my own conclusion that—that—I'm rather overdoing this blighted business—"

"Phil!"—in quick delight.

"Yes," he said, reddening nicely; "between you and Boots and myself I've decided that I'm going in for—for whatever any man is going in for—life! Ninette, life to the full and up to the hilt for mine!—not side-stepping anything. . . . Because I—because, Nina, it's shameful for a man to admit to himself that he cannot make good, no matter how thoroughly he's been hammered to the ropes. And so I'm starting out again—not hunting trouble like him of La Mancha—but, like him in this, that I shall not avoid it. . . . Is that plain to you, little sister?"

"Yes, oh, yes, it is!" she murmured; "I am so happy, so proud—but I knew it was in your blood, Phil; I knew that you were merely hurt and stunned—badly hurt, but not fatally!—you could not be; no weaklings come from our race."

"But still our race has always been law-abiding—observant of civil and religious law. If I make myself free again, I take some laws into my own hands.".

"How do you mean?" she asked.

"Well," he said grimly, "for example, I am forbidden, in some States, to marry again—"

"But you know there was no reason for that!"

"Yes, I do happen to know; but still I am taking the liberty of disregarding the law if I do. Then, what clergyman, of our faith, would marry me to anybody?"

"That, too, you know is not just, Phil. You were innocent of wrong-doing; you were chivalrous enough to make no defence—"

"Wrong-doing? Nina, I was such a fool that I was innocent of sense enough to do either good or evil. Yet I did do harm; there never was such a thing as a harmless fool. But all I can do is to go and sin no more; yet there is little merit in good conduct if one hides in a hole too small to admit temptation. No; there are laws civil and laws ecclesiastical; and sometimes I think a man is justified in repealing the form and retaining the substance of them, and remoulding it for purposes of self-government; as I do, now. . . . Once, oppressed by form and theory, I told you that to remarry after divorce was a slap at civilisation. . . . Which is true sometimes and sometimes not. Common sense, not laws, must govern a man in that matter. But if any motive except desire to be a decent citizen sways a self-punished man toward self-leniency, then is he unpardonable if he breaks those laws which truly were fashioned for such as he!"

"Saint Simon! Saint Simon! Will you please arise, stretch your limbs, and descend from your pillar?" said Nina; "because I am going to say something that is very, very serious; and very near my heart."

"I remember," he said; "it's about Eileen, isn't it?"

"Yes, it is about Eileen."

He waited; and again his sister's eyes began restlessly searching his for something that she seemed unable to find.

"You make it a little difficult, Phil; I don't believe I had better speak of it."

"Why not?"

"Why, just because you ask me 'why not?' for example."

"Is it anything that worries you about Eileen?"

"N-no; not exactly. It is—it may be a phase; and yet I know that if it is anything at all it is not a passing phase. She is different from the majority, you see—very intelligent, very direct. She never forgets—for example. Her loyalty is quite remarkable, Phil. She is very intense in her—her beliefs—the more so because she is unusually free from impulse—even quite ignorant of the deeper emotions; or so I believed until—until—"

"Is she in *love*?" he asked.

"A little, Phil."

"Does she admit it?" he demanded, unpleasantly astonished.

"She admits it in a dozen innocent ways to me who can understand her; but to herself she has not admitted it, I think—could not admit it yet; because—because—"

"Who is it?" asked Selwyn; and there was in his voice the slightest undertone of a growl.

"Dear, shall I tell you?"

"Why not?"

"Because—because—Phil, I think that our pretty Eileen is a little in love with—you."

He straightened out to his full height, scarlet to the temples; she dropped her linked fingers in her lap, gazing at him almost sadly.

"Dear, all the things you are preparing to shout at me are quite useless; I *know*; I don't imagine, I don't forestall, I don't predict. I am not discounting any hopes of mine, because, Phil, I had not thought—had not planned such a thing—between you and Eileen—I don't know why. But I had not; there was Suddy Gray—a nice boy, perfectly qualified; and there were alternates more worldly, perhaps. But I did not think of you; and that is what now amazes and humiliates me; because it was the obvious that I overlooked—the most perfectly natural—"

"Nina! you are madder than a March heiress!"

"Air your theories, Phil, then come back to realities. The conditions remain; Eileen is certainly a little in love with you; and a little with her means something. And you, evidently, have never harboured any serious intentions toward the child; I can see that, because you are the most transparent man I ever knew. Now, the question is, what is to be done?"

"Done? Good heavens! Nothing, of course! There's nothing to do anything about! Nina, you are the most credulous little matchmaker that ever—"

"Oh, Phil, *must* I listen to all those fulminations before you come down to the plain fact? And it's plain to me as the nose on your countenance; and I don't know what to do about it! I certainly was a perfect fool to confide in you, for you are exhibiting the coolness and sagacity of a stampeded chicken."

He laughed in spite of himself; then, realising a little what her confidence had meant, he turned a richer red and slowly lifted his fingers to his moustache, while his perplexed gray eyes began to narrow as though sun-dazzled.

"I am, of course, obliged to believe that you are mistaken," he said; "a man cannot choose but believe in that manner. . . . There is no very young girl—nobody, old or young, whom I like as thoroughly as I do Eileen Erroll. She knows it; so do you, Nina. It is open and above-board. . . . I should be very unhappy if anything marred or distorted our friendship. . . . I am quite confident that nothing will."

"In that frame of mind," said his sister, smiling, "you are the healthiest companion in the world for her, for you will either cure her, or she you; and it is all right either way."

"Certainly it will be all right," he said confidently.

For a few moments he paced the room, reflective, quickening his pace all the while; and his sister watched him, silent in her indecision.

"I'm going up to see the kids," he said abruptly.

The children, one and all, were in the Park; but Eileen was sewing in the nursery, and his sister did not call him back as he swung out of the room and up the stairs. But when he had disappeared, Nina dropped into her chair, aware that she had played her best card prematurely; forced by Rosamund, who had just told her that rumour continued to be very busy coupling her brother's name with the name of the woman who once had been his wife.

Nina was now thoroughly convinced of Alixe's unusual capacity for making mischief.

She had known Alixe always—and she had seen her develop from a talented, restless, erratic, emotional girl, easily moved to generosity, into an impulsive woman, reckless to the point of ruthlessness when ennui and unhappiness stampeded her; a woman not deliberately selfish, not wittingly immoral, for she lacked the passion which her emotion was sometimes mistaken for; and she was kind by instinct.

Sufficiently intelligent to suffer from the lack of it in others, cultured to the point of recognising culture, her dangerous unsoundness lay in her utter lack of mental stamina when conditions became unpleasant beyond her will, not her ability to endure them.

The consequences of her own errors she refused to be burdened with; to escape somehow, was her paramount impulse, and she always tried to—had always attempted it even in school-days—and farther back when Nina first remembered her as a thin, eager, restless little girl scampering from one scrape into another at full speed. Even in those days there were moments when Nina believed her to be actually irrational, but there was every reason not to say so to the heedless scatterbrain whose father, in the prime of life, sat all day in his room, his faded eyes fixed wistfully on the childish toys which his attendant brought to him from his daughter's nursery.

All this Nina was remembering; and again she wondered bitterly at Alixe's treatment of her brother, and what explanation there could ever be for it—except one.

Lately, too, Alixe had scarcely been at pains to conceal her contempt for her husband, if what Rosamund related was true. It was only one more headlong scrape, this second marriage, and Nina knew Alixe well enough to expect the usual stampede toward that gay phantom which was always beckoning onward to promised happiness—that goal of heart's desire already lying so far behind her—and farther still for every step her little flying feet were taking in the oldest, the vainest, the most hopeless chase in the world—the headlong hunt for happiness.

And if that blind hunt should lead once more toward Selwyn? Suppose, freed from Ruthven, she turned in her tracks and threw herself and her youthful unhappiness straight at the man who had not yet destroyed the picture that Nina found when she visited her brother's rooms with the desire to be good to him with rocking-chairs!

Not that she really believed or feared that Philip would consider such an impossible reconciliation; pride, and a sense of the absurd, must always check any such weird caprice of her brother's conscience; and yet—and yet other amazing and mismated couples had done it—had been reunited.

And Nina was mightily troubled, for Alixe's capacity for mischief was boundless; and that she, in some manner, had already succeeded in stirring up Philip, was a rumour that persisted and would not be annihilated.

To inform a man frankly that a young girl is a little in love with him is one of the oldest, simplest, and easiest methods of interesting that man—unless he happen to be in love with somebody else. And Nina had taken her chances that the picture of Alixe was already too unimportant for the ceremony of incineration. Besides, what she had ventured to say to him was her belief; the child appeared to be utterly absorbed in her increasing intimacy with Selwyn. She talked of little else; her theme was Selwyn—his influence on Gerald, and her delight in his companionship. They had, at his suggestion, taken up together the study of Cretan antiquities—a sort of tender pilgrimage for her, because, with the aid of her father's and mother's letters, note-books, and papers, she and Selwyn were following on the map the journeys and discoveries of her father.

But this was not all; Nina's watchful eyes opened wider and wider as she witnessed in Eileen the naissance of an unconscious and delicate coquetry, quite unabashed, yet the more significant for that; and Nina, intent on the new phenomena, began to divine more about Eileen in a single second, than the girl could have suspected of herself in a month of introspection and of prayer.

Love was not there; Nina understood that; but its germ was—still dormant, but bedded deliciously in congenial soil—the living germ in all its latent promise, ready to swell with the first sudden heart-beat, quicken with the first quickening of the pulse, unfold into perfect symmetry if ever the warm, even current in the veins grew swift and hot under the first scorching whisper of Truth.

Eileen, sewing by the nursery window, looked up; her little Alsatian maid, cross-legged on the floor at her feet, sewing away diligently, also looked up, then scrambled to her feet as Selwyn halted on the threshold of the room.

"Why, how odd you look!" said Eileen, laughing: "come in, please; Susanne and I are only mending some of my summer things. Were you in search of the children?—don't say so if you were, because I'm quite happy in believing that you knew I was here. Did you?"

"Where are the children?" he asked.

"In the Park, my very rude friend. You will find them on the Mall if you start at once."

He hesitated, but finally seated himself, omitting the little formal hand-shake with which they always met, even after an hour's separation. Of course she noticed this, and, bending low above her sewing, wondered why.

It seemed to him, for a moment, as though he were looking at a woman he had heard about and had just met for the first time. His observation of her now was leisurely, calm, and thorough—not so calm, however, when, impatient of his reticence, bending there over her work, she raised her dark-blue eyes to his, her head remaining lowered. The sweet, silent inspection lasted but a moment, then she resumed her stitches, aware that something in him had changed since she last had seen him; but she merely smiled quietly to herself, confident of his unaltered devotion in spite of the strangely hard and unresponsive gaze that had uneasily evaded hers.

As her white fingers flew with the glimmering needle she reflected on conditions as she had left them a week ago. A week ago, between him and her the most perfect of understandings existed; and the consciousness of it she had carried with her every moment in the country—amid the icy tumble of the surf, on long vigorous walks over the greening hills where wild moorland winds whipped like a million fairy switches till the young blood fairly sang, pouring through her veins.

Since that—some time within the week, *something*evidently had happened to him, here in the city while she had been away. What?

As she bent above the fine linen garment on her knee, needle flying, a sudden memory stirred coldly—the recollection of her ride with Rosamund; and instinctively her clear eyes flew open and she raised her head, turning directly toward him a disturbed gaze he did not this time evade.

In silence their regard lingered; then, satisfied, she smiled again, saying: "Have I been away so long that we must begin all over, Captain Selwyn?"

"Begin what, Eileen?"

"To remember that the silence of selfish preoccupation is a privilege I have not accorded you?"

"I didn't mean to be preoccupied—"

"Oh, worse and worse!" She shook her head and began to thread the needle. "I see that my week's absence has not been very good for you. I knew it the moment you came in with all that guilty absent-minded effrontery which I have forbidden. Now, I suppose I shall have to recommence your subjection. Ring for tea, please. And, Susanne"—speaking in French and gathering up a fluffy heap of mended summer waists—"these might as well be sent to the laundress—thank you, little one; your sewing is always beautiful."

The small maid, blushing with pleasure, left the room, both arms full of feminine apparel; Selwyn rang for tea, then strolled back to the window, where he stood with both hands thrust into his coat-pockets, staring out at the sunset.

A primrose light bathed the city. Below, through the new foliage of the Park, the little lake reflected it in tints of deeper gold and amber where children clustered together, sailing toy ships. But there was no wind; the tiny sails and flags hung motionless, and out and in, among the craft becalmed, steered a family of wild ducks, the downy yellow fledglings darting hither and thither in chase of gnats, the mother bird following in leisurely solicitude.

And, as he stood there, absently intent on sky and roof and foliage, her soft bantering voice aroused him; and turning he found her beside him, her humorous eyes fixed on his face.

"Suppose," she said, "that we go back to first principles and resume life properly by shaking hands. Shall we?"

He coloured up as he took her hand in his; then they both laughed at the very vigorous shake.

"What a horribly unfriendly creature you *can* be," she said. "Never a greeting, never even a formal expression of pleasure at my return—"

"You have not *returned!*" he said, smiling; "you have been with me every moment, Eileen."

"What a pretty tribute!" she exclaimed; "I am beginning to recognise traces of my training after all. And it is high time, Captain Selwyn, because I was half convinced that you had escaped to the woods again. What, if you please, have you been doing in town since I paroled you? Nothing? Oh, it's very likely. You're probably too ashamed to tell me. Now note the difference between us; *I* have been madly tearing over turf and dune, up hills, down hillocks, along headlands, shores, and shingle; and I had the happiness of being half-frozen in the surf before Nina learned of it and stopped me. . . . Come; sit over here; because I'm quite crazy to tell you everything as usual—about how I played marbles with the children—yes, indeed!—down on my knees and shooting hard! Oh, it is divine, that sea-girdled, wind-drenched waste of moor and thicket!—the strange little stunted forests in the hollows of the miniature hills—do you remember? The trees, you know, grow only to the wind-level, then spread out like those grotesque trees in fairy-haunted forests—so old, so fantastic are these curious patches of woods that I am for ever watching to see something magic moving far in the twilight of the trees! . . . And one night I went out on the moors; oh, heavenly! celestial!—under the stretch of stars! Elf-land in silence, save for the bewitched wind. And the fairy forests drew me toward their edges, down, down into the hollow, with delicious shivers.

"Once I trembled indeed, for the starlight on the swamp was suddenly splintered into millions of flashes; and my heart leaped in pure fright! . . . It was only a wild duck whirring headlong into the woodland waters—but oh, if you had been there to see the weird beauty of its coming—and the star-splashed blackness! You *must* see that with me, some time. . . . When are you coming to Silverside? We go back very soon, now. . . . And I don't feel at all like permitting you to run wild in town when I'm away and playing hopscotch on the lawn with Drina!"

She lay back in her chair, laughing, her hands linked together behind her head.

"Really, Captain Selwyn, I confess I missed you. It's much better fun when two can see all those things that I saw—the wild roses just a tangle of slender green-mossed stems, the new grass so intensely green, with a touch of metallic iridescence; the cat's-paws chasing each other across the purple inland ponds—and that cheeky red fox that came trotting out of the briers near Wonder Head, and, when he saw me, coolly attempted to stare me out of countenance! Oh, it's all very well to tell you about it, but there is a little something lacking in unshared pleasures. . . . Yes, a great deal lacking. . . . And here is our tea-tray at last."

Nina came up to join them. Her brother winced as she smiled triumphantly at him, and the colour continued vivid in his face while she remained in the room. Then the children charged upstairs, fresh from the Park, clamouring for food; and they fell upon Selwyn's neck, and disarranged his scarf-pin, and begged for buttered toast and crumpets, and got what they demanded before Nina's authority could prevent.

"I saw a rabbit at Silverside!" said Billy, "but do you know, Uncle Philip, that hunting pack of ours is no good! Not one dog paid any attention to the rabbit though Drina and I did our best—didn't we, Drina?"

"You should have seen them," murmured Eileen, leaning close to whisper to Selwyn; "the children had fits when the rabbit came hopping across the road out of the Hither Woods. But the dogs all ran madly the other way, and I thought Billy would die of mortification."

153

Nina stood up, waving a crumpet which she had just rescued from Winthrop. "Hark!" she said, "there's the nursery curfew!—and not one wretched infant bathed! Billy! March bathward, my son! Drina, sweetheart, take command. Prune soufflé for the obedient, dry bread for rebels! Come, children!—don't let mother speak to you twice."

"Let's go down to the library," said Eileen to Selwyn—"you are dining with us, of course. . . . What? Yes, indeed, you are. The idea of your attempting to escape to some dreadful club and talk man-talk all the evening when I have not begun to tell you what I did at Silverside!"

They left the nursery together and descended the stairs to the library. Austin had just come in, and he looked up from his solitary cup of tea as they entered:

"Hello, youngsters! What conspiracy are you up to now? I suppose you sniffed the tea and have come to deprive me. By the way, Phil, I hear that you've sprung the trap on those Siowitha people."

"Neergard has, I believe."

"Well, isn't it all one?"

"No, it is not!" retorted Selwyn so bluntly that Eileen turned from the window at a sound in his voice which she had never before heard.

"Oh!" Austin stared over his suspended teacup, then drained it. "Trouble with our friend Julius?" he inquired.

"No trouble. I merely severed my connection with him."

"Ah! When?"

"This morning."

"In that case," said Austin, laughing, "I've a job for you—"

"No, old fellow; and thank you with all my heart. I've half made up my mind to live on my income for a while and take up that Chaosite matter again—"

"And blow yourself to smithereens! Why spatter Nature thus?"

"No fear," said Selwyn, laughing. "And, if it promises anything, I may come to you for advice on how to start it commercially."

"If it doesn't start you heavenward you shall have my advice from a safe distance. I'll telegraph it," said Austin. "But, if it's not personal, why on earth have you shaken Neergard?"

And Selwyn answered simply: "I don't like him. That is the reason, Austin."

The children from the head of the stairs were now shouting demands for their father; and Austin rose, pretending to grumble:

154

"Those confounded kids! A man is never permitted a moment to himself. Is Nina up there, Eileen! Oh, all right. Excuses et cetera; I'll be back pretty soon. You'll stay to dine, Phil?"

"I don't think so—"

"Yes, he will stay," said Eileen calmly.

And, when Austin had gone, she walked swiftly over to where Selwyn was standing, and looked him directly in the eyes.

"Is all well with Gerald?"

"Y-yes, I suppose so."

"Is he still with Neergard & Co.?"

"Yes, Eileen."

"And *you* don't like Mr. Neergard?"

"N-no."

"Then Gerald must not remain."

He said very quietly: "Eileen, Gerald no longer takes me into his confidence. I am afraid—I know, in fact—that I have little influence with him now. I am sorry; it hurts; but your brother is his own master, and he is at liberty to choose his own friends and his own business policy. I cannot influence him; I have learned that thoroughly. Better that I retain what real friendship he has left for me than destroy it by any attempt, however gentle, to interfere in his affairs."

She stood before him, straight, slender, her face grave and troubled.

"I cannot understand," she said, "how he could refuse to listen to a man like you."

"A man like me, Eileen? Well, if I were worth listening to, no doubt he'd listen. But the fact remains that I have not been able to hold his interest—"

"Don't give him up," she said, still looking straight into his eyes. "If you care for me, don't give him up."

"Care for you, Eileen! You know I do."

"Yes, I know it. So you will not give up Gerald, will you? He is—is only a boy—you know that; you know he has been—perhaps—indiscreet. But Gerald is only a boy. Stand by him, Captain Selwyn; because Austin does not know how to manage him—really he doesn't. . . . There has been another unpleasant scene between them; Gerald told me."

"Did he tell you why, Eileen?"

"Yes. He told me that he had played cards for money, and he was in debt. I know that sounds—almost disgraceful; but is not his need of help all the greater?"

Selwyn's eyes suddenly narrowed: "Did *you* help him out, this time?"

"I—I—how do you mean, Captain Selwyn?" But the splendid colour in her face confirmed his certainty that she had used her own resources to help her brother pay the gambling debt; and he turned away his eyes, angry and silent.

"Yes," she said under her breath, "I did aid him. What of it? Could I refuse?"

"I know. Don't aid him again—*that* way."

She stared: "You mean—"

"Send him to me, child. I understand such matters; I—that is—" and in sudden exasperation inexplicable, for the moment, to them both: "Don't touch such matters again! They soil, I tell you. I will not have Gerald go to you about such things!"

"My own brother! What do you mean?"

"I mean that, brother or not, he shall not bring such matters near you!"

"Am I to count for nothing, then, when Gerald is in trouble?" she demanded, flushing up.

"Count! Count!" he repeated impatiently; "of course you count! Good heavens! it's women like you who count—and no others—not one single other sort is of the slightest consequence in the world or to it. Count? Child, you control us all; everything of human goodness, of human hope hinges and hangs on you—is made possible, inevitable, because of you! And you ask me whether you count! You, who control us all, and always will—as long as you are you!"

She had turned a little pale under his vehemence, watching him out of wide and beautiful eyes.

What she understood—how much of his incoherence she was able to translate, is a question; but in his eyes and voice there was something simpler to divine; and she stood very still while his roused emotions swept her till her heart leaped up and every vein in her ran fiery pride.

"I am—overwhelmed . . . I did not consider that I counted—so vitally—in the scheme of things. But I must try to—if you believe all this of me—only you must teach me how to count for something in the world. Will you?"

"Teach you, Eileen. What winning mockery! *I* teach*you*? Well, then—I teach you this—that a man's blunder is best healed by a man's sympathy; . . . I will stand by Gerald as long as he will let me do so—not

156

alone for your sake, nor only for his, but for my own. I promise you that. Are you contented?"

"Yes."

She slowly raised one hand, laying it fearlessly in both of his.

"He is all I have left," she said. "You know that."

"I know, child."

"Then—thank you, Captain Selwyn."

"No; I thank you for giving me this charge. It means that a man must raise his own standard of living before he can accept such responsibility. . . . You endow me with all that a man ought to be; and my task is doubled; for it is not only Gerald but I myself who require surveillance."

He looked up, smilingly serious: "Such women as you alone can fit your brother and me for an endless guard duty over the white standard you have planted on the outer walls of the world."

"You say things to me—sometimes—" she faltered, "that almost hurt with the pleasure they give."

"Did that give you pleasure?"

"Y-yes; the surprise of it was almost too—too keen. I wish you would not—but I am glad you did. . . . You see"—dropping into a great velvet chair—"having been of no serious consequence to anybody for so many years—to be told, suddenly, that I—that I count so vitally with men—a man like you—"

She sank back, drew one small hand across her eyes, and rested a moment; then leaning forward, she set her elbow on one knee and bracketed her chin between forefinger and thumb.

"*You* don't know," she said, smiling faintly, "but, oh, the exalted dreams young girls indulge in! And one and all centre around some power-inspired attitude of our own when a great crisis comes. And most of all we dream of counting heavily; and more than all we clothe ourselves in the celestial authority which dares to forgive. . . . Is it not pathetically amusing—the mental process of a young girl?—and the paramount theme of her dream is power!—such power as will permit the renunciation of vengeance; such power as will justify the happiness of forgiving? . . . And every dream of hers is a dream of power; and, often, the happiness of forbearing to wield it. All dreams lead to it, all mean it; for instance, half-awake, then faintly conscious in slumber, I lie dreaming of power—always power; the triumph of attainment, of desire for wisdom and knowledge satisfied. I dream of friendships—wonderful intimacies exquisitely satisfying; I dream of troubles, and my moral power to sweep them out of existence; I dream of self-sacrifice, and of the spiritual power to endure it; I dream—I dream—sometimes—of more

157

material power—of splendours and imposing estates, of a paradise all my own. And when I have been selfishly happy long enough, I dream of a vast material power fitting me to wipe poverty from the world; I plan it out in splendid generalities, sometimes in minute detail. . . . Of men, we naturally dream; but vaguely, in a curious and confused way. . . . Once, when I was fourteen, I saw a volunteer regiment passing; and it halted for a while in front of our house; and a brilliant being on a black horse turned lazily in his saddle and glanced up at our window. . . . Captain Selwyn, it is quite useless for you to imagine what fairy scenes, what wondrous perils, what happy adventures that gilt-corded adjutant and I went through in my dreams. Marry him? Indeed I did, scores of times. Rescue him? Regularly. He was wounded, he was attacked by fevers unnumbered, he fled in peril of his life, he vegetated in countless prisons, he was misunderstood, he was a martyr to suspicion, he was falsely accused, falsely condemned. And then, just before the worst occurred, *I* appear!—the inevitable I."

She dropped back into the chair, laughing. Her colour was high, her eyes brilliant; she laid her arms along the velvet arms of the chair and looked at him.

"I've not had you to talk to for a whole week," she said; "and you'll let me; won't you? I can't help it, anyway, because as soon as I see you—crack! a million thoughts wake up in me and clipper-clapper goes my tongue. . . . You are very good for me. You are so thoroughly satisfactory—except when your eyes narrow in that dreadful far-away gaze—which I've forbidden, you understand. . . . *What* have you done to your moustache?"

"Clipped it."

"Oh, I don't like it too short. Can you get hold of it to pull it? It's the only thing that helps you in perplexity to solve problems. You'd be utterly helpless, mentally, without your moustache. . . . When are we to take up our Etruscan symbols again?—or was it Evans's monograph we were laboriously dissecting? Certainly it was; don't you remember the Hittite hieroglyph of Jerabis?—and how you and I fought over those wretched floral symbols? You don't? And it was only a week ago? . . . And listen! Down at Silverside I've been reading the most delicious thing—the Mimes of Herodas!—oh, so charmingly quaint, so perfectly human, that it seems impossible that they were written two thousand years ago. There's a maid, in one scene, Threissa, who is precisely like anybody's maid—and an old lady, Gyllis—perfectly human, and not Greek, but Yankee of to-day! Shall we reread it together?—when you come down to stay with us at Silverside?"

"Indeed we shall," he said, smiling; "which also reminds me—"

He drew from his breast-pocket a thin, flat box, turned it round and round, glanced at her, balancing it teasingly in the palm of his hand.

"Is it for me? Really? Oh, please don't be provoking! Is it *really* for me? Then give it to me this instant!"

"Turning, looked straight at Selwyn."

He dropped the box into the pink hollow of her supplicating palms. For a moment she was very busy with the tissue-paper; then:

"Oh! it is perfectly sweet of you!" turning the small book bound in heavy Etruscan gold; "whatever can it be?" and, rising, she opened it, stepping to the window so that she could see.

Within, the pages were closely covered with the minute, careful handwriting of her father; it was the first note-book he ever kept; and Selwyn had had it bound for her in gold.

For an instant she gazed, breathless, lips parted; then slowly she placed the yellowed pages against her lips and, turning, looked straight at Selwyn, the splendour of her young eyes starred with tears.

CHAPTER VII

ERRANDS AND LETTERS

Alixe Ruthven had not yet dared tell Selwyn that her visit to his rooms was known to her husband. Sooner or later she meant to tell him; it was only fair to him that he should be prepared for anything that might happen; but as yet, though her first instinct, born of sheer fright, urged her to seek instant council with Selwyn, fear of him was greater than the alarm caused her by her husband's knowledge.

She was now afraid of her husband's malice, afraid of Selwyn's opinion, afraid of herself most of all, for she understood herself well enough to realise that, if conditions became intolerable, the first and easiest course out of it would be the course she'd take—wherever it led, whatever it cost, or whoever was involved.

In addition to her dread and excitement, she was deeply chagrined and unhappy; and, although Jack Ruthven did not again refer to the matter—indeed appeared to have forgotten it—her alarm and humiliation remained complete, for Gerald now came and played and went as he chose; and in her disconcerted cowardice she dared not do more than plead with Gerald in secret, until she began to find the emotion consequent upon such intimacy unwise for them both.

Neergard, too, was becoming a familiar figure in her drawing-room; and, though at first she detested him, his patience and unfailing good spirits, and his unconcealed admiration for her softened her manner toward him to the point of toleration.

And Neergard, from his equivocal footing in the house of Ruthven, obtained another no less precarious in the house of Fane—all in the beginning on a purely gaming basis. However, Gerald had already proposed him for the Stuyvesant and Proscenium clubs; and, furthermore, a stormy discussion was now in progress among the members of the famous Siowitha over an amazing proposition from their treasurer, Jack Ruthven.

This proposal was nothing less than to admit Neergard to membership in that wealthy and exclusive country club, as a choice of the lesser evil; for it appeared, according to Ruthven, that Neergard, if admitted, was willing to restore to the club, free of rent, the thousands of acres vitally necessary to the club's existence as a game preserve, merely retaining the title to these lands for himself.

Draymore was incensed at the proposal, Harmon, Orchil, and Fane were disgustedly non-committal, but Phoenix Mottly was perhaps the angriest man on Long Island.

"In the name of decency, Jack," he said, "what are you dreaming of? Is it not enough that this man, Neergard, holds us up once? Do I

160

understand that he has the impudence to do it again with your connivance? Are you going to let him sandbag us into electing him? Is that the sort of hold-up you stand for? Well, then, I tell you I'll never vote for him. I'd rather see these lakes and streams of ours dry up; I'd rather see the last pheasant snared and the last covey leave for the other end of the island, than buy off that Dutchman with a certificate of membership in the Siowitha!"

"In that case," retorted Ruthven, "we'd better wind up our affairs and make arrangements for an auctioneer."

"All right; wind up and be damned!" said Mottly; "there'll be at least sufficient self-respect left in the treasury to go round."

Which was all very fine, and Mottly meant it at the time; but, outside of the asset of self-respect, there was too much money invested in the lands, plant, and buildings, in the streams, lakes, hatcheries, and forests of the Siowitha. The enormously wealthy seldom stand long upon dignity if that dignity is going to be very expensive. Only the poor can afford disastrous self-respect.

So the chances were that Neergard would become a member—which was why he had acquired the tract—and the price he would have to pay was not only in taxes upon the acreage, but, secretly, a solid sum in addition to little Mr. Ruthven whom he was binding to him by every tie he could pay for.

Neergard did not regret the expense. He had long since discounted the cost; and he also continued to lose money at the card-table to those who could do him the most good.

Away somewhere in the back of his round, squat, busy head he had an inkling that some day he would even matters with some people. Meanwhile he was patient, good-humoured, amusing when given a chance, and, as the few people he knew found out, inventive and resourceful in suggesting new methods of time-killing to any wealthy and fashionable victim of a vacant mind.

And as this faculty has always been the real key to the inner Temple of the Ten Thousand Disenchantments, the entrance of Mr. Neergard appeared to be only a matter of time and opportunity, and his ultimate welcome at the naked altar a conclusion foregone.

In the interim, however, he suffered Gerald and little Ruthven to pilot him; he remained cheerfully oblivious to the snubs and indifference accorded him by Mrs. Ruthven, Mrs. Fane, and others of their entourage whom he encountered over the card-tables or at card-suppers. And all the while he was attending to his business with an energy and activity that ought to have shamed Gerald, and did, at times, particularly when he arrived at the office utterly unfit for the work before him.

But Neergard continued astonishingly tolerant and kind, lending him money, advancing him what he required, taking up or renewing notes for him, until the boy, heavily in his debt, plunged more heavily still in sheer desperation, only to flounder the deeper at every struggle to extricate himself.

Alixe Ruthven suspected something of this, but it was useless as well as perilous in other ways for her to argue with Gerald, for the boy had come to a point where even his devotion to her could not stop him. He *must* go on. He did not say so to Alixe; he merely laughed, assuring her that he was all right; that he knew how much he could afford to lose, and that he would stop when his limit was in sight. Alas, he had passed his limit long since; and already it was so far behind him that he dared not look back—dared no longer even look forward.

Meanwhile the Ruthvens were living almost lavishly, and keeping four more horses; but Eileen Erroll's bank balance had now dwindled to three figures; and Gerald had not only acted offensively toward Selwyn, but had quarrelled so violently with Austin that the latter, thoroughly incensed and disgusted, threatened to forbid him the house.

"The little fool!" he said to Selwyn, "came here last night, stinking of wine, and attempted to lay down the law to me!—tried to dragoon me into a compromise with him over the investments I have made for him. By God, Phil, he shall not control one cent until the trust conditions are fulfilled, though it was left to my discretion, too. And I told him so flatly; I told him he wasn't fit to be trusted with the coupons of a repudiated South American bond—"

"Hold on, Austin. That isn't the way to tackle a boy like that!"

"Isn't it? Well, why not? Do you expect me to dicker with him?"

"No; but, Austin, you've always been a little brusque with him. Don't you think—"

"No, I don't. It's discipline he needs, and he'll get it good and plenty every time he comes here."

"I—I'm afraid he may cease coming here. That's the worst of it. For his sister's sake I think we ought to try to put up with—"

"Put up! Put up! I've been doing nothing else since he came of age. He's turned out a fool of a puppy, I tell you; he's idle, lazy, dissipated, impudent, conceited, insufferable—"

"But not vicious, Austin, and not untruthful. Where his affections are centred he is always generous; where they should be centred he is merely thoughtless, not deliberately selfish—"

"See here, Phil, how much good has your molly-coddling done him? You warned him to be cautious in his intimacy with Neergard, and he was actually insulting to you—"

162

"I know; but I understood. He probably had some vague idea of loyalty to a man whom he had known longer than he knew me. That was all; that was what I feared, too. But it had to be done—I was determined to venture it; and it seems I accomplished nothing. But don't think that Gerald's attitude toward me makes any difference, Austin. It doesn't; I'm just as devoted to the boy, just as sorry for him, just as ready to step in when the chance comes, as it surely will, Austin. He's only running a bit wilder than the usual colt; it takes longer to catch and bridle him—"

"Somebody'll rope him pretty roughly before you run him down," said Gerard.

"I hope not. Of course it's a chance he takes, and we can't help it; but I'm trying to believe he'll tire out in time and come back to us for his salt. And, Austin, we've simply got to believe in him, you know—on Eileen's account."

Austin grew angrier and redder:

"Eileen's account? Do you mean her bank account? It's easy enough to believe in him if you inspect his sister's bank account. Believe in him? Oh, certainly I do; I believe he's pup enough to come sneaking to his sister to pay for all the damfooleries he's engaged in. . . . And I've positively forbidden her to draw another check to his order—"

"It's that little bangled whelp, Ruthven," said Selwyn between his teeth. "I warned Gerald most solemnly of that man, but—"He shrugged his shoulders and glanced about him at the linen-covered furniture and bare floors. After a moment he looked up: "The game there is of course notorious. I—if matters did not stand as they do"—he flushed painfully—"I'd go straight to Ruthven and find out whether or not this business could be stopped."

"Stopped? No, it can't be. How are you going to stop a man from playing cards in his own house? They all do it—that sort. Fane's rather notorious himself; they call his house the house of ill-Fane, you know. If you or I or any of our family were on any kind of terms with the Ruthvens, they might exclude Gerald to oblige us. We are not, however; and, anyway, if Gerald means to make a gambler and a souse of himself at twenty-one, he'll do it. But it's pretty rough on us."

"It's rougher on him, Austin; and it's roughest on his sister. Well"—he held out his hand—"good-bye. No, thanks, I won't stop to see Nina and Eileen; I'm going to try to think up some way out of this. And—if Gerald comes to you again—try another tack—just try it. You know, old fellow, that, between ourselves, you and I are sometimes short of temper and long of admonition. Let's try reversing the combination with Gerald."

But Austin only growled from the depths of his linen-shrouded arm-chair, and Selwyn turned away, wondering what in the world he could do in a matter already far beyond the jurisdiction of either Austin or himself.

If Alixe had done her best to keep Gerald away, she appeared to be quite powerless in the matter; and it was therefore useless to go to her. Besides, he had every inclination to avoid her. He had learned his lesson.

To whom then could he go? Through whom could he reach Gerald? Through Nina? Useless. And Gerald had already defied Austin. Through Neergard, then? But he was on no terms with Neergard; how could he go to him? Through Rosamund Fane? At the thought he made a wry face. Any advances from him she would wilfully misinterpret. And Ruthven? How on earth could he bring himself to approach him?

And the problem therefore remained as it was; the only chance of any solution apparently depending upon these friends of Gerald's, not one of whom was a friend of Selwyn; indeed some among them were indifferent to the verge of open enmity.

And yet he had promised Eileen to do what he could. What merit lay in performing an easy obligation? What courage was required to keep a promise easily kept? If he cared anything for her—if he really cared for Gerald, he owed them more than effortless fulfilment. And here there could be no fulfilment without effort, without the discarding from self of the last rags of pride. And even then, what hope was there—after the sacrifice of self and the disregard of almost certain humiliation?

It was horribly hard for him; there seemed to be no chance in sight. But forlorn hope was slowly rousing the soldier in him—the grim, dogged, desperate necessity of doing his duty to the full and of leaving consequences to that Destiny, which some call by a name more reverent.

So first of all, when at length he had decided, he nerved himself to strike straight at the centre; and within the hour he found Gerald at the Stuyvesant Club.

The boy descended to the visitors' rooms, Selwyn's card in his hand and distrust written on every feature. And at Selwyn's first frank and friendly words he reddened to the temples and checked him.

"I won't listen," he said. "They—Austin and—and everybody have been putting you up to this until I'm tired of it. Do they think I'm a baby? Do they suppose I don't know enough to take care of myself? Are they trying to make me ridiculous? I tell you they'd better let me alone. My friends are my friends, and I won't listen to any criticism of them, and that settles it."

"Gerald—"

"Oh, I know perfectly well that you dislike Neergard. I don't, and that's the difference."

"I'm not speaking of Mr. Neergard, Gerald; I'm only trying to tell you what this man Ruthven really is doing—"

"What do I care what he is doing!" cried Gerald angrily. "And, anyway, it isn't likely I'd come to you to find out anything about Mrs. Ruthven's second husband!"

Selwyn rose, very white and still. After a moment he drew a quiet breath, his clinched hands relaxed, and he picked up his hat and gloves.

"They are my friends," muttered Gerald, as pale as he. "You drove me into speaking that way."

"Perhaps I did, my boy. . . . I don't judge you. . . . If you ever find you need help, come to me; and if you can't come, and still need me, send for me. I'll do what I can—always. I know you better than you know yourself. Good-bye."

He turned to the door; and Gerald burst out: "Why can't you let my friends alone? I liked you before you began this sort of thing!"

"I will let them alone if you will," said Selwyn, halting. "I can't stand by and see you exploited and used and perverted. Will you give me one chance to talk it over, Gerald?"

"No, I wont!" returned Gerald hotly; "I'll stand for my friends every time! There's no treachery in me!"

"You are not standing by me very fast," said the elder man gently.

"I said I was standing by my *friends*!" repeated the boy.

"Very well, Gerald; but it's at the expense of your own people, I'm afraid."

"That's my business, and you're not one of 'em!" retorted the boy, infuriated; "and you won't be, either, if I can prevent it, no matter whether people say that you're engaged to her—"

"What!" whispered Selwyn, wheeling like a flash. The last vestige of colour had fled from his face; and Gerald caught his breath, almost blinded by the blaze of fury in the elder man's eyes.

Neither spoke again; and after a moment Selwyn's eyes fell, he turned heavily on his heel and walked away, head bent, gray eyes narrowing to slits.

Yet, through the brain's chaos and the heart's loud tumult and the clamour of pulses run wild at the insult flung into his very face, the grim instinct to go on persisted. And he went on, and on, for *her* sake—on—he knew not how—until he came to Neergard's apartment in one of the vast West-Side constructions, bearing the name of a sovereign state; and here, after an interval, he followed his card to Neergard's splendid suite, where a man-servant received him and left him seated by a sunny window overlooking the blossoming foliage of the Park.

When Neergard came in, and stood on the farther side of a big oak table, Selwyn rose, returning the cool, curt nod.

"Mr. Neergard," he said, "it is not easy for me to come here after what I said to you when I severed my connection with your firm. You have every reason to be unfriendly toward me; but I came on the chance that whatever resentment you may feel will not prevent you from hearing me out."

"Personal resentment," said Neergard slowly, "never interferes with my business. I take it, of course, that you have called upon a business matter. Will you sit down?"

"Thank you; I have only a moment. And what I am here for is to ask you, as Mr. Erroll's friend, to use your influence on Mr. Erroll—every atom of your influence—to prevent him from ruining himself financially through his excesses. I ask you, for his family's sake, to discountenance any more gambling; to hold him strictly to his duties in your office, to overlook no more shortcomings of his, but to demand from him what any trained business man demands of his associates as well as of his employees. I ask this for the boy's sake."

Neergard's close-set eyes focussed a trifle closer to Selwyn's, yet did not meet them.

"Mr. Selwyn," he said, "have you come here to criticise the conduct of my business?"

"Criticise! No, I have not. I merely ask you—"

"You are merely asking me," cut in Neergard, "to run my office, my clerks, and my associate in business after some theory of your own."

Selwyn looked at the man and knew he had lost; yet he forced himself to go on:

"The boy regards you as his friend. Could you not, as his friend, discourage his increasing tendency toward dissipation—"

"I am not aware that he is dissipated."

"What!"

"I say that I am not aware that Gerald requires any interference from me—or from you, either," said Neergard coolly. "And as far as that goes, I and my business require no interference either. And I believe that settles it."

He touched a button; the man-servant appeared to usher Selwyn out.

The latter set his teeth in his under lip and looked straight and hard at Neergard, but Neergard thrust both hands in his pockets, turned

166

squarely on his heel, and sauntered out of the room, yawning as he went.

It bid fair to become a hard day for Selwyn; he foresaw it, for there was more for him to do, and the day was far from ended, and his self-restraint was nearly exhausted!

An hour later he sent his card in to Rosamund Fane; and Rosamund came down, presently, mystified, flattered, yet shrewdly alert and prepared for anything since the miracle of his coming justified such preparation.

"Why in the world," she said with a flushed gaiety perfectly genuine, "did you ever come to see *me*? Will you please sit here, rather near me?—or I shall not dare believe that you are that same Captain Selwyn who once was so deliciously rude to me at the Minster's dance."

"Was there not a little malice—just a very little—on your part to begin it?" he asked, smiling.

"Malice? Why? Just because I wanted to see how you and Alixe Ruthven would behave when thrust into each other's arms? Oh, Captain Selwyn—what a harmless little jest of mine to evoke all that bitterness you so smilingly poured out on me! . . . But I forgave you; I'll forgive you more than that—if you ask me. Do you know"—and she laid her small head on one side and smiled at him out of her pretty doll's eyes—"do you know that there are very few things I might not be persuaded to pardon you? Perhaps"—with laughing audacity—"there are not any at all. Try, if you please."

"Then you surely will forgive me for what I have come to ask you," he said lightly. "Won't you?"

"Yes," she said, her pink-and-white prettiness challenging him from every delicate feature—"yes—I will pardon you—on one condition."

"And what is that, Mrs. Fane?"

"That you are going to ask me something quite unpardonable!" she said with a daring little laugh. "For if it's anything less improper than an impropriety I won't forgive you. Besides, there'd be nothing to forgive. So please begin, Captain Selwyn."

"It's only this," he said: "I am wondering whether you would do anything for me?"

"*Anything! Merci!* Isn't that extremely general, Captain Selwyn? But you never can tell; ask me."

So he bent forward, his clasped hands between his knees, and told her very earnestly of his fears about Gerald, asking her to use her undoubted influence with the boy to shame him from the card-tables, explaining how utterly disastrous to him and his family his present course was.

167

"He is very fond of you, Mrs. Fane—and you know how easy it is for a boy to be laughed out of excesses by a pretty woman of experience. You see I am desperately put to it or I would never have ventured to trouble you—"

"I see," she said, looking at him out of eyes bright with disappointment.

"Could you help us, then?" he asked pleasantly.

"Help *us*, Captain Selwyn? Who is the 'us,' please?"

"Why, Gerald and me—and his family," he added, meeting her eyes. The eyes began to dance with malice.

"His family," repeated Rosamund; "that is to say, his sister, Miss Erroll. His family, I believe, ends there; does it not?"

"Yes, Mrs. Fane."

"I see. . . . Miss Erroll is naturally worried over him. But I wonder why she did not come to me herself instead of sending you as her errant ambassador?"

"Miss Erroll did not send me," he said, flushing up. And, looking steadily into the smiling doll's face confronting him, he knew again that he had failed.

"I am not inclined to be very much flattered after all," said Rosamund. "You should have come on your own errand, Captain Selwyn, if you expected a woman to listen to you. Did you not know that?"

"It is not a question of errands or of flattery," he said wearily; "I thought you might care to influence a boy who is headed for serious trouble— that is all, Mrs. Fane."

She smiled: "Come to me on your *own* errand—for Gerald's sake, for anybody's sake—for your own, preferably, and I'll listen. But don't come to me on another woman's errands, for I won't listen—even to you."

"I *have* come on my own errand!" he repeated coldly. "Miss Erroll knew nothing about it, and shall not hear of it from me. Can you not help me, Mrs. Fane?"

But Rosamund's rose-china features had hardened into a polished smile; and Selwyn stood up, wearily, to make his adieux.

But, as he entered his hansom before the door, he knew the end was not yet; and once more he set his face toward the impossible; and once more the hansom rolled away over the asphalt, and once more it stopped—this time before the house of Ruthven.

Every step he took now was taken through sheer force of will—and in *her* service; because, had it been, now, only for Gerald's sake, he knew he must have weakened—and properly, perhaps, for a man owes something to himself. But what he was now doing was for a young girl

168

who trusted him with all the fervour and faith of her heart and soul; and he could spare himself in nowise if, in his turn, he responded heart and soul to the solemn appeal.

Mr. Ruthven, it appeared, was at home and would receive Captain Selwyn in his own apartment.

Which he did—after Selwyn had been seated for twenty minutes—strolling in clad only in silken lounging clothes, and belting about his waist, as he entered, the sash of a kimona, stiff with gold.

His greeting was a pallid stare; but, as Selwyn made no motion to rise, he lounged over to a couch and, half reclining among the cushions, shot an insolent glance at Selwyn, then yawned and examined the bangles on his wrist.

After a moment Selwyn said: "Mr. Ruthven, you are no doubt surprised that I am here—"

"I'm not surprised if it's my wife you've come to see," drawled Ruthven. "If I'm the object of your visit, I confess to some surprise—as much as the visit is worth, and no more."

The vulgarity of the insult under the man's own roof scarcely moved Selwyn to any deeper contempt, and certainly not to anger.

"I did not come here to ask a favour of you," he said coolly—"for that is out of the question, Mr. Ruthven. But I came to tell you that Mr. Erroll's family has forbidden him to continue his gambling in this house and in your company anywhere or at any time."

"Most extraordinary," murmured Ruthven, passing his ringed fingers over his minutely shaven face—that strange face of a boy hardened by the depravity of ages.

"So I must request you," continued Selwyn, "to refuse him the opportunity of gambling here. Will you do it—voluntarily?"

"No."

"Then I shall use my judgment in the matter."

"And what may your judgment in the matter be?"

"I have not yet decided; for one thing I might enter a complaint with the police that a boy is being morally and materially ruined in your private gambling establishment."

"Is that a threat?"

"No. I will act, not threaten."

"Ah," drawled Ruthven, "I may do the same the next time my wife spends the evening in your apartment."

169

"You lie," said Selwyn in a voice made low by surprise.

"Oh, no, I don't. Very chivalrous of you—quite proper for you to deny it like a gentleman—but useless, quite useless. So the less said about invoking the law, the better for—some people. You'll agree with me, I dare say. . . . And now, concerning your friend, Gerald Erroll—I have not the slightest desire to see him play cards. Whether or not he plays is a matter perfectly indifferent to me, and you had better understand it. But if you come here demanding that I arrange my guest-lists to suit you, you are losing time."

Selwyn, almost stunned at Ruthven's knowledge of the episode in his rooms, had risen as he gave the man the lie direct.

For an instant, now, as he stared at him, there was murder in his eye. Then the utter hopeless helplessness of his position overwhelmed him, as Ruthven, with danger written all over him, stood up, his soft smooth thumbs hooked in the glittering sash of his kimona.

"Scowl if you like," he said, backing away instinctively, but still nervously impertinent; "and keep your distance! If you've anything further to say to me, write it." Then, growing bolder as Selwyn made no offensive move, "Write to me," he repeated with a venomous smirk; "it's safer for you to figure as *my* correspondent than as my wife's co-respondent—L-let go of me! W-what the devil are you d-d-doing—"

For Selwyn had him fast—one sinewy hand twisted in his silken collar, holding him squirming at arm's length.

"M-murder!" stammered Mr. Ruthven.

"No," said Selwyn, "not this time. But be very, very careful after this."

And he let him go with an involuntary shudder, and wiped his hands on his handkerchief.

Ruthven stood quite still; and after a moment the livid terror died out in his face and a rushing flush spread over it—a strange, dreadful shade, curiously opaque; and he half turned, dizzily, hands outstretched for self-support.

Selwyn coolly watched him as he sank on to the couch and sat huddled together and leaning forward, his soft, ringed fingers covering his impurpled face.

Then Selwyn went away with a shrug of utter loathing; but after he had gone, and Ruthven's servants had discovered him and summoned a physician, their master lay heavily amid his painted draperies and cushions, his congested features set, his eyes partly open and possessing sight, but the whites of them had disappeared and the eyes themselves, save for the pupils, were like two dark slits filled with blood.

There was no doubt about it; the doctors, one and all, knew their business when they had so often cautioned Mr. Ruthven to avoid sudden and excessive emotions.

That night Selwyn wrote briefly to Mrs. Ruthven:

"I saw your husband this afternoon. He is at liberty to inform you of what passed. But in case he does not, there is one detail which you ought to know: your husband believes that you once paid a visit to my apartments. It is unlikely that he will repeat the accusation and I think there is no occasion for you to worry. However, it is only proper that you should know this—which is my only excuse for writing you a letter that requires no acknowledgment. Very truly yours,

"PHILIP SELWYN."

To this letter she wrote an excited and somewhat incoherent reply; and rereading it in troubled surprise, he began to recognise in it something of the strange, illogical, impulsive attitude which had confronted him in the first weeks of his wedded life.

Here was the same minor undertone of unrest sounding ominously through every line; the same illogical, unhappy attitude which implied so much and said so little, leaving him uneasy and disconcerted, conscious of the vague recklessness and veiled reproach—dragging him back from the present through the dead years to confront once more the old pain, the old bewilderment at the hopeless misunderstanding between them.

He wrote in answer:

"For the first time in my life I am going to write you some unpleasant truths. I cannot comprehend what you have written; I cannot interpret what you evidently imagine I must divine in these pages—yet, as I read, striving to understand, all the old familiar pain returns—the hopeless attempt to realise wherein I failed in what you expected of me.

"But how can I, now, be held responsible for your unhappiness and unrest—for the malicious attitude, as you call it, of the world toward you? Years ago you felt that there existed some occult coalition against you, and that I was either privy to it or indifferent. I was not indifferent, but I did not believe there existed any reason for your suspicions. This was the beginning of my failure to understand you; I was sensible enough that we were unhappy, yet could not see any reason for it— could see no reason for the increasing restlessness and discontent which came over you like successive waves following some brief happy interval when your gaiety and beauty and wit fairly dazzled me and everybody who came near you. And then, always hateful and irresistible, followed the days of depression, of incomprehensible impulses, of that strange unreasoning resentment toward me.

"What could I do? I don't for a moment say that there was nothing I might have done. Certainly there must have been something; but I did not know what. And often in my confusion and bewilderment I was quick-tempered, impatient to the point of exasperation—so utterly unable was I to understand wherein I was failing to make you contented.

"Of course I could not shirk or avoid field duty or any of the details which so constantly took me away from you. Also I began to understand your impatience of garrison life, of the monotony of the place, of the climate, of the people. But all this, which I could not help, did not account for those dreadful days together when I could see that every minute was widening the breach between us.

"Alixe—your letter has brought it all back, vivid, distressing, exasperating; and this time I *know* that I could have done nothing to render you unhappy, because the time when I was responsible for such matters is past.

"And this—forgive me if I say it—arouses a doubt in me—the first honest doubt I have had of my own unshared culpability. Perhaps after all a little more was due from you than what you brought to our partnership—a little more patience, a little more appreciation of my own inexperience and of my efforts to make you happy. You were, perhaps, unwittingly exacting—even a little bit selfish. And those sudden, impulsive caprices for a change of environment—an escape from the familiar—were they not rather hard on me who could do nothing—who had no choice in the matter of obedience to my superiors?

"Again and again I asked you to go to some decent climate and wait for me until I could get leave. I stood ready and willing to make any arrangement for you, and you made no decision.

"Then when Barnard's command moved out we had our last distressing interview. And, if that night I spoke of your present husband and asked you to be a little wiser and use a little more discretion to avoid malicious comment—it was not because I dreamed of distrusting you—it was merely for your own guidance and because you had so often complained of other people's gossip about you.

"To say I was stunned, crushed, when I learned of what had happened in my absence, is to repeat a trite phrase. What it cost me is of no consequence now; what it is now costing you I cannot help.

"Yet, your letter, in every line, seems to imply some strange responsibility on my part for what you speak of as the degrading position you now occupy.

"Degradation or not—let us leave that aside; you cannot now avoid being his wife. But as for any hostile attitude of society in your regard—any league or coalition to discredit you—that is not apparent to me. Nor can it occur if your personal attitude toward the world is correct.

Discretion and circumspection, a happy, confident confronting of life—these, and a wise recognition of conditions, constitute sufficient safeguard for a woman in your delicately balanced position.

"And now, one thing more. You ask me to meet you at Sherry's for a conference. I don't care to, Alixe. There is nothing to be said except what can be written on letter-paper. And I can see neither the necessity nor the wisdom of our writing any more letters."

For a few days no reply came; then he received such a strange, unhappy, and desperate letter, that, astonished, alarmed, and apprehensive, he went straight to his sister, who had run up to town for the day from Silverside, and who had telephoned him to take her somewhere for luncheon.

Nina appeared very gay and happy and youthful in her spring plumage, but she exclaimed impatiently at his tired and careworn pallor; and when a little later they were seated tête-à-tête in the rococo dining-room of a popular French restaurant, she began to urge him to return with her, insisting that a week-end at Silverside was what he needed to avert physical disintegration.

"What is there to keep you in town?" she demanded, breaking bits from the stick of crisp bread. "The children have been clamouring for you day and night, and Eileen has been expecting a letter—You promised to write her, Phil—!"

"I'm going to write to her," he said impatiently; "wait a moment, Nina—don't speak of anything pleasant or—or intimate just now—because—because I've got to bring up another matter—something not very pleasant to me or to you. May I begin?"

"What is it, Phil?" she asked, her quick, curious eyes intent on his troubled face.

"It is about—Alixe."

"What about her?" returned his sister calmly.

"You knew her in school—years ago. You have always known her—"

"Yes."

"You—did you ever visit her?—stay at the Varians' house?"

"Yes."

"In—in her own home in Westchester?"

"Yes."

There was a silence; his eyes shifted to his plate; remained fixed as he said:

"Then you knew her—father?"

173

"Yes, Phil," she said quietly, "I knew Mr. Varian."

"Was there anything—anything unusual—about him—in those days?"

"Have you heard that for the first time?" asked his sister.

He looked up: "Yes. What was it, Nina?"

She became busy with her plate for a while; he sat rigid, patient, one hand resting on his claret-glass. And presently she said without meeting his eyes:

"It was even farther back—her grandparents—one of them—" She lifted her head slowly—"That is why it so deeply concerned us, Phil, when we heard of your marriage."

"What concerned you?"

"The chance of inheritance—the risk of the taint—of transmitting it. Her father's erratic brilliancy became more than eccentricity before I knew him. I would have told you that had I dreamed that you ever could have thought of marrying Alixe Varian. But how could I know you would meet her out there in the Orient! It was—your cable to us was like a thunderbolt. . . . And when she—she left you so suddenly—Phil, dear— I *feared* the true reason—the only possible reason that could be responsible for such an insane act."

"What was the truth about her father?" he said doggedly. "He was eccentric; was he ever worse than that?"

"The truth was that he became mentally irresponsible before his death."

"You *know* this?"

"Alixe told me when we were schoolgirls. And for days she was haunted with the fear of what might one day be her inheritance. That is all I know, Phil."

He nodded and for a while made some pretence of eating, but presently leaned back and looked at his sister out of dazed eyes.

"Do you suppose," he said heavily, "that *she* was not entirely responsible when—when she went away?"

"I have wondered," said Nina simply. "Austin believes it."

"But—but—how in God's name could that be possible? She was so brilliant—so witty, so charmingly and capriciously normal—"

"Her father was brilliant and popular—when he was young. Austin knew him, Phil. I have often, often wondered whether Alixe realises what she is about. Her restless impulses, her intervals of curious resentment—so many things which I remember and which, now, I cannot believe were entirely normal. . . . It is a dreadful surmise to

174

make about anybody so youthful, so pretty, so lovable—and yet, it is the kindest way to account for her strange treatment of you—"

"I can't believe it," he said, staring at vacancy. "I refuse to." And, thinking of her last frightened and excited letter imploring an interview with him and giving the startling reason: "What a scoundrel that fellow Ruthven is," he said with a shudder.

"Why, what has he—"

"Nothing. I can't discuss it, Nina—"

"Please tell me, Phil!"

"There is nothing to tell."

She said deliberately: "I hope there is not, Phil. Nor do I credit any mischievous gossip which ventures to link my brother's name with the name of Mrs. Ruthven."

He paid no heed to what she hinted, and he was still thinking of Ruthven when he said: "The most contemptible and cowardly thing a man can do is to fail a person dependent on him—when that person is in prospective danger. The dependence, the threatened helplessness *must* appeal to any man! How can he, then, fail to stand by a person in trouble—a person linked to him by every tie, every obligation. Why—why to fail at such a time is dastardly—and to—to make a possible threatened infirmity a reason for abandoning a woman is monstrous—!"

"Phil! I never for a moment supposed that even if you suspected Alixe to be not perfectly responsible you would have abandoned her—"

"*I?* Abandon *her!*" He laughed bitterly. "I was not speaking of myself," he said. . . . And to himself he wondered: "Was it *that*—after all? Is that the key to my dreadful inability to understand? I cannot—I cannot accept it. I know her; it was not that; it—it must not be!"

And that night he wrote to her:

"If he threatens you with divorce on such a ground he himself is likely to be adjudged mentally unsound. It was a brutal, stupid threat, nothing more; and his insult to your father's memory was more brutal still. Don't be stampeded by such threats. Disprove them by your calm self-control under provocation; disprove them by your discretion and self-confidence. Give nobody a single possible reason for gossip. And above all, Alixe, don't become worried and morbid over anything you might dread as inheritance, for you are as sound to-day as you were when I first met you; and you shall not doubt that you could ever be anything else. Be the woman you can be! Show the pluck and courage to make the very best out of life. I have slowly learned to attempt it; and it is not difficult if you convince yourself that it can be done."

To this she answered the next day:

"I will do my best. There is danger and treachery everywhere; and if it becomes unendurable I shall put an end to it in one way or another. As for his threat—incident on my admitting that I did go to your room, and defying him to dare believe evil of me for doing it—I can laugh at it now—though, when I wrote you, I was terrified—remembering how mentally broken my father was when he died.

"But, as you say, I *am* sound, body and mind. I*know* it; I don't doubt it for one moment—except—at long intervals when, apropos of nothing, a faint sensation of dread comes creeping.

"But I am *sound!* I know it so absolutely that I sometimes wonder at my own perfect sanity and understanding; and so clearly, so faultlessly, so precisely does my mind work that—and this I never told you—I am often and often able to detect mental inadequacy in many people around me—the slightest deviation from the normal, the least degree of mental instability. Phil, so sensitive to extraneous impression is my mind that you would be astonished to know how instantly perceptible to me is mental degeneration in other people. And it would amaze you, too, if I should tell you how many, many people you know are, in some degree, more or less insane.

"But there is no use in going into such matters; all I meant to convey to you was that I am not frightened now at any threat of that sort from him.

"I don't know what passed between you and him; he won't tell me; but I do know from the servants that he has been quite ill—I was in Westchester that night—and that something happened to his eyes—they were dreadful for a while. I imagine it has something to do with veins and arteries; and it's understood that he's to avoid sudden excitement.

"However, he's only serenely disagreeable to me now, and we see almost nothing of one another except over the card-tables. Gerald has been winning rather heavily, I am glad to say—glad, as long as I cannot prevent him from playing. And yet I may be able to accomplish that yet—in a roundabout way—because the apple-visaged and hawk-beaked Mr. Neergard has apparently become my slavish creature; quite infatuated. And as soon as I've fastened on his collar, and made sure that Rosamund can't unhook it, I'll try to make him shut down on Gerald's playing. This for your sake, Phil—because you ask me. And because you must always stand for all that is upright and good and manly in my eyes. Ah, Phil! what a fool I was! And all, all my own fault, too.

"Alixe."

This ended the sudden eruption of correspondence; for he did not reply to this letter, though in it he read enough to make him gravely uneasy; and he fell, once more, into the habit of brooding, from which both Boots Lansing and Eileen had almost weaned him.

176

Also he began to take long solitary walks in the Park when not occupied in conferences with the representatives of the Lawn Nitro-Powder Works—a company which had recently approached him in behalf of his unperfected explosive, Chaosite.

This hermit life might have continued in town indefinitely had he not, one morning, been surprised by a note from Eileen—the first he had ever had from her.

It was only a very brief missive—piquant, amusing, innocently audacious in closing—a mere reminder that he had promised to write to her; and she ended it by asking him very plainly whether he had not missed her, in terms so frank, so sweet, so confident of his inevitable answer, that all the enchantment of their delightful intimacy surged back in one quick tremor of happiness, washing from his heart and soul the clinging, sordid, evil things which were creeping closer, closer to torment and overwhelm him.

And all that day he went about his business quite happily, her letter in his pocket; and that night, taking a new pen and pen holder, he laid out his very best letter-paper, and began the first letter he had ever written to Eileen Erroll.

"DEAR EILEEN: I have your charming little note from Silverside reminding me that I had promised to write you. But I needed no reminder; you know that. Then why have I not written? I couldn't, off-hand. And every day and evening except to-day and this evening I have been in conference with Edgerton Lawn and other representatives of the Lawn Nitro-Powder Company; and have come to a sort of semi-agreement with them concerning a high explosive called Chaosite, which they desire to control the sale of as soon as I can control its tendency to misbehave. This I expect to do this summer; and Austin has very kindly offered me a tiny cottage out on the moors too far from anybody or anything to worry people.

"I know you will be glad to hear that I have such attractive business prospects in view. I dare say I shall scarcely know what to do with my enormous profits a year or two hence. Have you any suggestions?

"Meanwhile, however, your letter and its questions await answers; and here they are:

"Yes, I saw Gerald once at his club and had a short talk with him. He was apparently well. You should not feel so anxious about him. He is very young, yet, but he comes from good stock. Sooner or later he is bound to find himself; you must not doubt that. Also he knows that he can always come to me when he wishes.

"No, I have not ridden in the Park since you and Nina and the children went to Silverside. I walked there Sunday, and it was most beautiful, especially through the Ramble. In his later years my father was fond of walking there with me. That is one reason I go there; he seems to be

177

very near me when I stand under the familiar trees or move along the flowering walks he loved so well. I wish you had known him. It is curious how often this wish recurs to me; and so persistent was it in the Park that lovely Sunday that, at moments, it seemed as though we three were walking there together—he and you and I—quite happy in the silence of companionship which seemed not of yesterday but of years.

"It is rather a comforting faculty I have—this unconscious companionship with the absent. Once I told you that you had been with me while you supposed yourself to be at Silverside. Do you remember? Now, here in the city, I walk with you constantly; and we often keep pace together through crowded streets and avenues; and in the quiet hours you are very often, seated not far from where I sit. . . . If I turned around now—so real has been your presence in my room to-night—that it seems as though I could not help but surprise you here—just yonder on the edges of the lamp glow—

"But I know you had rather remain at Silverside, so I won't turn around and surprise you here in Manhattan town.

"And now your next question: Yes, Boots is well, and I will give him Drina's love, and I will try my best to bring him to Silverside when I come. Boots is still crazed with admiration for his house. He has two cats, a housekeeper, and a jungle of shrubs and vines in the back yard, which he plays the hose on; and he has also acquired some really beautiful old rugs—a Herez which has all the tints of a living sapphire, and a charming antique Shiraz, rose, gold, and that rare old Persian blue. To mention symbols for a moment, apropos of our archaeological readings together, Boots has an antique Asia Minor rug in which I discovered not only the Swastika, but also a fire-altar, a Rhodian lily border, and a Mongolian motif which appears to resemble the cloud-band. It was quite an Anatshair jumble in fact, very characteristic. We must capture Nina some day and she and you and I will pay a visit to Boots's rugs and study these old dyes and mystic symbols of the East. Shall we?

"And now your last question. And I answer: Yes, I do miss you—so badly that I often take refuge in summoning you in spirit. The other day I had occasion to see Austin; and we sat in the library where all the curtains are in linen bags and all the furniture in overalls, and where the rugs are rolled in tarred paper and the pictures are muffled in cheese-cloth.

"And after our conference had ended and I was on my way to the hall below, suddenly on my ear, faint but clear, I heard your voice, sweet as the odour of blossoms in an empty room. No—it neither deceived nor startled me; I have often heard it before, when you were nowhere near. And, that I may answer your question more completely, I answer it again: Yes, I miss you; so that I hear your voice through every silence; all voids are gay with it; there are no lonely places where my steps pass,

178

because you are always near; no stillness through which your voice does not sound; no unhappiness, no sordid cares which the memory of you does not make easier to endure.

"Have I answered? And now, good-night. Gerald has just come in; I hear him passing through the hall to his own apartments. So I'll drop in for a smoke with him before I start to search for you in dreamland. Good-night, Eileen. PHILIP SELWYN."

When he had finished, sealed, and stamped his letter he leaned back in his chair, smiling to himself, still under the spell which the thought of her so often now cast over him. Life and the world were younger, cleaner, fresher; the charming energy of her physical vigour and youth and beauty tinted all things with the splendid hue of inspiration. But most of all it was the exquisite fastidiousness of her thoughts that had begun to inthral him—that crystal clear intelligence, so direct, so generous—the splendid wholesome attitude toward life—and her dauntless faith in the goodness of it.

Breathing deeply, he drew in the fragrance of her memory, and the bitterness of things was dulled with every quiet respiration.

He smiled again, too; how utterly had his sister mistaken their frank companionship! How stupidly superfluous was it to pretend to detect, in their comradeship, the commonplaces of sentiment—as though such a girl as Eileen Erroll were of the common self-conscious mould—as though in their cordial understanding there was anything less simple than community of taste and the mutual attraction of intelligence!

Then, the memory of what his sister had said drove the smile from his face and he straightened up impatiently. Love! What unfortunate hallucination had obsessed Nina to divine what did not exist?—what need not exist? How could a woman like his sister fall into such obvious error; how could she mistake such transparent innocence, such visible freedom from motive in this young girl's pure friendship for himself?

And, as for him, he had never thought of Eileen—he could not bring himself to think of her so materially or sentimentally. For, although he now understood that he had never known what love, might be—its coarser mask, infatuation, he had learned to see through; and, as that is all he had ever known concerning love, the very hint of it had astonished and repelled him, as though the mere suggestion had been a rudeness offered to this delicate and delicious friendship blossoming into his life—a life he had lately thought so barren and laid waste.

No, his sister was mistaken; but her mistake must not disturb the blossoming of this unstained flower. Sufficient that Eileen and he disdainfully ignore the trite interpretation those outside might offer them unasked; sufficient that their confidence in one another remain without motive other than the happiness of unembarrassed people who find a pleasure in sharing an intelligent curiosity concerning men and things and the world about them.

179

Thinking of these matters, lying back there in his desk chair, he suddenly remembered that Gerald had come in. They had scarcely seen one another since that unhappy meeting in the Stuyvesant Club; and now, remembering what he had written to Eileen, he emerged with a start from his contented dreaming, sobered by the prospect of seeking Gerald.

For a moment or two he hesitated; but he had said in his letter that he was going to do it; and now he rose, looked around for his pipe, found it, filled and lighted it, and, throwing on his dressing-gown, went out into the corridor, tying the tasselled cords around his waist as he walked.

His first knock remaining unanswered, he knocked more sharply. Then he heard from within the muffled creak of a bed, heavy steps across the floor. The door opened with a jerk; Gerald stood there, eyes swollen, hair in disorder, his collar crushed, and the white evening tie unknotted and dangling over his soiled shirt-front.

"Hello," said Selwyn simply; "may I come in?"

The boy passed his hand across his eyes as though confused by the light; then he turned and walked back toward the bed, still rubbing his eyes, and sat down on the edge.

Selwyn closed the door and seated himself, apparently not noticing Gerald's dishevelment.

"Thought I'd drop in for a good-night pipe," he said quietly. "By the way, Gerald, I'm going down to Silverside next week. Nina has asked Boots, too. Couldn't you fix it to come along with us?"

"I don't know," said the boy in a low voice; "I'd like to."

"Good business! That will be fine! What you and I need is a good stiff tramp across the moors, or a gallop, if you like. It's great for mental cobwebs, and my brain is disgracefully unswept. By the way, somebody said that you'd joined the Siowitha Club."

"Yes," said the boy listlessly.

"Well, you'll get some lively trout fishing there now. It's only thirty miles from Silverside, you know—you can run over in the motor very easily."

Gerald nodded, sitting silent, his handsome head supported in both hands, his eyes on the floor.

That something was very wrong with him appeared plainly enough; but Selwyn, touched to the heart and miserably apprehensive, dared not question him, unasked.

And so they sat there for a while, Selwyn making what conversation he could; and at length Gerald turned and dragged himself across the bed, dropping his head back on the disordered pillows.

"Go on," he said; "I'm listening."

So Selwyn continued his pleasant, inconsequential observations, and Gerald lay with closed eyes, quite motionless, until, watching him, Selwyn saw his hand was trembling where it lay clinched beside him. And presently the boy turned his face to the wall.

Toward midnight Selwyn rose quietly, removed his unlighted pipe from between his teeth, knocked the ashes from it, and pocketed it. Then he walked to the bed and seated himself on the edge.

"What's the trouble, old man?" he asked coolly.

There was no answer. He placed his hand over Gerald's; the boy's hand lay inert, then quivered and closed on Selwyn's convulsively.

"That's right," said the elder man; "that's what I'm here for—to stand by when you hoist signals. Go on."

The boy shook his head and buried it deeper in the pillow.

"Bad as that?" commented Selwyn quietly. "Well, what of it? I'm standing by, I tell you. . . . That's right"—as Gerald broke down, his body quivering under the spasm of soundless grief—"that's the safety-valve working. Good business. Take your time."

It took a long time; and Selwyn sat silent and motionless, his whole arm numb from its position and Gerald's crushing grasp. And at last, seeing that was the moment to speak:

"Now let's fix up this matter, Gerald. Come on!"

"Good heavens! h-how can it be f-fixed—"

"I'll tell you when you tell me. It's a money difficulty, I suppose; isn't it?"

"Yes."

"Cards?"

"P-partly."

"Oh, a note? Case of honour? Where is this I.O.U. that you gave?"

"It's worse than that. The—the note is paid. Good God—I can't tell you—"

"You must. That's why I'm here, Gerald."

"Well, then, I—I drew a check—knowing that I had no funds. If it—if they return it, marked—"

"I see. . . . What are the figures?"

The boy stammered them out; Selwyn's grave face grew graver still.

"That is bad," he said slowly—"very bad. Have you—but of course you couldn't have seen Austin—"

"I'd kill myself first!" said Gerald fiercely.

"No, you wouldn't do that. You're not *that* kind. . . . Keep perfectly cool, Gerald; because it is going to be fixed. The method only remains to be decided upon—"

"I can't take your money!" stammered the boy; "I can't take a cent from you—after what I've said—the beastly things I've said—"

"It isn't the things you say to me, Gerald, that matter. . . . Let me think a bit—and don't worry. Just lie quietly, and understand that I'll do the worrying. And while I'm amusing myself with a little quiet reflection as to ways and means, just take your own bearings from this reef; and set a true course once more, Gerald. That is all the reproach, all the criticism you are going to get from me. Deal with yourself and your God in silence."

And in silence and heavy dismay Selwyn confronted the sacrifice he must make to save the honour of the house of Erroll.

It meant more than temporary inconvenience to himself; it meant that he must go into the market and sell securities which were partly his capital, and from which came the modest income that enabled him to live as he did.

There was no other way, unless he went to Austin. But he dared not do that—dared not think what Austin's action in the matter might be. And he knew that if Gerald were ever driven into hopeless exile with Austin's knowledge of his disgrace rankling, the boy's utter ruin must result inevitably.

Yet—yet—how could he afford to do this—unoccupied, earning nothing, bereft of his profession, with only the chance in view that his Chaosite might turn out stable enough to be marketable? How could he dare so strip himself? Yet, there was no other way; it had to be done; and done at once—the very first thing in the morning before it became too late.

And at first, in the bitter resentment of the necessity, his impulse was to turn on Gerald and bind him to good conduct by every pledge the boy could give. At least there would be compensation. Yet, with the thought came the clear conviction of its futility. The boy had brushed too close to dishonour not to recognise it. And if this were not a lifelong lesson to him, no promises forced from him in his dire need and distress, no oaths, no pledges could bind him; no blame, no admonition, no scorn, no contempt, no reproach could help him to see more clearly the pit of destruction than he could see now.

"You need sleep, Gerald," he said quietly. "Don't worry; I'll see that your check is not dishonoured; all you have to see to is yourself. Good-night, my boy."

But Gerald could not speak; and so Selwyn left him and walked slowly back to his own room, where he seated himself at his desk, grave, absent-eyed, his unfilled pipe between his teeth.

And he sat there until he had bitten clean through the amber mouthpiece, so that the brier bowl fell clattering to the floor. By that time it was full daylight; but Gerald was still asleep. He slept late into the afternoon; but that evening, when Selwyn and Lansing came in to persuade him to go with them to Silverside, Gerald was gone.

They waited another day for him; he did not appear. And that night they left for Silverside without him.

CHAPTER VIII

SILVERSIDE

During that week-end at Silverside Boots behaved like a school-lad run wild. With Drina's hand in his, half a dozen dogs as advanced guard, and heavily flanked by the Gerard battalion, he scoured the moorlands from Surf Point to the Hither Woods; from Wonder Head to Sky Pond.

Ever hopeful of rabbit and fox, Billy urged on his cheerful waddling pack and the sea wind rang with the crack of his whip and the treble note of his whistle. Drina, lately inoculated with the virus of nature-study, carried a green gauze butterfly net, while Boots's pockets bulged with various lethal bottles and perforated tin boxes for the reception of caterpillars. The other children, like the puppies of Billy's pack, ran haphazard, tireless and eager little opportunists, eternal prisoners of hope, tripped flat by creepers, scratched and soiled in thicket and bog, but always up and forward again, ranging out, nose in the wind, dauntless, expectant, wonder-eyed.

Nina, Eileen, and Selwyn formed a lagging and leisurely rear-guard, though always within signalling distance of Boots and the main body; and, when necessary, the two ex-army men wig-wagged to each other across the uplands to the endless excitement and gratification of the children.

It was a perfect week-end; the sky, pale as a robin's egg at morn and even, deepened to royal blue under the noon-day sun; and all the world—Long Island—seemed but a gigantic gold-green boat stemming the running purple of the sea and Sound.

The air, when still, quivered in that deep, rich silence instinct with the perpetual monotone of the sea; stiller for the accentless call of some lone moorland bird, or the gauzy clatter of a dragon-fly in reedy reaches. But when the moon rose and the breeze awakened, and the sedges stirred, and the cat's-paws raced across the moonlit ponds, and the far surf off Wonder Head intoned the hymn of the four winds, the trinity, earth and sky and water, became one thunderous symphony—a harmony of sound and colour silvered to a monochrome by the moon.

Then, through the tinted mystery the wild ducks, low flying, drove like a flight of witches through the dusk; and unseen herons called from their heronry, fainter, fainter till their goblin yelps died out in the swelling murmur of a million wind-whipped leaves.

Then was the moorland waste bewitching in its alternation of softly checkered gray and shade, where acres of feathery grasses flowed in wind-blown furrows; where in the purple obscurity of hollows the strange and aged little forests grew restless and full of echoes; where shadowy reeds like elfin swords clattered and thrust and parried across the darkling pools of haunted waters unstirred save for the swirl of a startled fish or the smoothly spreading wake of some furry creature swimming without a sound.

Into this magic borderland, dimmer for moonlit glimpses in ghostly contrast to the shadow shape of wood and glade, Eileen conducted Selwyn; and they heard the whirr of painted wood-ducks passing in obscurity, and the hymn of the four winds off Wonder Head; and they heard the herons, noisy in their heronry, and a young fox yapping on a moon-struck dune.

But Selwyn cared more for the sun and the infinite blue above, and the vast cloud-forms piled up in argent splendour behind a sea of amethyst.

"The darker, vaguer phases of beauty," he said to Eileen, smiling, "attract and fascinate those young in experience. Tragedy is always better appreciated and better rendered by those who have never lived it. The anatomy of sadness, the subtler fascination of life brooding in shadow, appeals most keenly to those who can study and reflect, then dismiss it all and return again to the brightness of existence which has not yet for them been tarnished."

He had never before, even by slightest implication, referred to his own experience with life. She was not perfectly certain that he did so now.

They were standing on one of the treeless hills—a riotous tangle of grasses and wild flowers—looking out to sea across Sky Pond. He had a rod; and as he stood he idly switched the gaily coloured flies backward and forward.

"My tastes," he said, still smiling, "incline me to the garishly sunlit side of this planet." And, to tease her and arouse her to combat: "I prefer a farandole to a nocturne; I'd rather have a painting than an etching; Mr. Whistler bores me with his monochromatic mud; I don't like dull colours, dull sounds, dull intellects; and anything called 'an arrangement' on canvas, or anything called 'a human document' or 'an appreciation' in literature, or anything 'precious' in art, or any author who 'weaves' instead of writes his stories—all these irritate me when they do not first bore me to the verge of anæsthesia."

He switched his trout-flies defiantly, hopeful of an indignant retort from her; but she only laughed and glanced at him, and shook her pretty head.

"There's just enough truth in what you say to make a dispute quite profitless. Besides, I don't feel like single combat; I'm too glad to have you here."

Standing there—fairly swimming—in the delicious upper-air currents, she looked blissfully across the rolling moors, while the sunlight drenched her and the salt wind winnowed the ruddy glory of her hair, and from the tangle of tender blossoming green things a perfume mounted, saturating her senses as she breathed it deeper in the happiness of desire fulfilled and content quite absolute.

"After all," she said, "what more is there than this? Earth and sea and sky and sun, and a friend to show them to. . . . Because, as I wrote you, the friend is quite necessary in the scheme of things—to round out the symmetry of it all. . . . I suppose you're dying to dangle those flies in Brier Water to see whether there are any trout there. Well, there are; Austin stocked it years ago, and he never fishes, so no doubt it's full of fish. . . . What is that black thing moving along the edge of the Golden Marsh?"

"A mink," he said, looking.

She seated herself cross-legged on the hill-top to watch the mink at her leisure. But the lithe furry creature took to the water, dived, and vanished, and she turned her attention to the landscape.

"Do you see that lighthouse far to the south?" she asked; "that is Frigate Light. West of it lies Surf Point, and the bay between is Surf Bay. That's where I nearly froze solid in my first ocean bath of the year. A little later we can bathe in that cove to the north—the Bay of Shoals. You see it, don't you?—there, lying tucked in between Wonder Head and the Hither Woods; but I forgot! Of course you've been here before; and you know all this; don't you?"

"Yes," he said quietly, "my brother and I came here as boys."

"Have you not been here since?"

"Once." He turned and looked down at the sea-battered wharf jutting into the Bay of Shoals. "Once, since I was a boy," he repeated; "but I came alone. The transports landed at that wharf after the Spanish war. The hospital camp was yonder. . . . My brother died there."

She lifted her clear eyes to his; he was staring at the outline of the Hither Woods fringing the ochre-tinted heights.

185

"There was no companion like him," he said; "there is no one to take his place. Still, time helps—in a measure."

But he looked out across the sea with a grief for ever new.

She, too, had been helped by time; she was very young when the distant and fabled seas took father and mother; and it was not entirely their memory, but more the wistful lack of ability to remember that left her so hopelessly alone.

Sharper his sorrow; but there was the comfort of recollection in it; and she looked at him and, for an instant, envied him his keener grief. Then leaning a little toward him where he reclined, the weight of his body propped up on one arm, she laid her hand across his hand half buried in the grass.

"It's only another tie between us," she said—"the memory of your dead and mine. . . . Will you tell me about him?"

And leaning there, eyes on the sea, and her smooth, young hand covering his, he told her of the youth who had died there in the first flush of manhood and achievement.

His voice, steady and grave, came to her through hushed intervals when the noise of the surf died out as the wind veered seaward. And she listened, heart intent, until he spoke no more; and the sea-wind rose again filling her ears with the ceaseless menace of the surf.

After a while he picked up his rod, and sat erect and cross-legged as she sat, and flicked the flies, absently, across the grass, aiming at wind-blown butterflies.

"All these changes!" he exclaimed with a sweep of the rod-butt toward Widgeon Bay. "When I was here as a boy there were no fine estates, no great houses, no country clubs, no game preserves—only a few fishermen's hovels along the Bay of Shoals, and Frigate Light yonder. . . . Then Austin built Silverside out of a much simpler, grand-paternal bungalow; then came Sanxon Orchil and erected Hitherwood House on the foundations of his maternal great-grandfather's cabin; and then the others came; the Minsters built gorgeous Brookminster—you can just make out their big summer palace—that white spot beyond Surf Point!—and then the Lawns came and built Southlawn; and, beyond, the Siowitha people arrived on scout, land-hungry and rich; and the tiny hamlet of Wyossett grew rapidly into the town it now is. Truly this island with its hundred miles of length has become but a formal garden of the wealthy. Alas! I knew it as a stretch of woods, dunes, and old-time villages where life had slumbered for two hundred years!"

He fell silent, but she nodded him to go on.

"Brooklyn was a quiet tree-shaded town," he continued thoughtfully, "unvexed by dreams of traffic; Flatbush an old Dutch village buried in the scented bloom of lilac, locust, and syringa, asleep under its ancient

186

gables, hip-roofs, and spreading trees. Bath, Utrecht, Canarsie, Gravesend were little more than cross-road taverns dreaming in the sun; and that vile and noise-cursed island beyond the Narrows was a stretch of unpolluted beauty in an untainted sea—nothing but whitest sand and dunes and fragrant bayberry and a blaze of wild flowers. Why"—and he turned impatiently to the girl beside him—"why, I have seen the wild geese settle in Sheepshead Bay, and the wild duck circling over it; and I am not very aged. Think of it! Think of what this was but a few years ago, and think of what 'progress' has done to lay it waste! What will it be to-morrow?"

"Oh—oh!" she protested, laughing; "I did not suppose you were that kind of a Jeremiah!"

"Well, I am. I see no progress in prostrate forests, in soft-coal smoke, in noise! I see nothing gained in trimming and cutting and ploughing and macadamising a heavenly wilderness into mincing little gardens for the rich." He was smiling at his own vehemence, but she knew that he was more than half serious.

She liked him so; she always denied and disputed when he became declamatory, though usually, in her heart, she agreed with him.

"Oh—oh!" she protested, shaking her head; "your philosophy is that of all reactionaries—emotional arguments which never can be justified. Why, if the labouring man delights in the harmless hurdy-gurdy and finds his pleasure mounted on a wooden horse, should you say that the island of his delight is 'vile'? All fulfilment of harmless happiness is progress, my poor friend—"

"But my harmless happiness lay in seeing the wild-fowl splashing where nothing splashes now except beer and the bathing rabble. If progress is happiness—where is mine? Gone with the curlew and the wild duck! Therefore, there is no progress. *Quod erat*, my illogical friend."

"But *your* happiness in such things was an exception—"

"Exceptions prove anything!"

"Yes—but—no, they don't, either! What nonsense you can talk when you try to. . . . As for me I'm going down to the Brier Water to look into it. If there are any trout there foolish enough to bite at those gaudy-feathered hooks I'll call you—"

"I'm going with you," he said, rising to his feet. She smilingly ignored his offered hands and sprang erect unaided.

The Brier Water, a cold, deep, leisurely stream, deserved its name. Rising from a small spring-pond almost at the foot of Silverside lawn, it wound away through tangles of bull-brier and wild-rose, under arches of weed and grass and clustered thickets of mint, north through one of the strange little forests where it became a thread edged with a duck-haunted bog, then emerging as a clear deep stream once more it curved sharply south, recurved north again, and flowed into Shell Pond which, in turn, had an outlet into the Sound a mile east of Wonder Head.

If anybody ever haunted it with hostile designs upon its fishy denizens, Austin at least never did. Belted kingfisher, heron, mink, and perhaps a furtive small boy with pole and sinker and barnyard worm—these were the only foes the trout might dread. As for a man and a fly-rod, they knew him not, nor was there much chance for casting a line, because the water everywhere flowed under weeds, arched thickets of brier and grass, and leafy branches criss-crossed above.

"This place is impossible," said Selwyn scornfully. "What is Austin about to let it all grow up and run wild—"

"You *said*," observed Eileen, "that you preferred an untrimmed wilderness; didn't you?"

He laughed and reeled in his line until only six inches of the gossamer leader remained free. From this dangled a single silver-bodied fly, glittering in the wind.

"There's a likely pool hidden under those briers," he said; "I'm going to poke the tip of my rod under—this way—Hah!" as a heavy splash sounded from depths unseen and the reel screamed as he struck.

Up and down, under banks and over shallows rushed the invisible fish; and Selwyn could do nothing for a while but let him go when he insisted, and check and recover when the fish permitted.

Eileen, a spray of green mint between her vivid lips, watched the performance with growing interest; but when at length a big, fat, struggling speckled trout was cautiously but successfully lifted out into the grass, she turned her back until the gallant fighter had departed this life under a merciful whack from a stick.

"That," she said faintly, "is the part I don't care for. . . . Is he out of all pain? . . . What? Didn't feel any? Oh, are you quite sure?"

"Eileen watched the performance with growing interest."

She walked over to him and looked down at the beautiful victim of craft.

"Oh, well," she sighed, "you are very clever, of course, and I suppose I'll eat him; but I wish he were alive again, down there in those cool, sweet depths."

"Killing frogs and insects and his smaller brother fish?"

"Did he do *that*?"

189

"No doubt of it. And if I hadn't landed him, a heron or a mink would have done it sooner or later. That's what a trout is for: to kill and be killed."

She smiled, then sighed. The taking of life and the giving of it were mysteries to her. She had never wittingly killed anything.

"Do you say that it doesn't hurt the trout?" she asked.

"There are no nerves in the jaw muscles of a trout—Hah!" as his rod twitched and swerved under water and his reel sang again.

And again she watched the performance, and once more turned her back.

"Let me try," she said, when the *coup-de-grâce* had been administered to a lusty, brilliant-tinted bulltrout. And, rod in hand, she bent breathless and intent over the bushes, cautiously thrusting the tip through a thicket of mint.

She lost two fish, then hooked a third—a small one; but when she lifted it gasping into the sunlight, she shivered and called to Selwyn:

"Unhook it and throw it back! I—I simply can't stand that!"

Splash! went the astonished trout; and she sighed her relief.

"There's no doubt about it," she said, "you and I certainly do belong to different species of the same genus; men and women *are* separate species. Do you deny it?"

"I should hate to lose you that way," he returned teasingly.

"Well, you can't avoid it. I gladly admit that woman is not too closely related to man. We don't like to kill things; it's an ingrained distaste, not merely a matter of ethical philosophy. You like to kill; and it's a trait common also to children and other predatory animals. Which fact," she added airily, "convinces me of woman's higher civilisation."

"It would convince me, too," he said, "if woman didn't eat the things that man kills for her."

"I know; isn't it horrid! Oh, dear, we're neither of us very high in the scale yet—particularly you."

"Well, I've advanced some since the good old days when a man went wooing with a club," he suggested.

"*You* may have. But, anyway, you don't go wooing. As for man collectively, he has not progressed so very far," she added demurely. "As an example, that dreadful Draymore man actually hurt my wrist."

Selwyn looked up quickly, a shade of frank annoyance on his face and a vision of the fat sybarite before his eyes. He turned again to his fishing, but his shrug was more of a shudder than appeared to be complimentary to Percy Draymore.

She had divined, somehow, that it annoyed Selwyn to know that men had importuned her. She had told him of her experience as innocently as she had told Nina, and with even less embarrassment. But that had been long ago; and now, without any specific reason, she was not certain that she had acted wisely, although it always amused her to see Selwyn's undisguised impatience whenever mention was made of such incidents.

So, to torment him, she said: "Of course it is somewhat exciting to be asked to marry people—rather agreeable than otherwise—"

"What!"

Waist deep in bay-bushes he turned toward her where she sat on the trunk of an oak which had fallen across the stream. Her arms balanced her body; her ankles were interlocked. She swung her slim russet-shod feet above the brook and looked at him with a touch of *gaminerie* new to her and to him.

"Of course it's amusing to be told you are the only woman in the world," she said, "particularly when a girl has a secret fear that men don't consider her quite grown up."

"You once said," he began impatiently, "that the idiotic importunities of those men annoyed you."

"Why do you call them idiotic?"—with pretence of hurt surprise. "A girl is honoured—"

"Oh, bosh!"

"Captain Selwyn!"

"I beg your pardon," he said sulkily; and fumbled with his reel.

She surveyed him, head a trifle on one side—the very incarnation of youthful malice in process of satisfying a desire for tormenting. Never before had she experienced that desire so keenly, so unreasoningly; never before had she found such a curious pleasure in punishing without cause. A perfectly inexplicable exhilaration possessed her—a gaiety quite reasonless, until every pulse in her seemed singing with laughter and quickening with the desire for his torment.

"When I pretended I was annoyed by what men said to me, I was only a yearling," she observed. "Now I'm a two-year, Captain Selwyn. . . . Who can tell what may happen in my second season?"

"You said that you were *not* the—the marrying sort," he insisted.

"Nonsense. All girls are. Once I sat in a high chair and wore a bib and banqueted on cambric-tea and prunes. I don't do it now; I've advanced. It's probably part of that progress which you are so opposed to."

He did not answer, but stood, head bent, looping on a new leader.

"All progress is admirable," she suggested.

No answer.

So, to goad him:

"There *are* men," she said dreamily, "who might hope for a kinder reception next winter—"

"Oh, no," he said coolly, "there are no such gentlemen. If there were you wouldn't say so."

"Yes, I would. And there are!"

"How many?" jeeringly, and now quite reassured.

"One!"

"You can't frighten me"—with a shade less confidence. "You wouldn't tell if there was."

"I'd tell *you.*"

"Me?"—with a sudden slump in his remaining stock of reassurance.

"Certainly. I tell you and Nina things of that sort. And when I have fully decided to marry I shall, of course, tell you both before I inform other people."

How the blood in her young veins was racing and singing with laughter! How thoroughly she was enjoying something to which she could give neither reason nor name! But how satisfying it all was—whatever it was that amused her in this man's uncertainty, and in the faint traces of an irritation as unreasoning as the source of it!

"Really, Captain Selwyn," she said, "you are not one of those old-fashioned literary landmarks who objects through several chapters to a girl's marrying—are you?"

"Yes," he said, "I am."

"You are quite serious?"

"Quite."

"You won't *let* me?"

"No, I won't."

"Why?"

"I want you myself," he said, smiling at last.

"That is flattering but horridly selfish. In other words you won't marry me and you won't let anybody else do it."

"That is the situation," he admitted, freeing his line and trying to catch the crinkled silvery snell of the new leader. It persistently avoided him; he lowered the rod toward Miss Erroll; she gingerly imprisoned the feathered fly between pink-tipped thumb and forefinger and looked questioningly at him.

"Am I to sit here holding this?" she inquired.

"Only a moment; I'll have to soak that leader. Is the water visible under that log you're sitting on?"

She nodded.

So he made his way through the brush toward her, mounted the log, and, seating himself beside her, legs dangling, thrust the rod tip and leader straight down into the stream below.

Glancing around at her he caught her eyes, bright with mischief.

"You're capable of anything to-day," he said. "Were you considering the advisability of starting me overboard?" And he nodded toward the water beneath their feet.

"But you say that you won't let me throw you overboard, Captain Selwyn!"

"I mean it, too," he returned.

"And I'm not to marry that nice young man?"—mockingly sweet. "No? What!—not anybody at all—ever and ever?"

"Me," he suggested, "if you're as thoroughly demoralised as that."

"Oh! Must a girl be pretty thoroughly demoralised to marry you?"

"I don't suppose she'd do it if she wasn't," he admitted, laughing.

She considered him, head on one side:

"You are ornamental, anyway," she concluded.

"Well, then," he said, lifting the leader from the water to inspect it, "will you have me?"

"Oh, but is there nothing to recommend you except your fatal beauty?"

"My moustache," he ventured; "it's considered very useful when I'm mentally perplexed."

193

"It's clipped too close; I have told you again and again that I don't care for it clipped like that. Your mind would be a perfect blank if you couldn't get hold of it."

"And to become imbecile," he said, "I've only to shave it."

She threw back her head and her clear laughter thrilled the silence. He laughed, too, and sat with elbows on his thighs, dabbling the crinkled leader to and fro in the pool below.

"So you won't have me?" he said.

"You haven't asked me—have you?"

"Well, I do now."

She mused, the smile resting lightly on lips and eyes.

"*Wouldn't* such a thing astonish Nina!" she said.

He did not answer; a slight colour tinged the new sunburn on his cheeks.

She laughed to herself, clasped her hands, crossed her slender feet, and bent her eyes on the pool below.

"Marriage," she said, pursuing her thoughts aloud, "is curiously unnecessary to happiness. Take our pleasure in each other, for example. It has, from the beginning, been perfectly free from silliness and sentiment."

"Naturally," he said. "I'm old enough to be safe."

"You are not!" she retorted. "What a ridiculous thing to say!"

"Well, then," he said, "I'm dreadfully unsafe, but yet you've managed to escape. Is that it?"

"Perhaps. You *are* attractive to women! I've heard that often enough to be convinced. Why, even I can see what attracts them"—she turned to look at him—"the way your head and shoulders set—and—well, the—rest. . . . It's rather superior of me to have escaped sentiment, don't you think so?"

"Indeed I do. Few—few escape where many meet to worship at my frisky feet, and this I say without conceit is due to my mustachios. Tangled in those like web-tied flies, imprisoned hearts complain in sighs—in fact, the situation vies with moments in Boccaccio."

Her running comment was her laughter, ringing deliciously amid the trees until a wild bird, restlessly attentive, ventured a long, sweet response from the tangled green above them.

After their laughter the soberness of reaction left them silent for a while. The wild bird sang and sang, dropping fearlessly nearer from branch to branch, until in his melody she found the key to her dreamy thoughts.

"Because," she said, "you are so unconscious of your own value, I like you best, I think. I never before quite realised just what it was in you."

"My value," he said, "is what you care to make it."

"Then nobody can afford to take you away from me, Captain Selwyn."

He flushed with pleasure: "That is the prettiest thing a woman ever admitted to a man," he said.

"You have said nicer things to me. That is your reward. I wonder if you remember any of the nice things you say to me? Oh, don't look so hurt and astonished—because I don't believe you do. . . . Isn't it jolly to sit here and let life drift past us? Out there in the world"—she nodded backward toward the open—"out yonder all that 'progress' is whirling around the world, and here we sit—just you and I—quite happily, swinging our feet in perfect content and talking nonsense. . . . What more is there after all than a companionship that admits both sense and nonsense?"

She laughed, turning her chin on her shoulder to glance at him; and when the laugh had died out she still sat lightly poised, chin nestling in the hollow of her shoulder, considering him out of friendly beautiful eyes in which no mockery remained.

"What more is there than our confidence in each other and our content?" she said.

And, as he did not respond: "I wonder if you realise how perfectly lovely you have been to me since you have come into my life? Do you? Do you remember the first day—the very first—how I sent word to you that I wished you to see my first real dinner gown? Smile if you wish—Ah, but you don't, you *don't* understand, my poor friend, how much you became to me in that little interview. . . . Men's kindness is a strange thing; they may try and try, and a girl may know they are trying and, in her turn, try to be grateful. But it is all effort on both sides. Then—with a word— an impulse born of chance or instinct—a man may say and do that which a woman can never forget—and would not if she could."

"Have I done—that?"

"Yes. Didn't you understand? Do you suppose any other man in the world could have what you have had of me—of my real self? Do you suppose for one instant that any other man than you could ever obtain from me the confidence I offer you unasked? Do I not tell you everything that enters my head and heart? Do you not know that I care for you more than for anybody alive?"

"Gerald—"

She looked him straight in the eyes; her breath caught, but she steadied her voice:

"I've got to be truthful," she said; "I care for you more than for Gerald."

"And I for you more than anybody living," he said.

"Is it true?"

"It is the truth, Eileen."

"You—you make me very happy, Captain Selwyn."

"But—did you not know it before I told you?"

"I—y-yes; I hoped so." In the exultant reaction from the delicious tension of avowal she laughed lightly, not knowing why.

"The pleasure in it," she said, "is the certainty that I am capable of making you happy. You have no idea how I desire to do it. I've wanted to ever since I knew you—I've wanted to be capable of doing it. And you tell me that I do; and I am utterly and foolishly happy." The quick mischievous sparkle of *gaminerie* flashed up, transforming her for an instant—"Ah, yes; and I can make you unhappy, too, it seems, by talking of marriage! That, too, is something—a delightful power—but"—the malice dying to a spark in her brilliant eyes—"I shall not torment you, Captain Selwyn. Will it make you happier if I say, 'No; I shall never marry as long as I have you'? Will it really? Then I say it; never, never will I marry as long as I have your confidence and friendship. . . . But I want it *all!*—every bit, please. And if ever there is another woman—if ever you fall in love!—crack!—away I go"—she snapped her white fingers—"like that!" she added, "only quicker! Well, then! Be very, very careful, my friend! . . . I wish there were some place here where I could curl up indefinitely and listen to your views on life. You brought a book to read, didn't you?"

He gave her a funny embarrassed glance: "Yes; I brought a sort of a book."

"Then I'm all ready to be read to, thank you. . . . Please steady me while I try to stand up on this log—one hand will do—"

Scarcely in contact with him she crossed the log, sprang blithely to the ground, and, lifting the hem of her summer gown an inch or two, picked her way toward the bank above.

"We can see Nina when she signals us from the lawn to come to luncheon," she said, gazing out across the upland toward the silvery tinted hillside where Silverside stood, every pane glittering with the white eastern sunlight.

In the dry, sweet grass she found a place for a nest, and settled into it, head prone on a heap of scented bay leaves, elbows skyward, and fingers linked across her chin. One foot was hidden, the knee, doubled, making a tent of her white skirt, from an edge of which a russet shoe projected, revealing the contour of a slim ankle.

"What book did you bring?" she asked dreamily.

He turned red: "It's—it's just a chapter from a little book I'm trying to write—a—a sort of suggestion for the establishment of native regiments in the Philippines. I thought, perhaps, you might not mind listening—"

Her delighted surprise and quick cordiality quite overwhelmed him, so, sitting flat on the grass, hat off and the hill wind furrowing his bright crisp hair, he began, naïvely, like a schoolboy; and Eileen lay watching him, touched and amused at his eager interest in reading aloud to her this mass of co-ordinated fact and detail.

There was, in her, one quality to which he had never appealed in vain— her loyalty. Confident of that, and of her intelligence, he wasted no words in preliminary explanation, but began at once his argument in favour of a native military establishment erected on the general lines of the British organisation in India.

He wrote simply and without self-consciousness; loyalty aroused her interest, intelligence sustained it; and when the end came, it came too quickly for her, and she said so frankly, which delighted him.

At her invitation he outlined for her the succeeding chapters with terse military accuracy; and what she liked best and best understood was avoidance of that false modesty which condescends, turning technicality into pabulum.

Lying there in the fragrant verdure, blue eyes skyward or slanting sideways to watch his face, she listened, answered, questioned, or responded by turns; until their voices grew lazy and the light reaction from things serious awakened the gaiety always latent when they were together.

"Proceed," she smiled; "*Arma virumque*—a noble theme, Captain Selwyn. Sing on!"

He shook his head, quoting from "The Dedication":

"Arms   and   the   Man!
A   noble   theme   I   ween!
Alas!   I   cannot   sing   of   these,   Eileen;
Only   of   maids   and   men   and   meadow-grass,
Of   sea   and   tree   and   woodlands   where   I   pass—
Nothing but these I know, Eileen—alas!

Clear   eyes,   that   lifted   up   to   me
Free   heart   and   soul   of   vanity;
Blue   eyes,   that   speak   so   wistfully—
Nothing but these I know, alas!"

She laughed her acknowledgment, and lying there, face to the sky, began to sing to herself, under her breath, fragments of that ancient war-song:

"Le   bon   Roi   Dagobert
Avait   un   grand   sabre   de   fer;
Le   grand   Saint   Éloi
Lui   dit: 'O   mon   Roi
Vôtre   Majesté
Pourrait   se   blesser!'
'C'est   vrai,'   lui   dit   le   Roi,
'Qu'on me donne un sabre de bois!'"

"In that verse," observed Selwyn, smiling, "lies the true key to the millennium—international disarmament and moral suasion."

"Nonsense," she said lazily; "the millennium will arrive when the false balance between man and woman is properly adjusted—not before. And that means universal education. . . . Did you ever hear that old, old song, written two centuries ago—the 'Education of Phyllis'? No? Listen then and be ashamed."

And lying there, the back of one hand above her eyes, she sang in a sweet, childish, mocking voice, tremulous with hidden laughter, the song of Phyllis the shepherdess and Sylvandre the shepherd—how Phyllis, more avaricious than sentimental, made Sylvandre pay her thirty sheep for one kiss; how, next day, the price shifted to one sheep for thirty kisses; and then the dreadful demoralisation of Phyllis:

"Le   lendemain,   Philis,   plus   tendre
Fut   trop   heureuse   de   lui   rendre
Trente moutons pour un baiser!

Le   lendemain,   Philis,   peu   sage,
Aurait   donné   moutons   et   chien
Pour   un   baiser   que   le   volage
À Lisette donnait pour rien!"

"And there we are," said Eileen, sitting up abruptly and levelling the pink-tipped finger of accusation at him—"*there*, if you please, lies the woe of the world—not in the armaments of nations! That old French poet understood in half a second more than your Hague tribunal could comprehend in its first Cathayan cycle! There lies the hope of your millennium—in the higher education of the modern Phyllis."

"And the up-to-date Sylvandre," added Selwyn.

"He knows too much already," she retorted, delicate nose in the air. . . . "Hark! Ear to the ground! My atavistic and wilder instincts warn me that somebody is coming!"

"Boots and Drina," said Selwyn; and he hailed them as they came into view above. Then he sprang to his feet, calling out: "And Gerald, too! Hello, old fellow! This is perfectly fine! When did you arrive?"

"Oh, Gerald!" cried Eileen, both hands outstretched—"it's splendid of you to come! Dear fellow! have you seen Nina and Austin? And were they not delighted? And you've come to stay, haven't you? There, I won't begin to urge you. . . . Look, Gerald—look, Boots—and Drina, too—only look at those beautiful big plump trout in Captain Selwyn's creel!"

"Oh, I say!" exclaimed Gerald, "you didn't take those in that little brook—did you, Philip? Well, wouldn't that snare you! I'm coming down here after luncheon; I sure am."

"You will, too, won't you?" asked Drina, jealous lest Boots, her idol, miss his due share of piscatorial glory. "If you'll wait until I finish my French I'll come with you."

"Of course I will," said Lansing reproachfully; "you don't suppose there's any fun anywhere for me without you, do you?"

"No," said Drina simply, "I don't."

"Another Phyllis in embryo," murmured Eileen to Selwyn. "Alas! for education!"

Selwyn laughed and turned to Gerald. "I hunted high and low for you before I came to Silverside. You found my note?"

"Yes; I—I'll explain later," said the boy, colouring. "Come ahead, Eily; Boots and I will take you on at tennis—and Philip, too. We've an hour or so before luncheon. Is it a go?"

"Certainly," replied his sister, unaware of Selwyn's proficiency, but loyal even in doubt. And the five, walking abreast, moved off across the uplands toward the green lawns of Silverside, where, under a gay lawn parasol, Nina sat, a "Nature book" in hand, the centre of an attentive gathering composed of dogs, children, and the cat, Kit-Ki, blinking her topaz-tinted eyes in the sunshine.

The young mother looked up happily as the quintet came strolling across the lawn: "Please don't wander away again before luncheon," she said; "Gerald, I suppose you are starved, but you've only an hour to wait—Oh, Phil! what wonderful trout! Children, kindly arise and admire the surpassing skill of your frivolous uncle!" And, as the children and dogs came crowding around the opened fish-basket she said to her brother in a low, contented voice: "Gerald has quite made it up with Austin, dear; I think we have to thank you, haven't we?"

"Has he really squared matters with Austin? That's good—that's fine! Oh, no, I had nothing to do with it—practically nothing. The boy is sound at the core—that's what did it." And to Gerald, who was hailing him from the veranda, "Yes, I've plenty of tennis-shoes. Help yourself, old chap."

Eileen had gone to her room to don a shorter skirt and rubber-soled shoes; Lansing followed her example; and Selwyn, entering his own room, found Gerald trying on a pair of white foot-gear.

The boy looked up, smiled, and, crossing one knee, began to tie the laces:

"I told Austin that I meant to slow down," he said. "We're on terms again. He was fairly decent."

"Good business!" commented Selwyn vigorously.

"And I'm cutting out cards and cocktails," continued the boy, eager as a little lad who tells how good he has been all day—"I made it plain to the fellows that there was nothing in it for me. And, Philip, I'm boning down like thunder at the office—I'm horribly in debt and I'm hustling to pay up and make a clean start. You," he added, colouring, "will come first—"

"At your convenience," said Selwyn, smiling.

"Not at all! Yours is the first account to be squared; then Neergard—"

"Do you owe *him*, Gerald?"

"Do I? Oh, Lord! But he's a patient soul—really, Philip, I wish you didn't dislike him so thoroughly, because he's good company and besides that he's a very able man. . . . Well, we won't talk about him, then. Come on; I'll lick the very life out of you over the net!"

A few moments later the white balls were flying over the white net, and active white-flannelled figures were moving swiftly over the velvet turf.

Drina, aloft on the umpire's perch, calmly scored and decided each point impartially, though her little heart was beating fast in desire for her idol's supremacy; and it was all her official composure could endure to see how Eileen at the net beat down his defence, driving him with her volleys to the service line.

Selwyn's game proved to be steady, old-fashioned, but logical; Eileen, sleeves at her elbows, red-gold hair in splendid disorder, carried the game through Boots straight at her brother—and the contest was really a brilliant duel between them, Lansing and Selwyn assisting when a rare chance came their way. The pace was too fast for them, however; they were in a different class and they knew it; and after two terrific sets had gone against Gerald and Boots, the latter, signalling Selwyn, dropped out and climbed up beside Drina to watch a furious single between Eileen and Gerald.

"Oh, Boots, Boots!" said Drina, "why *didn't* you stay forward and kill her drives and make her lob? I just know you could do it if you had only thought to play forward! What on earth was the matter?"

"Age," said Mr. Lansing serenely—"decrepitude, Drina. I am a Was, sweetheart, but Eileen still remains an Is."

"I won't let you say it! You are *not* a Was!" said the child fiercely. "After luncheon you can take me on for practice. Then you can just give it to her!"

"It would gratify me to hand a few swift ones to somebody," he said. "Look at that demon girl, yonder! She's hammering Gerald to the service line! Oh, my, oh, me! I'm only fit for hat-ball with Billy or cat's-cradle with Kit-Ki. Drina, do you realise that I am nearly thirty?"

"Pooh! I'm past thirteen. In five years I'll be eighteen. I expect to marry you at eighteen. You promised."

"Sure thing," admitted Boots; "I've bought the house, you know."

"I know it," said the child gravely.

Boots looked down at her; she smiled and laid her head, with its clustering curls, against his shoulder, watching the game below with the quiet composure of possession.

Their relations, hers and Lansing's, afforded infinite amusement to the Gerards. It had been a desperate case from the very first; and the child took it so seriously, and considered her claim on Boots so absolute, that neither that young man nor anybody else dared make a jest of the affair within her hearing.

From a dimple-kneed, despotic, strenuous youngster, ruling the nursery with a small hand of iron, in half a year Drina had grown into a rather slim, long-legged, coolly active child; and though her hair had not been put up, her skirts had been lowered, and shoes and stockings substituted for half-hose and sandals.

Weighted with this new dignity she had put away dolls, officially. Unofficially she still dressed, caressed, forgave, or spanked Rosalinda and Beatrice—but she excluded the younger children from the nursery when she did it.

201

However, the inborn necessity for mimicry and romance remained; and she satisfied it by writing stories—marvellous ones—which she read to Boots. Otherwise she was the same active, sociable, wholesome, intelligent child, charmingly casual and inconsistent; and the list of her youthful admirers at dancing-school and parties required the alphabetical classification of Mr. Lansing.

But Boots was her own particular possession; he was her chattel, her thing; and he and other people knew that it was no light affair to meddle with the personal property of Drina Gerard.

Her curly head resting against his arm, she was now planning his future movements for the day:

"You may do what you please while I'm having French," she said graciously; "after that we will go fishing in Brier Water; then I'll come home to practice, while you sit on the veranda and listen; then I'll take you on at tennis, and by that time the horses will be brought around and we'll ride to the Falcon. You won't forget any of this, will you? Come on; Eileen and Gerald have finished and there's Dawson to announce luncheon!" And to Gerald, as she climbed down to the ground: "Oh, what a muff! to let Eileen beat you six—five, six—three! . . . Where's my hat? . . . Oh, the dogs have got it and are tearing it to rags!"

And she dashed in among the dogs, slapping right and left, while a facetious dachshund seized the tattered bit of lace and muslin and fled at top speed.

"That is pleasant," observed Nina; "it's her best hat, too—worn to-day in your honour, Boots. . . . Children! Hands and faces! There is Bridget waiting! Come, Phil; there's no law against talking at table, and there's no use trying to run an establishment if you make a mockery of the kitchen."

Eileen, one bare arm around her brother's shoulders, strolled houseward across the lawn, switching the shaven sod with her tennis-bat.

"What are you doing this afternoon?" she said to Selwyn. "Gerald"—she touched her brother's smooth cheek—"means to fish; Boots and Drina are keen on it, too; and Nina is driving to Wyossett with the children."

"And you?" he asked, smiling.

"Whatever you wish"—confident that he wanted her, whatever he had on hand.

"I ought to walk over to Storm Head," he said, "and get things straightened out."

"Your laboratory?" asked Gerald. "Austin told me when I saw him in town that you were going to have the cottage on Storm Head to make powder in."

"Only in minute quantities, Gerald," explained Selwyn; "I just want to try a few things. . . . And if they turn out all right, what do you say to taking a look in—if Austin approves?"

"Oh, please, Gerald," whispered his sister.

"Do you really believe there is anything in it?" asked the boy. "Because, if you are sure—"

"There certainly is if I can prove that my powder is able to resist heat, cold, and moisture. The Lawn people stand ready to talk matters over as soon as I am satisfied. . . . There's plenty of time—but keep the suggestion in the back of your head, Gerald."

The boy smiled, nodded importantly, and went off to remove the stains of tennis from his person; and Eileen went, too, turning around to look back at Selwyn:

"Thank you for asking Gerald! I'm sure he will love to go into anything you think safe."

"Will you join us, too?" he called back, smilingly—"we may need capital!"

"I'll remember that!" she said; and, turning once more as she reached the landing: "Good-bye—until luncheon!" And touched her lips with the tips of her fingers, flinging him a gay salute.

In parting and meeting—even after the briefest of intervals—it was always the same with her; always she had for him some informal hint of the formality of parting; always some recognition of their meeting—in the light touching of hands as though the symbol of ceremony, at least, was due to him, to herself, and to the occasion.

Luncheon at Silverside was anything but a function—with the children at table and the dogs in a semicircle, and the nurses tying bibs and admonishing the restless or belligerent, and the wide French windows open, and the sea wind lifting the curtains and stirring the cluster of wild flowers in the centre of the table.

Kit-Ki's voice was gently raised at intervals; at intervals some grinning puppy, unable to longer endure the nourishing odours, lost self-control and yapped, then lowered his head, momentarily overcome with mortification.

All the children talked continuously, unlimited conversation being permitted until it led to hostilities or puppy-play. The elders conducted such social intercourse as was possible under the conditions, but luncheon was the children's hour at Silverside.

Nina and Eileen talked garden talk—they both were quite mad about their fruit-trees and flower-beds; Selwyn, Gerald, and Boots discussed stables, golf links, and finally the new business which Selwyn hoped to develop.

Afterward, when the children had been excused, and Drina had pulled her chair close to Lansing's to listen—and after that, on the veranda, when the men sat smoking and Drina was talking French, and Nina and Eileen had gone off with baskets, trowels, and pruning-shears—Selwyn still continued in conference with Boots and Gerald; and it was plain that his concise, modest explanation of what he had accomplished in his experiments with Chaosite seriously impressed the other men.

Boots frankly admitted it: "Besides," he said, "if the Lawn people are so anxious for you to give them first say in the matter I don't see why we shouldn't have faith in it—enough, I mean, to be good to ourselves by offering to be good to you, Phil."

"Wait until Austin comes down—and until I've tried one or two new ideas," said Selwyn. "Nothing on earth would finish me quicker than to get anybody who trusted me into a worthless thing."

"It's plain," observed Boots, "that although you may have been an army captain you're no captain of industry—you're not even a non-com.!"

Selwyn laughed: "Do you really believe that ordinary decency is uncommon?"

"Look at Long Island," returned Boots. "Where does the boom of worthless acreage and paper cities land investors when it explodes?"

Gerald had flushed up at the turn in the conversation; and Selwyn steered Lansing into other and safer channels until Gerald went away to find a rod.

And, as Drina had finished her French lesson, she and Lansing presently departed, brandishing fishing-rods adorned with the gaudiest of flies.

The house and garden at Silverside seemed to be logical parts of a landscape, which included uplands, headlands, sky, and water—a silvery harmonious ensemble, where the artificial portion was neither officiously intrusive nor, on the other hand, meagre and insignificant.

The house, a long two-storied affair with white shutters and pillared veranda, was built of gray stone; the garden was walled with it—a precaution against no rougher intruder than the wind, which would have whipped unsheltered flowers and fruit-trees into ribbons.

Walks of hardened earth, to which green mould clung in patches, wound through the grounds and threaded the three little groves of oak, chestnut, and locust, in the centres of which, set in circular lawns, were the three axes of interest—the stone-edged fish-pond, the spouting fountain, and the ancient ship's figurehead—a wind-worn, sea-battered mermaid cuddling a tiny, finny sea-child between breast and lips.

Whoever the unknown wood-carver had been he had been an artist, too, and a good one; and when the big China trader, the *First Born*, went to pieces off Frigate Light, fifty years ago, this figurehead had been cast up from the sea.

Wandering into the garden, following the first path at random, Selwyn chanced upon it, and stood, pipe in his mouth, hands in his pockets, surprised and charmed.

Plunkitt, the head gardener, came along, trundling a mowing-machine.

"Ain't it kind 'er nice," he said, lingering. "When I pass here moonlight nights, it seems like that baby was a-smilin' right up into his mamma's face, an' that there fish-tailed girl was laughin' back at him. Come here some night when there's a moon, Cap'in Selwyn."

Selwyn stood for a while listening to the musical click of the machine, watching the green shower flying into the sunshine, and enjoying the raw perfume of juicy, new-cut grass; then he wandered on in quest of Miss Erroll.

Tulips, narcissus, hyacinths, and other bulbs were entirely out of bloom, but the earlier herbaceous borders had come into flower, and he passed through masses of pink and ivory-tinted peonies—huge, heavy, double blossoms, fragrant and delicate as roses. Patches of late iris still lifted crested heads above pale sword-bladed leaves; sheets of golden pansies gilded spaces steeped in warm transparent shade, but larkspur and early rocket were as yet only scarcely budded promises; the phlox-beds but green carpets; and zinnia, calendula, poppy, and coreopsis were symphonies in shades of green against the dropping pink of bleeding-hearts or the nascent azure of flax and spiderwort.

In the rose garden, and along that section of the wall included in it, the rich, dry, porous soil glimmered like gold under the sun; and here Selwyn discovered Nina and Eileen busily solicitous over the tender shoots of favourite bushes. A few long-stemmed early rosebuds lay in their baskets; Selwyn drew one through his buttonhole and sat down on a wheelbarrow, amiably disposed to look on and let the others work.

"Not much!" said Nina. "You can start in and 'pinch back' this prairie climber—do you hear, Phil? I won't let you dawdle around and yawn while I'm pricking my fingers every instant! Make him move, Eileen."

Eileen came over to him, fingers doubled into her palm and small thumb extended.

"Thorns and prickles, please," she said; and he took her hand in his and proceeded to extract them while she looked down at her almost invisible wounds, tenderly amused at his fear of hurting her.

"Do you know," she said, "that people are beginning to open their houses yonder?" She nodded toward the west: "The Minsters are on the way to Brookminster, the Orchils have already arrived at Hitherwood House, and the coachmen and horses were housed at Southlawn last night. I rather dread the dinners and country formality that always interfere with the jolly times we have; but it will be rather good fun at the bathing-beach. . . . Do you swim well? But of course you do."

"Pretty well; do you?"

"I'm a fish. Gladys Orchil and I would never leave the surf if they didn't literally drag us home. . . . You know Gladys Orchil? . . . She's very nice; so is Sheila Minster; you'll like her better in the country than you do in town. Kathleen Lawn is nice, too. Alas! I see many a morning where Drina and I twirl our respective thumbs while you and Boots are off with a gayer set. . . . Oh, don't interrupt! No mortal man is proof against Sheila and Gladys and Kathleen—and you're not a demi-god—are you? . . . Thank you for your surgery upon my thumb—" She naïvely placed the tip of it between her lips and looked at him, standing there like a schoolgirl in her fresh gown, burnished hair loosened and curling in riotous beauty across cheeks and ears.

He had seated himself on the wheelbarrow again; she stood looking down at him, hands now bracketed on her narrow hips—so close that the fresh fragrance of her grew faintly perceptible—a delicate atmosphere of youth mingling with the perfume of the young garden.

Nina, basket on her arm, snipping away with her garden shears, glanced over her shoulder—and went on, snipping. They did not notice how far away her agricultural ardour led her—did not notice when she stood a moment at the gate looking back at them, or when she passed out, pretty head bent thoughtfully, the shears swinging loose at her girdle.

The prairie rosebuds in Eileen's basket exhaled their wild, sweet odour; and Selwyn, breathing it, removed his hat like one who faces a cooling breeze, and looked up at the young girl standing before him as though she were the source of all things sweet and freshening in this opening of the youngest year of his life.

She said, smiling absently at his question: "Certainly one can grow younger; and you have done it in a day, here with me."

She looked down at his hair; it was bright and inclined to wave a little, but whether the lighter colour at the temples was really silvered or only a paler tint she was not sure.

"You are very like a boy, sometimes," she said—"as young as Gerald, I often think—especially when your hat is off. You always look so perfectly groomed: I wonder—I wonder what you would look like if your hair were rumpled?"

"Try it," he suggested lazily.

"I? I don't think I dare—" She raised her hand, hesitated, the gay daring in her eyes deepening to audacity. "Shall I?"

"Why not?"

"T-touch your hair?—rumple it?—as I would Gerald's! . . . I'm tempted to—only—only—"

"What?"

"I don't know; I couldn't. I—it was only the temptation of a second—" She laughed uncertainly. The suggestion of the intimacy tinted her cheeks with its reaction; she took a short step backward; instinct, blindly stirring, sobered her; and as the smile faded from eye and lip, his face changed, too. And far, very far away in the silent cells of his heart a distant pulse awoke.

She turned to her roses again, moving at random among the bushes, disciplining with middle-finger and thumb a translucent, amber-tinted shoot here and there. And when the silence had lasted too long, she broke it without turning toward him:

"After all, if it were left to me, I had rather be merciful to these soft little buds and sprays, and let the sun and the showers take charge. A whole cluster of blossoms left free to grow as Fate fashions them!—Why not? It is certainly very officious of me to strip a stem of its hopes just for the sake of one pampered blossom. . . . Non-interference is a safe creed, isn't it?"

But she continued moving along among the bushes, pinching back here, snipping, trimming, clipping there; and after a while she had wandered quite beyond speaking distance; and, at leisurely intervals she straightened up and turned to look back across the roses at him— quiet, unsmiling gaze in exchange for his unchanging eyes, which never left her.

She was at the farther edge of the rose garden now where a boy knelt, weeding; and Selwyn saw her speak to him and give him her basket and shears; and saw the boy start away toward the house, leaving her leaning idly above the sun-dial, elbows on the weather-beaten stone, studying the carved figures of the dial. And every line and contour and curve of her figure—even the lowered head, now resting between both hands—summoned him.

She heard his step, but did not move; and when he leaned above the dial, resting on his elbows, beside her, she laid her finger on the shadow of the dial.

"Time," she said, "is trying to frighten me. It pretends to be nearly five o'clock; do you believe it?"

"Time is running very fast with me," he said.

207

"With me, too; I don't wish it to; I don't care for third speed forward all the time."

He was bending closer above the stone dial, striving to decipher the inscription on it:

"Under   blue   skies
My   shadow   lies.
Under   gray   skies
My   shadow   dies.

"If   over   me
Two   Lovers   leaning
Would   solve   my   Mystery
And   read   my   Meaning,
—Or   clear,   or   overcast   the   Skies—
The   Answer   always   lies   within   their   Eyes.
Look   long!   Look   long!   For   there,   and   there   alone
Time solves the Riddle graven on this Stone!"

Elbows almost touching they leaned at ease, idly reading the almost obliterated lines engraved there.

"I never understood it," she observed, lightly scornful. "What occult meaning has a sun-dial for the spooney? *I'm* sure I don't want to read riddles in a strange gentleman's optics."

"The verses," he explained, "are evidently addressed to the spooney, so why should you resent them?"

"I don't. . . . I can be spoons, too, for that matter; I mean I could once."

"But you're past spooning now," he concluded.

"Am I? I rather resent your saying it—your calmly excluding me from anything I might choose to do," she said. "If I cared—if I chose—if I really wanted to—"

"You could still spoon? Impossible! At your age? Nonsense!"

"It isn't at all impossible. Wait until there's a moon, and a canoe, and a nice boy who is young enough to be frightened easily!"

"And I," he retorted, "am too old to be frightened; so there's no moon, no canoe, no pretty girl, no spooning for me. Is that it, Eileen?"

"Oh, Gladys and Sheila will attend to you, Captain Selwyn."

"Why Gladys Orchil? Why Sheila Minster? And why *not*Eileen Erroll?"

"Spoon? With *you!*"

"You are quite right," he said, smiling; "it would be poor sport."

208

There had been no change in his amused eyes, in his voice; yet, sensitive to the imperceptible, the girl looked up quickly. He laughed and straightened up; and presently his eyes grew absent and his sunburned hand sought his moustache.

"Have you misunderstood me?" she asked in a low voice.

"How, child?"

"I don't know. . . . Shall we walk a little?"

When they came to the stone fish-pond she seated herself for a moment on a marble bench, then, curiously restless, rose again; and again they moved forward at hazard, past the spouting fountain, which was a driven well, out of which a crystal column of water rose, geyser-like, dazzling in the westering sun rays.

"Nina tells me that this water rises in the Connecticut hills," he said, "and flows as a subterranean sheet under the Sound, spouting up here on Long Island when you drive a well."

She looked at the column of flashing water, nodding silent assent.

They moved on, the girl curiously reserved, non-communicative, head slightly lowered; the man vague-eyed, thoughtful, pacing slowly at her side. Behind them their long shadows trailed across the brilliant grass.

Traversing the grove which encircled the newly clipped lawn, now fragrant with sun-crisped grass-tips left in the wake of the mower, he glanced up at the pretty mermaid mother cuddling her tiny offspring against her throat. Across her face a bar of pink sunlight fell, making its contour exquisite.

"Plunkitt tells me that they really laugh at each other in the moonlight," he said.

She glanced up; then away from him:

"You seem to be enamoured of the moonlight," she said.

"I like to prowl in it."

"Alone?"

"Sometimes."

"And—at other times?"

He laughed: "Oh, I'm past that, as you reminded me a moment ago."

"Then you *did* misunderstand me!"

"Why, no—"

"Yes, you did! But I supposed you knew."

209

"Knew what, Eileen?" "What I meant."

"You meant that I am *hors de concours.*"

"I didn't!"

"But I am, child. I was, long ago."

She looked up: "Do you really think that, Captain Selwyn? If you do—I am glad."

He laughed outright. "You are glad that I'm safely past the spooning age?" he inquired, moving forward.

She halted: "Yes. Because I'm quite sure of you if you are; I mean that I can always keep you for myself. Can't I?"

She was smiling and her eyes were clear and fearless, but there was a wild-rose tint on her cheeks which deepened a little as he turned short in his tracks, gazing straight at her.

"You wish to keep me—for yourself?" he repeated, laughing.

"Yes, Captain Selwyn."

"Until you marry. Is that it, Eileen?"

"Yes, until I marry."

"And then we'll let each other go; is that it?"

"Yes. But I think I told you that I would never marry. Didn't I?"

"Oh! Then ours is to be a lifelong and anti-sentimental contract!"

"Yes, unless *you* marry."

"I promise not to," he said, "unless you do."

"I promise not to," she said gaily, "unless you do."

"There remains," he observed, "but one way for you and I ever to marry anybody. And as I'm *hors de concours*, even that hope is ended."

She flushed; her lips parted, but she checked what she had meant to say, and they walked forward together in silence for a while until she had made up her mind what to say and how to express it:

"Captain Selwyn, there are two things that you do which seem to me unfair. You still have, at times, that far-away, absent expression which excludes me; and when I venture to break the silence, you have a way of answering, 'Yes, child,' and 'No, child'—as though you were inattentive, and I had not yet become an adult. *That* is my first complaint! . . . *What* are you laughing at? It is true; and it confuses and hurts me; because I *know* I am intelligent enough and old enough to—to be treated as a woman!—a woman attractive enough to be reckoned with! But I never seem to be wholly so to you."

The laugh died out as she ended; for a moment they stood there, confronting one another.

"Do you imagine," he said in a low voice, "that I do not know all that?"

"I don't know whether you do. For all your friendship—for all your liking and your kindness to me—somehow—I—I don't seem to stand with you as other women do; I don't seem to stand their chances."

"What chances?"

"The—the consideration; you don't call any other woman 'child,' do you? You don't constantly remind other women of the difference in your ages, do you? You don't *feel* with other women that you are—as you please to call it—*hors de concours*—out of the running. And somehow, with me, it humiliates. Because even if I—if I am the sort of a girl who never means to marry, you—your attitude seems to take away the possibility of my changing my mind; it dictates to me, giving me no choice, no liberty, no personal freedom in the matter. . . . It's as though you considered me somehow utterly out of the question—radically unthinkable as a woman. And you assume to take for granted that I also regard you as— as *hors de concours*. . . . Those are my grievances, Captain Selwyn. . . . And I *don't* regard you so. And I—and it troubles me to be excluded—to be found wanting, inadequate in anything that a woman should be. I know that you and I have no desire to marry each other—but—but please don't make the reason for it either your age or my physical immaturity or intellectual inexperience."

Another of those weather-stained seats of Georgia marble stood embedded under the trees near where she had halted; and she seated herself, outwardly composed, and inwardly a little frightened at what she had said.

As for Selwyn, he remained where he had been standing on the lawn's velvet edge; and, raising her eyes again, her heart misgave her that she had wantonly strained a friendship which had been all but perfect; and now he was moving across the path toward her—a curious look in his face which she could not interpret. She looked up as he approached and stretched out her hand:

"Forgive me, Captain Selwyn," she said. "I *am* a child—a spoiled one; and I have proved it to you. Will you sit here beside me and tell me very gently what a fool I am to risk straining the friendship dearest to me in the whole world? And will you fix my penance?"

"You have fixed it yourself," he said.

"How?"

"By the challenge of your womanhood."

"I did not challenge—"

"No; you defended. You are right. The girl I cared for—the girl who was there with me on Brier Water—so many, many centuries ago—the girl who, years ago, leaned there beside me on the sun-dial—has become a memory."

"What do you mean?" she asked faintly.

"Shall I tell you?"

"Yes."

"You will not be unhappy if I tell you?"

"N-no."

"Have you any idea what I am going to say, Eileen?"

She looked up quickly, frightened at the tremor in his voice:

"Don't—don't say it, Captain Selwyn!"

"Will you listen—as a penance?"

"I—no, I cannot—"

He said quietly: "I was afraid you could not listen. You see, Eileen, that, after all, a man does know when he is done for—"

"Captain Selwyn!" She turned and caught his hands in both of hers, her eyes bright with tears: "Is that the penalty for what I said? Did you think I invited this—"

"Invited! No, child," he said gently. "I was fool enough to believe in myself; that is all. I have always been on the edge of loving you. Only in dreams did I ever dare set foot across that frontier. Now I have dared. I love you. That is all; and it must not distress you."

"But it does not," she said; "I have always loved you—dearly, dearly. . . . Not in that way. . . . I don't know how. . . . Must it be in *that* way, Captain Selwyn? Can we not go on in the other way—that dear way which I—I have—almost spoiled? Must we be like other people—must sentiment turn it all to commonplace? . . . Listen to me; I do love you; it is perfectly easy and simple to say it. But it is not emotional, it is not sentimental. Can't you see that in little things—in my ways with you? I—if I were sentimental about you I would call you Ph—by your first name, I suppose. But I can't; I've tried to—and it's very, very hard—and makes me self-conscious. It is an effort, you see—and so would it be for me to think of you sentimentally. Oh, I couldn't! I couldn't!—you, so much of a man, so strong and generous and experienced and clever—so perfectly the embodiment of everything I care for in a man! I love you dearly; but—you saw! I could—could not bring myself to touch even your hair—even in pure mischief. . . . And—sentiment chills me; I— there are times when it would be unendurable—I could not use an

212

endearing term—nor suffer a—a caress. . . . So you see—don't you? And won't you take me for what I am?—and as I am?—a girl—still young, devoted to you with all her soul—happy with you, believing implicitly in you, deeply, deeply sensible of your goodness and sweetness and loyalty to her. I am not a woman; I was a fool to say so. But you—you are so overwhelmingly a man that if it were in me to love—in that way—it would be you! . . . Do you understand me? Or have I lost a friend? Will you forgive my foolish boast? Can you still keep me first in your heart—as you are in mine? And pardon in me all that I am not? Can you do these things because I ask you?"

"Yes," he said.

CHAPTER IX

A NOVICE

Gerald came to Silverside two or three times during the early summer, arriving usually on Friday and remaining until the following Monday morning.

All his youthful admiration and friendship for Selwyn had returned; that was plainly evident—and with it something less of callow self-sufficiency. He did not appear to be as cock-sure of himself and the world as he had been; there was less bumptiousness about him, less aggressive complacency. Somewhere and somehow somebody or something had come into collision with him; but who or what this had been he did not offer to confide in Selwyn; and the older man, dreading to disturb the existing accord between them, forbore to question him or invite, even indirectly, any confidence not offered.

Selwyn had slowly become conscious of this change in Gerald. In the boy's manner toward others there seemed to be hints of that seriousness which maturity or the first pressure of responsibility brings, even to the more thoughtless. Plainly enough some experience, not wholly agreeable, was teaching him the elements of consideration for others; he was less impulsive, more tolerant; yet, at times, Selwyn and Eileen also noticed that he became very restless toward the end of his visits at Silverside; as though something in the city awaited him—some duty, or responsibility not entirely pleasant.

There was, too, something of soberness, amounting, at moments, to discontented listlessness—not solitary brooding; for at such moments he stuck to Selwyn, following him about and remaining rather close to him, as though the elder man's mere presence was a comfort—even a protection.

At such intervals Selwyn longed to invite the boy's confidence, knowing that he had some phase of life to face for which his experience was evidently inadequate. But Gerald gave no sign of invitation; and Selwyn dared not speak lest he undo what time and his forbearance were slowly repairing.

So their relations remained during the early summer; and everybody supposed that Gerald's two weeks' vacation would be spent there at Silverside. Apparently the boy himself thought so, too, for he made some plans ahead, and Austin sent down a very handsome new motor-boat for him.

Then, at the last minute, a telegram arrived, saying that he had sailed for Newport on Neergard's big yacht! And for two weeks no word was received from him at Silverside.

Late in August, however, he wrote a rather colourless letter to Selwyn, saying that he was tired and would be down for the week-end.

He came, thinner than usual, with the city pallor showing through traces of the sea tan. And it appeared that he was really tired; for he seemed inclined to lounge on the veranda, satisfied as long as Selwyn remained in sight. But, when Selwyn moved, he got up and followed.

So subdued, so listless, so gentle in manner and speech had he become that somebody, in his temporary absence, wondered whether the boy were perfectly well—which voiced the general doubt hitherto unexpressed.

But Austin laughed and said that the boy was merely finding himself; and everybody acquiesced, much relieved at the explanation, though to Selwyn the explanation was not at all satisfactory.

There was trouble somewhere, stress of doubt, pressure of apprehension, the gravity of immaturity half realising its own inexperience. And one day in September he wrote Gerald, asking him to bring Edgerton Lawn and come down to Silverside for the purpose of witnessing some experiments with the new smokeless explosive, Chaosite.

Young Lawn came by the first train; Gerald wired that he would arrive the following morning.

He did arrive, unusually pallid, almost haggard; and Selwyn, who met him at the station and drove him over from Wyossett, ventured at last to give the boy a chance.

But Gerald remained utterly unresponsive—stolidly so—and the other instantly relinquished the hope of any confidence at that time—shifting the conversation at once to the object and reason of Gerald's coming, and gaily expressing his belief that the time was very near at hand when Chaosite would figure heavily in the world's list of commercially valuable explosives.

It was early in August that Selwyn had come to the conclusion that his Chaosite was likely to prove a commercial success. And now, in September, his experiments had advanced so far that he had ventured to invite Austin, Gerald, Lansing, and Edgerton Lawn, of the Lawn Nitro-Powder Company, to witness a few tests at his cottage laboratory on Storm Head; but at the same time he informed them with characteristic modesty that he was not yet prepared to guarantee the explosive.

About noon his guests arrived before the cottage in a solemn file, halted, and did not appear overanxious to enter the laboratory on Storm Head. Also they carefully cast away their cigars when they did enter, and seated themselves in a nervous circle in the largest room of the cottage. Here their eyes instantly became glued to a great bowl which was piled high with small rose-tinted cubes of some substance which resembled symmetrical and translucent crystals of pink quartz. That was Chaosite enough to blow the entire cliff into smithereens; and they were aware of it, and they eyed it with respect.

First of all Selwyn laid a cubic crystal on an anvil, and struck it sharply and repeatedly with a hammer. Austin's thin hair rose, and Edgerton Lawn swallowed nothing several times; but nobody went to heaven, and the little cube merely crumbled into a flaky pink powder.

Then Selwyn took three cubes, dropped them into boiling milk, fished them out again, twisted them into a waxy taper, placed it in a candle-stick, and set fire to it. The taper burned with a flaring brilliancy but without odour.

Then Selwyn placed several cubes in a mortar, pounded them to powder with an iron pestle, and, measuring out the tiniest pinch—scarcely enough to cover the point of a penknife, placed a few grains in several paper cartridges. Two wads followed the powder, then an ounce and a half of shot, then a wad, and then the crimping.

The guests stepped gratefully outside; Selwyn, using a light fowling-piece, made pattern after pattern for them; and then they all trooped solemnly indoors again; and Selwyn froze Chaosite and boiled it and baked it and melted it and took all sorts of hair-raising liberties with it; and after that he ground it to powder, placed a few generous pinches in a small hand-grenade, and affixed a primer, the secret composition of which he alone knew. That was the key to the secret—the composition of the primer charge.

"I used to play base-ball in college," he observed smiling—"and I used to be a pretty good shot with a snowball."

They followed him to the cliff's edge, always with great respect for the awful stuff he handled with such apparent carelessness. There was a black sea-soaked rock jutting out above the waves; Selwyn pointed at it, poised himself, and, with the long, overhand, straight throw of a trained ball player, sent the grenade like a bullet at the rock.

There came a blinding flash, a stunning, clean-cut report—but what the others took to be a vast column of black smoke was really a pillar of dust—all that was left of the rock. And this slowly floated, settling like mist over the waves, leaving nothing where the rock had been.

"I think," said Edgerton Lawn, wiping the starting perspiration from his forehead, "that you have made good, Captain Selwyn. Dense or bulk, your Chaosite and impact primer seem to do the business; and I think I may say that the Lawn Nitro-Powder Company is ready to do business, too. Can you come to town to-morrow? It's merely a matter of figures and signatures now, if you say so. It is entirely up to you."

But Selwyn only laughed. He looked at Austin.

"I suppose," said Edgerton Lawn good-naturedly, "that you intend to make us sit up and beg; or do you mean to absorb us?"

But Selwyn said: "I want more time on this thing. I want to know what it does to the interior of loaded shells and in fixed ammunition when it is stored for a year. I want to know whether it is necessary to use a solvent after firing it in big guns. As a bursting charge I'm practically satisfied with it; but time is required to know how it acts on steel in storage or on the bores of guns when exploded as a propelling charge. Meanwhile," turning to Lawn, "I'm tremendously obliged to you for coming—and for your offer. You see how it is, don't you? I couldn't risk taking money for a thing which might, at the end, prove dear at any price."

"I cheerfully accept that risk," insisted young Lawn; "I am quite ready to do all the worrying, Captain Selwyn."

But Selwyn merely shook his head, repeating: "You see how it is, don't you?"

"I see that you possess a highly developed conscience," said Edgerton Lawn, laughing; "and when I tell you that we are more than willing to take every chance of failure—"

But Selwyn shook his head: "Not yet," he said; "don't worry; I need the money, and I'll waste no time when a square deal is possible. But I ought to tell you this: that first of all I must offer it to the Government. That is only decent, you see—"

"Who ever heard of the Government's gratitude?" broke in Austin. "Nonsense, Phil; you are wasting time!"

"I've got to do it," said Selwyn; "you must see that, of course."

"But I don't see it," began Lawn—"because you are not in the Government service now—"

"Besides," added Austin, "you were not a West Pointer; you never were under obligations to the Government!"

"Are we not all under obligation?" asked Selwyn so simply that Austin flushed.

"Oh, of course—patriotism and all that—naturally—Confound it, I don't suppose you'd go and offer it to Germany or Japan before our own Government had the usual chance to turn it down and break your heart. But why can't the Government make arrangements with Lawn's Company—if it desires to?"

"A man can't exploit his own Government; you all know that as well as I do," returned Selwyn, smiling. "*Pro aris et focis*, you know—*ex necessitate rei.*"

"When the inventor goes to the Government," said Austin, with a shrug—"*vestigia nulla retrorsum.*"

"*Spero meliora*," retorted Selwyn, laughing; but there remained the obstinate squareness of jaw, and his amused eyes were clear and steady. Young Lawn looked into them and the hope in him flickered; Austin looked, and shrugged; but as they all turned away to retrace their steps across the moors in the direction of Silverside, Lansing lightly hooked his arm into Selwyn's; and Gerald, walking thoughtfully on the other side, turned over and over in his mind the proposition offered him—the spectacle of a modern and needy man to whom money appeared to be the last consideration in a plain matter of business. Also he turned over other matters in his mind; and moved closer to Selwyn, walking beside him with grave eyes bent on the ground.

The matter of business arrangements apparently ended then and there; Lawn's company sent several men to Selwyn and wrote him a great many letters—unlike the Government, which had not replied to his briefly tentative suggestion that Chaosite be conditionally examined, tested, and considered.

So the matter remained in abeyance, and Selwyn employed two extra men and continued storage tests and experimented with rifled and smooth-bore tubes, watchfully uncertain yet as to the necessity of inventing a solvent to neutralise possible corrosion after a propelling charge had been exploded.

Everybody in the vicinity had heard about his experiments; everybody pretended interest, but few were sincere; and of the sincere, few were unselfishly interested—his sister, Eileen, Drina, and Lansing—and maybe one or two others.

However, the younger set, now predominant from Wyossett to Wonder Head, made up parties to visit Selwyn's cottage, which had become known as The Chrysalis; and Selwyn good-naturedly exploded a pinch

217

or two of the stuff for their amusement, and never betrayed the slightest annoyance or boredom. In fact, he behaved so amiably during gratuitous interruptions that he won the hearts of the younger set, who presently came to the unanimous conclusion that there was Romance in the air. And they sniffed it with delicate noses uptilted and liked the aroma.

Kathleen Lawn, a big, leisurely, blond-skinned girl, who showed her teeth when she laughed and shook hands like a man, declared him "adorable" but "unsatisfactory," which started one of the Dresden-china twins, Dorothy Minster, and she, in turn, ventured the innocent opinion that Selwyn was misunderstood by most people—an inference that she herself understood him. And she smiled to herself when she made this observation, up to her neck in the surf; and Eileen, hearing the remark, smiled to herself, too. But she felt the slightest bit uncomfortable when that animated brunette Gladys Orchil, climbing up dripping on to the anchored float beyond the breakers, frankly confessed that the tinge of mystery enveloping Selwyn's career made him not only adorable, but agreeably "unfathomable"; and that she meant to experiment with him at every opportunity.

Sheila Minster, seated on the raft's edge, swinging her stockinged legs in the green swells that swept steadily shoreward, modestly admitted that Selwyn was "sweet," particularly in a canoe on a moonlight night— in spite of her weighty mother heavily afloat in the vicinity.

"He's nice every minute," she said—"every fibre of him is nice in the nicest sense. He never talks 'down' at you—like an insufferable undergraduate; and he is so much of a man—such a real man!—that I like him," she added naïvely; "and I'm quite sure he likes me, because he said so."

"I like him," said Gladys Orchil, "because he has a sense of humour and stands straight. I like a sense of humour and—good shoulders. He's an enigma; and I like that, too. . . . I'm going to investigate him every chance I get."

Dorothy Minster liked him, too: "He's such a regular boy at times," she explained; "I do love to see him without his hat sauntering along beside me—and not talking every minute when you don't wish to talk. Friends," she added—"true friends are most eloquent in their mutual silence. Ahem!"

Eileen Erroll, standing near on the pitching raft, listened intently, but curiously enough said nothing either in praise or blame.

"He is exactly the right age," insisted Gladys—as though somebody had said he was not—"the age when a man is most interesting."

The Minster twins twiddled their legs and looked sentimentally at the ocean. They were a pair of pink and white little things with china-blue eyes and the fairest of hair, and they were very impressionable; and when they thought of Selwyn they looked unutterable things at the Atlantic Ocean.

One man, often the least suitable, is usually the unanimous choice of the younger sort where, in the disconcerting summer time, the youthful congregate in garrulous segregation.

Their choice they expressed frankly and innocently; they admitted cheerfully that Selwyn was their idol. But that gentleman remained totally unconscious that he had been set up by them upon the shores of the summer sea.

In leisure moments he often came down to the bathing-beach at the hour made fashionable; he conducted himself amiably with dowager and chaperon, with portly father and nimble brother, with the late débutantes of the younger set and the younger matrons, individually, collectively, impartially.

He and Gerald usually challenged the rollers in a sponson canoe when Gerald was there for the week-end; or, when Lansing came down, the two took long swims seaward or cruised about in Gerald's dory, clad in their swimming-suits; and Selwyn's youth became renewed in a manner almost ridiculous, so that the fine lines which had threatened the corners of his mouth and eyes disappeared, and the clear sun tan of the tropics, which had never wholly faded, came back over a smooth skin as clear as a boy's, though not as smoothly rounded. His hair, too, crisped and grew lighter under the burning sun, which revealed, at the temples, the slightest hint of silver. And this deepened the fascination of the younger sort for the idol they had set up upon the sands of Silverside.

Gladys was still eloquent on the subject, lying flat on the raft where all were now gathered in a wet row, indulging in sunshine and the two minutes of gossip which always preceded their return swim to the beach.

"It is partly his hair," she said gravely, "that makes him so distinguished in his appearance—just that touch of silver; and you keep looking and looking until you scarcely know whether it's really beginning to turn a little gray or whether it's only a lighter colour at the temples. How insipid is a mere boy after such a man as Captain Selwyn! . . . I have dreamed of such a man—several times."

The Minster twins gazed soulfully at the Atlantic; Eileen Erroll bit her under lip and stood up suddenly. "Come on," she said; joined her hands skyward, poised, and plunged. One after another the others followed and, rising to the surface, struck out shoreward.

On the sunlit sands dozens of young people were hurling tennis-balls at each other. Above the beach, under the long pavilions, sat mothers and chaperons. Motors, beach-carts, and victorias were still arriving to discharge gaily dressed fashionables—for the hour was early—and up and down the inclined wooden walk leading from the bathing-pavilion to the sands, a constant procession of bathers passed with nod and gesture of laughing salutation, some already retiring to the showers after a brief ocean plunge, the majority running down to the shore, eager for the first frosty and aromatic embrace of the surf rolling in under a cloudless sky of blue.

As Eileen Erroll emerged from the surf and came wading shoreward through the seething shallows, she caught sight of Selwyn sauntering across the sands toward the water, and halted, knee-deep, smilingly expectant, certain that he had seen her.

Gladys Orchil, passing her, saw Selwyn at the same moment, and her clear, ringing salute and slender arm aloft, arrested his attention; and the next moment they were off together, swimming toward the sponson canoe which Gerald had just launched with the assistance of Sandon Craig and Scott Innis.

For a moment Eileen stood there, motionless. Knee-high the flat ebb boiled and hissed, dragging at her stockinged feet as though to draw her seaward with the others. Yesterday she would have gone, without a thought, to join the others; but yesterday is yesterday. It seemed to her, as she stood there, that something disquieting had suddenly come into the world; something unpleasant—but indefinite—yet sufficient to leave her vaguely apprehensive.

The saner emotions which have their birth in reason she was not ignorant of; emotion arising from nothing at all disconcerted her—nor could she comprehend the slight quickening of her heart-beats as she waded to the beach, while every receding film of water tugged at her limbs as though to draw her backward in the wake of her unquiet thoughts.

Somebody threw a tennis-ball at her; she caught it and hurled it in return; and for a few minutes the white, felt-covered balls flew back and forth from scores of graceful, eager hands. A moment or two passed when no balls came her way; she turned and walked to the foot of a dune and seated herself cross-legged on the hot sand.

Sometimes she watched the ball players, sometimes she exchanged a word of amiable commonplace with people who passed or halted to greet her. But she invited nobody to remain, and nobody ventured to, not even several very young and ardent gentlemen who had acquired only the rudiments of social sense. For there was a sweet but distant look in her dark-blue eyes and a certain reserved preoccupation in her acknowledgment of salutations. And these kept the would-be adorer moving—wistful, lagging, but still moving along the edge of that invisible barrier set between her and the world with her absent-minded greeting, and her serious, beautiful eyes fixed so steadily on a distant white spot—the sponson canoe where Gladys and Selwyn sat, their paddle blades flashing in the sun.

How far away they were. . . . Gerald was with them. . . . Curious that Selwyn had not seen her waiting for him, knee-deep in the surf—curious that he had seen Gladys instead. . . . True, Gladys had called to him and signalled him, white arm upflung. . . . Gladys was very pretty—with her heavy, dark hair and melting, Spanish eyes, and her softly rounded, olive-skinned figure. . . . Gladys had called to him, and *she* had not. . . . That was true; and lately—for the last few days—or perhaps more—she herself had been a trifle less impulsive in her greeting of Selwyn—a little less *sans-façon* with him. . . . After all, a man comes when it pleases him. Why should a girl call him?—unless she—unless—unless—

Perplexed, her grave eyes fixed on the sea where now the white canoe pitched nearer, she dropped both hands to the sand—those once wonderfully white hands, now creamed with sun tan; and her arms, too, were tinted from shoulder to finger-tip. Then she straightened her legs, crossed her feet, and leaned a trifle forward, balancing her body on both palms flat on the sand. The sun beat down on her; she loosened her hair to dry it, and as she shook her delicate head the superb red-gold mass came tumbling about her face and shoulders. Under its glimmering splendour, and through it, she stared seaward out of wide, preoccupied eyes; and in her breast, stirring uneasily, a pulse, intermittent yet dully importunate, persisted.

The canoe, drifting toward the surf, was close in, now. Gerald rose and dived; Gladys, steadying herself by a slim hand on Selwyn's shoulder, stood up on the bow, ready to plunge clear when the canoe capsized.

How wonderfully pretty she was, balanced there, her hand on his shoulder, ready for a leap, lest the heavy canoe, rolling over in the froth, strike her under the smother of foam and water. . . . How marvellously pretty she was. . . . Her hand on his shoulder. . . .

Miss Erroll sat very still; but the pulse within her was not still.

When the canoe suddenly capsized, Gladys jumped, but Selwyn went with it, boat and man tumbling into the tumult over and over; and the usual laughter from the onlookers rang out, and a dozen young people rushed into the surf to right the canoe and push it out into the surf again and clamber into it.

Gerald was among the number; Gladys swam toward it, beckoning imperiously to Selwyn; but he had his back to the sea and was moving slowly out through the flat swirling ebb. And as Eileen looked, she saw a dark streak leap across his face—saw him stoop and wash it off and stand, looking blindly about, while again the sudden dark line criss-crossed his face from temple to chin, and spread wider like a stain.

"Philip!" she called, springing to her feet and scarcely knowing that she had spoken.

He heard her, and came toward her in a halting, dazed way, stopping twice to cleanse his face of the bright blood that streaked it.

"It's nothing," he said—"the infernal thing hit me. . . . Oh, don't use *that!*" as she drenched her kerchief in cold sea-water and held it toward him with both hands.

"Take it!—I—I beg of you," she stammered. "Is it s-serious?"

"Why, no," he said, his senses clearing; "it was only a rap on the head—and this blood is merely a nuisance. . . . Thank you, I will use your kerchief if you insist. . . . It'll stop in a moment, anyway."

"Please sit here," she said—"here where I've been sitting."

He did so, muttering: "What a nuisance. It will stop in a second. . . . You needn't remain here with me, you know. Go in; it is simply glorious."

"I've been in; I was drying my hair."

He glanced up, smiling; then, as the wet kerchief against his forehead reddened, he started to rise, but she took it from his fingers, hastened to the water's edge, rinsed it, and brought it back cold and wet.

"Please sit perfectly still," she said; "a girl likes to do this sort of thing for a man."

"If I'd known that," he laughed, "I'd have had it happen frequently."

She only shook her head, watching him unsmiling. But the pulse in her had become very quiet again.

"It's no end of fun in that canoe," he observed. "Gladys Orchil and I work it beautifully."

"I saw you did," she nodded.

"Oh! Where were you? Why didn't you come?"

"I don't know. Gladys called you. I was waiting for you—expecting you. Then Gladys called you."

"I didn't see you," he said.

"I didn't call you," she observed serenely. And, after a moment: "Do you see only those who hail you, Captain Selwyn?"

He laughed: "In this life's cruise a good sailor always answers a friendly hail."

"So do I," she said. "Please hail me after this—because I don't care to take the initiative. If you neglect to do it, don't count on my hailing you . . . any more."

The stain spread on the kerchief; once more she went to the water's edge, rinsed it, and returned with it.

"I think it has almost stopped bleeding," she remarked as he laid the cloth against his forehead. "You frightened me, Captain Selwyn. I am not easily frightened."

"I know it."

"Did you know I was frightened?"

"Of course I did."

"Oh," she said, vexed, "how could you know it? I didn't do anything silly, did I?"

"No; you very sensibly called me Philip. That's how I knew you were frightened."

A slow bright colour stained face and neck.

"So I was silly, after all," she said, biting at her under lip and trying to meet his humorous gray eyes with unconcern. But her face was burning now, and, aware of it, she turned her gaze resolutely on the sea. Also, to her further annoyance, her heart awoke, beating unwarrantably, absurdly, until the dreadful idea seized her that he could hear it. Disconcerted, she stood up—a straight youthful figure against the sea. The wind blowing her dishevelled hair across her cheeks and shoulders, fluttered her clinging skirts as she rested both hands on her hips and slowly walked toward the water's edge.

"Shall we swim?" he asked her.

She half turned and looked around and down at him.

"I'm all right; it's stopped bleeding. Shall we?" he inquired, looking up at her. "You've got to wash your hair again, anyhow."

She said, feeling suddenly stupid and childish, and knowing she was speaking stupidly: "Would you not rather join Gladys again? I thought that—that—"

"Thought *what?*"

"Nothing," she said, furious at herself; "I am going to the showers. Good-bye."

"Good-bye," he said, troubled—"unless we walk to the pavilion together—"

"But you are going in again; are you not?"

"Not unless you do."

"W-what have I to do with it, Captain Selwyn?"

"It's a big ocean—and rather lonely without you," he said so seriously that she looked around again and laughed.

"It's full of pretty girls just now. Plunge in, my melancholy friend. The whole ocean is a dream of fair women to-day."

"'If they be not fair to me, what care I how fair they be,'" he paraphrased, springing to his feet and keeping step beside her.

"Really, that won't do," she said; "much moonlight and Gladys and the Minster twins convict you. Do you remember that I told you one day in early summer—that Sheila and Dorothy and Gladys would mark you for their own? Oh, my inconstant courtier, they are yonder!—And I absolve you. Adieu!"

"Do you remember what *I* told *you*—one day in early summer?" he returned coolly.

Her heart began its absurd beating again—but now there was no trace of pain in it—nothing of apprehension in the echo of the pulse either.

"You protested so many things, Captain Selwyn—"

"Yes; and one thing in particular. You've forgotten it, I see." And he looked her in the eye.

"No," she said, "you are wrong. I have not forgotten."

"Nor I."

He halted, looking out over the shining breakers. "I'm glad you have not forgotten what I said; because, you see, I'm forbidden to repeat it. So I shall be quite helpless to aid you in case your memory fails."

"I don't think it will fail," she said, looking at the flashing sea. A curious tingling sensation of fright had seized her—something entirely unknown to her heretofore. She spoke again because frightened; the heavy, hard pulse in breast and throat played tricks with her voice and she swallowed and attempted to steady it: "I—if—if I ever forget, you will know it as soon as I do—"

Her throat seemed to close in a quick, unsteady breath; she halted, both small hands clinched:

"*Don't* talk this way!" she said, exasperated under a rush of sensations utterly incomprehensible—stinging, confused emotions that beat chaotic time to the clamour of her pulses. "Why d-do you speak of such things?" she repeated with a fierce little indrawn breath—"why do you?—when you know—when I said—explained everything?" She looked at him fearfully: "You are somehow spoiling our friendship," she said; "and I don't exactly know how you are doing it, but something of the comfort of it is being taken away from me—and don't! don't! don't do it!"

She covered her eyes with her clinched hands, stood a moment, motionless; then her arms dropped, and she turned sharply with a gesture which left him standing there and walked rapidly across the beach to the pavilion.

After a little while he followed, pursuing his way very leisurely to his own quarters. Half an hour later when she emerged with her maid, Selwyn was not waiting for her as usual; and, scarcely understanding that she was finding an excuse for lingering, she stood for ten minutes on the step of the Orchils' touring-car, talking to Gladys about the lantern fête and dance to be given that night at Hitherwood House.

Evidently Selwyn had already gone home. Gerald came lagging up with Sheila Minster; but his sister did not ask him whether Selwyn had gone. Yesterday she would have done so; but to-day had brought to her the strangest sensation of her young life—a sudden and overpowering fear of a friend; and yet, strangest of all, the very friend she feared she was waiting for—contriving to find excuses to wait for. Surely he could not have finished dressing and have gone. He had never before done that. Why did he not come? It was late; people were leaving the pavilion; victorias and beach-phaetons were trundling off loaded to the water-line with fat dowagers; gay groups passed, hailing her or waving adieux; Drina drove up in her village-cart, calling out: "Are you coming, Eileen, or are you going to walk over? Hurry up! I'm hungry."

"I'll go with you," she said, nodding adieu to Gladys; and she swung off the step and crossed the shell road.

"Jump in," urged the child; "I'm in a dreadful hurry, and Odin can't trot very fast."

"I'd prefer to drive slowly," said Miss Erroll in a colourless voice; and seated herself in the village-cart.

"Why must I drive slowly?" demanded the child. "I'm hungry; besides, I haven't seen Boots this morning. I don't want to drive slowly; must I?"

"Which are you most in a hurry for?" asked Eileen curiously; "luncheon or Boots?"

"Both—I don't know. What a silly question. Boots of course! But I'm starving, too."

"Boots? Of course?"

"Certainly. He always comes first—just like Captain Selwyn with you."

"Like Captain Selwyn with me," she repeated absently; "certainly; Captain Selwyn should be first, everything else second. But how did you find out that, Drina?"

"Why, anybody can see that," said the child contemptuously; "you are as fast friends with Uncle Philip as I am with Boots. And why you don't marry him I can't see—unless you're not old enough. Are you?"

"Yes. . . . I am old enough, dear."

"Then why don't you? If I was old enough to marry Boots I'd do it. Why don't you?"

"I don't know," said Miss Erroll, as though speaking to herself.

Drina glanced at her, then flourished her be-ribboned whip, which whistling threat had no perceptible effect on the fat, red, Norwegian pony.

"I'll tell you what," said the child, "if you don't ask Uncle Philip pretty soon somebody will ask him first, and you'll be too late. As soon as I saw Boots I knew that I wanted him for myself, and I told him so. He said he was very glad I had spoken, because he was expecting a proposal by wireless from the young Sultana-elect of Leyte. Now," added the child with satisfaction, "she can't have him. It's better to be in time, you see."

Eileen nodded: "Yes, it is better to be in plenty of time. You can't tell what Sultana may forestall you."

"So you'll tell him, won't you?" inquired Drina with business-like briskness.

Miss Erroll looked absently at her: "Tell who what?"

"Uncle Philip—that you're going to marry him when you're old enough."

"Yes—when I'm old enough—I'll tell him, Drina."

"Oh, no; I mean you'll marry him when you're old enough, but you'd better tell him right away."

"I see; I'd better speak immediately. Thank you, dear, for suggesting it."

"You're quite welcome," said the child seriously; "and I hope you'll be as happy as I am."

"I hope so," said Eileen as the pony-cart drew up by the veranda and a groom took the pony's head.

Luncheon being the children's hour, Miss Erroll's silence remained unnoticed in the jolly uproar; besides, Gerald and Boots were discussing the huge house-party, lantern fête, and dance which the Orchils were giving that night for the younger sets; and Selwyn, too, seemed to take unusual interest in the discussion, though Eileen's part in the conference was limited to an occasional nod or monosyllable.

Drina was wild to go and furious at not having been asked, but when Boots offered to stay home, she resolutely refused to accept the sacrifice.

"No," she said; "they are pigs not to ask girls of my age, but you may go, Boots, and I'll promise not to be unhappy." And she leaned over and added in a whisper to Eileen: "You see how sensible it is to make arrangements beforehand! Because somebody, grown-up, might take him away at this very party. That's the reason why it is best to speak promptly. Please pass me another peach, Eileen."

"What are you two children whispering about?" inquired Selwyn, glancing at Eileen.

"Oho!" exclaimed Drina; "you may know before long! May he not, Eileen? It's about you," she said; "something splendid that somebody is going to do to you! Isn't it, Eileen?"

Miss Erroll looked smilingly at Selwyn, a gay jest on her lips; but the sudden clamour of pulses in her throat closed her lips, cutting the phrase in two, and the same strange fright seized her—an utterly unreasoning fear of him.

At the same moment Mrs. Gerard gave the rising signal, and Selwyn was swept away in the rushing herd of children, out on to the veranda, where for a while he smoked and drew pictures for the younger Gerards. Later, some of the children were packed off for a nap; Billy with his assorted puppies went away with Drina and Boots, ever hopeful of a fox or rabbit; Nina Gerard curled herself up in a hammock, and Selwyn seated himself beside her, an uncut magazine on his knees. Eileen had disappeared.

For a while Nina swung there in silence, her pretty eyes fixed on her brother. He had nearly finished cutting the leaves of the magazine before she spoke, mentioning the fact of Rosamund Fane's arrival at the Minsters' house, Brookminster.

The slightest frown gathered and passed from her brother's sun-bronzed forehead, but he made no comment.

"Mr. Neergard is a guest, too," she observed.

"What?" exclaimed Selwyn, in disgust.

"Yes; he came ashore with the Fanes."

Selwyn flushed a little but went on cutting the pages of the magazine. When he had finished he flattened the pages between both covers, and said, without raising his eyes:

"I'm sorry that crowd is to be in evidence."

"They always are and always will be," smiled his sister.

He looked up at her: "Do you mean that anybody *else* is a guest at Brookminster?"

"Yes, Phil."

"Alixe?"

"Yes."

He looked down at the book on his knees and began to furrow the pages absently.

227

"Phil," she said, "have you heard anything this summer—lately—about the Ruthvens?"

"No."

"Nothing at all?"

"Not a word."

"You knew they were at Newport as usual."

"I took it for granted."

"And you have heard no rumours?—no gossip concerning them? Nothing about a yacht?"

"Where was I to hear it? What gossip? What yacht?"

His sister said very seriously: "Alixe has been very careless."

"Everybody is. What of it?"

"It is understood that she and Jack Ruthven have separated."

He looked up quickly: "Who told you that?"

"A woman wrote me from Newport. . . . And Alixe is here and Jack Ruthven is in New York. Several people have—I have heard about it from several sources. I'm afraid it's true, Phil."

They looked into each other's troubled eyes; and he said: "If she has done this it is the worse of two evils she has chosen. To live with him was bad enough, but this is the limit."

"I know it. She cannot afford to do such a thing again. . . . Phil, what is the matter with her? She simply cannot be sane and do such a thing—can she?"

"I don't know," he said.

"Well, I do. She is not sane. She has made herself horridly conspicuous among conspicuous people; she has been indiscreet to the outer edge of effrontery. Even that set won't stand it always—especially as their men folk are quite crazy about her, and she leads a train of them about wherever she goes—the little fool!

"And now, if it's true, that there's to be a separation—what on earth will become of her? I ask you, Phil, for I don't know. But men know what becomes eventually of women who slap the world across the face with over-ringed fingers.

"If—if there's any talk about it—if there's newspaper talk—if there's a divorce—who will ask her to their houses? Who will condone this thing? Who will tolerate it, or her? Men—and men only—the odious sort that fawn on her now and follow her about half-sneeringly. They'll tolerate it; but their wives won't; and the kind of women who will receive and tolerate her are not included in my personal experience. What a fool she has been!—good heavens, what a fool!"

A trifle paler than usual, he said: "There is no real harm in her. I know there is not."

"You are very generous, Phil—"

"No, I am trying to be truthful. And I say there is no harm in her. I have made up my mind on that score." He leaned nearer his sister and laid one hand on hers where it lay across the hammock's edge:

"Nina; no woman could have done what she has done, and continue to do what she does, and be mentally sound. This, at last, is my conclusion."

"It has long been my conclusion," she said under her breath.

He stared at the floor out of gray eyes grown dull and hopeless.

"Phil," whispered his sister, "suppose—suppose—what happened to her father—"

"I know."

She said again: "It was slow at first, a brilliant eccentricity—that gradually became—something else less pleasant. Oh, Phil! Phil!"

"It was softening of the brain," he said, "was it not?"

"Yes—he entertained a delusion of conspiracy against him—also a complacent conviction of the mental instability of others. Yet, at intervals he remained clever and witty and charming."

"And then?"

"Phil—he became violent at times."

"Yes. And the end?" he asked quietly.

"A little child again—quite happy and content—playing with toys—very gentle, very pitiable—" The hot tears filled her eyes. "Oh, Phil!" she sobbed and hid her face on his shoulder.

Over the soft, faintly fragrant hair he stared stupidly, lips apart, chin loose.

A little later, Nina sat up in the hammock, daintily effacing the traces of tears. Selwyn was saying: "If this is so, that Ruthven man has got to stand by her. Where could she go—if such trouble is to come upon her? To whom can she turn if not to him? He is responsible for her—doubly so, if her condition is to be—*that*! By every law of manhood he is bound to stand by her now; by every law of decency and humanity he cannot desert her now. If she does these—these indiscreet things—and if he

229

knows she is not altogether mentally responsible—he cannot fail to stand by her! How can he, in God's name!"

"Phil," she said, "you speak like a man, but she has no man to stand loyally by her in the direst need a human soul may know. He is only a thing—no man at all—only a loathsome accident of animated decadence."

He looked up quickly, amazed at her sudden bitterness; and she looked back at him almost fiercely.

"I may as well tell you what I've heard," she said; "I was not going to, at first; but it will be all around town sooner or later. Rosamund told me. She learned—as she manages to learn everything a little before anybody else hears of it—that Jack Ruthven found out that Alixe was behaving very carelessly with some man—some silly, callow, and probably harmless youth. But there was a disgraceful scene on Mr. Neergard's yacht, the *Niobrara*. I don't know who the people were, but Ruthven acted abominably. . . . The *Niobrara* anchored in Widgeon Bay yesterday; and Alixe is aboard, and her husband is in New York, and Rosamund says he means to divorce her in one way or another! Ugh! the horrible little man with his rings and bangles!"

She shuddered: "Why, the mere bringing of such a suit means her social ruin no matter what verdict is brought in! Her only salvation has been in remaining inconspicuous; and a sane girl would have realised it. But"—and she made a gesture of despair—"you see what she has done. . . . And Phil—you know what she has done to you—what a mad risk she took in going to your rooms that night—"

"Who said she had ever been in my rooms?" he demanded, flushing darkly in his surprise.

"Did you suppose I didn't know it?" she asked quietly. "Oh, but I did; and it kept me awake nights, worrying. Yet I knew it must have been all right—knowing you as I do. But do you suppose other people would hold you as innocent as I do? Even Eileen—the sweetest, whitest, most loyal little soul in the world—was troubled when Rosamund hinted at some scandal touching you and Alixe. She told me—but she did not tell me what Rosamund had said—the mischief maker!"

His face had become quite colourless; he raised an unsteady hand to his mouth, touching his moustache; and his gray eyes narrowed menacingly.

"Rosamund—spoke of scandal to—Eileen?" he repeated. "Is that possible?"

"How long do you suppose a girl can live and not hear scandal of some sort?" said Nina. "It's bound to rain some time or other, but I prepared my little duck's back to shed some things."

"You say," insisted Selwyn, "that Rosamund spoke of me—in that way—to Eileen?"

"Yes. It only made the child angry, Phil; so don't worry."

"No; I won't worry. No, I—I won't. You are quite right, Nina. But the pity of it; that tight, hard-shelled woman of the world—to do such a thing—to a young girl."

"Rosamund is Rosamund," said Nina with a shrug; "the antidote to her species is obvious."

"Right, thank God!" said Selwyn between his teeth; "*Mens sana in corpore sano*! bless her little heart! I'm glad you told me this, Nina."

He rose and laughed a little—a curious sort of laugh; and Nina watched him, perplexed.

"Where are you going, Phil?" she asked.

"I don't know. I—where is Eileen?"

"She's lying down—a headache; probably too much sun and salt water. Shall I send for her?"

"No; I'll go up and inquire how she is. Susanne is there, isn't she?"

And he entered the house and ascended the stairs.

The little Alsatian maid was seated in a corner of the upper hall, sewing; and she informed Selwyn that mademoiselle "had bad in ze h'ead."

But at the sound of conversation in the corridor Eileen's gay voice came to them from her room, asking who it was; and she evidently knew, for there was a hint of laughter in her tone.

"It is I. Are you better?" said Selwyn.

"Yes. D-did you wish to see me?"

"I always do."

"Thank you. . . . I mean, do you wish to see me now? Because I'm very much occupied in trying to go to sleep."

"Yes, I wish to see you at once."

"Particularly?"

"Very particularly."

"Oh, if it's as serious as that, you alarm me. I'm afraid to come."

"I'm afraid to have you. But please come."

He heard her laugh to herself; then her clear, amused voice: "What are you going to say to me if I come out?"

231

"Something dreadful! Hurry!"

"Oh, if that's the case I'll hurry," she returned, and a moment later the door opened and she emerged in a breezy flutter of silvery ribbons and loosened ruddy hair.

She was dressed in some sort of delicate misty stuff that alternately clung and floated, outlining or clouding her glorious young figure as she moved with leisurely free-limbed grace across the hall to meet him.

The pretty greeting she always reserved for him, even if their separation had been for a few minutes only, she now offered, hand extended; a cool, fragrant hand which lay for a second in his, closed, and withdrew, leaving her eyes very friendly.

"Come out on the west veranda," she said; "I know what you wish to say to me. Besides, I have something to confide to you, too. And I'm very impatient to do it."

He followed her to the veranda; she seated herself in the broad swing, and moved so that her invitation to him was unmistakable. Then when he had taken the place beside her she turned toward him very frankly, and he looked up to encounter her beautiful direct gaze.

"What is disturbing our friendship?" she asked. "Do you know? I don't. I went to my room after luncheon and lay down on my bed and quietly deliberated. And do you know what conclusion I have reached?"

"What?" he asked.

"That there is nothing at all to disturb our friendship. And that what I said to you on the beach was foolish. I don't know why I said it; I'm not the sort of girl who says such stupid things—though I was apparently, for that one moment. And what I said about Gladys was childish; I am not jealous of her, Captain Selwyn. Don't think me silly or perverse or sentimental, will you?"

"No, I won't."

She smiled at him with a trifle less courage—a trifle more self-consciousness: "And—and as for what I called you—"

"You mean when you called me by my first name, and I teased you?"

"Y-es. I was silly to do it; sillier to be ashamed of doing it. There's a great deal of the callow schoolgirl in me yet, you see. The wise, amused smile of a man can sometimes stampede my self-possession and leave me blushing like any ninny in dire confusion. . . . It was very, very mean of you—for the blood across your face did shock me. . . . And, by myself, and in my very private thoughts, I do sometimes call you—by your first name. . . . And that explains it. . . . Now, what have you to say to me?"

"I wish to ask you something."

"With pleasure," she said; "go ahead." And she settled back, fearlessly expectant.

"Very well, then," he said, striving to speak coolly. "It is this: Will you marry me, Eileen?"

She turned perfectly white and stared at him, stunned. And he repeated his question, speaking slowly, but unsteadily.

"N-no," she said; "I cannot. Why—why, you know that, don't you?"

"Will you tell me why, Eileen?"

"I—I don't know why. I think—I suppose that it is because I do not love you—that way."

"Yes," he said, "that, of course, is the reason. I wonder—do you suppose that—in time—perhaps—you might care for me—that way?"

"I don't know." She glanced up at him fearfully, fascinated, yet repelled. "I don't know," she repeated pitifully. "Is it—can't you help thinking of me in that way? Can't you be as you were?"

"No, I can no longer help it. I don't want to help it, Eileen."

"But—I wish you to," she said in a low voice. "It is that which is coming between us. Oh, don't you see it is? Don't you feel it—feel what it is doing to us? Don't you understand how it is driving me back into myself? Whom am I to go to if not to you? What am I to do if your affection turns into this—this different attitude toward me? You were so perfectly sweet and reasonable—so good, so patient; and now—and now I am losing confidence in you—in myself—in our friendship. I'm no longer frank with you; I'm afraid at times—afraid and self-conscious— conscious of you, too—afraid of what seemed once the most natural of intimacies. I—I loved you so dearly—so fearlessly—"

Tears blinded her; she bent her head, and they fell on the soft delicate stuff of her gown, flashing downward in the sunlight.

"Dear," he said gently, "nothing is altered between us. I love you in that way, too."

"D-do you—really?" she stammered, shrinking away from him.

"Truly. Nothing is altered; nothing of the bond between us is weakened. On the contrary, it is strengthened. You cannot understand that now. But what you are to believe and always understand is that our friendship must endure. Will you believe it?"

"Y-yes—" She buried her face in her handkerchief and sat very still for a long time. He had risen and walked to the farther end of the veranda; and for a minute he stood there, his narrowed eyes following the sky flight of the white gulls off Wonder Head.

When at length he returned to her she was sitting low in the swing, both arms extended along the back of the seat. Evidently she had been waiting for him; and her face was very grave and sorrowful.

"I want to ask you something," she said—"merely to prove that you are a little bit illogical. May I?"

He nodded, smiling.

"Could you and I care for each other more than we now do, if we were married?"

"I think so," he said.

"Why?" she demanded, astonished. Evidently she had expected another answer.

He made no reply; and she lay back among the cushions considering what he had said, the flush of surprise still lingering in her cheeks.

"How can I marry you," she asked, "when I would—would not care to endure a—a caress from any man—even from you? It—such things—would spoil it all. I *don't* love you—that way. . . . Oh! *Don't* look at me that way! Have I hurt you?—dear Captain Selwyn? . . . I did not mean to. . . . Oh, what has become of our happiness! What has become of it!" And she turned, full length in the swing, and hid her face in the silken pillows.

For a long while she lay there, the western sun turning her crown of hair to fire above the white nape of her slender neck; and he saw her hands clasping, unclasping, or crushing the tiny handkerchief deep into one palm.

There was a chair near; he drew it toward her, and sat down, steadying the swing with one hand on the chain.

"Dearest," he said under his breath, "I am very selfish to have done this; but I—I thought—perhaps—you might have cared enough to—to venture—"

"I do care; you are very cruel to me." The voice was childishly broken and muffled. He looked down at her, slowly realising that it was a child he still was dealing with—a child with a child's innocence, repelled by the graver phase of love, unresponsive to the deeper emotions, bewildered by the glimpse of the mature rôle his attitude had compelled her to accept. That she already had reached that mile-stone and, for a moment, had turned involuntarily to look back and find her childhood already behind her, frightened her.

Thinking, perhaps, of his own years, and of what lay behind him, he sighed and looked out over the waste of moorland where the Atlantic was battering the sands of Surf Point. Then his patient gaze shifted to the east, and he saw the surface of Sky Pond, blue as the eyes of the girl who lay crouching in the cushioned corner of the swinging seat, small hands clinched over the handkerchief—a limp bit of stuff damp with her tears.

"There is one thing," he said, "that we mustn't do—cry about it—must we, Eileen?"

"No-o."

"Certainly not. Because there is nothing to make either of us unhappy; is there?"

"Oh-h, no."

"Exactly. So we're not going to be unhappy; not one bit. First because we love each other, anyway; don't we?"

"Y-yes."

"Of course we do. And now, just because I happen to love you in that way and also in a different sort of way, in addition to that way, why, it's nothing for anybody to cry about it; is it, Eileen?"

"No. . . . No, it is not. . . . But I c-can't help it."

"Oh, but you're going to help it, aren't you?"

"I—I hope so."

He was silent; and presently she said: "I—the reason of it—my crying—is b-b-because I don't wish you to be unhappy."

"But, dear, dear little girl, I am not!"

"Really?"

"No, indeed! Why should I be? You do love me; don't you?"

"You know I do."

"But not in *that* way."

"N-no; not in *that* way. . . . I w-wish I did."

A thrill passed through him; after a moment he relaxed and leaned forward, his chin resting on his clinched hands: "Then let us go back to the old footing, Eileen."

"Can we?"

"Yes, we can; and we will—back to the old footing—when nothing of deeper sentiment disturbed us. . . . It was my fault, little girl. Some day you will understand that it was not a wholly selfish fault—because I believed—perhaps only dreamed—that I could make you happier by loving you in—both ways. That is all; it is your happiness—our happiness that we must consider; and if it is to last and endure, we must be very, very careful that nothing really disturbs it again. And that means that the love, which is sometimes called friendship, must be recognised as sufficient. . . . You know how it is; a man who is locked up in Paradise is never satisfied until he can climb the wall and look over! Now I have climbed and looked; and now I climb back into the garden of your dear friendship, very glad to be there again with you—very, very thankful, dear. . . . Will you welcome me back?"

She lay quite still a minute, then sat up straight, stretching out both hands to him, her beautiful, fearless eyes brilliant as rain-washed stars.

"Don't go away," she said—"don't ever go away from our garden again."

"No, Eileen."

"Is it a promise . . . Philip?"

Her voice fell exquisitely low.

"Yes, a promise. Do you take me back, Eileen?"

"Yes; I take you. . . . Take me back, too, Philip." Her hands tightened in his; she looked up at him, faltered, waited; then in a fainter voice: "And—and be of g-good courage. . . . I—I am not very old yet."

She withdrew her hands and bent her head, sitting there, still as a white-browed novice, listlessly considering the lengthening shadows at her feet. But, as he rose and looked out across the waste with enchanted eyes that saw nothing, his heart suddenly leaped up quivering, as though his very soul had been drenched in immortal sunshine.

An hour later, when Nina discovered them there together, Eileen, curled up among the cushions in the swinging seat, was reading aloud "Evidences of Asiatic Influence on the Symbolism of Ancient Yucatan"; and Selwyn, astride a chair, chin on his folded arms, was listening with evident rapture.

"Heavens!" exclaimed Nina, "the blue-stocking and the fogy!—and yours *are* pale blue, Eileen!—you're about as self-conscious as Drina—slumping there with your hair tumbling *à la* Mérode! Oh, it's very picturesque, of course, but a straight spine and good grooming is better. Get up, little blue-stockings and we'll have our hair done—if you expect to appear at Hitherwood House with me!"

Eileen laughed, calmly smoothing out her skirt over her slim ankles; then she closed the book, sat up, and looked happily at Selwyn.

"Fogy and *Bas-bleu*," she repeated. "But it *is* fascinating, isn't it?—even if my hair is across my ears and you sit that chair like a polo player! Nina, dearest, what is your mature opinion concerning the tomoya and the Buddhist cross?"

"I know more about a tomboy-a than a tomoya, my saucy friend," observed Nina, surveying her with disapproval—"and I can be as cross about it as any Buddhist, too. You are, to express it as pleasantly as possible, a sight! Child, what on earth have you been doing? There are two smears on your cheeks!"

"I've been crying," said the girl, with an amused sidelong flutter of her lids toward Selwyn.

"Crying!" repeated Nina incredulously. Then, disarmed by the serene frankness of the girl, she added: "A blue-stocking is bad enough, but a grimy one is impossible. *Allons! Vite!*" she insisted, driving Eileen before her; "the country is demoralising you. Philip, we're dining early, so please make your arrangements to conform. Come, Eileen; have you never before seen Philip Selwyn?"

"I am not sure that I ever have," she replied, with a curious little smile at Selwyn. Nina had her by the hand, but she dragged back like a mischievously reluctant child hustled bedward:

"Good-bye," she said, stretching out her hand to Selwyn—"good-bye, my unfortunate fellow fogy! I go, slumpy, besmudged, but happy; I return, superficially immaculate—but my stockings will still be blue! . . . Nina, dear, if you don't stop dragging me I'll pick you up in my arms!—indeed I will—"

There was a laugh, a smothered cry of protest; and Selwyn was the amused spectator of his sister suddenly seized and lifted into a pair of vigorous young arms, and carried into the house by this tall, laughing girl who, an hour before, had lain there among the cushions, frightened, unconvinced, clinging instinctively to the last gay rags and tatters of the childhood which she feared were to be stripped from her for ever.

It was clear starlight when they were ready to depart. Austin had arrived unexpectedly, and he, Nina, Eileen, and Selwyn were to drive to Hitherwood House, Lansing and Gerald going in the motor-boat.

There was a brief scene between Drina and Boots—the former fiercely pointing out the impropriety of a boy like Gerald being invited where she, Drina, was ignored. But there was no use in Boots offering to remain and comfort her as Drina had to go to bed, anyway; so she kissed him good-bye very tearfully, and generously forgave Gerald; and comforted herself before she retired by putting on one of her mother's gowns and pinning up her hair and parading before a pier-glass until her nurse announced that her bath was waiting.

The drive to Hitherwood House was a dream of loveliness; under the stars the Bay of Shoals sparkled in the blue darkness set with the gemmed ruby and sapphire and emerald of ships' lanterns glowing from unseen yachts at anchor.

The great flash-light on Wonder Head broke out in brilliancy, faded, died to a cinder, grew perceptible again, and again blazed blindingly in its endless monotonous routine; far lights twinkled on the Sound, and farther away still, at sea. Then the majestic velvety shadow of the Hither Woods fell over them; and they passed in among the trees, the lamps of the depot wagon shining golden in the forest gloom.

Selwyn turned instinctively to the young girl beside him. Her face was in shadow, but she responded with the slightest movement toward him:

"This dusk is satisfying—like sleep—this wide, quiet shadow over the world. Once—and not so very long ago—I thought it a pity that the sun should ever set. . . . I wonder if I am growing old—because I feel the least bit tired to-night. For the first time that I can remember a day has been a little too long for me."

She evidently did not ascribe her slight sense of fatigue to the scene on the veranda; perhaps she was too innocent to surmise that any physical effect could follow that temporary stress of emotion. A quiet sense of relief in relaxation from effort came over her as she leaned back, conscious that there was happiness in rest and silence and the soft envelopment of darkness.

"If it would only last," she murmured lazily.

"What, Eileen?"

"This heavenly darkness—and our drive, together. . . . You are quite right not to talk to me; I won't, either. . . . Only I'll drone on and on from time to time—so that you won't forget that I am here beside you."

She lay so still for a while that at last Nina leaned forward to look at her; then laughed.

"She's asleep," she said to Austin.

"No, I'm not," murmured the girl, unclosing her eyes; "Captain Selwyn knows; don't you? . . . What is that sparkling—a fire-fly?"

But it was the first paper lantern glimmering through the Hitherwood trees from the distant lawn.

"Oh, dear," sighed Eileen, sitting up with an effort, and looking sleepily at Selwyn. "*J'ai sommeil—besoin—dormir—*"

But a few minutes later they were in the great hall of Hitherwood House, opened from end to end to the soft sea wind, and crowded with the gayest, noisiest throng that had gathered there in a twelvemonth.

Everywhere the younger set were in evidence; slim, fresh, girlish figures passed and gathered and crowded the stairs and galleries with a flirt and flutter of winnowing skirts, delicate and light as powder-puffs.

238

Mrs. Sanxon Orchil, a hard, highly coloured, tight-lipped little woman with electric-blue eyes, was receiving with her slim brunette daughter, Gladys.

"A tight little craft," was Austin's invariable comment on the matron; and she looked it, always trim and trig and smooth of surface like a converted yacht cleared for action.

Near her wandered her husband, orientally bland, invariably affable, and from time to time squinting sideways, as usual, in the ever-renewed expectation that he might catch a glimpse of his stiff, retroussé moustache.

The Lawns were there, the Minsters, the Craigs from Wyossett, the Grays of Shadow Lake, the Draymores, Fanes, Mottlys, Cardwells—in fact, it seemed as though all Long Island had been drained from Cedarhurst to Islip and from Oyster Bay to Wyossett, to pour a stream of garrulous and animated youth and beauty into the halls and over the verandas and terraces and lawns of Hitherwood House.

It was to be a lantern frolic and a lantern dance and supper, all most formally and impressively *sans façon*. And it began with a candle-race for a big silver gilt cup—won by Sandon Craig and his partner, Evelyn Cardwell, who triumphantly bore their lighted taper safely among the throngs of hostile contestants, through the wilderness of flitting lights, and across the lawn to the goal where they planted it, unextinguished, in the big red paper lantern.

Selwyn and Eileen came up breathless and laughing with the others, she holding aloft their candle, which somebody had succeeded in blowing out; and everybody cheered the winners, significantly, for it was expected that Miss Cardwell's engagement to young Craig would be announced before very long.

Then rockets began to rush aloft, starring the black void with iridescent fire; and everybody went to the lawn's edge where, below on the bay, a dozen motor-boats, dressed fore and aft with necklaces of electric lights, crossed the line at the crack of a cannon in a race for another trophy.

Bets flew as the excitement grew, Eileen confining hers to gloves and bonbons, and Selwyn loyally taking any offers of any kind as he uncompromisingly backed Gerald and Boots in the new motor-boat—the *Blue Streak*—Austin's contribution to the Silverside navy.

And sure enough, at last a blue rocket soared aloft, bursting into azure magnificence in the zenith; and Gerald and Boots came climbing up to the lawn to receive prize and compliments, and hasten away to change their oilskins for attire more suitable.

Eileen, turning to Selwyn, held up her booking list in laughing dismay: "I've won about a ton of bonbons," she said, "and too many pairs of gloves to feel quite comfortable."

"You needn't wear them all at once, you know," he assured her.

"Nonsense! I mean that I don't care to win things. Oh!"—and she laid her hand impulsively on his arm as a huge sheaf of rockets roared skyward, apparently from the water.

Then, suddenly, Neergard's yacht sprang into view, outlined in electricity from stem to stern, every spar and funnel and contour of hull and superstructure twinkling in jewelled brilliancy.

On a great improvised open pavilion set up in the Hither Woods, garlanded and hung thick with multi-coloured paper lanterns, dancing had already begun; but Selwyn and Eileen lingered on the lawn for a while, fascinated by the beauty of the fireworks pouring skyward from the *Niobrara*.

"They seem to be very gay aboard her," murmured the girl. "Once you said that you did not like Mr. Neergard. Do you remember saying it?"

He replied simply, "I don't like him; and I remember saying so."

"It is strange," she said, "that Gerald does."

Selwyn looked at the illuminated yacht. . . . "I wonder whether any of Neergard's crowd is expected ashore here. Do you happen to know?"

She did not know. A moment later, to his annoyance, Edgerton Lawn came up and asked her to dance; and she went with a smile and a whispered: "Wait for me—if you don't mind. I'll come back to you."

It was all very well to wait for her—and even to dance with her after that; but there appeared to be no peace for him in prospect, for Scott Innis came and took her away, and Gladys Orchil offered herself to him very prettily, and took him away; and after that, to his perplexity and consternation, a perfect furor for him seemed to set in and grow among the younger set, and the Minster twins had him, and Hilda Innis appropriated him, and Evelyn Cardwell, and even Mrs. Delmour-Carnes took a hand in the badgering.

At intervals he caught glimpses of Eileen through the gay crush around him; he danced with Nina, and suggested to her it was time to leave, but that young matron had tasted just enough to want more; and Eileen, too, was evidently having a most delightful time. So he settled into the harness of pleasure and was good to the pink-and-white ones; and they told each other what a "dear" he was, and adored him more inconveniently than ever.

Truly enough, as he had often said, these younger ones were the charmingly wholesome and refreshing antidote to the occasional misbehaviour of the mature. They were, as he also asserted, the hope and promise of the social fabric of a nation—this younger set—always a little better, a little higher-minded than their predecessors as the wheel of the years slowly turned them out in gay, eager, fearless throngs to teach a cynical generation the rudiments of that wisdom which blossoms most perfectly in the hearts of the unawakened.

Yes, he had frequently told himself all this; told it to others, too. But, now, the younger set, *en masse* and in detail, had become a little bit *cramponné*—a trifle too all-pervading. And it was because his regard for them, in the abstract, had become centred in a single concrete example that he began to find the younger set a nuisance. But others, it seemed, were quite as mad about Eileen Erroll as he was; and there seemed to be small chance for him to possess himself of her, unless he were prepared to make the matter of possession a pointed episode. This he knew he had no right to do; she had conferred no such privilege upon him; and he was obliged to be careful of what he did and said lest half a thousand bright unwinking eyes wink too knowingly—lest frivolous tongues go clip-clap, and idle brains infer that which, alas! did not exist except in his vision of desire.

The Hither Woods had been hung with myriads of lanterns. From every branch they swung in clusters or stretched away into perspective, turning the wooded aisles to brilliant vistas. Under them the more romantic and the dance-worn strolled in animated groups or quieter twos; an army of servants flitted hither and thither, serving the acre or so of small tables over each of which an electric cluster shed yellow light.

Supper, and then the Woodland cotillon was the programme; and almost all the tables were filled before Selwyn had an opportunity to collect Nina and Austin and capture Eileen from a very rosy-cheeked and indignant boy who had quite lost his head and heart and appeared to be on the verge of a headlong declaration.

"It's only Percy Draymore's kid brother," she explained, passing her arm through his with a little sigh of satisfaction. "Where have you been all the while?—and with whom have you danced, please?—and who is the pretty girl you paid court to during that last dance? What? *Didn't* pay court to her? Do you expect me to believe that? . . . Oh, here comes Nina and Austin. . . . How pretty the tables look, all lighted up among the trees! And such an uproar!"—as they came into the jolly tumult and passed in among a labyrinth of tables, greeted laughingly from every side.

Under a vigorous young oak-tree thickly festooned with lanterns Austin found an unoccupied table. There was a great deal of racket and laughter from the groups surrounding them, but this seemed to be the only available spot; besides, Austin was hungry, and he said so.

Nina, with Selwyn on her left, looked around for Gerald and Lansing. When the latter came sauntering up, Austin questioned him, but he replied carelessly that Gerald had gone to join some people whom he, Lansing, did not know very well.

"Why, there he is now!" exclaimed Eileen, catching sight of her brother seated among a very noisy group on the outer edge of the illuminated zone. "Who are those people, Nina? Oh! Rosamund Fane is there, too; and—and—"

She ceased speaking so abruptly that Selwyn turned around; and Nina bit her lip in vexation and glanced at her husband. For, among the overanimated and almost boisterous group which was attracting the attention of everybody in the vicinity sat Mrs. Jack Ruthven. And Selwyn saw her.

For a moment he looked at her—looked at Gerald beside her, and Neergard on the other side, and Rosamund opposite; and at the others, whom he had never before seen. Then quietly, but with heightened colour, he turned his attention to the glass which the servant had just filled for him, and, resting his hand on the stem, stared at the bubbles crowding upward through it to the foamy brim.

Nina and Boots had begun, ostentatiously, an exceedingly animated conversation; and they became almost aggressive, appealing to Austin, who sat back with a frown on his heavy face—and to Eileen, who was sipping her mineral water and staring thoughtfully at a big, round, orange-tinted lantern which hung like the harvest moon behind Gerald, throwing his curly head into silhouette.

"Gerald beside her, and Neergard on the other side."

What conversation there was to carry, Boots and Nina carried. Austin silently satisfied his hunger, eating and drinking with a sullen determination to make no pretence of ignoring a situation that plainly angered him deeply. And from minute to minute he raised his head to glare across at Gerald, who evidently was unconscious of the presence of his own party.

When Nina spoke to Eileen, the girl answered briefly but with perfect composure. Selwyn, too, added a quiet word at intervals, speaking in a voice that sounded a little tired and strained.

It was that note of fatigue in his voice which aroused Eileen to effort— the instinctive move to protect—to sustain him. Conscious of Austin's suppressed but increasing anger at her brother, amazed and distressed at what Gerald had done—for the boy's very presence there was an affront to them all—she was still more sensitive to Selwyn's voice; and in her heart she responded passionately.

Nina looked up, surprised at the sudden transformation in the girl, who had turned on Boots with a sudden flow of spirits and the gayest of challenges; and their laughter and badinage became so genuine and so persistent that, combining with Nina, they fairly swept Austin from his surly abstraction into their toils; and Selwyn's subdued laugh, if forced, sounded pleasantly, now, and his drawn face seemed to relax a little for the time being.

Once she turned, under cover of the general conversation which she had set going, and looked straight into Selwyn's eyes, flashing to him a message of purest loyalty; and his silent gaze in response sent the colour flying to her cheeks.

It was all very well for a while—a brave, sweet effort; but ears could not remain deaf to the increasing noise and laughter—to familiar voices, half-caught phrases, indiscreet even in the fragments understood. Besides, Gerald had seen them, and the boy's face had become almost ghastly.

Alixe, unusually flushed, was conducting herself without restraint; Neergard's snickering laugh grew more significant and persistent; even Rosamund spoke too loudly at moments; and once she looked around at Nina and Selwyn while her pretty, accentless laughter, rippling with its undertone of malice, became more frequent in the increasing tumult.

There was no use in making a pretence of further gaiety. Austin had begun to scowl again; Nina, with one shocked glance at Alixe, leaned over toward her brother:

"It is incredible!" she murmured; "she must be perfectly mad to make such an exhibition of herself. Can't anybody stop her? Can't anybody send her home?"

Austin said sullenly but distinctly: "The thing for us to do is to get out. . . . Nina—if you are ready—"

"But—but what about Gerald?" faltered Eileen, turning piteously to Selwyn. "We can't leave him—there!"

The man straightened up and turned his drawn face toward her:

"Do you wish me to get him?"

"Y-you can't do that—can you?"

"Yes, I can; if you wish it. Do you think there is anything in the world I can't do, if you wish it?"

As he rose she laid her hand on his arm:

"I—I don't ask it—" she began.

"You do not have to ask it," he said with a smile almost genuine. "Austin, I'm going to get Gerald—and Nina will explain to you that he's to be left to me if any sermon is required. I'll go back with him in the motor-boat. Boots, you'll drive home in my place."

As he turned, still smiling and self-possessed, Eileen whispered rapidly: "Don't go. I care for you too much to ask it."

He said under his breath: "Dearest, you cannot understand."

"Yes—I do! Don't go. Philip—don't go near—her—"

"I must."

"If you do—if you go—h-how can you c-care for me as you say you do?—when I ask you not to—when I cannot endure—to—"

She turned swiftly and stared across at Alixe; and Alixe, unsteady in the flushed brilliancy of her youthful beauty, half rose in her seat and stared back.

Instinctively the young girl's hand tightened on Selwyn's arm: "She—she is beautiful!" she faltered; but he turned and led her from the table, following Austin, his sister, and Lansing; and she clung to him almost convulsively when he halted on the edge of the lawn.

"I must go back," he whispered—"dearest—dearest—I must."

"T-to Gerald? Or—*her*?"

But he only muttered: "They don't know what they're doing. Let me go, Eileen"—gently detaching her fingers, which left her hands lying in both of his.—

She said, looking up at him: "If you go—if you go—whatever time you return—no matter what hour—knock at my door. Do you promise? I shall be awake. Do you promise?"

"Yes," he said with a trace of impatience—the only hint of his anger at the prospect of the duty before him.

So she went away with Nina and Austin and Boots; and Selwyn turned back, sauntering quietly toward the table where already the occupants had apparently forgotten him and the episode in the riotous gaiety increasing with the accession of half a dozen more men.

When Selwyn approached, Neergard saw him first, stared at him, and snickered; but he greeted everybody with smiling composure, nodding to those he knew—a trifle more formally to Mrs. Ruthven—and, coolly pulling up a chair, seated himself beside Gerald.

"Boots has driven home with the others," he said in a low voice; "I'm going back in the motor-boat with you. Don't worry about Austin. Are you ready?"

The boy had evidently let the wine alone, or else fright had sobered him, for he looked terribly white and tired: "Yes," he said, "I'll go when you wish. I suppose they'll never forgive me for this. Come on."

"One moment, then," nodded Selwyn; "I want to speak to Mrs. Ruthven." And, quietly turning to Alixe, and dropping his voice to a tone too low for Neergard to hear—for he was plainly attempting to listen:

"You are making a mistake; do you understand? Whoever is your hostess—wherever you are staying—find her and go there before it is too late."

She inclined her pretty head thoughtfully, eyes on the wine-glass which she was turning round and round between her slender fingers. "What do you mean by 'too late'?" she asked. "Don't you know that everything is too late for me now?"

"What do *you* mean, Alixe?" he returned, watching her intently.

"What I say. I have not seen Jack Ruthven for two months. Do you know what that means? I have not heard from him for two months. Do you know what *that* means? No? Well, I'll tell you, Philip; it means that when I do hear from him it will be through his attorneys."

He turned slightly paler: "Why"?"

"Divorce," she said with a reckless little laugh—"and the end of things for me."

"On what grounds?" he demanded doggedly. "Does he threaten you?"

She made no movement or reply, reclining there, one hand on her wine-glass, the smile still curving her lips. And he repeated his question in a low, distinct voice—too low for Neergard to hear; and he was still listening.

"Grounds? Oh, he thinks I've misbehaved with—never mind who. It is not true—but he cares nothing about that, either. You see"—and she bent nearer, confidentially, with a mysterious little nod of her pretty head—"you see, Jack Ruthven is a little insane. . . . You are surprised? Pooh! I've suspected it for months."

He stared at her; then: "Where are you stopping?"

"Aboard the *Niobrara*."

"Is Mrs. Fane a guest there, too?"

He spoke loud enough for Rosamund to hear; and she answered for herself with a smile at him, brimful of malice:

"Delighted to have you come aboard, Captain Selwyn. Is that what you are asking permission to do?"

"Thanks," he returned dryly; and to Alixe: "If you are ready, Gerald and I will take you over to the *Niobrara* in the motor-boat—"

"Oh, no, you won't!" broke in Neergard with a sneer—"you'll mind your own business, my intrusive friend, and I'll take care of my guests without your assistance."

Selwyn appeared not to hear him: "Come on, Gerald," he said pleasantly; "Mrs. Ruthven is going over to the *Niobrara*—"

"For God's sake," whispered Gerald, white as a sheet, "don't force me into trouble with Neergard."

Selwyn turned on him an astonished gaze: "Are you *afraid* of that whelp?"

"Yes," muttered the boy—"I—I'll explain later. But don't force things now, I beg you."

Mrs. Ruthven coolly leaned over and spoke to Gerald in a low voice; then, to Selwyn, she said with a smile: "Rosamund and I are going to Brookminster, anyway, so you and Gerald need not wait. . . . And thank you for coming over. It was rather nice of you"—she glanced insolently at Neergard—"considering the crowd we're with. *Good*-night, Captain Selwyn! *Good*-night, Gerald. So very jolly to have seen you again!" And, under her breath to Selwyn: "You need not worry; I am going in a moment. Good-bye and—thank you, Phil. It *is* good to see somebody of one's own caste again."

A few moments later, Selwyn and Gerald in their oilskins were dashing eastward along the coast in the swiftest motor-boat south of the Narrows.

The boy seemed deathly tired as they crossed the dim lawn at Silverside. Once, on the veranda steps he stumbled, and Selwyn's arm sustained him; but the older man forbore to question him, and Gerald, tight-lipped and haggard, offered no confidence until, at the door of his bedroom, he turned and laid an unsteady hand on Selwyn's shoulder: "I want to talk with you—to-morrow. May I?"

"You know you may, Gerald. I am always ready to stand your friend."

"I know. . . . I must have been crazy to doubt it. You are very good to me. I—I am in a very bad fix. I've got to tell you."

"Then we'll get you out of it, old fellow," said Selwyn cheerfully. "That's what friends are for, too."

The boy shivered—looked at the floor, then, without raising his eyes, said good-night, and, entering his bedroom, closed the door.

As Selwyn passed back along the corridor, the door of his sister's room opened, and Austin and Nina confronted him.

"Has that damfool boy come in?" demanded his brother-in-law, anxiety making his voice tremulous under its tone of contempt.

"Yes. Leave him to me, please. Good-night"—submitting to a tender embrace from his sister—"I suppose Eileen has retired, hasn't she? It's an ungodly hour—almost sunrise."

"I don't know whether Eileen is asleep," said Nina; "she expected a word with you, I understand. But don't sit up—don't let her sit up late. We'll be a company of dreadful wrecks at breakfast, anyway."

And his sister gently closed the door while he continued on to the end of the corridor and halted before Eileen's room. A light came through the transom; he waited a moment, then knocked very softly.

"Is it you?" she asked in a low voice.

"Yes. I didn't wake you, did I?"

"No. Is Gerald here?"

"Yes, in his own room. . . . Did you wish to speak to me about anything?"

"Yes."

He heard her coming to the door; it opened a very little. "Good-night," she whispered, stretching toward him her hand—"that was all I wanted—to—to touch you before I closed my eyes to-night."

He bent and looked at the hand lying within his own—the little hand with its fresh fragrant palm upturned and the white fingers relaxed, drooping inward above it—at the delicate bluish vein in the smooth wrist.

Then he released the hand, untouched by his lips; and she withdrew it and closed the door; and he heard her laugh softly, and lean against it, whispering:

"Now that I am safely locked in—I merely wish to say that—in the old days—a lady's hand was sometimes—kissed. . . . Oh, but you are too late, my poor friend! I can't come out; and I wouldn't if I could—not after what I dared to say to you. . . . In fact, I shall probably remain locked up here for days and days. . . . Besides, what I said is out of fashion—has no significance nowadays—or, perhaps, too much. . . . No, I won't dress and come out—even for you. *Je me déshabille—je fais ma toilette de nuit, monsieur—et je vais maintenant m'agenouiller et faire ma prière. Donc—bon soir—et bonne nuit—*"

And, too low for him to hear even the faintest breathing whisper of her voice—"Good-night. I love you with all my heart—with all my heart—in my own fashion."

He had been asleep an hour, perhaps more, when something awakened him, and he found himself sitting bolt upright in bed, dawn already whitening his windows.

Somebody was knocking. He swung out of bed, stepped into his bath-slippers, and, passing swiftly to the door, opened it. Gerald stood there, fully dressed.

"I'm going to town on the early train," began the boy—"I thought I'd tell you—"

"Nonsense! Gerald, go back to bed!"

"I can't sleep, Philip—"

"Can't sleep? Oh, that's the trouble, is it? Well, then, sit here and talk to me." He gave a mighty yawn—"I'm not sleepy, either; I can go days without it. Here!—here's a comfortable chair to sprawl in. . . . It's daylight already; doesn't the morning air smell sweet? I've a jug of milk and some grapes and peaches in my ice-cupboard if you feel inclined. No? All right; stretch out, sight for a thousand yards, and fire at will."

Gerald strove to smile; for a while he lay loosely in the arm-chair, his listless eyes intent on the strange, dim light which fell across the waste of sea fog. Only the water along the shore's edge remained visible; all else was a blank wall behind which, stretching to the horizon, lay the unseen ocean. Already a few restless gulls were on the wing, sheering inland; and their raucous, treble cries accented the pallid stillness.

But the dawn was no paler than the boy's face—no more desolate. Trouble was his, the same old trouble that has dogged the trail of folly since time began; and Selwyn knew it and waited.

At last the boy broke out: "This is a cowardly trick—this slinking in to you with all my troubles after what you've done for me—after the rotten way I've treated you—"

"Look here, my boy!" said Selwyn coolly, crossing one knee over the other and dropping both hands into the pockets of his pajamas—"I asked you to come to me, didn't I? Well, then; don't criticise my judgment in doing it. It isn't likely I'd ask you to do a cowardly thing."

"You don't understand what a wretched scrape I'm in—"

"I don't yet; but you're going to tell me—"

"Philip, I can't—I simply cannot. It's so contemptible—and you warned me—and I owe you already so much—"

"You owe me a little money," observed Selwyn with a careless smile, "and you've a lifetime to pay it in. What is the trouble now; do you need more? I haven't an awful lot, old fellow—worse luck!—but what I have is at your call—as you know perfectly well. Is that all that is worrying you?"

"No—not all. I—Neergard has lent me money—done things—placed me under obligations. . . . I liked him, you know; I trusted him. . . . People he desired to know I made him known to. He was a—a trifle peremptory at times—as though my obligations to him left me no choice but to take him to such people as he desired to meet. . . . We—we had trouble—recently."

"What sort?"

"Personal. I felt—began to feel—the pressure on me. There was, at moments, something almost of menace in his requests and suggestions—an importunity I did not exactly understand. . . . And then he said something to me—"

"Go on; what?"

"He'd been hinting at it before; and even when I found him jolliest and most amusing and companionable I never thought of him as a—a social possibility—I mean among those who really count—like my own people—"

"Oh! he asked you to introduce him into your own family circle?"

"Yes—I didn't understand it at first—until somehow I began to feel the pressure of it—the vague but constant importunity. . . . He was a good fellow—at least I thought so; I hated to hurt him—to assume any attitude that might wound him. But, good heavens!—he couldn't seem to understand that nobody in our family would receive him—although he had a certain footing with the Fanes and Harmons and a few others—like the Siowitha people—or at least the men of those families. Don't you see, Philip?"

"Yes, my boy, I see. Go on! When did he ask to be presented to—your sister?"

"W-who told you that?" asked the boy with an angry flush.

"You did—almost. You were going to, anyway. So that was it, was it? That was when you realised a few things—understood one or two things; was it not? . . . And how did you reply? Arrogantly, I suppose."

"Yes."

"With—a—some little show of—a—contempt?"

"Yes, I suppose so."

"Exactly. And Neergard—was put out—slightly?"

"Yes," said the boy, losing some of his colour. "I—a moment afterward I was sorry I had spoken so plainly; but I need not have been. . . . He was very ugly about it."

"Threats of calling loans?" asked Selwyn, smiling.

"Hints; not exactly threats. I was in a bad way, too—" The boy winced and swallowed hard; then, with sudden white desperation stamped on his drawn face: "Oh, Philip—it—it is disgraceful enough—but how am I going to tell you the rest?—how can I speak of this matter to you—"

"What matter?"

"A—about—about Mrs. Ruthven—"

"*What* matter?" repeated Selwyn. His voice rang a little, but the colour had fled from his face.

"She was—Jack Ruthven charged her with—and me—charged me with—"

"*You!*"

"Yes."

"Well—it was a lie, wasn't it?" Selwyn's ashy lips scarcely moved, but his eyes were narrowing to a glimmer. "It was a lie, wasn't it?" he repeated.

"Yes—a lie. I'd say it, anyway, you understand—but it really was a lie."

Selwyn quietly leaned back in his chair; a little colour returned to his cheeks.

"All right—old fellow"—his voice scarcely quivered—"all right; go on. I knew, of course, that Ruthven lied, but it was part of the story to hear you say so. Go on. What did Ruthven do?"

"There has been a separation," said the boy in a low voice. "He behaved like a dirty cad—she had no resources—no means of support—" He hesitated, moistening his dry lips with his tongue. "Mrs. Ruthven has been very, very kind to me. I was—I am fond of her; oh, I know well enough I never had any business to meet her; I behaved abominably toward you—and the family. But it was done; I knew her, and liked her tremendously. She was the only one who was decent to me—who tried to keep me from acting like a fool about cards—"

Did she try?"

"Yes—indeed, yes! . . . and, Phil—she—I don't know how to say it—but she—when she spoke of—of you—begged me to try to be like you. . . . And it is a lie what people say about her!—what gossip says. I know; I have known her so well—and—I was like other men—charmed and fascinated by her; but the women of that set are a pack of cats, and the men—well, none of them ever ventured to say anything to me! . . . And

251

that is all, Philip. I was horribly in debt to Neergard; then Ruthven turned on me—and on her; and I borrowed more from Neergard and went to her bank and deposited it to the credit of her account—but she doesn't know it was from me—she supposes Jack Ruthven did it out of ordinary decency, for she said so to me. And that is how matters stand; Neergard is ugly, and grows more threatening about those loans—and I haven't any money, and Mrs. Ruthven will require more very soon—"

"Is that *all*?" demanded Selwyn sharply.

"Yes—all. . . . I know I have behaved shamefully—"

"I've seen," observed Selwyn in a dry, hard voice, "worse behaviour than yours. . . . Have you a pencil, Gerald? Get a sheet of paper from that desk. Now, write out a list of the loans made you by Neergard. . . . Every cent, if you please. . . . And the exact amount you placed to Mrs. Ruthven's credit. . . . Have you written that? Let me see it."

The boy handed him the paper. He studied it without the slightest change of expression—knowing all the while what it meant to him; knowing that this burden must be assumed by himself because Austin would never assume it.

And he sat there staring at space over the top of the pencilled sheet of paper, striving to find some help in the matter. But he knew Austin; he knew what would happen to Gerald if, after the late reconciliation with his ex-guardian, he came once more to him with such a confession of debt and disgrace.

No; Austin must be left out; there were three things to do: One of them was to pay Neergard; another to sever Gerald's connection with him for ever; and the third thing to be done was something which did not concern Gerald or Austin—perhaps, not even Ruthven. It was to be done, no matter what the cost. But the thought of the cost sent a shiver over him, and left his careworn face gray.

His head sank; he fixed his narrowing eyes on the floor and held them there, silent, unmoved, while within the tempests of terror, temptation, and doubt assailed him, dragging at the soul of him, where it clung blindly to its anchorage. And it held fast—raging, despairing in the bitterness of renunciation, but still held on through the most dreadful tempest that ever swept him. Courage, duty, reparation—the words drummed in his brain, stupefying him with their dull clamour; but he understood and listened, knowing the end—knowing that the end must always be the same for him. It was the revolt of instinct against drilled and ingrained training, inherited and re-schooled—the insurgent clamour of desire opposed to that stern self-repression characteristic of generations of Selwyns, who had held duty important enough to follow, even when their bodies died in its wake.

And it were easier for him, perhaps, if his body died.

He rose and walked to the window. Over the Bay of Shoals the fog was lifting; and he saw the long gray pier jutting northward—the pier where the troopships landed their dead and dying when the Spanish war was ended.

And he looked at the hill where the field hospital had once been. His brother died there—in the wake of that same duty which no Selwyn could ignore.

After a moment he turned to Gerald, a smile on his colourless face:

"It will be all right, my boy. You are not to worry—do you understand me? Go to bed, now; you need the sleep. Go to bed, I tell you—I'll stand by you. You must begin all over again, Gerald—and so must I; and so must I."

CHAPTER X

LEX NON SCRIPTA

Selwyn had gone to New York with Gerald, "for a few days," as he expressed it; but it was now the first week in October, and he had not yet returned to Silverside.

A brief note to Nina thanking her for having had him at Silverside, and speaking vaguely of some business matters which might detain him indefinitely—a briefer note to Eileen regretting his inability to return for the present—were all the communication they had from him except news brought by Austin, who came down from town every Friday.

A long letter to him from Nina still remained unanswered; Austin had seen him only once in town; Lansing, now back in New York, wrote a postscript in a letter to Drina, asking for Selwyn's new address—the first intimation anybody had that he had given up his lodgings on Lexington Avenue.

"I was perfectly astonished to find he had gone, leaving no address," wrote Boots; "and nobody knows anything about him at his clubs. I have an idea that he may have gone to Washington to see about the Chaosite affair; but if you have any address except his clubs, please send it to me."

Eileen had not written him; his sudden leave-taking nearly a month ago had so astounded her that she could not believe he meant to be gone more than a day or two. Then came his note, written at the Patroons' Club—very brief, curiously stilted and formal, with a strange tone of finality through it, as though he were taking perfunctory leave of people who had come temporarily into his life, and as though the chances were agreeably even of his ever seeing them again.

The girl was not hurt, as yet; she remained merely confused, incredulous, unreconciled. That there was to be some further explanation of his silence she never dreamed of doubting; and there seemed to be nothing to do in the interval but await it. As for writing him, some instinct forbade it, even when Nina suggested that she write, adding laughingly that nothing else seemed likely to stir her brother.

For the first few days the children clamoured intermittently for him; but children forget, and Billy continued to cast out his pack in undying hope of a fox or bunny, and the younger children brought their butterfly-nets and sand-shovels to Austin and Nina for repairs; and Drina, when Boots deserted her for his Air Line Company, struck up a wholesome and lively friendship with a dozen subfreshmen and the younger Orchil girls, and began to play golf like a little fiend.

It was possible, now, to ride cross-country; and Nina, who was always in terror of an added ounce to her perfect figure, rode every day with Eileen; and Austin, on a big hunter, joined them two days in the week.

There were dances, too, and Nina went to some of them. So did Eileen, who had created a furor among the younger brothers and undergraduates; and the girl was busy enough with sailing and motoring and dashing through the Sound in all sorts of power boats.

Once, under Austin's and young Craig's supervision, she tried shore-bird shooting; but the first broken wing from the gun on her left settled the thing for ever for her, and the horror of the blood-sprinkled, kicking mass of feathers haunted her dreams for a week.

Youths, however, continued to hover numerously about her. They sat in soulful rows upon the veranda at Silverside; they played guitars at her in canoes, accompanying the stringy thrumming with the peculiarly exasperating vocal noises made only by very young undergraduates; they rode with her and Nina; they pervaded her vicinity with a tireless constancy amounting to obsession.

She liked it well enough; she was as interested in everything as usual; as active at the nets, playing superbly, and with all her heart in the game—while it lasted; she swung her slim brassy with all the old-time fire and satisfaction in the clean, sharp whack, as the ball flew through the sunshine, rising beautifully in a long, low trajectory against the velvet fair-green.

It was unalloyed happiness for her to sit her saddle, feeling under her the grand stride of her powerful hunter on a headlong cross-country gallop; it was purest pleasure for her to lean forward in her oilskins, her eyes almost blinded with salt spray, while the low motor-boat rushed on and on through cataracts of foam, and the heaving, green sea-miles fled away, away, in the hissing furrow of the wake.

Truly, for her, the world was still green, the sun bright, the high sky blue; but she had not forgotten that the earth had been greener, the sun brighter, the azure above her more splendid—once upon a time— like the first phrase of a tale that is told. And if she were at times listless, absent-eyed, subdued—a trifle graver, or unusually silent, seeking the still paths of the garden as though in need of youthful meditation and the quiet of the sunset hour, she never doubted that that tale would be retold for her again. Only—alas!—the fair days were passing, and the russet rustle of October sounded already among the curling leaves in the garden; and he had been away a long time—a very long time. And she could not understand.

On one of Austin's week-end visits, the hour for conjugal confab having arrived and husband and wife locked in the seclusion of their bedroom—being old-fashioned enough to occupy the same—he said, with a trace of irritation in his voice:

"I don't know where Phil is, or what he's about. I'm wondering—he's got the Selwyn conscience, you know—what he's up to—and if it's any kind of dam-foolishness. Haven't you heard a word from him, Nina?"

Nina, in her pretty night attire, had emerged from her dressing-room, locked out Kit-Ki and her maid, and had curled up in a big, soft armchair, cradling her bare ankles in her hand.

"I haven't heard from him," she said. "Rosamund saw him in Washington—passed him on the street. He was looking horridly thin and worn, she wrote. He did not see her."

"Now what in the name of common sense is he doing in Washington!" exclaimed Austin wrathfully. "Probably breaking his heart because nobody cares to examine his Chaosite. I told him, as long as he insisted on bothering the Government with it instead of making a deal with the Lawn people, that I'd furnish him with a key to the lobby. I told him I knew the right people, could get him the right lawyers, and start the thing properly. Why didn't he come to me about it? There's only one way to push such things, and he's as ignorant of it as a boatswain in the marine cavalry."

Nina said thoughtfully: "You always were impatient of people, dear. Perhaps Phil may get them to try his Chaosite without any wire-pulling. . . . I do wish he'd write. I can't understand his continued silence. Hasn't Boots heard from him? Hasn't Gerald?"

"Not a word. And by the way, Nina, Gerald has done rather an unexpected thing. I saw him last night; he came to the house and told me that he had just severed his connection with Julius Neergard's company."

"I'm glad of it!" exclaimed Nina; "I'm glad he showed the good sense to do it!"

255

"Well—yes. As a matter of fact, Neergard is going to be a very rich man some day; and Gerald might have—But I am not displeased. What appeals to me is the spectacle of the boy acting with conviction on his own initiative. Whether or not he is making a mistake has nothing to do with the main thing, and that is that Gerald, for the first time in his rather colourless career, seems to have developed the rudiments of a backbone out of the tail which I saw so frequently either flourishing defiance at me or tucked sullenly between his hind legs. I had quite a talk with him last night; he behaved very decently, and with a certain modesty which may, one day, develop into something approaching dignity. We spoke of his own affairs—in which, for the first time, he appeared to take an intelligent interest. Besides that, he seemed willing enough to ask my judgment in several matters—a radical departure from his cub days."

"What are you going to do for him, dear?" asked his wife, rather bewildered at the unexpected news. "Of course he must go into some sort of business again—"

"Certainly. And, to my astonishment, he actually came and solicited my advice. I—I was so amazed, Nina, that I could scarcely credit my own senses. I managed to say that I'd think it over. Of course he can, if he chooses, begin everything again and come in with me. Or—if I am satisfied that he has any ability—he can set up some sort of a real-estate office on his own hook. I could throw a certain amount of business in his way—but it's all in the air, yet. I'll see him Monday, and we'll have another talk. By gad! Nina," he added, with a flush of half-shy satisfaction on his ruddy face, "it's—it's almost like having a grown-up son coming bothering me with his affairs; ah—rather agreeable than otherwise. There's certainly something in that boy. I—perhaps I have been, at moments, a trifle impatient. But I did not mean to be. You know that, dear, don't you?"

His wife looked up at her big husband in quiet amusement. "Oh, yes! I know a little about you," she said, "and a little about Gerald, too. He is only a masculine edition of Eileen—the irresponsible freedom of life brought out all his faults at once, like a horrid rash; it's due to the masculine notion of masculine education. His sister's education was essentially the contrary: humours were eradicated before first symptoms became manifest. The moral, mental, and physical drilling and schooling was undertaken and accepted without the slightest hope—and later without the slightest desire—for any relaxation of the rigour when she became of age and mistress of herself. That's the difference: a boy looks forward to the moment when he can flourish his heels and wag his ears and bray; a girl has no such prospect. Gerald has brayed; Eileen never will flourish her heels unless she becomes fashionable after marriage—which isn't very likely—"

Nina hesitated, another idea intruding.

256

"By the way, Austin; the Orchil boy—the one in Harvard—proposed to Eileen—the little idiot! She told me—thank goodness! she still does tell me things. Also the younger and chubbier Draymore youth has offered himself—after a killingly proper interview with me. I thought it might amuse you to hear of it."

"It might amuse me more if Eileen would get busy and bring Philip into camp," observed her husband. "And why the devil they don't make up their minds to it is beyond me. That brother of yours is the limit sometimes. I'm fond of him—you know it—but he certainly can be the limit sometimes."

"Do you know," said Nina, "that I believe he is in love with her?"

"Then, why doesn't—"

"I don't know. I was sure—I am sure now—that the girl cares more for him than for anybody. And yet—and yet I don't believe she is actually in love with him. Several times I supposed she was—or near it, anyway. . . . But they are a curious pair, Austin—so quaint about it; so slow and old-fashioned. . . . And the child is the most innocent being—in some ways. . . . Which is all right unless she becomes one of those pokey, earnest, knowledge-absorbing young things with the very germ of vitality dried up and withered in her before she awakens. . . . I don't know—I really don't. For a girl *must* have something of the human about her to attract a man, and be attracted. . . . Not that she need know anything about love—or even suspect it. But there must be some response in her, some—some—"

"Deviltry?" suggested Austin.

His pretty wife laughed and dropped one knee over the other, leaning back to watch him finish his good-night cigarette. After a moment her face grew grave, and she bent forward.

"Speaking of Rosamund a moment ago reminds me of something else she wrote—it's about Alixe. Have you heard anything?"

"Not a word," said Austin, with a frank scowl, "and don't want to."

"It's only this—that Alixe is ill. Nobody seems to know what the matter is; nobody has seen her. But she's at Clifton, with a couple of nurses, and Rosamund heard rumours that she is very ill indeed. . . . People go to Clifton for shattered nerves, you know."

"Yes; for bridge-fidgets, neurosis, pip, and the various jumps that originate in the simpler social circles. What's the particular matter with her? Too many cocktails? Or a dearth of grand slams?"

"You are brutal, Austin. Besides, I don't know. She's had a perfectly dreary life with her husband. . . . I—I can't forget how fond I was of her in spite of what she did to Phil. . . . Besides, I'm beginning to be certain that it was not entirely her fault."

"What? Do you think Phil—"

"No, no, no! Don't be an utter idiot. All I mean to say is that Alixe was always nervous and high-strung; odd at times; eccentric—*more* than merely eccentric—"

"You mean dippy?"

"Oh, Austin, you're horrid. I mean that there is mental trouble in that family. You have heard of it as well as I; you know her father died of it—"

"The usual defence in criminal cases," observed Austin, flicking his cigarette-end into the grate. "I'm sorry, dear, that Alixe has the jumps; hope she'll get over 'em. But as for pretending I've any use for her, I can't and don't and won't. She spoiled life for the best man I know; she kicked his reputation into a cocked hat, and he, with his chivalrous Selwyn conscience, let her do it. I did like her once; I don't like her now, and that's natural and it winds up the matter. Dear friend, shall we, perhaps, to bed presently our way wend—yess?"

"Yes, dear; but you are not very charitable about Alixe. And I tell you I've my own ideas about her illness—especially as she is at Clifton. . . . I wonder where her little beast of a husband is?"

But Austin only yawned and looked at the toes of his slippers, and then longingly at the pillows.

Had Nina known it, the husband of Mrs. Ruthven, whom she had characterised so vividly, was at that very moment seated in a private card-room at the Stuyvesant Club with Sanxon Orchil, George Fane, and Bradley Harmon; and the game had been bridge, as usual, and had gone very heavily against him.

Several things had gone against Mr. Ruthven recently; for one thing, he was beginning to realise that he had made a vast mistake in mixing himself up in any transactions with Neergard.

When he, at Neergard's cynical suggestion, had consented to exploit his own club—the Siowitha—and had consented to resign from it to do so, he had every reason to believe that Neergard meant to either mulct them heavily or buy them out. In either case, having been useful to Neergard, his profits from the transaction would have been considerable.

But, even while he was absorbed in figuring them up—and he needed the money, as usual—Neergard coolly informed him of his election to the club, and Ruthven, thunder-struck, began to perceive the depth of the underground mole tunnels which Neergard had dug to undermine and capture the stronghold which had now surrendered to him.

Rage made him ill for a week; but there was nothing to do about it. He had been treacherous to his club and to his own caste, and Neergard knew it—and knew perfectly well that Ruthven dared not protest—dared not even whimper.

Then Neergard began to use Ruthven when he needed him; and he began to permit himself to win at cards in Ruthven's house—a thing he had not dared to do before. He also permitted himself more ease and freedom in that house—a sort of intimacy *sans façon*—even a certain jocularity. He also gave himself the privilege of inviting the Ruthvens on board the *Niobrara*; and Ruthven went, furious at being forced to stamp with his open approval an episode which made Neergard a social probability.

How it happened that Rosamund divined something of the situation is not quite clear; but she always had a delicate nose for anything not intended for her, and the thing amused her immensely, particularly because what viciousness had been so long suppressed in Neergard was now tentatively making itself apparent in his leering ease among women he so recently feared.

This, also, was gall and wormwood to Ruthven, so long the official lap-dog of the very small set he kennelled with; and the women of that set were perverse enough to find Neergard amusing, and his fertility in contriving new extravagances for them interested these people, whose only interest had always been centred in themselves.

Meanwhile, Neergard had almost finished with Gerald—he had only one further use for him; and as his social success became more pronounced with the people he had crowded in among, he became bolder and more insolent, no longer at pains to mole-tunnel toward the object desired, no longer overcareful about his mask. And one day he asked the boy very plainly why he had never invited him to meet his sister. And he got an answer that he never forgot.

And all the while Ruthven squirmed under the light but steadily inflexible pressure of the curb which Neergard had slipped on him so deftly; he had viewed with indifference Gerald's boyish devotion to his wife, which was even too open and naïve to be of interest to those who witnessed it. But he had not counted on Neergard's sudden hatred of Gerald; and the first token of that hatred fell upon the boy like a thunderbolt when Neergard whispered to Ruthven, one night at the Stuyvesant Club, and Ruthven, exasperated, had gone straight home, to find his wife in tears, and the boy clumsily attempting to comfort her, both her hands in his.

"Perhaps," said Ruthven coldly, "you have some plausible explanation for this sort of thing. If you haven't, you'd better trump up one together, and I'll send you my attorney to hear it. In that event," he added, "you'd better leave your joint address when you find a more convenient house than mine."

As a matter of fact, he had really meant nothing more than the threat and the insult, the situation permitting him a heavier hold upon his wife and a new grip on Gerald in case he ever needed him; but threat and insult were very real to the boy, and he knocked Mr. Ruthven flat on his back—the one thing required to change that gentleman's pretence to deadly earnest.

Ruthven scrambled to his feet; Gerald did it again; and, after that, Mr. Ruthven prudently remained prone during the delivery of a terse but concise opinion of him expressed by Gerald.

After Gerald had gone, Ruthven opened first one eye, then the other, then his mouth, and finally sat up; and his wife, who had been curiously observing him, smiled.

"It is strange," she said serenely, "that I never thought of that method. I wonder why I never thought of it," lazily stretching her firm young arms and glancing casually at their symmetry and smooth-skinned strength. "Go into your own quarters," she added, as he rose, shaking with fury: "I've endured the last brutality I shall ever suffer from you."

She dropped her folded hands into her lap, gazing coolly at him; but there was a glitter in her eyes which arrested his first step toward her.

"I think," she said, "that you mean my ruin. Well, we began it long ago, and I doubt if I have anything of infamy to learn, thanks to my thorough schooling as your wife. . . . But knowledge is not necessarily practice, and it happens that I have not cared to commit the particular indiscretion so fashionable among the friends you have surrounded me with. I merely mention this for your information, not because I am particularly proud of it. It is not anything to be proud of, in my case—it merely happened so; a matter, perhaps of personal taste, perhaps because of lack of opportunity; and there is a remote possibility that belated loyalty to a friend I once betrayed may have kept me personally chaste in this rotting circus circle you have driven me around in, harnessed to your vicious caprice, dragging the weight of your corruption—"

She laughed. "I had no idea that I could be so eloquent, Jack. But my mind has become curiously clear during the last year—strangely and unusually limpid and precise. Why, my poor friend, every plot of yours and of your friends—every underhand attempt to discredit and injure me has been perfectly apparent to me. You supposed that my headaches, my outbursts of anger, my wretched nights, passed in tears—and the long, long days spent kneeling in the ashes of dead memories—all these you supposed had weakened—perhaps unsettled— my mind. . . . You lie if you deny it, for you have had doctors watching me for months. . . . You didn't know I was aware of it, did you? But I was, and I am. . . . And you told them that my father died of—of brain trouble, you coward!"

Still he stood there, jaw loose, gazing at her as though fascinated; and she smiled and settled deeper in her chair, framing the gilded foliations of the back with her beautiful arms.

"We might as well understand one another now," she said languidly. "If you mean to get rid of me, there is no use in attempting to couple my name with that of any man; first, because it is untrue, and you not only know it, but you know you can't prove it. There remains the cowardly method you have been nerving yourself to attempt, never dreaming that I was aware of your purpose."

A soft, triumphant little laugh escaped her. There was something almost childish in her delight at outwitting him, and, very slowly, into his worn and faded eyes a new expression began to dawn—the flickering stare of suspicion. And in it the purely personal impression of rage and necessity of vengeance subsided; he eyed her intently, curiously, and with a cool persistence which finally began to irritate her.

"What a credulous fool you are," she said, "to build your hopes of a separation on any possible mental disability of mine."

He stood a moment without answering, then quietly seated himself. The suspicious glimmer in his faded eyes had become the concentration of a curiosity almost apprehensive.

"Go on," he said; "what else?"

"What do you mean?"

"You have been saying several things—about doctors whom I have set to watch you—for a year or more."

"Do you deny it?" she retorted angrily.

"No—no, I do not deny anything. But—who are these doctors—whom you have noticed?"

"I don't know who they are," she replied impatiently. "I've seen them often enough—following me on the street, or in public places—watching me. They are everywhere—you have them well paid, evidently; I suppose you can afford it. But you are wasting your time."

"You think so?"

"Yes!" she cried in a sudden violence that startled him, "you are wasting your time! And so am I—talking to you—enduring your personal affronts and brutal sneers. Sufficient for you that I know my enemies, and that I am saner, thank God, than any of them!" She flashed a look of sudden fury at him, and rose from her chair. He also rose with a promptness that bordered on precipitation.

261

"For the remainder of the spring and summer," she said, "I shall make my plans regardless of you. I shall not go to Newport; you are at liberty to use the house there as you choose. And as for this incident with Gerald, you had better not pursue it any further. Do you understand?"

He nodded, dropping his hands into his coat-pockets.

"Now you may go," she said coolly.

He went—not, however, to his room, but straight to the house of the fashionable physician who ministered to wealth with an unction and success that had permitted him, in summer time, to occupy his own villa at Newport and dispense further ministrations when requested.

On the night of the conjugal conference between Nina Gerard and her husband—and almost at the same hour—Jack Ruthven, hard hit in the card-room of the Stuyvesant Club, sat huddled over the table, figuring up what sort of checks he was to draw to the credit of George Fane and Sanxon Orchil.

Matters had been going steadily against him for some time—almost everything, in fact, except the opinions of several physicians in a matter concerning his wife. For, in that scene between them in early spring, his wife had put that into his head which had never before been there—suspicion of her mental soundness.

And now, as he sat there, pencil in hand, adding up the score-cards, he remembered that he was to interview his attorney that evening at his own house—a late appointment, but necessary to insure the presence of one or two physicians at a consultation to definitely decide what course of action might be taken.

He had not laid eyes on his wife that summer, but for the first time he had really had her watched during her absence. What she lived on—how she managed—he had not the least idea, and less concern. All he knew was that he had contributed nothing, and he was quite certain that her balance at her own bank had been nonexistent for months.

But any possible additional grounds for putting her away from him that might arise in a question as to her sources of support no longer interested him. That line of attack was unnecessary; besides, he had no suspicion concerning her personal chastity. But Alixe, that evening in early spring, had unwittingly suggested to him the use of a weapon the existence of which he had never dreamed of. And he no longer entertained any doubts of its efficiency as a means of finally ridding him of a wife whom he had never been able to fully subdue or wholly corrupt, and who, as a mate for him in his schemes for the pecuniary maintenance of his household, had proven useless and almost ruinous.

262

He had not seen her during the summer. In the autumn he had heard of her conduct at Hitherwood House. And, a week later, to his astonishment, he learned of her serious illness, and that she had been taken to Clifton. It was the only satisfactory news he had had of her in months.

So now he sat there at the bridge-table in the private card-room of the Stuyvesant Club, deftly adding up the score that had gone against him, but consoled somewhat at the remembrance of his appointment, and of the probability of an early release from the woman who had been to him only a source of social mistakes, domestic unhappiness, and financial disappointment.

When he had finished his figuring he fished out a check-book, detached a tiny gold fountain-pen from the bunch of seals and knick-knacks on his watch-chain, and, filling in the checks, passed them over without comment.

Fane rose, stretching his long neck, gazed about through his spectacles, like a benevolent saurian, and finally fixed his mild, protruding eyes upon Orchil.

"There'll be a small game at the Fountain Club," he said, with a grin which creased his cheeks until his retreating chin almost disappeared under the thick lower lip.

Orchil twiddled his long, crinkly, pointed moustache and glanced interrogatively at Harmon; then he yawned, stretched his arms, and rose, pocketing the check, which Ruthven passed to him, with a careless nod of thanks.

As they filed out of the card-room into the dim passageway, Orchil leading, a tall, shadowy figure in evening dress stepped back from the door of the card-room against the wall to give them right of way, and Orchil, peering at him without recognition in the dull light, bowed suavely as he passed, as did Fane, craning his curved neck, and Harmon also, who followed in his wake.

But when Ruthven came abreast of the figure in the passage and bowed his way past, a low voice from the courteous unknown, pronouncing his name, halted him short.

"I want a word with you, Mr. Ruthven," added Selwyn; "that card-room will suit me, if you please."

But Ruthven, recovering from the shock of Selwyn's voice, started to pass him without a word.

"I said that I wanted to speak to you!" repeated Selwyn.

Ruthven, deigning no reply, attempted to shove by him; and Selwyn, placing one hand flat against the other's shoulder, pushed him violently back into the card-room he had just left, and, stepping in behind him, closed and locked the door.

"W-what the devil do you mean!" gasped Ruthven, his hard, minutely shaven face turning a deep red.

"What I say," replied Selwyn; "that I want a word or two with you."

He stood still for a moment, in the centre of the little room, tall, gaunt of feature, and very pale. The close, smoky atmosphere of the place evidently annoyed him; he glanced about at the scattered cards, the empty oval bottles in their silver stands, the half-burned remains of cigars on the green-topped table. Then he stepped over and opened the only window.

"Sit down," he said, turning on Ruthven; and he seated himself and crossed one leg over the other. Ruthven remained standing.

"This—this thing," began Ruthven in a voice made husky and indistinct through fury, "this ruffianly behaviour amounts to assault."

"As you choose," nodded Selwyn, almost listlessly, "but be quiet; I've something to think of besides your convenience."

For a few moments he sat silent, thoughtful, narrowing eyes considering the patterns on the rug at his feet; and Ruthven, weak with rage and apprehension, was forced to stand there awaiting the pleasure of a man of whom he had suddenly become horribly afraid.

And at last Selwyn, emerging from his pallid reverie, straightened out, shaking his broad shoulders as though to free him of that black spectre perching there.

"Ruthven," he said, "a few years ago you persuaded my wife to leave me; and I have never punished you. There were two reasons why I did not: the first was because I did not wish to punish her, and any blow at you would have reached her heavily. The second reason, subordinate to the first, is obvious: decent men, in these days, have tacitly agreed to suspend a violent appeal to the unwritten law as a concession to civilisation. This second reason, however, depends entirely upon the first, as you see."

He leaned back in his chair thoughtfully, and recrossed his legs.

"I did not ask you into this room," he said, with a slight smile, "to complain of the wrong you have committed against me, or to retail to you the consequences of your act as they may or may not have affected me and my career; I have—ah—invited you here to explain to you the present condition of your own domestic affairs"—he looked at Ruthven full in the face—"to explain them to you, and to lay down for you the course of conduct which you are to follow."

"By God!—" began Ruthven, stepping back, one hand reaching for the door-knob; but Selwyn's voice rang out clean and sharp:

264

"Sit down!"

And, as Ruthven glared at him out of his little eyes:

"You'd better sit down, I think," said Selwyn softly.

Ruthven turned, took two unsteady steps forward, and laid his heavily ringed hand on the back of a chair. Selwyn smiled, and Ruthven sat down.

"Now," continued Selwyn, "for certain rules of conduct to govern you during the remainder of your wife's lifetime. . . . And your wife is ill, Mr. Ruthven—sick of a sickness which may last for a great many years, or may be terminated in as many days. Did you know it?"

Ruthven snarled.

"Yes, of course you knew it, or you suspected it. Your wife is in a sanitarium, as you have discovered. She is mentally ill—rational at times—violent at moments, and for long periods quite docile, gentle, harmless—content to be talked to, read to, advised, persuaded. But during the last week a change of a certain nature has occurred which— which, I am told by competent physicians, not only renders her case beyond all hope of ultimate recovery, but threatens an earlier termination than was at first looked for. It is this: your wife has become like a child again—occupied contentedly and quite happily with childish things. She has forgotten much; her memory is quite gone. How much she does remember it is impossible to say."

His head fell; his brooding eyes were fixed again on the rug at his feet. After a while he looked up.

"It is pitiful, Mr. Ruthven—she is so young—with all her physical charm and attraction quite unimpaired. But the mind is gone—quite gone, sir. Some sudden strain—and the tension has been great for years—some abrupt overdraft upon her mental resource, perhaps; God knows how it came—from sorrow, from some unkindness too long endured—"

Again he relapsed into his study of the rug; and slowly, warily, Ruthven lifted his little, inflamed eyes to look at him, then moistened his dry lips with a thick-coated tongue, and stole a glance at the locked door.

"I understand," said Selwyn, looking up suddenly, "that you are contemplating proceedings against your wife. Are you?"

Ruthven made no reply.

"*Are* you?" repeated Selwyn. His face had altered; a dim glimmer played in his eyes like the reflection of heat lightning at dusk.

"Yes, I am," said Ruthven.

"On the grounds of her mental incapacity?"

"Yes."

"Then, as I understand it, the woman whom you persuaded to break every law, human and divine, for your sake, you now propose to abandon. Is that it?"

Ruthven made no reply.

"You propose to publish her pitiable plight to the world by beginning proceedings; you intend to notify the public of your wife's infirmity by divorcing her."

"Sane or insane," burst out Ruthven, "she was riding for a fall—and she's going to get it! What the devil are you talking about? I'm not accountable to you. I'll do what I please; I'll manage my own affairs—"

"No," said Selwyn, "I'll manage this particular affair. And now I'll tell you how I'm going to do it. I have in my lodgings—or rather in the small hall bedroom which I now occupy—an army service revolver, in fairly good condition. The cylinder was a little stiff this morning when I looked at it, but I've oiled it with No. 27—an excellent rust solvent and lubricant, Mr. Ruthven—and now the cylinder spins around in a manner perfectly trustworthy. So, as I was saying, I have this very excellent and serviceable weapon, and shall give myself the pleasure of using it on you if you ever commence any such action for divorce or separation against your wife. This is final."

Ruthven stared at him as though hypnotised.

"Don't mistake me," added Selwyn, a trifle wearily. "I am not compelling you to decency for the purpose of punishing *you*; men never trouble themselves to punish vermin—they simply exterminate them, or they retreat and avoid them. I merely mean that you shall never again bring publicity and shame upon your wife—even though now, mercifully enough, she has not the faintest idea that you are what a complacent law calls her husband."

A slow blaze lighted up his eyes, and he got up from his chair.

"You decadent little beast!" he said slowly, "do you suppose that the dirty accident of your intrusion into an honest man's life could dissolve the divine compact of wedlock? Soil it—yes; besmirch it, render it superficially unclean, unfit, nauseous—yes. But neither you nor your vile code nor the imbecile law you invoked to legalise the situation really ever deprived me of my irrevocable status and responsibility. . . . I—even I—was once—for a while—persuaded that it did; that the laws of the land could do this—could free me from a faithless wife, and regularise her position in your household. The laws of the land say so, and I—I said so at last—persuaded because I desired to be persuaded. . . . It was a lie. My wife, shamed or unshamed, humbled or unhumbled, true to her marriage vows or false to them, now legally the wife of another, has never ceased to be my wife. And it is a higher law that corroborates me—higher than you can understand—a law unwritten because axiomatic; a law governing the very foundation of the social fabric, and on which that fabric is absolutely dependent for its existence intact. But"—with a contemptuous shrug—"you won't understand; all you can understand is the gratification of your senses and the fear of something interfering with that gratification—like death, for instance. Therefore I am satisfied that you understand enough of what I said to discontinue any legal proceedings which would tend to discredit, expose, or cast odium on a young wife very sorely stricken—very, very ill—whom God, in his mercy, has blinded to the infamy where you have dragged her—under the law of the land."

He turned on his heel, paced the little room once or twice, then swung round again:

"Keep your filthy money—wrung from women and boys over card-tables. Even if some blind, wormlike process of instinct stirred the shame in you, and you ventured to offer belated aid to the woman who bears your name, I forbid it—I do not permit you the privilege. Except that she retains your name—and the moment you attempt to rob her of that I shall destroy you!—except for that, you have no further relations with her—nothing to do or undo; no voice as to the disposal of what remains of her; no power, no will, no influence in her fate. *I* supplant you; I take my own again; I reassume a responsibility temporarily taken from me. And *now*, I think, you understand!"

He gave him one level and deadly stare; then his pallid features relaxed, he slowly walked past Ruthven, grave, preoccupied; unlocked the door, and passed out.

His lodgings were not imposing in their furnishings or dimensions—a very small bedroom in the neighbourhood of Sixth Avenue and Washington Square—but the heavy and increasing drain on his resources permitted nothing better now; and what with settling Gerald's complications and providing two nurses and a private suite at Clifton for Alixe Ruthven, he had been obliged to sell a number of securities, which reduced his income to a figure too absurd to worry over.

However, the Government had at last signified its intention of testing his invention—Chaosite—and there was that chance for better things in prospect. Also, in time, Gerald would probably be able to return something of the loans made. But these things did not alleviate present stringent conditions, nor were they likely to for a long while; and Selwyn, tired and perplexed, mounted the stairs of his lodging-house and laid his overcoat on the iron bed, and, divesting himself of the garments of ceremony as a matter of economy, pulled on an old tweed shooting-jacket and trousers.

Then, lighting his pipe—cigars being now on the expensive and forbidden list—he drew a chair to his table and sat down, resting his worn face between both hands. Truly the world was not going very well with him in these days.

For some time, now, it had been his custom to face his difficulties here in the silence of his little bedroom, seated alone at his table, pipe gripped between his firm teeth, his strong hands framing his face. Here he would sit for hours, the long day ended, staring steadily at the blank wall, the gas-jet flickering overhead; and here, slowly, painfully, with doubt and hesitation, out of the moral confusion in his weary mind he evolved the theory of personal responsibility.

With narrowing eyes, from which slowly doubt faded, he gazed at duty with all the calm courage of his race, not at first recognising it as duty in its new and dreadful guise.

But night after night, patiently perplexed, he retraced his errant pathway through life, back to the source of doubt and pain; and, once arrived there, he remained, gazing with impartial eyes upon the ruin two young souls had wrought of their twin lives; and always, always somehow, confronting him among the débris, rose the spectre of their deathless responsibility to one another; and the inexorable life-sentence sounded ceaselessly in his ears: "For better or for worse—for better or for worse—till death do us part—till death—till death!"

Dreadful his duty—for man already had dared to sunder them, and he had acquiesced to save her in the eyes of the world! Dreadful, indeed—because he knew that he had never loved her, never could love her! Dreadful—doubly dreadful—for he now knew what love might be; and it was not what he had believed it when he executed the contract which must bind him while life endured.

Once, and not long since, he thought that, freed from the sad disgrace of the shadowy past, he had begun life anew. They told him—and he told himself—that a man had that right; that a man was no man who stood stunned and hopeless, confronting the future in fetters of conscience. And by that token he had accepted the argument as truth—because he desired to believe it—and he had risen erect and shaken himself free of the past—as he supposed; as though the past, which becomes part of us, can be shaken from tired shoulders with the first shudder of revolt!

No; he understood now that the past was part of him—as his limbs and head and body and mind were part of him. It had to be reckoned with—what he had done to himself, to the young girl united to him in bonds indissoluble except in death.

That she had strayed—under man-made laws held guiltless—could not shatter the tie. That he, blinded by hope, had hoped to remake a life already made, and had dared to masquerade before his own soul as a man free to come, to go, and free to love, could not alter what had been done. Back, far back of it all lay the deathless pact—for better or for worse. And nothing man might wish or say or do could change it.

Always, always he must remain bound by that, no matter what others did or thought; always, always he was under obligations to the end.

And now, alone, abandoned, helplessly sick, utterly dependent upon the decency, the charity, the mercy of her legal paramour, the young girl who had once been his wife had not turned to him in vain.

Before the light of her shaken mind had gone out she had written him, incoherently, practically *in extremis*; and if he had hitherto doubted where his duty lay, from that moment he had no longer any doubt. And very quietly, hopelessly, and irrevocably he had crushed out of his soul the hope and promise of the new life dawning for him above the dead ashes of the past.

It was not easy to do; he had not ended it yet. He did not know how. There were ties to be severed, friendships to be gently broken, old scenes to be forgotten, memories to kill. There was also love—to be disposed of. And he did not know how.

First of all, paramount in his hopeless trouble, the desire to save others from pain persisted.

For that reason he had been careful that Gerald should not know where and how he was now obliged to live—lest the boy suspect and understand how much of Selwyn's little fortune it had taken to settle his debts of "honour" and free him from the sinister pressure of Neergard's importunities.

For that reason, too, he dreaded to have Austin know, because, if the truth were exposed, nothing in the world could prevent a violent and final separation between him and the foolish boy who now, at last, was beginning to show the first glimmering traces of character and common sense.

So he let it be understood that his address was his club for the present; for he also desired no scene with Boots, whom he knew would attempt to force him to live with him in his cherished and brand-new house. And even if he cared to accept and permit Boots to place him under such obligations, it would only hamper him in his duties.

Because now, what remained of his income must be devoted to Alixe.

Even before her case had taken the more hopeless turn, he had understood that she could not remain at Clifton. Such cases were neither desired nor treated there; he understood that. And so he had taken, for her, a pretty little villa at Edgewater, with two trained nurses to care for her, and a phaeton for her to drive.

And now she was installed there, properly cared for, surrounded by every comfort, contented—except in the black and violent crises which still swept her in recurrent storms—indeed, tranquil and happy; for through the troubled glimmer of departing reason, her eyes were already opening in the calm, unearthly dawn of second childhood.

Pain, sadness, the desolate awakening to dishonour had been forgotten; to her, the dead now lived; to her, the living who had been children with her were children again, and she a child among them. Outside of that dead garden of the past, peopled by laughing phantoms of her youth, but one single extraneous memory persisted—the memory of Selwyn—curiously twisted and readjusted to the comprehension of a child's mind—vague at times, at times wistfully elusive and incoherent—but it remained always a memory, and always a happy one.

He was obliged to go to her every three or four days. In the interim she seemed quite satisfied and happy, busy with the simple and pretty things she now cared for; but toward the third day of his absence she usually became restless, asking for him, and why he did not come. And then they telegraphed him, and he left everything and went, white-faced, stern of lip, to endure the most dreadful ordeal a man may face—to force the smile to his lips and gaiety into the shrinking soul of him, and sit with her in the pretty, sunny room, listening to her prattle, answering the childish questions, watching her, seated in her rocking-chair, singing contentedly to herself, and playing with her dolls and ribbons—dressing them, undressing, mending, arranging—until the heart within him quivered under the misery of it, and he turned to the curtained window, hands clinching convulsively, and teeth set to force back the strangling agony in his throat.

And the dreadful part of it all was that her appearance had remained unchanged—unless, perhaps, she was prettier, lovelier of face and figure than ever before; but in her beautiful dark eyes only the direct intelligence of a child answered his gaze of inquiry; and her voice, too, had become soft and hesitating, and the infantile falsetto sounded in it at times, sweet, futile, immature.

Thinking of these things now, he leaned heavily forward, elbows on the little table. And, suddenly unbidden, before his haunted eyes rose the white portico of Silverside, and the greensward glimmered, drenched in sunshine, and a slim figure in white stood there, arms bare, tennis-bat swinging in one tanned little hand.

Voices were sounding in his ears—Drina's laughter, Lansing's protest; Billy shouting to his eager pack; his sister's calm tones, admonishing the young—and through it all, *her* voice, clear, hauntingly sweet, pronouncing his name.

And he set his lean jaws tight and took a new grip on his pipe-stem, and stared, with pain-dulled eyes, at the white wall opposite.

But on the blank expanse the faintest tinge of colour appeared, growing clearer, taking shape as he stared; and slowly, slowly, under the soft splendour of her hair, two clear eyes of darkest blue opened under the languid lids and looked at him, and looked and looked until he closed his own, unable to endure the agony.

But even through his sealed lids he saw her; and her clear gaze pierced him, blinded as he was, leaning there, both hands pressed across his eyes.

Sooner or later—sooner or later he must write to her and tell what must be told. How to do it, when to do it, he did not know. What to say he did not know; but that there was something due her from him—something to say, something to confess—to ask her pardon for—he understood.

Happily for her—happily for him, alas!—love, in its full miracle, had remained beyond her comprehension. That she cared for him with all her young heart he knew; that she had not come to love him he knew, too. So that crowning misery of happiness was spared him.

Yet he knew, too, that there had been a chance for him; that her awakening had not been wholly impossible. Loyal in his soul to the dread duty before him, he must abandon hope; loyal in his heart to her, he must abandon her, lest, by chance, in the calm, still happiness of their intimacy the divine moment, unheralded, flash out through the veil, dazzling, blinding them with the splendour of its truth and beauty.

And now, leaning there, his face buried in his hands, hours that he spent with her came crowding back upon him, and in his ears her voice echoed and echoed, and his hands trembled with the scented memory of her touch, and his soul quivered and cried out for her.

Storm after storm swept him; and in the tempest he abandoned reason, blinded, stunned, crouching there with head lowered and his clenched hands across his face.

But storms, given right of way, pass on and over, and tempests sweep hearts cleaner; and after a long while he lifted his bowed head and sat up, squaring his shoulders.

Presently he picked up his pipe again, held it a moment, then laid it aside. Then he leaned forward, breathing deeply but quietly, and picked up a pen and a sheet of paper. For the time had come for his letter to her, and he was ready.

The letter he wrote was one of those gay, cheerful, inconsequential letters which, from the very beginning of their occasional correspondence, had always been to her most welcome and delightful.

Ignoring that maturity in her with which he had lately dared to reckon, he reverted to the tone which he had taken and maintained with her before the sweetness and seriousness of their relations had deepened to an intimacy which had committed him to an avowal.

News of all sorts humorously retailed—an amusing sketch of his recent journey to Washington and its doubtful results—matters that they both were interested in, details known only to them, a little harmless gossip—these things formed the body of his letter. There was never a hint of sorrow or discouragement—nothing to intimate that life had so utterly and absolutely changed for him—only a jolly, friendly badinage— an easy, light-hearted narrative, ending in messages to all and a frank regret that the pursuit of business and happiness appeared incompatible at the present moment.

His address, he wrote, was his club; he sent her, he said, under separate cover, a rather interesting pamphlet—a monograph on the symbolism displayed by the designs in Samarcand rugs and textiles of the Ming dynasty. And he ended, closing with a gentle jest concerning blue-stockings and rebellious locks of ruddy hair.

And signed his name.

Nina and Eileen, in travelling gowns and veils, stood on the porch at Silverside, waiting for the depot wagon, when Selwyn's letter was handed to Eileen.

The girl flushed up, then, avoiding Nina's eyes, turned and entered the house. Once out of sight, she swiftly mounted to her own room and dropped, breathless, on the bed, tearing the envelope from end to end. And from end to end, and back again and over again, she read the letter—at first in expectancy, lips parted, colour brilliant, then with the smile still curving her cheeks—but less genuine now—almost mechanical—until the smile stamped on her stiffening lips faded, and the soft contours relaxed, and she lifted her eyes, staring into space with a wistful, questioning lift of the pure brows.

What more had she expected? What more had she desired? Nothing, surely, of that emotion which she declined to recognise; surely not that sentiment of which she had admitted her ignorance to him. Again her eyes sought the pages, following the inked writing from end to end. What was she seeking there that he had left unwritten? What was she searching for, of which there was not one hint in all these pages?

And now Nina was calling her from the hall below; and she answered gaily and, hiding the letter in her long glove, came down the stairs.

272

"I'll tell you all about the letter in the train," she said; "he is perfectly well, and evidently quite happy; and Nina—"

"What, dear?"

"I want to send him a telegram. May I?"

"A dozen, if you wish," said Mrs. Gerard, "only, if you don't climb into that vehicle, we'll miss the train."

So on the way to Wyossette station Eileen sat very still, gloved hands folded in her lap, composing her telegram to Selwyn. And, once in the station, having it by heart already, she wrote it rapidly:

"Nina and I are on our way to the Berkshires for a week. House-party at the Craigs'. We stay overnight in town. E.E."

But the telegram went to his club, and waited for him there; and meanwhile another telegram arrived at his lodgings, signed by a trained nurse; and while Miss Erroll, in the big, dismantled house, lay in a holland-covered armchair, waiting for him, while Nina and Austin, reading their evening papers, exchanged significant glances from time to time, the man she awaited sat in the living-room in a little villa at Edgewater. And a slim young nurse stood beside him, cool and composed in her immaculate uniform, watching the play of light and shadow on a woman who lay asleep on the couch, fresh, young face flushed and upturned, a child's doll cradled between arm and breast.

"How long has she been asleep?" asked Selwyn under his breath.

"An hour. She fretted a good deal because you had not come. This afternoon she said she wished to drive, and I had the phaeton brought around; but when she saw it she changed her mind. I was rather afraid of an outburst—they come sometimes from less cause than that—so I did not urge her to go out. She played on the piano for a long while, and sang some songs—those curious native songs she learned in Manila. It seemed to soothe her; she played with her little trifles quite contentedly for a time, but soon began fretting again, and asking why you had not come. She had a bad hour later—she is quite exhausted now. Could you stay to-night, Captain Selwyn?"

"Y-es, if you think it better. . . . Wait a moment; I think she has awakened."

Alixe had turned her head, her lovely eyes wide open.

"Phil!" she cried, "is it you?"

He went forward and took the uplifted hands, smiling down at her.

"Such a horrid dream!" she said pettishly, "about a soft, plump man with ever so many rings on his hands. . . . Oh, I am glad you came. . . . Look at this child of mine!" cuddling the staring wax doll closer; "she's not undressed yet, and it's long, long after bedtime. Hand me her night-clothes, Phil."

The slim young nurse bent and disentangled a bit of lace and cambric from a heap on the floor, offering it to Selwyn. He laid it in the hand Alixe held out, and she began to undress the doll in her arms, prattling softly all the while:

"Late—oh, so very, very late! I must be more careful of her, Phil; because, if you and I grow up, some day we may marry, and we ought to know all about children. It would be great fun, wouldn't it?"

He nodded, forcing a smile.

"Don't you think so?" she persisted.

"Yes—yes, indeed," he said gently.

She laughed, contented with his answer, and laid her lips against the painted face of the doll.

"When we grow up, years from now—then we'll understand, won't we, Phil? . . . I am tired with playing. . . . And Phil—let me whisper something. Is that person gone?"

He turned and signed to the nurse, who quietly withdrew.

"Is she gone?" repeated Alixe.

"Yes."

"Then listen, Phil. Do you know what she and the other one are about all day? *I* know; I pretend not to, but I know. They are watching me every moment—always watching me, because they want to make you believe that I am forgetting you. But I am not. That is why I made them send for you so I could tell you myself that I could never, never forget you. . . . I think of you always while I am playing—always—always I am thinking of you. You will believe it, won't you?"

"Yes," he said.

Contented, she turned to her doll again, undressing it deftly, tenderly.

"At moments," she said, "I have an odd idea that it is real. I am not quite sure even now. Do you believe it is alive, Phil? Perhaps, at night, when I am asleep, it becomes alive. . . . This morning I awoke, laughing, laughing in delight—thinking I heard you laughing, too—as once—in the dusk where there were many roses and many stars—big stars, and very, very bright—I saw you—saw you—and the roses—"

She paused with a pained, puzzled look of appeal.

"Where was it, Phil?"

"In Manila town."

"Yes; and there were roses. But I was never there."

"You came out on the veranda and pelted me with roses. There were others there—officers and their wives. Everybody was laughing."

"Yes—but I was not there, Phil. . . . Who—who was the tall, thin bugler who sounded taps?"

"Corrigan."

"And—the little, girl-shaped, brown men?"

"My constabulary."

"I can't recollect," she said listlessly, laying the doll against her breast. "I think, Phil, that you had better be a little quiet now—she may wish to sleep. And I am sleepy, too," lifting her slender hand as a sign for him to take his leave.

As he went out the nurse said: "If you wish to return to town, you may, I think. She will forget about you for two or three days, as usual. Shall I telegraph if she becomes restless?"

"Yes. What does the doctor say to-day?"

The slim nurse looked at him under level brows.

"There is no change," she said.

"No hope." It was not even a question.

"No hope, Captain Selwyn."

He stood silent, tapping his leg with the stiff brim of his hat; then, wearily: "Is there anything more I can do for her?"

"Nothing, sir."

"Thank you."

He turned away, bidding her good-night in a low voice.

He arrived in town about midnight, but did not go to any of his clubs. At one of them a telegram was awaiting him; and in a dismantled and summer-shrouded house a young girl was still expecting him, lying with closed eyes in a big holland-covered arm-chair, listening to the rare footfalls in the street outside.

But of these things he knew nothing; and he went wearily to his lodgings and climbed the musty stairs, and sat down in his old attitude before the table and the blank wall behind it, waiting for the magic frescoes to appear in all the vague loveliness of their hues and dyes, painting for him upon his chamber-walls the tinted paradise now lost to him for ever.

CHAPTER XI

HIS OWN WAY

The winter promised to be a busy one for Selwyn. If at first he had had any dread of enforced idleness, that worry, at least, vanished before the first snow flew. For there came to him a secret communication from the Government suggesting, among other things, that he report, three times a week, at the proving grounds on Sandy Hook; that experiments with Chaosite as a bursting charge might begin as soon as he was ready with his argon primer; that officers connected with the bureau of ordnance and the marine laboratory had recommended the advisability of certain preliminary tests, and that the general staff seemed inclined to consider the matter seriously.

This meant work—hard, constant, patient work. But it did not mean money to help him support the heavy burdens he had assumed. If there were to be any returns, all that part of it lay in the future, and the future could not help him now.

Yet, unless still heavier burdens were laid upon him, he could hold on for the present; his bedroom cost him next to nothing; breakfast he cooked for himself, luncheon he dispensed with, and he dined at random—anywhere that appeared to promise seclusion, cheapness, and immunity from anybody he had ever known.

A minute and rather finicky care of his wardrobe had been second nature to him—the habits of a soldier systematised the routine—and he was satisfied that his clothes would outlast winter demands, although laundry expenses appalled him.

As for his clubs, he hung on to them, knowing the importance of appearances in a town which is made up of them. But this expense was all he could carry, for the demands of the establishment at Edgewater were steadily increasing with the early coming of winter; he was sent for oftener, and a physician was now in practically continual attendance.

Also, three times a week he boarded the Sandy Hook boat, returning always at night because he dared not remain at the reservation lest an imperative telegram from Edgewater find him unable to respond.

276

So, when in November the first few hurrying snow-flakes whirled in among the city's canons of masonry and iron, Selwyn had already systematised his winter schedule; and when Nina opened her house, returning from Lenox with Eileen to do so, she found that Selwyn had made his own arrangements for the winter, and that, according to the programme, neither she nor anybody else was likely to see him oftener than one evening in a week.

To Boots she complained bitterly, having had visions of Selwyn and Gerald as permanent fixtures of family support during the season now imminent.

"I cannot understand," she said, "why Philip is acting this way. He need not work like that; there is no necessity, because he has a comfortable income. If he is determined to maintain a stuffy apartment somewhere, of course I won't insist on his coming to us as he ought to, but to abandon us in this manner makes me almost indignant. Besides, it's having anything but a salutary effect on Eileen."

"What effect is it having on Eileen?" inquired Boots curiously.

"Oh, I don't know," said Nina, coming perilously close to a pout; "but I see symptoms—indeed I do, Boots!—symptoms of shirking the winter's routine. It's to be a gay season, too, and it's only her second. The idea of a child of that age informing me that she's had enough of the purely social phases of this planet! Did you ever hear anything like it? One season, if you please—and she finds it futile, stale, and unprofitable to fulfil the duties expected of her!"

Boots began to laugh, but it was no laughing matter to Nina, and she said so vigorously.

"It's Philip's fault. If he'd stand by us this winter she'd go anywhere—and enjoy it, too. Besides, he's the only man able to satisfy the blue-stocking in her between dances. But he's got this obstinate mania for seclusion, and he seldom comes near us, and it's driving Eileen into herself, Boots—and every day I catch her hair slumping over her ears—and once I discovered a lead-pencil behind 'em!—and a monograph on the Ming dynasty in her lap, all marked up with notes! Oh, Boots! Boots! I've given up all hopes of that brother of mine for her—but she could marry anybody, if she chose—*anybody!*—and she could twist the entire social circus into a court of her own and dominate everything. Everybody knows it; everybody says it! . . . And look at her!—indifferent, listless, scarcely civil any longer to her own sort, but galvanised into animation the moment some impossible professor or artist or hairy scientist flutters batlike into a drawing-room where he doesn't belong unless he's hired to be amusing! And that sounds horridly snobbish, I know; I *am* a snob about Eileen, but not about myself because it doesn't harm me to make round wonder-eyes at a Herr Professor or gaze intensely into the eyes of an artist when he's ornamental; it doesn't make my hair come down over my ears to do that sort of thing, and it doesn't corrupt me into slinking off to museum lectures or spending mornings prowling about the Society Library or the Chinese jades in the Metropolitan—"

Boots's continuous and unfeigned laughter checked the pretty, excited little matron, and after a moment she laughed, too.

"Dear Boots," she said, "can't you help me a little? I really am serious. I don't know what to do with the girl. Philip never comes near us—once a week for an hour or two, which is nothing—and the child misses him. There—the murder is out! Eileen misses him. Oh, she doesn't say so—she doesn't hint it, or look it; but I know her; I know. She misses him; she's lonely. And what to do about it I don't know, Boots, I don't know."

Lansing had ceased laughing. He had been indulging in tea—a shy vice of his which led him to haunt houses where that out-of-fashion beverage might still be had. And now he sat, cup suspended, saucer held meekly against his chest, gazing out at the pelting snow-flakes.

"Boots, dear," said Nina, who adored him, "tell me what to do. Tell me what has gone amiss between my brother and Eileen. Something has. And whatever it is, it began last autumn—that day when—you remember the incident?"

Boots nodded.

"Well, it seemed to upset everybody, somehow. Philip left the next day; do you remember? And Eileen has never been quite the same. Of course, I don't ascribe it to that unpleasant episode—even a young girl gets over a shock in a day. But the—the change—or whatever it is—dated from that night. . . . They—Philip and Eileen—had been inseparable. It was good for them—for her, too. And as for Phil—why, he looked about twenty-one! . . . Boots, I—I had hoped—expected—and I was right! They *were* on the verge of it!"

"I think so, too," he said.

She looked up curiously.

"Did Philip ever say—"

"No; he never *says*, you know."

"I thought that men—close friends—sometimes did."

"Sometimes—in romantic fiction. Phil wouldn't; nor," he added smilingly, "would I."

"How do you know, Boots?" she asked, leaning back to watch him out of mischievous eyes. "How do you know what you'd do if you were in love—with Gladys, for example?"

"I know perfectly well," he said, "because I am."

"In love!" incredulously.

278

"Of course."

"Oh—you mean Drina."

"Who else?" he asked lightly.

"I thought you were speaking seriously. I"—all her latent instinct for such meddling aroused—"I thought perhaps you meant Gladys."

"Gladys who?" he asked blandly.

"Gladys Orchil, silly! People said—"

"Oh, Lord!" he exclaimed; "if people 'said,' then it's all over. Nina! do I look like a man on a still hunt for a million?"

"Gladys is a beauty!" retorted Nina indignantly.

"With the intellect of a Persian kitten," he nodded. "I—that was not a nice thing to say. I'm sorry. I'm ashamed. But, do you know, I have come to regard my agreement with Drina so seriously that I take absolutely no interest in anybody else."

"Try to be serious, Boots," said Nina. "There are dozens of nice girls you ought to be agreeable to. Austin and I were saying only last night what a pity it is that you don't find either of the Minster twins interesting—"

"I might find them compoundly interesting," he admitted, "but unfortunately there's no chance in this country for multiple domesticity and the simpler pleasures of a compound life. It's no use, Nina; I'm not going to marry any girl for ever so long—anyway, not until Drina releases me on her eighteenth birthday. Hello!—somebody's coming—and I'm off!"

"I'm not at home; don't go!" said Nina, laying one hand on his arm to detain him as a card was brought up. "Oh, it's only Rosamund Fane! I *did* promise to go to the Craigs' with her. . . . Do you mind if she comes up?"

"Not if you don't," said Boots blandly. He could not endure Rosamund and she detested him; and Nina, who was perfectly aware of this, had just enough of perversity in her to enjoy their meeting.

Rosamund came in breezily, sables powdered with tiny flecks of snow, cheeks like damask roses, eyes of turquoise.

"How d'ye do!" she nodded, greeting Boots askance as she closed with Nina. "I came, you see, but *do* you want to be jammed and mauled and trodden on at the Craigs'? No? That's perfect!—neither do I. Where is the adorable Eileen? Nobody sees her any more."

"She was at the Delmour-Carnes's yesterday."

"Was she? Curious I didn't see her. Tea? With gratitude, dear, if it's Scotch."

She sat erect, the furs sliding to the back of the chair, revealing the rather accented details of her perfectly turned figure; and rolling up her gloves she laid her pretty head on one side and considered Boots with very bright and malicious eyes.

"They say," she said, smiling, "that some very heavy play goes on in that cunning little new house of yours, Mr. Lansing."

"Really?" he asked blandly.

"Yes; and I'm wondering if it is true."

"I shouldn't think you'd care, Mrs. Fane, as long as it makes a good story."

Rosamund flushed. Then, always alive to humour, laughed frankly.

"What a nasty thing to say to a woman!" she observed; "it fairly reeks impertinence. Mr. Lansing, you don't like me very well, do you?"

"I dare not," he said, "because you are married. If you were only free *a vinculo matrimonii*—"

Rosamund laughed again, and sat stroking her muff and smiling. "Curious, isn't it?" she said to Nina—"the inborn antipathy of two agreeable human bipeds for one another. *Similis simili gaudet*—as my learned friend will admit. But with us it's the old, old case of that eminent practitioner, the late Dr. Fell. *Esto perpetua!* Oh, well! We can't help it, can we, Mr. Lansing?" And again to Nina: "Dear, *have* you heard anything about Alixe Ruthven? I think it is the strangest thing that nobody seems to know where she is. And all anybody can get out of Jack is that she's in a nerve factory—or some such retreat—and a perfect wreck. She might as well be dead, you know."

"In that case," observed Lansing, "it might be best to shift the centre of gossip. *De mortuis nil nisi bonum*—which is simple enough for anybody to comprehend."

"That is rude, Mr. Lansing," flashed out Rosamund; and to his astonishment he saw the tears start to her eyes.

"I beg your pardon," he said sulkily.

"You do well to. I care more for Alixe Ruthven than—than you give me credit for caring about anybody. People are never wholly worthless, Mr. Lansing—only the very young think that. Give me credit for one wholly genuine affection, and you will not be too credulous; and perhaps in future you and I may better be able to endure one another when Fate lands us at the same tea-table."

Boots said respectfully: "I am sorry for what I said, Mrs. Pane. I hope that your friend Mrs. Ruthven will soon recover."

280

Rosamund looked at Nina, the tears still rimming her lids. "I miss her frightfully," she said. "If somebody would only tell me where she is—I—I know it could do no harm for me to see her. I *can* be as gentle and loyal as anybody—when I really care for a person. . . . Do *you* know where she might be, Nina?"

"I? No, I do not. I'd tell you if I did, Rosamund."

"*Don't* you know?"

"Why, no," said Nina, surprised at her persistence.

"Because," continued Rosamund, "your brother does."

Nina straightened up, flushed and astonished.

"Why do you say that?" she asked.

"Because he does know. He sent her to Clifton. The maid who accompanied her is in my service now. It's a low way of finding out things, but we all do it."

"He—sent Alixe to—to Clifton!" repeated Nina incredulously. "Your maid told you that?"

Rosamund finished the contents of her slim glass and rose. "Yes; and it was a brave and generous and loyal thing for him to do. I supposed you knew it. Jack has been too beastly to her; she was on the verge of breaking down when I saw her on the *Niobrara*, and she told me then that her husband had practically repudiated her. . . . Then she suddenly disappeared; and her maid, later, came to me seeking a place. That's how I knew, and that's all I know. And I care for Alixe; and I honour your brother for what he did."

She stood with pretty golden head bent, absently arranging the sables around her neck and shoulders.

"I have been very horrid to Captain Selwyn," she said quietly. "Tell him I am sorry; that he has my respect. . . . And—if he cares to tell me where Alixe is I shall be grateful and do no harm."

She turned toward the door, stopped short, came back, and made her adieux, then started again toward the door, not noticing Lansing.

"With your permission," said Boots at her shoulder in a very low voice.

She looked up, surprised, her eyes still wet. Then comprehending the compliment of his attendance, acknowledged it with a faint smile.

"Good-night," he said to Nina. Then he took Rosamund down to her brougham with a silent formality that touched her present sentimental mood.

She leaned from her carriage-window, looking at him where he stood, hat in hand, in the thickly falling snow.

281

"Please—without ceremony, Mr. Lansing." And, as he covered himself, "May I not drop you at your destination?"

"Thank you"—in refusal.

"I thank you for being nice to me. . . . Please believe there is often less malice than perversity in me. I—I have a heart, Mr. Lansing—such as it is. And often those I torment most I care for most. It was so with Alixe. Good-bye."

Boots's salute was admirably formal; then he went on through the thickening snow, swung vigorously across the Avenue to the Park-wall, and, turning south, continued on parallel to it under the naked trees.

It must have been thick weather on the river and along the docks, for the deep fog-horns sounded persistently over the city, and the haunted warning of the sirens filled the leaden sky lowering through the white veil descending in flakes that melted where they fell.

And, as Lansing strode on, hands deep in his overcoat, more than one mystery was unravelling before his keen eyes that blinked and winked as the clinging snow blotted his vision.

Now he began to understand something of the strange effacement of his friend Selwyn; he began to comprehend the curious economies practised, the continued absence from club and coterie, the choice of the sordid lodging whither Boots, one night, seeing him on the street by chance, had shamelessly tracked him—with no excuse for the intrusion save his affection for this man and his secret doubts of the man's ability to take care of himself and his occult affairs.

Now he was going there, exactly what to do he did not yet know, but with the vague determination to do something.

On the wet pavements and reeking iron overhead structure along Sixth Avenue the street lights glimmered, lending to the filthy avenue under its rusty tunnel a mystery almost picturesque.

Into it he turned, swung aboard a car as it shot groaning and clanking around the curve from Fifty-ninth Street, and settled down to brood and ponder and consider until it was time for him to swing off the car into the slimy street once more.

Silvery pools of light inlaid the dim expanse of Washington Square. He turned east, then south, then east again, and doubled into a dim street, where old-time houses with toppling dormers crowded huddling together as though in the cowering contact there was safety from the destroyer who must one day come, bringing steel girders and cement to mark their graves with sky-scraping monuments of stone.

Into the doorway of one of these houses Lansing turned. When the town was young a Lansing had lived there in pomp and circumstance—his own great-grandfather—and he smiled grimly, amused at the irony of things terrestrial.

A slattern at the door halted him:

"Nobody ain't let up them stairs without my knowin' why," she mumbled.

"I want to see Captain Selwyn," he explained.

"Hey?"

"Captain Selwyn!"

"Hey? I'm a little deef!" screeched the old crone. "Is it Cap'n Selwyn you want?"

Above, Selwyn, hearing his name screamed through the shadows of the ancient house, came to the stairwell and looked down into the blackness.

"What is it, Mrs. Glodden?" he said sharply; then, catching sight of a dim figure springing up the stairs:

"Here! this way. Is it for me?" and as Boots came into the light from his open door: "Oh!" he whispered, deadly pale under the reaction; "I thought it was a telegram. Come in."

Boots shook the snow from his hat and coat into the passageway and took the single chair; Selwyn, tall and gaunt in his shabby dressing-gown, stood looking at him and plucking nervously at the frayed and tasselled cord around his waist.

"I don't know how you came to stumble in here," he said at length, "but I'm glad to see you."

"Thanks," replied Boots, gazing shamelessly and inquisitively about. There was nothing to see except a few books, a pipe or two, toilet articles, and a shaky gas-jet. The flat military trunk was under the iron bed.

"I—it's not much of a place," observed Selwyn, forcing a smile. "However, you see I'm so seldom in town; I'm busy at the Hook, you know. So I don't require anything elaborate."

"Yes, I know," said Boots solemnly. A silence.

"H—have a pipe?" inquired Selwyn uneasily. He had nothing else to offer.

Boots leaned back in his stiff chair, crossed his legs, and filled a pipe. When he had lighted it he said:

"How are things, Phil?"

"All right. First rate, thank you."

283

Boots removed the pipe from his lips and swore at him; and Selwyn listened with head obstinately lowered and lean hands plucking at his frayed girdle. And when Boots had ended his observations with an emphatic question, Selwyn shook his head:

"No, Boots. You're very good to ask me to stop with you, but I can't. I'd be hampered; there are matters—affairs that concern me—that need instant attention at times—at certain times. I must be free to go, free to come. I couldn't be in your house. Don't ask me. But I'm—I thank you for offering—"

"Phil!"

"What?"

"Are you broke?"

"Ah—a little"—with a smile.

"Will you take what you require from me?"

"No."

"Oh—very well. I was horribly afraid you would."

Selwyn laughed and leaned back, indenting his meagre pillow.

"Come, Boots," he said, "you and I have often had worse quarters than this. To tell you the truth I rather like it than otherwise."

"Oh, damn!" said Boots, disgusted; "the same old conscience in the same old mule! Who likes squalidity? I don't. You don't! What if Fate has hit you a nasty swipe! Suppose Fortune has landed you a few in the slats! It's only temporary and you know it. All business in the world is conducted on borrowed capital. It's your business to live in decent quarters, and I'm here to lend you the means of conducting that business. Oh, come on, Phil, for Heaven's sake! If there were really any reason—any logical reason for this genius-in-the-garret business, I'd not say a word. But there isn't; you're going to make money—"

"Oh, yes, I've got to," said Selwyn simply.

"Well, then! In the meanwhile—"

"No. Listen, Boots; I couldn't be free in your house. I—they—there are telegrams—unexpected ones—at all hours."

"What of it?"

"You don't understand."

"Wait a bit! How do you know I don't? Do the telegrams come from Sandy Hook?"

"No."

Boots looked him calmly in the eye. "Then I *do* understand, old man. Come on out of this, in Heaven's name! Come, now! Get your dressing-gown off and your coat on! Don't you think I understand? I tell you I *do*! Yes, the whole blessed, illogical, chivalrous business. . . . Never mind how I know—for I won't tell you! Oh, I'm not trying to interfere with you; I know enough to shun buzz-saws. All I want is for you to come and take that big back room and help a fellow live in a lonely house—help a man to make it cheerful. I can't stand it alone any longer; and it will be four years before Drina is eighteen."

"Drina!" repeated Selwyn blankly—then he laughed. It was genuine laughter, too; and Boots grinned and puffed at his pipe, and recrossed his legs, watching Selwyn out of eyes brightening with expectancy.

"Then it's settled," he said.

"What? Your ultimate career with Drina?"

"Oh, yes; that also. But I referred to your coming to live with me."

"Boots—"

"Oh, fizz! Come on. I don't like the way you act, Phil."

Selwyn said slowly: "Do you make it a personal matter—"

"Yes, I do; dam'f I don't! You'll be perfectly free there. I don't care what you do or where you go or what hours you keep. You can run up and down Broadway all night, if you want to, or you can stop at home and play with the cats. I've three fine ones"—he made a cup of his hands and breathed into them, for the room was horribly cold—"three fine tabbies, and a good fire for 'em to blink at when they start purring."

He looked kindly but anxiously at Selwyn, waiting for a word; and as none came he said:

"Old fellow, you can't fool me with your talk about needing nothing better because you're out of town all the time. You know what you and I used to talk about in the old days—our longing for a home and an open fire and a brace of cats and bedroom slippers. Now I've got 'em, and I make Ardois signals at you. If your shelter-tent got afire or blew away, wouldn't you crawl into mine? And are you going to turn down an old tent-mate because his shack happens to be built of bricks?"

"Do you put it that way?"

"Yes, I do. Why, in Heaven's name, do you want to stay in a vile hole like this—unless you're smitten with Mrs. Glodden? Phil, I *want* you to come. Will you?"

"Then—I'll accept a corner of your blanket—for a day or two," said Selwyn wearily. . . . "You'll let me go when I want to?"

"I'll do more; I'll make you go when *I* want you to. Come on; pay Mrs. Glodden and have your trunk sent."

Selwyn forced a laugh, then sat up on the bed's edge and looked around at the unpapered walls.

"Boots—you won't say to—to anybody what sort of a place I've been living in—"

"No; but I will if you try to come back here."

So Selwyn stood up and began to remove his dressing-gown, and Lansing dragged out the little flat trunk and began to pack it.

An hour later they went away together through the falling snow.

For a week Boots let him alone. He had a big, comfortable room, dressing-closet, and bath adjoining the suite occupied by his host; he was absolutely free to go and come, and for a week or ten days Boots scarcely laid eyes on him, except at breakfast, for Selwyn's visits to Sandy Hook became a daily routine except when a telegram arrived from Edgewater calling him there.

But matters at Edgewater were beginning to be easier in one way for him. Alixe appeared to forget him for days at a time; she was less irritable, less restless and exacting. A sweet-tempered and childish docility made the care of her a simpler matter for the nurses and for him; her discontent had disappeared; she made fewer demands. She did ask for a sleigh to replace the phaeton, and Selwyn managed to get one for her; and Miss Casson, one of the nurses, wrote him how delighted Alixe had been, and how much good the sleighing was doing her.

"Yesterday," continued the nurse in her letter, "there was a consultation here between Drs. Vail, Wesson, and Morrison—as you requested. They have not changed their opinions—indeed, they are convinced that there is no possible chance of the recovery you hoped for when you talked with Dr. Morrison. They all agree that Mrs. Ruthven is in excellent physical condition—young, strong, vigorous—and may live for years; may outlive us all. But there is nothing else to expect."

The letter ran on:

"I am enclosing the bills you desired to have sent you. Fuel is very expensive, as you will see. The items for fruits, too, seems unreasonably large, but grapes are two dollars a pound and fresh vegetables dreadfully expensive.

"Mrs. Ruthven is comfortable and happy in the luxury provided. She is very sweet and docile with us all—and we are careful not to irritate her or to have anything intrude which might excite or cause the slightest shock to her.

"Yesterday, standing at the window, she caught sight of a passing negro, and she turned to me like a flash and said:

"'The Tenth Cavalry were there!'

"She seemed rather excited for a moment—not unpleasantly—but when I ventured to ask her a question, she had quite forgotten it all.

"I meant to thank you for sending me the revolver and cartridges. It seemed a silly request, but we are in a rather lonely place, and I think Miss Bond and I feel a little safer knowing that, in case of necessity, we have *something* to frighten away any roaming intruder who might take it into his head to visit us.

"One thing we must be careful about: yesterday Mrs. Ruthven had a doll on my bed, and I sat sewing by the window, not noticing what she was doing until I heard her pretty, pathetic little laugh.

"And *what* do you think she had done? She had discovered your revolver under my pillow, and she had tied her handkerchief around it, and was using it as a doll!

"I got it away with a little persuasion, but at times she still asks for her 'army' doll—saying that a boy she knew, named Philip, had sent it to her from Manila, where he was living.

"This, Captain Selwyn, is all the news. I do not think she will begin to fret for you again for some time. At first, you remember, it was every other day, then every three or four days. It has now been a week since she asked for you. When she does I will, as usual, telegraph you.

"With many thanks for your kindness to us all, "Very respectfully yours,

"Mary Casson."

Selwyn read this letter sitting before the fire in the living-room, feet on the fender, pipe between his teeth. It was the first day of absolute rest he had had in a long while.

The day before he had been at the Hook until almost dark, watching the firing of a big gun, and the results had been so satisfactory that he was venturing to give himself a holiday—unless wanted at Edgewater.

But the morning had brought this letter; Alixe was contented and comfortable. So when Boots, after breakfast, went off to his Air Line office, Selwyn permitted himself the luxury of smoking-jacket and slippers, and settled down before the fire to reread the letter and examine the enclosed bills, and ponder and worry over them at his ease. To have leisure to worry over perplexities was something; to worry in such luxury as this seemed something so very near to happiness that as he refolded the last bill for household expenses he smiled faintly to himself.

Boots's three tabby-cats were disposed comfortably before the blaze, fore paws folded under, purring and blinking lazily at the grate. All around were evidences of Boots's personal taste in pretty wall-paper and hangings, a few handsome Shiraz rugs underfoot, deep, comfortable chairs, low, open bookcases full of promising literature—the more promising because not contemporary.

Selwyn loved such a room as this—where all was comfort, and nothing in the quiet, but cheerful, ensemble disturbed the peaceful homeliness.

Once—and not very long since—he had persuaded himself that there had been a chance for him to have such a home, and live in it—*not* alone. That chance had gone—had never really existed, he knew now. For sooner or later he must have awakened from the pleasant dreams of self-persuasion to the reality of his relentless responsibility. No, there had never been such a chance; and he thanked God that he had learned before it was too late that for him there could be no earthly paradise, no fireside *à deux*, no home, no hope of it.

As long as Alixe lived his spiritual responsibility must endure. And they had just told him that she might easily outlive them all.

He turned heavily in his chair and stared at the fire. Perhaps he saw infernal visions in the flames; perhaps the blaze meant nothing more to him than an example of chemical reaction, for his face was set and colourless and vacant, and his hands lay loosely along the padded arms of his easy-chair.

The hardest lesson he had to learn in these days was to avoid thinking. Or, if he must surrender to the throbbing, unbidden memories which came crowding in hordes to carry him by the suddenness of their assault, that he learn to curb and subdue and direct them in pity toward that hopeless, helpless, stricken creature who was so utterly dependent upon him in her dreadful isolation.

And he could not so direct them.

Loyal in act and deed, his thoughts betrayed him. Memories, insurgent, turned on him to stab him; and he shrank from them, cowering among his pillows at midnight. But memory is merciless, and what has been is without pity; and so remembrance rose at midnight from its cerements, like a spectre, floating before his covered eyes, wearing the shape of youth and love, crowned with the splendour of *her* hair, looking at him out of those clear, sweet eyes whose gaze was purity and truth eternal.

And truth is truth, though he might lie with hands clinched across his brow to shut out the wraith of it that haunted him; though he might set his course by the faith that was in him, and put away the hope of the world—whose hope is love—the truth was there, staring, staring at him out of Eileen Erroll's dark-blue eyes.

He had seen her seldom that winter. When he had seen her their relations appeared to be as happy, as friendly as before; there was no apparent constraint, nothing from her to indicate that she noticed an absence for which his continual business with the Government seemed sufficient excuse.

Besides, her days were full days, consequent upon Nina's goading and indefatigable activity; and Eileen danced and received, and she bridged and lunched, and she heard opera Wednesdays and was good to the poor on Fridays; and there were balls, and theatres, and classes for intellectual improvement, and routine duties incident to obligations born with those inhabitants of Manhattan who are numbered among the thousand caryatides that support upon their jewelled necks and naked shoulders the social structure of the metropolis.

But Selwyn, unable longer to fulfil his social obligations, was being quietly eliminated from the social scheme of things. Passed over here, dropped there, counted out as one more man not to be depended upon, it was not a question of loss of caste; he simply stayed away, and his absence was accepted by people who, in the breathless pleasure chase, have no leisure to inquire why a man has lagged behind.

There were rumours, however, that he had merely temporarily donned overalls for the purpose of making a gigantic fortune; and many an envious young fellow asked his pretty partner in the dance if it was true, and many a young girl frankly hoped it was, and that the fortune would be quick in the making. For Selwyn was well liked in the younger set, and that he was in process of becoming eligible interested everybody except Gladys and the Minster twins, who considered him sufficiently eligible without the material additions required by their cynical seniors, and would rather have had him penniless and present than absent and opulent.

But they were young and foolish, and after a while they forgot to miss him, particularly Gladys, whose mother had asked her not to dance quite so often with Gerald, and to favour him a trifle less frequently in cotillon. Which prevoyance had been coped with successfully by Nina, who, noticing it, at first took merely a perverse pleasure in foiling Mrs. Orchil; but afterward, as the affair became noticeable, animated by the instinct of the truly clever opportunist, she gave Gerald every fighting chance. Whatever came of it—and, no doubt, the Orchils had more ambitious views for Gladys—it was well to have Gerald mentioned in such a fashionable episode, whether anything came of it or not.

Gerald, in the early days of his affair with Gladys, and before even it had assumed the proportions of an affair, had shyly come to Selwyn, not for confession but with the crafty purpose of introducing her name into the conversation so that he might have the luxury of talking about her to somebody who would neither quiz him nor suspect him.

Selwyn, of course, ultimately suspected him; but as he never quizzed him, Gerald continued his elaborate system of subterfuges to make her personality and doings a topic for him to expand upon and Selwyn to listen to.

It had amused Selwyn; he thought of it now—a gay memory like a ray of light flung for a moment across the sombre background of his own sadness. Fortunate or unfortunate, Gerald was still lucky in his freedom to hazard it with chance and fate.

Freedom to love! That alone was blessed, though that love be unreturned. Without that right—the right to love—a man was no man. Lansing had been correct: such a man was a spectre in a living world— the ghost of what he had been. But there was no help for it, and there Lansing had been in the wrong. No hope, no help, nothing for it but to set a true course and hang to it.

And Selwyn's dull eyes rested upon the ashes of the fire, and he saw his dead youth among them; and, in the flames, his maturity burning to embers.

If he outlived Alixe, his life would lie as the ashes lay at his feet. If she outlived him—and they had told him there was every chance of it—at least he would have something to busy himself with in life if he was to leave her provided for when he was no longer there to stand between her and charity.

That meant work—the hard, incessant, blinding, stupefying work which stuns thought and makes such a life endurable.

Not that he had ever desired death as a refuge or as a solution of despair; there was too much of the soldier in him. Besides, it is so impossible for youth to believe in death, to learn to apply the word to themselves. He had not learned to, and he had seen death, and watched it; but for himself he had not learned to believe in it. When one turns forty it is easier to credit it.

Thinking of death, impersonally, he sat watching the flames playing above the heavy log; and as he lay there in his chair, the unlighted pipe drooping in his hands, the telephone on the desk rang, and he rose and unhooked the receiver.

Drina's voice sounded afar, and: "Hello, sweetheart!" he said gaily; "is there anything I can do for your youthful highness?"

"I've been talking over the 'phone to Boots," she said. "You know, whenever I have nothing to do I call up Boots at his office and talk to him."

"That must please him," suggested Selwyn gravely.

"It does. Boots says you are not going to business to-day. So I thought I'd call you up."

"Thank you," said Selwyn.

"You are welcome. What are you doing over there in Boots's house?"

"Looking at the fire, Drina, and listening to the purring of three fat tabby-cats."

"Oh! Mother and Eileen have gone somewhere. I haven't anything to do for an hour. Can't you come around?"

"Why, yes, if you want me."

"Yes, I do. Of course I can't have Boots, and I prefer you next. The children are fox-hunting, and it bores me. Will you come?"

"Yes. When?"

"Now. And would you mind bringing me a box of mint-paste? Mother won't object. Besides, I'll tell her, anyway, after I've eaten them."

"All right!" said Selwyn, laughing and hanging up the receiver.

On his way to the Gerards' he bought a box of the confection dear to Drina. But as he dropped the packet into his overcoat-pocket, the memory of the past rose up suddenly, halting him. He could not bear to go to the house without some little gift for Eileen, and it was violets now as it was in the days that could never dawn again—a great, fragrant bunch of them, which he would leave for her after his brief play-hour with Drina was ended.

The child was glad to see him, and expressed herself so, coming across to the chair where he sat and leaning against him, one arm on his shoulder.

"Do you know," she said, "that I miss you ever so much? Do you know, also, that I am nearly fourteen, and that there is nobody in this house near enough my age to be very companionable? I have asked them to send me to school, and mother is considering it."

She leaned against his shoulder, curly head bent, thoughtfully studying the turquoise ring on her slim finger. It was her first ring. Nina had let Boots give it to her.

"What a tall girl you are growing into!" he said, encircling her waist with one arm. "Your mother was like you at fourteen. . . . Did she ever tell you how she first met your father? Well, I'll tell you then. Your father was a schoolboy of fifteen, and one day he saw the most wonderful little girl riding a polo pony out of the Park. Her mother was riding with her. And he lost his head, and ran after her until she rode into the Academy stables. And in he went, headlong, after her, and found her dismounted and standing with her mother; and he took off his hat, and he said to her mother: 'I've run quite a long way to tell you who I am: I am Colonel Gerard's son, Austin. Would you care to know me?'

"And he looked at the little girl, who had curls precisely like yours, and the same little nose and mouth. And that little girl, who is now your mother, said very simply: 'Won't you come home to luncheon with us? May he, mother? He has run a very long way to be polite to us.'

"And your mother's mother looked at the boy for a moment, smiling, for he was the image of his father, who had been at school with her. Then she said: 'Come to luncheon and tell me about your father. Your father once came a thousand miles to see me, but I had started the day before on my wedding-trip.'

"And that is how your father first met your mother, when she was a little girl."

Drina laughed: "What a funny boy father was to run after a strange girl on a polo pony! . . . Suppose—suppose he had not seen her, and had not run after her. . . . Where would I be now, Uncle Philip? . . . Could you please tell me?"

"Still aloft among the cherubim, sweetheart."

"But—whose uncle would you be? And who would Boots have found for a comrade like me? . . . It's a good thing that father ran after that polo pony. . . . Probably God arranged it. Do you think so?"

"There is no harm in thinking it," he said, smiling.

"No; no harm. I've known for a long while that He was taking care of Boots for me until I grow up. Meanwhile, I know some very nice Harvard freshmen and two boys from St. Paul and five from Groton. That helps, you know."

"Helps what?" asked Selwyn, vastly amused.

"To pass the time until I am eighteen," said the child serenely, helping herself to another soft, pale-green chunk of the aromatic paste. "Uncle Philip, mother has forbidden me—and I'll tell her and take my punishment—but would you mind telling me how you first met my Aunt Alixe?"

Selwyn's arm around her relaxed, then tightened.

"Why do you ask, dear?" he said very quietly.

"Because I was just wondering whether God arranged that, too."

Selwyn looked at her a moment. "Yes," he said grimly; "nothing happens by chance."

"Then, when God arranges such things, He does not always consider our happiness."

"He gives us our chance, Drina."

"Oh! Did you have a chance? I heard mother say to Eileen that you had never had a chance for happiness. I thought it was very sad. I had gone into the clothes-press to play with my dolls—you know I still do play with them—that is, I go into some secret place and look at them at times when the children are not around. So I was in there, sitting on the cedar-chest, and I couldn't help hearing what they said."

She extracted another bonbon, bit into it, and shook her head:

"And mother said to Eileen: 'Dearest, can't you learn to care for him?' And Eileen—"

"Drina!" he interrupted sharply, "you must not repeat things you overhear."

"Oh, I didn't hear anything more," said the child, "because I remembered that I shouldn't listen, and I came out of the closet. Mother was standing by the bed, and Eileen was lying on the bed with her hands over her eyes; and I didn't know she had been crying until I said: 'Please excuse me for listening,' and she sat up very quickly, and I saw her face was flushed and her eyes wet. . . . Isn't it possible for you to marry anybody, Uncle Philip?"

"No, Drina."

"Not even if Eileen would marry you?"

"No."

"Why?"

"You could not understand, dear. Even your mother cannot quite understand. So we won't ever speak of it again, Drina."

The child balanced a bonbon between thumb and forefinger, considering it very gravely.

"I know something that mother does not," she said. And as he betrayed no curiosity:

"Eileen *is* in love. I heard her say so."

He straightened up sharply, turning to look at her.

293

"I was sleeping with her. I was still awake, and I heard her say: 'I *do* love you—I *do* love you.' She said it very softly, and I cuddled up, supposing she meant me. But she was asleep."

"She certainly meant you," said Selwyn, forcing his stiffened lips into a smile.

The child shook her head, looking down at the ring which she was turning on her finger:

"No; she did not mean me."

"H-how do you know?"

"Because she said a man's name."

The silence lengthened; he sat, tilted a little forward, blank gaze focussed on the snowy window; Drina, standing, leaned back into the hollow of his arm, absently studying her ring.

A few moments later her music-teacher arrived, and Drina was obliged to leave him.

"If you don't wait until I have finished my music," she said, "you won't see mother and Eileen. They are coming to take me to the riding-school at four o'clock."

He said that he couldn't stay that day; and when she had gone away to the schoolroom he walked slowly to the window and looked out across the snowy Park, where hundreds of children were floundering about with gaily painted sleds. It was a pretty scene in the sunshine; crimson sweaters and toboggan caps made vivid spots of colour on the white expanse. Beyond, through the naked trees, he could see the drive, and the sleighs with their brilliant scarlet plumes and running-gear flashing in the sun. Overhead was the splendid winter blue of the New York sky, in which, at a vast height, sea-birds circled.

Meaning to go—for the house and its associations made him restless— he picked up the box of violets and turned to ring for a maid to take charge of them—and found himself confronting Eileen, who, in her furs and gloves, was just entering the room.

"I came up," she said; "they told me you were here, calling very formally upon Drina, if you please. What with her monopoly of you and Boots, there seems to be no chance for Nina and me."

They shook hands pleasantly; he offered her the box of violets, and she thanked him and opened it, and, lifting the heavy, perfumed bunch, bent her fresh young face to it. For a moment she stood inhaling the scent, then stretched out her arm, offering their fragrance to him.

"The first night I ever knew you, you sent me about a wagon-load of violets," she said carelessly.

He nodded pleasantly; she tossed her muff on to the library table, stripped off her gloves, and began to unhook her fur coat, declining his aid with a quick shake of her head.

"It is easy—you see!"—as the sleeves slid from her arms and the soft mass of fur fell into a chair. "And, by the way, Drina said that you couldn't wait to see Nina," she continued, turning to face a mirror and beginning to withdraw the jewelled pins from her hat, "so you won't for a moment consider it necessary to remain just because I wandered in— will you?"

He made no reply; she was still busy with her veil and hat and her bright, glossy hair, the ends of which curled up at the temples—a burnished frame for her cheeks which the cold had delicately flushed to a wild-rost tint. Then, brushing back the upcurled tendrils of her hair, she turned to confront him, faintly smiling, brows lifted in silent repetition of her question.

"I will stay until Nina comes, if I may," he said slowly.

She seated herself. "You may," she said mockingly; "we don't allow you in the house very often, so when you do come you may remain until the entire family can congregate to inspect you." She leaned back, looking at him; then look and manner changed, and she bent impulsively forward:

"You don't look very well, Captain Selwyn; are you?"

"Perfectly. I"—he laughed—"I am growing old; that is all."

"Do you say that to annoy me?" she asked, with a disdainful shrug, "or to further impress me?"

He shook his head and touched the hair at his temples significantly.

"Pooh!" she retorted. "It is becoming—is that what you mean?"

"I hope it is. There's no reason why a man should not grow old gracefully—"

"Captain Selwyn! But of course you only say it to bring out that latent temper of mine. It's about the only thing that does it, too. . . . And please don't plague me—if you've only a few moments to stay. . . . It may amuse you to know that I, too, am exhibiting signs of increasing infirmity; my temper, if you please, is not what it once was."

"Worse than ever?" he asked in pretended astonishment.

"Far worse. It is vicious. Kit-Ki took a nap on a new dinner-gown of mine, and I slapped her. And the other day Drina hid in a clothes-press while Nina was discussing my private affairs, and when the little imp emerged I could have shaken her. Oh, I am certainly becoming infirm; so if you are, too, comfort yourself with the knowledge that I am keeping pace with you through the winter of our discontent."

At the mention of the incident of which Drina had already spoken to him, Selwyn raised his head and looked at the girl curiously. Then he laughed.

"I am wondering," he said in a bantering voice, "what secrets Drina heard. I think I'd better ask her—"

"You had better not! Besides, *I* said nothing at all."

"But Nina did."

She nodded, lying there, arms raised, hands clasping the upholstered wings of the big chair, and gazing at him out of indolent, amused eyes.

"Would you like to know what Nina was saying to me?" she asked.

"I'd rather hear what you said to her."

"I told you that I said nothing."

"Not a word?" he insisted.

"Not a word."

"Not even a sound?"

"N—well—I won't answer that."

"Oho!" he laughed. "So you did make some sort of inarticulate reply! Were you laughing or weeping?"

"Perhaps I was yawning. How do you know?" she smiled.

After a moment he said, still curious: "*Why* were you crying, Eileen?"

"Crying! I didn't say I was crying."

"I assume it."

"To prove or disprove that assumption," she said coolly, amused, "let us hunt up a motive for a possible display of tears. What, Captain Selwyn, have I to cry about? Is there anything in the world that I lack? Anything that I desire and cannot have?"

"*Is* there?" he repeated.

"I asked you, Captain Selwyn."

"And, unable to reply," he said, "I ask you."

"And I," she retorted, "refuse to answer."

"Oho! So there *is*, then, something you lack? There *is* a motive for possible tears?"

"You have not proven it," she said.

"You have not denied it."

She tipped back her head, linked her fingers under her chin, and looked at him across the smooth curve of her cheeks.

"Well—yes," she admitted, "I was crying—if you insist on knowing. Now that you have so cleverly driven me to admit that, can you also force me to tell you *why* I was so tearful?"

"Certainly," he said promptly; "it was something Nina said that made you cry."

They both laughed.

"Oh, what a come-down!" she said teasingly. "You knew that before. But can you force me to confess to you *what* Nina was saying? If you can you are the cleverest cross-examiner in the world, for I'd rather perish than tell you—"

"Oh," he said instantly, "then it was something about love!"

He had not meant to say it; he had spoken too quickly, and the flush of surprise on the girl's face was matched by the colour rising to his own temples. And, to retrieve the situation, he spoke too quickly again—and too lightly.

"A girl would rather perish than admit that she is in love?" he said, forcing a laugh. "That is rather a clever deduction, I think. Unfortunately, however, I happen to know to the contrary, so all my cleverness comes to nothing."

The surprise had faded from her face, but the colour remained; and with it something else—something in the blue eyes which he had never before encountered there—the faintest trace of recoil, of shrinking away from him.

And she herself did not know it was there—did not quite realise that she had been hurt. Surprise that he had chanced so abruptly, so unerringly upon the truth had startled and confused her; but that he had made free of the truth so lightly, so carelessly, laughingly amused, left her without an answering smile.

That it had been an accident—a chance surmise which perhaps he himself did not credit—which he could not believe—made it no easier for her. For the first time in his life he had said something which left her unresponsive, with a sense of bruised delicacy and of privacy invaded. A tinge of fear of him crept in, too. She did not misconstrue what he had said under privilege of a jest, but after what had once passed between them she had not considered that love, even in the abstract, might serve as a mocking text for any humour or jesting sermon from a man who had asked her what he once asked—the man she had loved enough to weep for when she had refused him only because she lacked what he asked for. Knowing that she loved him in her own innocent fashion, scarcely credulous that he ever could be dearer to her, yet shyly wistful for whatever more the years might add to her knowledge of a love so far immune from stress or doubt or the mounting thrill of a deeper emotion, she had remained confidently passive, warmly loyal, reverencing the mystery of the love he offered, though she could not understand it or respond.

And now—now a chance turn; of a word—a trend to an idle train of thought, jestingly followed!—and, without warning, they had stumbled on a treasured memory, too frail, too delicately fragile, to endure the shock.

And now fear crept in—fear that he had forgotten, had changed. Else how could he have spoken so? . . . And the tempered restraint of her quivered at the thought—all the serenity, the confidence in life and in him began to waver. And her first doubt crept in upon her.

She turned her expressionless face from him and, resting her cheek against the velvet back of the chair, looked out into the late afternoon sunshine.

All the long autumn without him, all her long, lonely, leisure hours in the golden weather, his silence, his withdrawal into himself, and his work, hitherto she had not misconstrued, though often she confused herself in explaining it. Impatience of his absence, too, had stimulated her to understand the temporary state of things—to know that time away from him meant for her only existence in suspense.

Very, very slowly, by degrees imperceptible, alone with memories of him and of their summer's happiness already behind her, she had learned that time added things to what she had once considered her full capacity for affection.

Alone with her memories of him, at odd moments during the day—often in the gay clamour and crush of the social routine—or driving with Nina, or lying, wide-eyed, on her pillow at night, she became conscious that time, little by little, very gradually but very surely, was adding to her regard for him frail, new, elusive elements that stole in to awake an unquiet pulse or stir her heart into a sudden thrill, leaving it fluttering, and a faint glow gradually spreading through her every vein.

She was beginning to love him no longer in her own sweet fashion, but in his; and she was vaguely aware of it, yet curiously passive and content to put no question to herself whether it was true or false. And how it might be with him she evaded asking herself, too; only the quickening of breath and pulse questioned the pure thoughts unvoiced; only the increasing impatience of her suspense confirmed the answer which now, perhaps, she might give him one day while the blessed world was young.

At the thought she moved uneasily, shifting her position in the chair. Sunset, and the swift winter twilight, had tinted, then dimmed, the light in the room. On the oak-beamed ceiling, across the ivory rosettes, a single bar of red sunlight lay, broken by rafter and plaster foliation. She watched it turn to rose, to ashes. And, closing her eyes, she lay very still and motionless in the gray shadows closing over all.

He had not yet spoken when again she lifted her eyes and saw him sitting in the dusk, one arm resting across his knee, his body bent slightly forward, his gaze vacant.

Into himself again!—silently companioned by the shadows of old thoughts; far from her—farther than he had ever been. For a while she lay there, watching him, scarcely breathing; then a faint shiver of utter loneliness came over her—of desire for his attention, his voice, his friendship, and the expression of it. But he never moved; his eyes seemed dull and unseeing; his face strangely gaunt to her, unfamiliar, hard. In the dim light he seemed but the ghost of what she had known, of what she had thought him—a phantom, growing vaguer, more unreal, slipping away from her through the fading light. And the impulse to arouse herself and him from the dim danger—to arrest the spell, to break it, and seize what was their own in life overwhelmed her; and she sat up, grasping the great arms of her chair, slender, straight, white-faced in the gloom.

But he did not stir. Then unreasoning, instinctive fear confused her, and she heard her own voice, sounding strangely in the twilight:

"What has come between us, Captain Selwyn? What has happened to us? Something is all wrong, and I—I ask you what it is, because I don't know. Tell me."

He had lifted his head at her first word, hesitatingly, as though dazed.

"Could you tell me?" she asked faintly.

"Tell you what, child?"

"Why you are so silent with me; what has crept in between us. I"—the innocent courage sustaining her—"I have not changed—except a little in—in the way you wished. Have you?"

"No," he said in an altered voice.

"Then—what is it? I have been—you have left me so much alone this winter—and I supposed I understood—"

"My work," he said; but she scarcely knew the voice for his.

"I know; you have had no time. I know that; I ought to know it by this time, for I have told myself often enough. And yet—when we *are* together, it is—it has been—different. Can you tell me why? Do you think me changed?"

"You must not change," he said.

"No," she breathed, wondering, "I could not—except—a little, as I told you."

299

"You must not change—not even that way!" he repeated in a voice so low she could scarcely hear him—and believed she had misunderstood him.

"I did not hear you," she said faintly. "What did you say to me?"

"I cannot say it again."

She slowly shook her head, not comprehending, and for a while sat silent, struggling with her own thoughts. Then, suddenly instinct with the subtle fear which had driven her into speech:

"When I said—said that to you—last summer; when I cried in the swinging seat there—because I could not answer you—as I wished to— did *that* change you, Captain Selwyn?"

"No."

"Then y-you are unchanged?"

"Yes, Eileen."

The first thrill of deep emotion struck through and through her.

"Then—then *that* is not it," she faltered. "I was afraid—I have sometimes wondered if it was. . . . I am very glad, Captain Selwyn. . . . Will you wait a—a little longer—for me to—to change?"

He stood up suddenly in the darkness, and she sprang to her feet, breathless; for she had caught the low exclamation, and the strange sound that stifled it in his throat.

"Tell me," she stammered, "w-what has happened. D-don't turn away to the window; don't leave me all alone to endure this—this *something* I have known was drawing you away—I don't know where! What is it? Could you not tell*me*, Captain Selwyn? I—I have been very frank with you; I have been truthful—and loyal. I gave you, from the moment I knew you, all of me there was to give. And—and if there is more to give—now—it was yours when it came to me.

"Do you think I am too young to know what I am saying? Solitude is a teacher. I—I am still a scholar, perhaps, but I think that you could teach me what my drill-master, Solitude, could not . . . if it—it is true you love me."

The mounting sea of passion swept him; he turned on her, unsteadily, his hands clenched, not daring to touch her. Shame, contrition, horror that the damage was already done, all were forgotten; only the deadly grim duty of the moment held him back.

"Dear," he said, "because I am unchanged—because I—I love you so— help me!—and God help us both."

"Tell me," she said steadily, but it was fear that stilled her voice. She laid one slim hand on the table, bearing down on the points of her fingers until the nails whitened, but her head was high and her eyes met his, straight, unwavering.

"I—I knew it," she said; "I understood there was something. If it is trouble—and I see it is—bring it to me. If I am the woman you took me for, give me my part in this. It is the quickest way to my heart, Captain Selwyn."

But he had grown afraid, horribly afraid. All the cowardice in him was in the ascendant. But that passed; watching his worn face, she saw it passing. Fear clutched at her; for the first time in her life she desired to go to him, hold fast to him, seeking in contact the reassurance of his strength; but she only stood straighter, a little paler, already half divining in the clairvoyance of her young soul what lay still hidden.

"Do you ask a part in this?" he said at last.

"I ask it."

"Why?"

Her eyes wavered, then returned his gaze:

"For love of you," she said, as white as death.

He caught his breath sharply and straightened out, passing one hand across his eyes. When she saw his face again in the dim light it was ghastly.

"There was a woman," he said, "for whom I was once responsible." He spoke wearily, head bent, resting the weight of one arm on the table against which she leaned. "Do you understand?" he asked.

"Yes. You mean—Mrs. Ruthven."

"I mean—her. Afterward—when matters had altered—I came—home."

He raised his head and looked about him in the darkness.

"Came home," he repeated, "no longer a man; the shadow of a man, with no hope, no outlook, no right to hope."

He leaned heavily on the table, his arm rigid, looking down at the floor as he spoke.

"No right to hope. Others told me that I still possessed that right. I knew they were wrong; I do not mean that they persuaded me—I persuaded myself that, after all, perhaps my right to hope remained to me. I persuaded myself that I might be, after all, the substance, not the shadow."

He looked up at her:

"And so I dared to love you."

She gazed at him, scarcely breathing.

301

"Then," he said, "came the awakening. My dream had ended."

She waited, the lace on her breast scarce stirring, so still she stood, so pitifully still.

"Such responsibility cannot die while those live who undertook it. I believed it until I desired to believe it no longer. But a man's self-persuasion cannot alter such laws—nor can human laws confirm or nullify them, nor can a great religion do more than admit their truth, basing its creed upon such laws. . . . No man can put asunder, no laws of man undo the burden. . . . And, to my shame and disgrace, I have had to relearn this after offering you a love I had no right to offer—a life which is not my own to give."

He took one step toward her, and his voice fell so low that she could just hear him:

"She has lost her mind, and the case is hopeless. Those to whom the laws of the land have given care of her turned on her, threatened her with disgrace. And when one friend of hers halted this miserable conspiracy, her malady came swiftly upon her, and suddenly she found herself helpless, penniless, abandoned, her mind already clouded, and clouding faster! . . . Eileen, was there then the shadow of a doubt as to the responsibility? Because a man's son was named in the parable, does the lesson end there—and are there no others as prodigal—no other bonds that hold as inexorably as the bond of love?

"Men—a lawyer or two—a referee—decided to remove a burden; but a higher court has replaced it."

He came and stood directly before her:

"I dare not utter one word of love to you; I dare not touch you. What chance is there for such a man as I?"

"No chance—for us," she whispered. "Go!"

For a second he stood motionless, then, swaying slightly, turned on his heel.

And long after he had left the house she still stood there, eyes closed, colourless lips set, her slender body quivering, racked with the first fierce grief of a woman's love for a man.

CHAPTER XII

HER WAY

Neergard had already begun to make mistakes. The first was in thinking that, among those whose only distinction was their wealth, his own wealth permitted him the same insolence and ruthlessness that so frequently characterised them.

Clever, vindictively patient, circumspect, and commercially competent as he had been, his intelligence was not of a high order. The intelligent never wilfully make enemies; Neergard made them gratuitously, cynically kicking from under him the props he used in mounting the breach, and which he fancied he no longer needed as a scaffolding now that he had obtained a foothold on the outer wall. Thus he had sneeringly dispensed with Gerald; thus he had shouldered Fane and Harmon out of his way when they objected to the purchase of Neergard's acreage adjoining the Siowitha preserve, and its incorporation as an integral portion of the club tract; thus he was preparing to rid himself of Ruthven for another reason. But he was not yet quite ready to spurn Ruthven, because he wanted a little more out of him—just enough to place himself on a secure footing among those of the younger set where Ruthven, as hack cotillon leader, was regarded by the young with wide-eyed awe.

Why Neergard, who had forced himself into the Siowitha, ever came to commit so gross a blunder as to dragoon, or even permit, the club to acquire the acreage, the exploiting of which had threatened their existence, is not very clear.

Once within the club he may have supposed himself perpetually safe, not only because of his hold on Ruthven, but also because, back of his unflagging persistence, back of his determination to shoulder and push deep into the gilded, perfumed crush where purse-strings and morals were loosened with every heave and twist in the panting struggle around the raw gold altar—back of the sordid past, back of all the resentment, and the sinister memory of wrongs and grievances, still unbalanced, lay an enormous vanity.

It was the vanity in him—even in the bitter days—that throbbed with the agony of the bright world's insolence; it was vanity which sustained him in better days where he sat nursing in his crooked mind the crooked thoughts that swarmed there. His desire for position and power was that; even his yearning for corruption was but the desire for the satiation of a vanity as monstrous as it was passionless. His to have what was shared by those he envied—the power to pick and choose, to ignore, to punish. His to receive, not to seek; to dispense, not to stand waiting for his portion; his the freedom of the forbidden, of everything beyond him, of all withheld, denied by this bright, loose-robed, wanton-eyed goddess from whose invisible altar he had caught a whiff of sacrificial odours, standing there through the wintry years in the squalor and reek of things.

Now he had arrived among those outlying camps where camp-followers and masters mingled. Certain card-rooms were open to him, certain drawing-rooms, certain clubs. Through them he shouldered, thrilled as he advanced deeper into the throng, fired with the contact of the crush around him.

Already the familiarity of his appearance and his name seemed to sanction his presence; two minor clubs, but good ones—in need of dues—had strained at this social camel and swallowed him. Card-rooms welcomed him—not the rooms once flung open contemptuously for his plucking—but rooms where play was fiercer, and where those who faced him expected battle to the limit.

And they got it, for he no longer felt obliged to lose. And that again was a mistake: he could not yet afford to win.

Thick in the chance and circumstance of the outer camp, heavily involved financially and already a crushing financial force, meshed in, or spinning in his turn the strands and counter-strands of intrigue, with a dozen men already mortally offended and a woman or two alarmed or half-contemptuously on guard, flattered, covetous, or afraid, the limit of Neergard's intelligence was reached; his present horizon ended the world for him because he could not imagine anything beyond it; and that smirking vanity which had 'squired him so far, hat in hand, now plucked off its mask and leered boldly about in the wake of its close-eyed master.

George Fane, unpleasantly involved in Block Copper, angry, but not very much frightened, turned in casual good faith to Neergard to ease matters until he could cover. And Neergard locked him in the tighter and shouldered his way through Rosamund's drawing-room to the sill of Sanxon Orchil's outer office, treading brutally on Harmon's heels.

Harmon in disgust, wrath, and fear went to Craig; Craig to Maxwell Hunt; Hunt wired Mottly; Mottly, cold and sleek in his contempt, came from Palm Beach.

The cohesive power of caste is an unknown element to the outsider.

That he had unwittingly and prematurely aroused some unsuspected force on which he had not counted and of which he had no definite knowledge was revealed to Neergard when he desired Rosamund to obtain for him an invitation to the Orchils' ball.

It appeared that she could not do so—that even the threatened tendency of Block Copper could not sharpen her wits to devise a way for him. Very innocently she told him that Jack Ruthven was leading the Chinese Cotillon with Mrs. Delmour-Carnes from one end, Gerald Erroll with Gladys from the other—a hint that a card ought to be easy enough to obtain in spite of the strangely forgetful Orchils.

Long since he had fixed upon Gladys Orchil as the most suitable silent partner for the unbuilt house of Neergard, unconcerned that rumour was already sending her abroad for the double purpose of getting rid of

Gerald and of giving deserving aristocracy a look-in at the fresh youth of her and her selling price.

Nothing, so far, had checked his progress; why should rumour? Elbow and money had shoved him on and on, shoulder-deep where his thin nose pointed, crowding aside and out of his way whatever was made to be crowded out; and going around, hat off, whatever remained arrogantly immovable.

So he had come, on various occasions, close to the unruffled skirts of this young girl—not yet, however, in her own house. But Sanxon Orchil had recently condescended to turn around in his office chair and leave his amusing railroad combinations long enough to divide with Neergard a quarter of a million copper profits; and there was another turn to be expected when Neergard gave the word.

Therefore, it puzzled and confused Neergard to be overlooked where the gay world had been summoned with an accompanying blast from the public press; therefore he had gone to Rosamund with the curtest of hints; but he had remained, standing before her, checked, not condescending to irritation, but mentally alert to a new element of resistance which he had not expected—a new force, palpable, unlooked for, unclassified as yet in his schedule for his life's itinerary. That force was the cohesive power of abstract caste in the presence of a foreign irritant threatening its atomic disintegration. That foreign and irritating substance was himself. But he had forgotten in his vanity that which in his rawer shrewdness he should have remembered. Eternal vigilance was the price; not the cancelled vouchers of the servitude of dead years and the half-servile challenge of the strange new days when his vanity had dared him to live.

Rosamund, smoothly groomed, golden-headed, and smiling, rose as Neergard moved slowly forward to take his leave.

"So stupid of them to have overlooked you," she said; "and I should have thought Gladys would have remembered—unless—"

His close-set eyes focussed so near her own that she stopped, involuntarily occupied with the unusual phenomenon.

"Unless what?" he asked.

She was all laughing polished surface again. "Unless Gladys's intellect, which has only room for one idea at a time, is already fully occupied."

"With what?" he demanded.

"Oh, with that Gerald boy "—she shrugged indulgently—"perhaps with her pretty American Grace and the outlook for the Insular invasion."

Neergard's apple face was dull and mottled, and on the thin bridge of his nose the sweat glistened. He did not know what she meant; and she knew he did not.

As he turned to go she paced him a step or two across the rose-and-gold reception-room, hands linked behind her back, bending forward slightly as she moved beside him.

"Gerald, poor lad, is to be disciplined," she observed. "The prettiest of American duchesses takes her over next spring; and Heaven knows the household cavalry needs green forage . . . Besides, even Jack Ruthven may stand the chance they say he stands if it is true he has made up his mind to sue for his divorce."

Neergard wheeled on her; the sweat on his nose had become a bright bead.

"Where did you hear that?" he asked.

"What? About Jack Ruthven?" Her smooth shoulders fluttered her answer.

"You mean it's talked about?" he insisted.

"In some sets," she said with an indifference which coolly excluded the probability that he could have been in any position to hear what was discussed in those sets.

Again he felt the check of something intangible but real; and the vanity in him, flicked on the raw, peered out at her from his close-set eyes. For a moment he measured her from the edge of her skirt to her golden head, insolently.

"You might remind your husband," he said, "that I'd rather like to have a card to the Orchil affair."

"There is no use in speaking to George," she replied regretfully, shaking her head.

"Try it," returned Neergard with the hint of a snarl; and he took his leave, and his hat from the man in waiting, who looked after him with the slightest twitching of his shaven upper lip. For the lifting of an eyebrow in the drawing-rooms becomes warrant for a tip that runs very swiftly below stairs.

That afternoon, alone in his office, Neergard remembered Gerald. And for the first time he understood the mistake of making an enemy out of what he had known only as a friendly fool.

But it was a detail, after all—merely a slight error in assuming too early an arrogance he could have afforded to wait for. He had waited a long, long while for some things.

306

As for Fane, he had him locked up with his short account. No doubt he'd hear from the Orchils through the Fanes. However, to clinch the matter, he thought he might as well stop in to see Ruthven. A plain word or two to Ruthven indicating his own wishes—perhaps outlining his policy concerning the future house of Neergard—might as well be delivered now as later.

So that afternoon he took a hansom at Broad and Wall streets and rolled smoothly uptown, not seriously concerned, but willing to have a brief understanding with Ruthven on one or two subjects.

As his cab drove up to the intricately ornamental little house of gray stone, a big touring limousine wheeled out from the curb, and he caught sight of Sanxon Orchil and Phoenix Mottly inside, evidently just leaving Ruthven.

His smiling and very cordial bow was returned coolly by Orchil, and apparently not observed at all by Mottly. He sat a second in his cab, motionless, the obsequious smile still stencilled on his flushed face; then the flush darkened; he got out of his cab and, bidding the man wait, rang at the house of Ruthven.

Admitted, it was a long while before he was asked to mount the carved stairway of stone. And when he did, on every step, hand on the bronze rail, he had the same curious sense of occult resistance to his physical progress; the same instinct of a new element arising into the scheme of things the properties of which he felt a sudden fierce desire to test and comprehend.

Ruthven in a lounging suit of lilac silk, sashed in with flexible silver, stood with his back to the door as Neergard was announced; and even after he was announced Ruthven took his time to turn and stare and nod with a deliberate negligence that accented the affront.

Neergard sat down; Ruthven gazed out of the window, then, soft thumbs hooked in his sash, turned leisurely in impudent interrogation.

"What the hell is the matter with you?" asked Neergard, for the subtle something he had been encountering all day had suddenly seemed to wall him out of all he had conquered, forcing him back into the simpler sordid territory where ways and modes of speech were more familiar to him—where the spontaneous crudity of expression belonged among the husks of all he had supposed discarded for ever.

"Really," observed Ruthven, staring at the seated man, "I scarcely understand your remark."

"Well, you'll understand it perhaps when I choose to explain it," said Neergard. "I see there's some trouble somewhere. What is it? What's the matter with Orchil, and that hatchet-faced beagle-pup, Mottly? *Is* there anything the matter, Jack?"

"Nothing important," said Ruthven with an intonation which troubled Neergard. "Did you come here to—ah—ask anything of me? Very glad to do anything, I'm sure."

"Are you? Well, then, I want a card to the Orchils'."

Ruthven raised his brows slightly; and Neergard waited, then repeated his demand.

Ruthven began to explain, rather languidly, that it was impossible; but—"I want it," insisted the other doggedly.

"I can't be of any service to you in this instance."

"Oh, yes, I think you can. I tell you I want that card. Do you understand plain speech?"

"Ya-as," drawled Ruthven, seating himself a trifle wearily among his cushions, "but yours is so—ah—very plain—quite elemental, you know. You ask for a bid to the Orchils'; I tell you quite seriously I can't secure one for you."

"You'd better think it over," said Neergard menacingly.

"Awfully sorry."

"You mean you won't?"

"Ah—quite so."

Neergard's thin nose grew white and tremulous:

"Why?"

"You insist?" in mildly bored deprecation.

"Yes, I insist. Why can't you—or why won't you?"

"Well, if you really insist, they—ah—don't want you, Neergard."

"Who—why—how do you happen to know that they don't? Is this some petty spite of that young cub, Gerald? Or"—and he almost looked at Ruthven—"is this some childish whim of yours?"

"Oh, really now—"

"Yes, really now," sneered Neergard, "you'd better tell me. And you'd better understand, now, once for all, just exactly what I've outlined for myself—so you can steer clear of the territory I operate in." He clasped his blunt fingers and leaned forward, projecting his whole body, thick legs curled under; but his close-set eyes still looked past Ruthven.

"I need a little backing," he said, "but I can get along without it. And what I'm going to do is to marry Miss Orchil. Now you know; now you understand. I don't care a damn about the Erroll boy; and I think I'll discount right now any intentions of any married man to bother Miss

308

Orchil after some Dakota decree frees him from the woman whom he's driven into an asylum."

Ruthven looked at him curiously:

"So that is discounted, is it?"

"I think so," nodded Neergard. "I don't think that man will try to obtain a divorce until I say the word."

"Oh! Why not?"

"Because of my knowledge concerning that man's crooked methods in obtaining for me certain options that meant ruin to his own country club," said Neergard coolly.

"I see. How extraordinary! But the club has bought in all that land, hasn't it?"

"Yes—but the stench of your treachery remains, my friend."

"Not treachery, only temptation," observed Ruthven blandly. "I've talked it all over with Orchil and Mottly—"

"You—*what*!" gasped Neergard.

"Talked about it," repeated Ruthven, hard face guileless, and raising his eyebrows—a dreadful caricature of youth in the misleading smoothness of the minutely shaven face; "I told Orchil what you persuaded me to do—"

"You—you damned—"

"Not at all, not at all!" protested Ruthven, languidly settling himself once more among the cushions. "And by the way," he added, "there's a law— by-law—something or other, that I understand may interest you"—he looked up at Neergard, who had sunk back in his chair—"about unpaid assessments—"

Neergard now for the first time was looking directly at him.

"Unpaid assessments," repeated Ruthven. "It's a, detail—a law—never enforced unless we—ah—find it convenient to rid ourselves of a member. It's rather useful, you see, in such a case—a technical pretext, you know. . . . I forget the exact phrasing; something about' ceases to retain his membership, and such shares of stock as he may own in the said club shall be appraised and delivered to the treasurer upon receipt of the value'—or something like that."

Still Neergard looked at him, hunched up in his chair, chin sunk on his chest.

"Thought it just as well to mention it," said Ruthven blandly, "as they've seen fit to take advantage of the—ah—opportunity—under legal advice.

You'll hear from the secretary, I fancy—Mottly, you know. . . .*Is there anything more, Neergard?*"

Neergard scarcely heard him. He had listened, mechanically, when told in as many words that he had been read out of the Siowitha Club; he understood that he stood alone, discarded, disgraced, with a certain small coterie of wealthy men implacably hostile to him. But it was not that which occupied him: he was face to face with the new element of which he had known nothing—the subtle, occult resistance to himself and his personality, all that he represented, embodied, stood for, hoped for.

And for the first time he realised that among the ruthless, no ruthlessness was permitted him; among the reckless, circumspection had been required of him; no arrogance, no insolence had been permitted him among the arrogant and insolent; for, when such as he turned threateningly upon one of those belonging to that elemental matrix of which he dared suppose himself an integral part, he found that he was mistaken. Danger to one from such as he endangered their common caste—such as it was. And, silently, subtly, all through that portion of the social fabric, he became slowly sensible of resistance— resistance everywhere, from every quarter.

Now, hunched up there in his chair, he began to understand. If Ruthven had been a blackguard—it was not for him to punish him—no, not even threaten to expose him. His own caste would take care of that; his own sort would manage such affairs. Meanwhile Neergard had presumed to annoy them, and the society into which he had forced himself and which he had digestively affected, was now, squid-like, slowly turning itself inside out to expel him as a foreign substance from which such unimportant nutrition as he had afforded had been completely extracted.

He looked at Ruthven, scarcely seeing him. Finally he gathered his thick legs under to support him as he rose, stupidly, looking about for his hat.

Ruthven rang for a servant; when he came Neergard followed him without a word, small eyes vacant, the moisture powdering the ridge of his nose, his red blunt hands dangling as he walked. Behind him a lackey laughed.

In due time Neergard, who still spent his penny on a morning paper, read about the Orchil ball. There were three columns and several pictures. He read all there was to read about—the sickeningly minute details of jewels and costumes, the sorts of stuffs served at supper, the cotillon, the favours—then, turning back, he read about the dozen-odd separate hostesses who had entertained the various coteries and sets at separate dinners before the ball—read every item, every name, to the last imbecile period.

Then he rose wearily, and started downtown to see what his lawyers could do toward reinstating him in a club that had expelled him—to find out if there remained the slightest trace of a chance in the matter. But even as he went he knew there could be none. The squid had had its will with him, not he with the squid; and within him rose again all the old hatred and fear of these people from whom he had desired to extract full payment for the black days of need he had endured, for the want, the squalor, the starvation he had passed through.

But the reckoning left him where he had started—save for the money they had used when he forced it on them—not thanking him.

So he went to his lawyers—every day for a while, then every week, then, toward the end of winter, less often, for he had less time now, and there was a new pressure which he was beginning to feel vaguely hostile to him in his business enterprises—hitches in the negotiations of loans, delays, perhaps accidental, but annoying; changes of policy in certain firms who no longer cared to consider acreage as investment; and a curiously veiled antagonism to him in a certain railroad, the reorganisation of which he had dared once to aspire to.

And one day, sitting alone in his office, a clerk brought him a morning paper with one column marked in a big blue-pencilled oval.

It was only about a boy and a girl who had run away and married because they happened to be in love, although their parents had prepared other plans for their separate disposal. The column was a full one, the heading in big type—a good deal of pother about a boy and a girl, after all, particularly as it appeared that their respective families had determined to make the best of it. Besides, the girl's parents had other daughters growing up; and the prettiest of American duchesses would no doubt remain amiable. As for the household cavalry, probably some of them were badly in need of forage, but that thin red line could hold out until the younger sisters shed pinafores. So, after all, in spite of double leads and the full column, the runaways could continue their impromptu honeymoon without fear of parents, duchess, or a rescue charge from that thin, red, and impecunious line.

It took Neergard all day to read that column before he folded it away and pigeonholed it among a lot of dusty documents—uncollected claims, a memorandum of a deal with Ruthven, a note from an actress, and the papers in his case against the Siowitha Club which would never come to a suit—he knew it now—never amount to anything. So among these archives of dead desires, dead hopes, and of vengeance deferred *sine die*, he laid away the soiled newspaper.

311

Then he went home, very tired with a mental lassitude that depressed him and left him drowsy in his great arm-chair before the grate—too drowsy and apathetic to examine the letters and documents laid out for him by his secretary, although one of them seemed to be important— something about alienation of affections, something about a yacht and Mrs. Ruthven, and a heavy suit to be brought unless other settlement was suggested as a balm to Mr. Ruthven.

To dress for dinner was an effort—a purely mechanical operation which was only partly successful, although his man aided him. But he was too tired to continue the effort; and at last it was his man alone who disembarrassed him of his heavy clothing and who laid him among the bedclothes, where he sank back, relaxed, breathing loudly in the dreadful depressed stupor of utter physical and neurotic prostration.

Meaningless to him the hurriedly intrusive attorneys—his own and Ruthven's—who forced their way in that night—or was it the next, or months later? A weight like the weight of death lay on him, mind and body. If he comprehended what threatened, what was coming, he did not care. The world passed on, leaving him lying there, nerveless, exhausted, a derelict on a sea too stormy for such as he—a wreck that might have sailed safely in narrower waters.

And some day he'd be patched up and set afloat once more to cruise and operate and have his being in the safer and smaller seas; some day, when the nerve crash had subsided and the slow, wounded mind came back to itself, and its petty functions were once more resumed—its envious scheming, its covetous capability, its vicious achievement. For with him achievement could embody only the meaner imitations of the sheer colossal *coups* by which the great financiers gutted a nation with kid-gloved fingers, and changed their gloves after the operation so that no blood might stick to Peter's pence or smear the corner-stones of those vast and shadowy institutions upreared in restitution—black silhouettes against the infernal sunset of lives that end in the shadowy death of souls.

Even before Neergard's illness Ruthven's domestic and financial affairs were in a villainous mess. Rid of Neergard, he had meant to deal him a crashing blow at the breakaway which would settle him for ever and incidentally bring to a crisis his own status in regard to his wife.

Whether or not his wife was mentally competent he did not know; he did not know anything about her. But he meant to. Selwyn's threat, still fairly fresh in his memory, had given him no definite idea of Alixe, her whereabouts, her future plans, and whether or not her mental condition was supposed to be permanently impaired or otherwise.

That she had been, and probably now was, under Selwyn's protection he believed; what she and Selwyn intended to do he did not know. But he wanted to know; he dared not ask Selwyn—dared not, because he was horribly afraid of Selwyn; dared not yet make a legal issue of their relations, of her sequestration, or of her probable continued infirmity, because of his physical fear of the man.

But there was—or he thought that there had been—one way to begin the matter, because the matter must sooner or later be begun: and that was to pretend to assume Neergard responsible; and, on the strength of his wife's summer sojourn aboard the *Niobrara*, turn on Neergard and demand a reckoning which he believed Selwyn would never hear of, because he did not suppose Neergard dared defend the suit, and would sooner or later compromise. Which would give him what he wanted to begin with, money, and the entering wedge against the wife he meant to be rid of in one way or another, even if he had to swear out a warrant against Selwyn before he demanded a commission to investigate her mental condition.

Ruthven was too deadly afraid of Selwyn to begin suit at that stage of the proceedings. All he could do was to start, through his attorneys, a search for his wife, and meanwhile try to formulate some sort of definite plan in regard to Gladys Orchil; for if that featherbrained youngster went abroad in the spring he meant to follow her and not only have the Atlantic between him and Selwyn when he began final suit for freedom, but also be in a position to ride off any of the needy household cavalry who might come caracolling and cavorting too close to the young girl he had selected to rehabilitate the name, fortune, and house of Ruthven.

This, in brief, was Ruthven's general scheme of campaign; and the entire affair had taken some sort of shape, and was slowly beginning to move, when Neergard's illness came as an absolute check, just as the first papers were about to be served on him.

There was nothing to do but wait until Neergard got well, because his attorneys simply scoffed at any suggestion of settlement *ex curia*, and Ruthven didn't want a suit involving his wife's name while he and Selwyn were in the same hemisphere.

But he could still continue an unobtrusive search for the whereabouts of his wife, which he did. And the chances were that his attorneys would find her without great difficulty, because Selwyn had not the slightest suspicion that he was being followed.

In these days Selwyn's life was methodical and colourless in its routine to the verge of dreariness.

313

When he was not at the Government proving grounds on Sandy Hook he remained in his room at Lansing's, doggedly forcing himself into the only alternate occupation sufficient to dull the sadness of his mind—the preparation of a history of British military organisation in India, and its possible application to present conditions in the Philippines.

He had given up going out—made no further pretense; and Boots let him alone.

Once a week he called at the Gerards', spending most of his time while there with the children. Sometimes he saw Nina and Eileen, usually just returned or about to depart for some function; and his visit, as a rule, ended with a cup of tea alone with Austin, and a quiet cigar in the library, where Kit-Ki sat, paws folded under, approving of the fireside warmth in a pleasureable monotone.

On such evenings, late, if Nina and Eileen had gone to a dance, or to the opera with Boots, Austin, ruddy with well-being and shamelessly slippered, stretched luxuriously in the fire warmth, lazily discussing what was nearest to him—his children and wife, and the material comfort which continued to attend him with the blessing of that heaven which seems so largely occupied in fulfilling the desires of the good for their own commercial prosperity.

Too, he had begun to show a peculiar pride in the commercial development of Gerald, speaking often of his gratifying application to business, the stability of his modest position, the friends he was making among men of substance, their regard for him.

"Not that the boy is doing much of a business yet," he would say with a tolerant shrug of his big fleshy shoulders, "but he's laying the foundation for success—a good, upright, solid foundation—with the doubtful scheming of Neergard left out"—at that time Neergard had not yet gone to pieces, physically—"and I expect to aid him when aid is required, and to extend to him, judiciously, such assistance, from time to time, as I think he may require. . . . There's one thing—"

Austin puffed once or twice at his cigar and frowned; and Selwyn, absently watching the dying embers on the hearth, waited in silence.

"One thing," repeated Austin, reaching for the tongs and laying a log of white birch across the coals; "and that is Gerald's fondness for pretty girls. . . . Not that it isn't all right, too, but I hope he isn't going to involve himself—hang a millstone around his neck before he can see his way clear to some promise of a permanent income based on—"

"Pooh!" said Selwyn.

"What's that?" demanded Austin, turning red.

Selwyn laughed. "What did you have when you married my sister?"

Austin, still red and dignified, said:

314

"Your sister is a very remarkable woman—extremely unusual. I had the good sense to see that the first time I ever met her."

"Gerald will see the same thing when his time comes," said Selwyn quietly. "Don't worry, Austin; he's sound at the core."

Austin considered his cigar-end, turning it round and round. "There's good stock in the boy; I always knew it—even when he acted like a yellow pup. You see, Phil, that my treatment of him was the proper treatment. I was right in refusing to mollycoddle him or put up with any of his callow, unbaked impudence. You know yourself that you wanted me to let up on him—make all kinds of excuses. Why, man, if I had given him an inch leeway he'd have been up to his ears in debt. But I was firm. He saw I'd stand no fooling. He didn't dare contract debts which he couldn't pay. So now, Phil, you can appreciate the results of my attitude toward him."

"I can, indeed," said Selwyn thoughtfully.

"I think I've made a man of him," persisted Austin.

"He's certainly a manly fellow," nodded Selwyn.

"You admit it?"

"Certainly, Austin."

"Well, I'm glad of it. You thought me harsh—oh, I know you did!—but I don't blame you. I knew what I was about. Why, Phil, if I hadn't taken the firm stand I took that boy would have been running to Nina and Eileen—he did go to his sister once, but he never dared try it again!—and he'd probably have borrowed money of Neergard and—by Jove! he might even have come to you to get him out of his scrapes!"

"Oh, scarcely that," protested Selwyn with grave humour.

"That's all you know about it," nodded Austin, wise-eyed, smoking steadily. "And all I have to say is that it's fortunate for everybody that I stood my ground when he came around looking for trouble. For you're just the sort of a man, Phil, who'd be likely to strip yourself if that young cub came howling for somebody to pay his debts of honour. Admit it, now; you know you are."

But Selwyn only smiled and looked into the fire.

After a few moments' silence Austin said curiously: "You're a frugal bird. You used to be fastidious. Do you know that coat of yours is nearly the limit?"

"Nonsense," said Selwyn, colouring.

"It is. . . . What do you do with your money? Invest it, of course; but you ought to let me place it. You never spend any; you should have a decent little sum tucked away by this time. Do your Chaosite experiments cost anything now?"

"No; the Government is conducting them."

"Good business. What does the bally Government think of the powder, now?"

"I can't tell yet," said Selwyn listlessly. "There's a plate due to arrive to-morrow; it represents a section of the side armour of one of the new 22,000-ton battleships. . . . I hope to crack it."

"Oh!—with a bursting charge?"

Selwyn nodded, and rested his head on his hand.

A little later Austin cast the remains of his cigar from him, straightened up, yawned, patted his waistcoat, and looked wisely at the cat.

"I'm going to bed," he announced. "Boots is to bring back Nina and Eileen. . . . You don't mind, do you, Phil? I've a busy day to-morrow. . . . There's Scotch over there—you know where things are. Ring if you have a sudden desire for anything funny like peacock feathers on toast. There's cold grouse somewhere underground if you're going to be an owl. . . . And don't feed that cat on the rugs. . . . Good-night."

"Good-night," nodded Selwyn, relighting his cigar.

He had no intention of remaining very long; he supposed that his sister and Eileen would be out late, wherever they were, and he merely meant to dream a bit longer before going back to bed.

He had been smoking for half an hour perhaps, lying deep in his chair, worn features dully illuminated by the sinking fire; and he was thinking about going—had again relighted his partly consumed cigar to help him with its fragrant companionship on his dark route homeward, when he heard a footfall on the landing, and turned to catch a glimpse of Gerald in overcoat and hat, moving silently toward the stairs.

"Hello, old fellow!" he said, surprised. "I didn't know you were in the house."

The boy hesitated, turned, placed something just outside the doorway, and came quickly into the room.

"Philip!" he said with a curious, excited laugh, "I want to ask you something. I never yet came to you without asking something and—you never have failed me. Would you tell me now what I had better do?"

"Certainly," said Selwyn, surprised and smiling; "ask me, old fellow. You're not eloping with some nice girl, are you?"

"Yes," said Gerald, calm in his excitement, "I am."

"What?" repeated Selwyn gravely; "what did you say?

316

"You guessed it. I came home and dressed and I'm going back to the Craigs' to marry a girl whose mother and father won't let me have her."

"Sit down, Gerald," said Selwyn, removing the cigar from his lips; but:

"I haven't time," said the boy. "I simply want to know what you'd do if you loved a girl whose mother means to send her to London to get rid of me and marry her to that yawning Elliscombe fellow who was over here. . . . What would you do? She's too young to stand much of a siege in London—some Englishman will get her if he persists—and I mean to make her love me."

"Oh! Doesn't she?"

"Y-es. . . . You know how young girls are. Yes, she does—now. But a year or two with that crowd—and the duchess being good to her, and Elliscombe yawning and looking like a sleepy Lohengrin or some damned prince in his Horse Guards' helmet!—Selwyn, I can see the end of it. She can't stand it; she's too young not to get over it. . . . So, what would you do?"

"Who is she, Gerald?"

"I won't tell you."

"Oh! . . . Of course she's the right sort?"

"Perfectly."

"Young?"

"Very. Out last season."

Selwyn rose and began to pace the floor; Kit-Ki, disturbed, looked up, then resumed her purring.

"There's nothing dishonourable in this, of course," said Selwyn, halting short.

"No," said the boy. "I went to her mother and asked for her, and was sent about my business. Then I went to her father. You know him. He was decent, bland, evasive, but decent. Said his daughter needed a couple of seasons in London; hinted of some prior attachment. Which is rot; because she loves me—she admits it. Well, I said to him, 'I'm going to marry Gladys'; and he laughed and tried to look at his moustache; and after a while he asked to be excused. I took the count. Then I saw Gladys at the Craigs', and I said, 'Gladys, if you'll give up the whole blooming heiress business and come with me, I'll make you the happiest girl in Manhattan.' And she looked me straight in the eyes and said, 'I'd rather grow up with you than grow old forgetting you.'"

"Did she say that?" asked Selwyn.

"She said,'We've the greatest chance in the world, Gerald, to make something of each other. Is it a good risk?' And I said, 'It is the best risk

317

in the world if you love me.' And she said, 'I do, dearly; I'll take my chance.' And that's how it stands, Philip. . . . She's at the Craigs'—a suit-case and travelling-gown upstairs. Suddy Gray and Betty Craig are standing for it, and"—with a flush—"there's a little church, you know—"

"Around the corner. I know. Did you telephone?"

"Yes."

There was a pause; the older man dropped his hands into his pockets and stepped quietly in front of Gerald; and for a full minute they looked squarely at one another, unwinking.

"Well?" asked Gerald, almost tremulously. "Can't you say, 'Go ahead!'?"

"Don't ask me."

"No, I won't," said the boy simply. "A man doesn't ask about such matters; he does them. . . . Tell Austin and Nina. . . . And give this note to Eileen." He opened a portfolio and laid an envelope in Selwyn's hands. "And—by George!—I almost forgot! Here"—and he laid a check across the note in Selwyn's hand—"here's the balance of what you've advanced me. Thank God, I've made it good, every cent. But the debt is only the deeper. . . . Good-bye, Philip."

Selwyn held the boy's hand a moment. Once or twice Gerald thought he meant to speak, and waited, but when he became aware of the check thrust back at him he forced it on Selwyn again, laughing:

"No! no! If I did not stand clear and free in my shoes do you think I'd dare do what I'm doing? Do you suppose I'd ask a girl to face with me a world in which I owed a penny? Do you suppose I'm afraid of that world?—or of a soul in it? Do you suppose I can't take a living out of it?"

Suddenly Selwyn crushed the boy's hand.

"Then take it!—and her, too!" he said between his teeth; and turned on his heel, resting his arms on the mantel and his head face downward between them.

So Gerald went away in the pride and excitement of buoyant youth to take love as he found it and where he found it—though he had found it only as the green bud of promise which unfolds, not to the lover, but to love. And the boy was only one of many on whom the victory might have fallen; but such a man becomes the only man when he takes what he finds for himself—green bud, half blown, or open to its own deep fragrant heart. To him that hath shall be given, and much forgiven. For it is the law of the strong and the prophets: and a little should be left to that Destiny which the devout revere under a gentler name.

The affair made a splash in the social puddle, and the commotion spread outside of it. Inside the nine-and-seventy cackled; outside similar gallinaceous sounds. Neergard pored all day over the blue-pencilled column, and went home, stunned; the social sheet which is taken below stairs and read above was full of it, as was the daily press and the mouths of people interested, uninterested, and disinterested, legitimately or otherwise, until people began to tire of telling each other exactly how it happened that Gerald Erroll ran away with Gladys Orchil.

Sanxon Orchil was widely quoted as suavely and urbanely deploring the premature consummation of an alliance long since decided upon by both families involved; Mrs. Orchil snapped her electric-blue eyes and held her peace—between her very white teeth; Austin Gerard, secretly astounded with admiration for Gerald, received the reporters with a countenance expressive of patient pain, but downtown he made public pretence of busy indifference, as though not fully alive to the material benefit connected with the unexpected alliance. Nina wept—happily at moments—at moments she laughed—because she had heard all about the famous British invasion planned by the Orchils and abetted by Anglo-American aristocracy. She did not laugh too maliciously; she simply couldn't help it. Her set was not the Orchils' set, their ways were not her ways; their orbits merely intersected occasionally; and, left to herself and the choice hers, she would not have troubled herself to engineer any such alliance, even to stir up Mrs. Sanxon Orchil. Besides, deep in her complacent little New York soul she had the faintest germ of contempt for the Cordova ancestors of the house of Orchil.

But the young and silly pair had now relieved her as well as Mrs. Orchil of any further trouble concerning themselves, the American duchess, the campaign, and the Horse Guards: they had married each other rather shamelessly one evening while supposed to be dancing at the Sandon Craigs', and had departed expensively for Palm Beach, whither Austin, grim, reticent, but inwardly immensely contented, despatched the accumulated exclamatory letters of the family with an intimation of his own that two weeks was long enough to cut business even with a honeymoon as excuse.

Meanwhile the disorganisation in the nursery was tremendous; the children, vaguely aware of the household demoralisation and excitement, took the opportunity to break loose on every occasion; and Kit-Ki, to her infinite boredom and disgust, was hunted from garret to cellar; and Drina, taking advantage, contrived to over-eat herself and sit up late, and was put to bed sick; and Eileen, loyal, but sorrowfully amazed at her brother's exclusion of her in such a crisis, became slowly overwhelmed with the realisation of her loneliness, and took to the seclusion of her own room, feeling tearful and abandoned, and very much like a very little girl whose heart was becoming far too full of all sorts of sorrows.

Nina misunderstood her, finding her lying on her bed, her pale face pillowed in her hair.

"Only horridly ordinary people will believe that Gerald wanted her money," said Nina; "as though an Erroll considered such matters at all—or needed to. Clear, clean English you are, back to the cavaliers whose flung purses were their thanks when the Cordovans held their horses' heads. . . . What are you crying for?"

"I don't know," said Eileen; "not for anything that you speak of. Neither Gerald nor I ever wasted any emotion over money, or what others think about it. . . . Is Drina ill?"

"No; only sick. Calomel will fix her, but she believes she's close to dissolution and she's sent for Boots to take leave of him—the little monkey! I'm so indignant. She's taken advantage of the general demoralisation to eat up everything in the house. . . . Billy fell downstairs, fox-hunting, and his nose bled all over that pink Kirman rug. . . . Boots is a dear; do you know what he's done?"

"What?" asked Eileen listlessly, raising the back of her slender hand from her eyes to peer at Nina through the glimmer of tears.

"Well, he and Phil have moved out of Boots's house, and Boots has wired Gerald and Gladys that the house is ready for them until they can find a place of their own. Of course they'll both come here—in fact, their luggage is upstairs now—Boots takes the blue room and Phil his old quarters, . . . But don't you think it is perfectly sweet of Boots? And isn't it good to have Philip back again?"

"Y-es," said Eileen faintly. Lying there, the deep azure of her eyes starred with tears, a new tremor altered her mouth, and the tight-curled upper lip quivered. Her heart, too, had begun its heavy, unsteady response in recognition of her lover's name; she turned partly away from Nina, burying her face in her brilliant hair; and beside her slim length, straight and tense, her arms lay, the small hands contracting till they had closed as tightly as her teeth.

It was no child, now, who lay there, fighting down the welling desolation; no visionary adolescent grieving over the colourless ashes of her first romance; not even the woman, socially achieved, intelligently and intellectually in love. It was a girl, old enough to realise that the adoration she had given was not wholly spiritual, that her delight in her lover and her response to him was not wholly of the mind, not so purely of the intellect; that there was still more, something sweeter, more painful, more bewildering that she could give him, desired to give—nay, that she could not withhold even with sealed eyes and arms outstretched in the darkness of wakeful hours, with her young heart straining in her breast and her set lips crushing back the unuttered cry.

Love! So that was it!—the need, the pain, the bewilderment, the hot sleeplessness, the mad audacity of a blessed dream, the flushed awakening, stunned rapture—and then the gray truth, bleaching the rose tints from the fading tapestries of slumberland, leaving her flung across her pillows, staring at daybreak.

Nina had laid a cool smooth hand across her forehead, pushing back the hair—a light caress, sensitive as an unasked question.

But there was no response, and presently the elder woman rose and went out along the landing, and Eileen heard her laughingly greeting Boots, who had arrived post-haste on news of Drina's plight.

"Don't be frightened; the little wretch carried tons of indigestible stuff to her room and sat up half the night eating it. Where's Philip?"

"I don't know. Here's a special delivery for him. I signed for it and brought it from the house. He'll be here from the Hook directly, I fancy. Where is Drina?"

"In bed. I'll take you up. Mind you, there'll be a scene, so nerve yourself."

They went upstairs together. Nina knocked, peeped in, then summoned Mr. Lansing.

"Oh, Boots, Boots!" groaned Drina, lifting her arms and encircling his neck, "I don't think I am ever going to get well—I don't believe it, no matter what they say. I am glad you have come; I wanted you—and I'm very, very sick. . . . Are you happy to be with me?"

Boots sat on the bedside, the feverish little head in his arms, and Nina was a trifle surprised to see how seriously he took it.

"Boots," she said, "you look as though your last hour had come. Are you letting that very bad child frighten you? Drina, dear, mother doesn't mean to be horrid, but you're too old to whine. . . . It's time for the medicine, too—"

"Oh, mother! the nasty kind?"

"Certainly. Boots, if you'll move aside—"

"Let Boots give it to me!" exclaimed the child tragically. "It will do no good; I'm not getting better; but if I must take it, let Boots hold me—and the spoon!"

She sat straight up in bed with a superb gesture which would have done credit to that classical gentleman who heroically swallowed the hemlock cocktail. Some of the dose bespattered Boots, and when the deed was done the child fell back and buried her head on his breast, incidentally leaving medicinal traces on his collar.

Half an hour later she was asleep, holding fast to Boots's sleeve, and that young gentleman sat in a chair beside her, discussing with her pretty mother the plans made for Gladys and Gerald on their expected arrival.

Eileen, pale and heavy-lidded, looked in on her way to some afternoon affair, nodding unsmiling at Boots.

"Have you been rifling the pantry, too?" he whispered. "You lack your usual chromatic symphony."

"No, Boots; I'm just tired. If I wasn't physically afraid of Drina, I'd get you to run off with me—anywhere. . . . What is that letter, Nina? For me?"

"It's for Phil. Boots brought it around. Leave it on the library table, dear, when you go down."

Eileen took the letter and turned away. A few moments later as she laid it on the library table, her eyes involuntarily noted the superscription written in the long, angular, fashionable writing of a woman.

And slowly the inevitable question took shape within her.

How long she stood there she did not know, but the points of her gloved fingers were still resting on the table and her gaze was still concentrated on the envelope when she felt Selwyn's presence in the room, near, close; and looked up into his steady eyes. And knew he loved her.

And suddenly she broke down—for with his deep gaze in hers the overwrought spectre had fled!—broke down, no longer doubting, bowing her head in her slim gloved hands, thrilled to the soul with the certitude of their unhappiness eternal, and the dreadful pleasure of her share.

"What is it?" he made out to say, managing also to keep his hands off her where she sat, bowed and quivering by the table.

"N-nothing. A—a little crisis—over now—nearly over. It was that letter^other women writing you. . . . And I—outlawed—tongue-tied. . . . Don't look at me, don't wait. I—I am going out."

He went to the window, stood a moment, came back to the table, took his letter, and walked slowly again to the window.

After a while he heard the rustle of her gown as she left the room, and a little later he straightened up, passed his hand across his tired eyes, and, looking down at the letter in his hand, broke the seal.

It was from one of the nurses, Miss Casson, and shorter than usual:

"Mrs. Ruthven is physically in perfect health, but yesterday we noted a rather startling change in her mental condition. There were, during the day, intervals that seemed perfectly lucid. Once she spoke of Miss Bond as 'the other nurse,' as though she realised something of the conditions surrounding her. Once, too, she seemed astonished when I brought her a doll, and asked me:' Is there a child here? Or is it for a charity bazaar?'

"Later I found her writing a letter at my desk. She left it unfinished when she went to drive—a mere scrap. I thought it best to enclose it, which I do, herewith."

The enclosure he opened:

"Phil, dear, though I have been very ill I know you are my own husband. All the rest was only a child's dream of terror—"

And that was all—only this scrap, firmly written in the easy flowing hand he knew so well. He studied it for a moment or two, then resumed Miss Casson's letter:

"A man stopped our sleigh yesterday, asking if he was not speaking to Mrs. Ruthven. I was a trifle worried, and replied that any communication for Mrs. Ruthven could be sent to me.

"That evening two men—gentlemen apparently—came to the house and asked for me. I went down to receive them. One was a Dr. Mallison, the other said his name was Thomas B. Hallam, but gave no business address.

"When I found that they had come without your knowledge and authority, I refused to discuss Mrs. Ruthven's condition, and the one who said his name was Hallam spoke rather peremptorily and in a way that made me think he might be a lawyer.

"They got nothing out of me, and they left when I made it plain that I had nothing to tell them.

"I thought it best to let you know about this, though I, personally, cannot guess what it might mean."

Selwyn turned the page:

"One other matter worries Miss Bond and myself. The revolver you sent us at my request has disappeared. We are nearly sure Mrs. Ruthven has it—you know she once dressed it as a doll—calling it her army doll!—but now we can't find it. She has hidden it somewhere, out of doors in the shrubbery, we think, and Miss Bond and I expect to secure it the next time she takes a fancy to have all her dolls out for a 'lawn-party.'

"Dr. Wesson says there is no danger of her doing any harm with it, but wants us to secure it at the first opportunity—"

He turned the last page; on the other side was merely the formula of leave-taking and Miss Casson's signature.

For a while he stood in the centre of the room, head bent, narrowing eyes fixed; then he folded the letter, pocketed it, and walked to the table where a directory lay.

323

He found the name, Hallam, very easily—Thomas B. Hallam, lawyer, junior in the firm of Spencer, Boyd & Hallam. They were attorneys for Jack Ruthven; he knew that.

Mallison he also found—Dr. James Mallison, who, it appeared, conducted some sort of private asylum on Long Island.

And when he had found what he wanted, he went to the telephone and rang up Mr. Ruthven, but the servant who answered the telephone informed him that Mr. Ruthven was not in town.

So Selwyn hung up the receiver and sat down, thoughtful, grim, the trace of a scowl creeping across his narrowing gray eyes.

Of the abject cowardice of Ruthven he had been so certain that he had hitherto discounted any interference from him. Yet, now, the man was apparently preparing for some sort of interference. What did he want? Selwyn had contemptuously refused to permit him to seek a divorce on the ground of his wife's infirmity. What was the man after?

The man was after his divorce, that was what it all meant. His first check on the long trail came with the stupefying news of Gerald's runaway marriage to the young girl he was laying his own plans to marry some day in the future, and at first the news staggered him, leaving him apparently no immediate incentive for securing his freedom.

But Ruthven instantly began to realise that what he had lost he might not have lost had he been free to shoulder aside the young fellow who had forestalled him. The chance had passed—that particular chance. But he'd never again allow himself to be caught in a position where such a chance could pass him by because he was not legally free to at least make the effort to seize it.

Fear in his soul had kept him from blazoning his wife's infirmity to the world as cause for an action against her; but he remembered Neergard's impudent cruise with her on the Niobrara, and he had temporarily settled on that as a means to extort revenue, not intending such an action should ever come to trial. And then he learned that Neergard had gone to pieces. That was the second check.

Ruthven needed money. He needed it because he meant to put the ocean between himself and Selwyn before commencing any suit—whatever ground he might choose for entering such a suit. He required capital on which to live abroad during the proceedings, if that could be legally arranged. And meanwhile, preliminary to any plan of campaign, he desired to know where his wife was and what might he her actual physical and mental condition.

324

He had supposed her to be, or to have been, ill—at least erratic and not to be trusted with her own freedom; therefore he had been quite prepared to hear from those whom he employed to trace and find her that she was housed in some institution devoted to the incarceration of such unfortunates.

But Ruthven was totally unprepared for the report brought him by a private agency to the effect that Mrs. Ruthven was apparently in perfect health, living in the country, maintaining a villa and staff of servants; that she might be seen driving a perfectly appointed Cossack sleigh any day with a groom on the rumble and a companion beside her; that she seemed to be perfectly sane, healthy in body and mind, comfortable, happy, and enjoying life under the protection of a certain Captain Selwyn, who paid all her bills and, at certain times, was seen entering or leaving her house at Edgewater.

Excited, incredulous, but hoping for the worst, Ruthven had posted off to his attorneys. To them he naïvely confessed his desire to be rid of Alixe; he reported her misconduct with Neergard—which he knew was a lie—her pretence of mental prostration, her disappearance, and his last interview with Selwyn in the card-room. He also gave a vivid description of that gentleman's disgusting behaviour, and his threats of violence during that interview.

To all of which his attorneys listened very attentively, bade him have no fear of his life, requested him to make several affidavits, and leave the rest to them for the present.

Which he did, without hearing from them until Mr. Hallam telegraphed him to come to Edgewater if he had nothing better to do.

And Ruthven had just arrived at that inconspicuous Long Island village when his servant, at the telephone, replied to Selwyn's inquiry that his master was out of town.

Mr. Hallam was a very busy, very sanguine, very impetuous young man; and when he met Ruthven at the Edgewater station he told him promptly that he had the best case on earth; that he, Hallam, was going to New York on the next train, now almost due, and that Ruthven had better drive over and see for himself how gaily his wife maintained her household; for the Cossack sleigh, with its gay crimson tchug, had but just returned from the usual afternoon spin, and the young chatelaine of Willow Villa was now on the snow-covered lawn, romping with the coachman's huge white wolf-hound. . . . It might he just as well for Ruthven to stroll up that way and see for himself. The house was known as the Willow Villa. Any hackman could drive him past it.

325

As Hallam was speaking the New York train came thundering in, and the young lawyer, facing the snowy clouds of steam, swung his suit-case and himself aboard. On the Pullman platform he paused and looked around and down at Ruthven.

"It's just as you like," he said. "If you'd rather come back with me on this train, come ahead! It isn't absolutely necessary that you make a personal inspection now; only that fellow Selwyn is not here to-day, and I thought if you wanted to look about a bit you could do it this afternoon without chance of running into him and startling the whole mess boiling."

"Is Captain Selwyn in town?" asked Ruthven, reddening.

"Yes; an agency man telephoned me that he's just back from Sandy Hook—"

The train began to move out of the station. Ruthven hesitated, then stepped away from the passing car with a significant parting nod to Hallam.

As the train, gathering momentum, swept past him, he stared about at the snow-covered station, the guard, the few people congregated there.

"There's another train at four, isn't there?" he asked an official.

"Four-thirty, express. Yes, sir."

A hackman came up soliciting patronage. Ruthven motioned him to follow, leading the way to the edge of the platform.

"I don't want to drive to the village. What have you got there, a sleigh?"

It was the usual Long Island depot-wagon, on runners instead of wheels.

"Do you know the Willow Villa?" demanded Ruthven.

"Wilier Viller, sir? Yes, sir. Step right this way—"

"Wait!" snapped Ruthven. "I asked you if you knew it; I didn't say I wanted to go there."

The hackman in his woolly greatcoat stared at the little dapper, smooth-shaven man, who eyed him in return, coolly insolent, lighting a cigar.

"I don't want to go to the Willow Villa," said Ruthven; "I want you to drive me past it."

"Sir?"

"*Past* it. And then turn around and drive back here. Is that plain?"

"Yes, sir."

326

Ruthven got into the closed body of the vehicle, rubbed the frost from the window, and peeked out. The hackman, unhitching his lank horse, climbed to the seat, gathered the reins, and the vehicle started to the jangling accompaniment of a single battered cow-bell.

The melancholy clamour of the bell annoyed little Mr. Ruthven; he was horribly cold, too, even in his fur coat. Also the musty smell of the ancient vehicle annoyed him as he sat, half turned around, peeping out of the rear window into the white tree-lined road.

There was nothing to see but the snowy road flanked by trees and stark hedges; nothing but the flat expanse of white on either side, broken here and there by patches of thin woodlands or by some old-time farmhouse with its slab shingles painted white and its green shutters and squat roof.

"What a God-forsaken place," muttered little Mr. Ruthven with a hard grimace. "If she's happy in this sort of a hole there's no doubt she's some sort of a lunatic."

He looked out again furtively, thinking of what the agency had reported to him. How was it possible for any human creature to live in such a waste and be happy and healthy and gay, as they told him his wife was. What could a human being do to kill the horror of such silent, deathly white isolation? Drive about in it in a Cossack sleigh, as they said she did? Horror!

The driver pulled up short, then began to turn his horse. Ruthven squinted out of the window, but saw no sign of a villa. Then he rapped sharply on the forward window, motioning the driver to descend, come around, and open the door.

When the man appeared Ruthven demanded why he had turned his horse, and the hackman, pointing to a wooded hill to the west, explained that the Willow Villa stood there.

Ruthven had supposed that the main road passed the house; he got out of the covered wagon, looked across at the low hill, and dug his gloved hands deeper into his fur-lined pockets.

For a while he stood in the snow, stolid, thoughtful, puffing his cigar. A half-contemptuous curiosity possessed him to see his wife once more before he discarded her; see what she looked like, whether she appeared normal and in possession of the small amount of sense he had condescended to credit her with.

Besides, here was a safe chance to see her. Selwyn was in New York, and the absolute certainty of his personal safety attracted him strongly, rousing all the latent tyranny in his meagre soul.

Probably—but he didn't understand the legal requirements of the matter, and whether or not it was necessary for him personally to see this place where Selwyn maintained her, and see her in it—probably he would be obliged to come here again with far less certainty of personal security from Selwyn. Perhaps that future visit might even be avoided if he took this opportunity to investigate. Whether it was the half-sneering curiosity to see his wife, or the hope of doing a thing now which, by the doing, he need not do later—whether it was either of these that moved him to the impulse, is not quite clear.

He said to the hackman: "You wait here. I'm going over to the Willow Villa for a few moments, and then I'll want you to drive me back to the station in time for that four-thirty. Do you understand?"

The man said he understood, and Ruthven, bundled in his fur coat, picked his way across the crust, through a gateway, and up what appeared to be a hedged lane.

The lane presently disclosed itself as an avenue, now doubly lined with tall trees; this avenue he continued to follow, passing through a grove of locusts, and came out before a house on the low crest of a hill.

There were clumps of evergreens about, tall cedars, a bit of bushy foreland, and a stretch of snow. And across this open space of snow a young girl was moving, followed by a white wolf-hound. Once she paused, hesitated, looked cautiously around her. Ruthven, hiding behind a bush, saw her thrust her arm into a low evergreen shrub and draw out a shining object that glittered like glass. Then she started toward the house again.

At first Ruthven thought she was his wife, then he was not sure, and he cast his cigar away and followed, slinking forward among the evergreens. But the youthful fur-clad figure kept straight on to the veranda of the house, and Ruthven, curious and determined to find out whether it was Alixe or not, left the semi-shelter of the evergreens and crossed the open space just as the woman's figure disappeared around an angle of the veranda.

Vexed, determined not to return without some definite discovery, Ruthven stepped upon the veranda. Just around the angle of the porch he heard a door opening, and he hurried forward impatient and absolutely unafraid, anxious to get one good look at his wife and be off.

But when he turned the angle of the porch there was no one there; only an open door confronted him, with a big, mild-eyed wolf-hound standing in the doorway, looking steadily up at him.

Ruthven glanced somewhat dubiously at the dog, then, as the animal made no offensive movement, he craned his fleshy neck, striving to see inside the house.

He did see—nothing very much—only the same young girl, still in her furs, emerging from an inner room, her arms full of dolls.

In his eagerness to see more, Ruthven pushed past the great white dog, who withdrew his head disdainfully from the unceremonious contact, but quietly followed Ruthven into the house, standing beside him, watching him out of great limpid, deerlike eyes.

But Ruthven no longer heeded the dog. His amused and slightly sneering gaze was fastened on the girl in furs who had entered what appeared to be a living room to the right, and now, down on her knees beside a couch, smiling and talking confidentially and quite happily to herself, was placing her dolls in a row against the wall.

The dolls were of various sorts, some plainly enough home-made, some very waxy and gay in sash and lace, some with polished smiling features of porcelain. One doll, however, was different—a bit of ragged red flannel and something protruding to represent the head, something that glittered. And the girl in the fur jacket had this curious doll in her hands when Ruthven, to make sure of her identity, took a quick impulsive step forward.

"With the acrid smell of smoke choking her."

Then the great white dog growled, very low, and the girl in the fur jacket looked around and up quickly.

Alixe! He realised it as she caught his pale eyes fixed on her; and she stared, sprang to her feet still staring. Then into her eyes leaped terror, the living horror of recognition distorting her face. And, as she saw he meant to speak she recoiled, shrinking away, turning in her fright like a hunted thing. The strange doll in her hand glittered; it was a revolver wrapped in a red rag.

"W-what's the matter?" he stammered, stepping forward, fearful of the weapon she clutched.

But at the sound of his voice she screamed, crept back closer against the wall, screamed again, pushing the shining muzzle of the weapon deep into her fur jacket above her breast.

"F-for God's sake!" he gasped, "don't fire!—don't—"

She closed both eyes and pulled the trigger; something knocked her flat against the wall, but she heard no sound of a report, and she pulled the trigger again and felt another blow.

The second blow must have knocked her down, for she found herself rising to her knees, reaching for the table to aid her. But her hand was all red and slippery; she looked at it stupidly, fell forward, rose again, with the acrid smell of smoke choking her, and her pretty fur jacket all soaked with the warm wet stuff which now stained both hands.

Then she got to her knees once more, groped in the rushing darkness, and swayed forward, falling loosely and flat. And this time she did not try to rise.

It was her way; it had always been her way out of trouble; the quickest, easiest escape from what she did not choose to endure. And even when in her mind the light of reason had gone out for ever, she had not lost that instinct for escape; and, wittingly or not, she had taken the old way out of trouble—the shortest, quickest way. And where it leads—she knew at last, lying there on her face, her fur jacket and her little hands so soiled and red.

As for the man, they finally contrived to drag the dog from him, and lift him to the couch, where he lay twitching among the dolls for a while; then stopped twitching.

Later in the night men came with lanterns who carried him away. A doctor said that there was the usual chance for partial recovery. But it was the last excitement he could ever venture to indulge in. His own doctors had warned him often enough. Now he had learned something, but not as much as Alixe had already learned. And perhaps he never would; but no man knows such things with the authority to speak of them.

ARS AMORIS

Nine days is the period of time allotted the human mind in which to wonder at anything. In New York the limit is much less; no tragedy can hold the boards as long as that where the bill must be renewed three times u day to hold even the passing attention of those who themselves are eternal understudies in the continuous metropolitan performance. It is very expensive for the newspapers, but fortunately for them there is always plenty of trouble in the five boroughs, and an occasional catastrophe elsewhere to help out.

So they were grateful enough that the Edgewater tragedy lasted them forty-eight hours, and on the forty-ninth they forgot it.

In society it was about the same. Ruthven was evidently done for; that the spark of mere vitality might linger for years in the exterior shell of him familiar to his world, concerned that world no more. Interest in him was laid aside with the perfunctory finality with which the memory of Alixe was laid away.

As for Selwyn, a few people noticed his presence at the services; but even that episode was forgotten before he left the city, six hours later, under an invitation from Washington which admitted of no delay on the score of private business or of personal perplexity. For the summons was peremptory, and his obedience so immediate that a telegram to Austin comprised and concluded the entire ceremony of his leave-taking.

Later he wrote a great many letters to Eileen Erroll—not one of which he ever sent. But the formality of his silence was no mystery to her; and her response was silence as profound as the stillness in her soul. But deep into her young heart something new had been born, faint fire, latent, unstirred; and her delicate lips rested one on the other in the sensitive curve of suspense; and her white fingers, often now interlinked, seemed tremulously instinct with the exquisite tension hushing body and soul in breathless accord as they waited in unison.

Toward the end of March the special service battleship squadron of the North Atlantic fleet commenced testing Chaosite in the vicinity of the Southern rendezvous. Both main and secondary batteries were employed. Selwyn had been aboard the flag-ship for nearly a month.

In April the armoured ships left the Southern drill ground and began to move northward. A destroyer took Selwyn across to the great fortress inside the Virginia Capes and left him there. During his stay there was almost constant firing; later he continued northward as far as Washington; but it was not until June that he telegraphed Austin:

"Government satisfied. Appropriation certain next session. Am on my way to New York."

Austin, in his house, which was now dismantled for the summer, telephoned Nina at Silverside that he had been detained and might not be able to grace the festivities which were to consist of a neighbourhood dinner to the younger set in honour of Mrs. Gerald. But he said nothing about Selwyn, and Nina did not suspect that her brother's arrival in New York had anything to do with Austin's detention.

There was in Austin a curious substreak of sentiment which seldom came to the surface except where his immediate family was involved. In his dealings with others he avoided it; even with Gerald and Eileen there had been little of this sentiment apparent. But where Selwyn was concerned, from the very first days of their friendship, he had always felt in his heart very close to the man whose sister he had married, and was always almost automatically on his guard to avoid any expression of that affection. Once he had done so, or attempted to, when Selwyn first arrived from the Philippines, and it made them both uncomfortable to the verge of profanity, but remained as a shy source of solace to them both.

And now as Selwyn came leisurely up the front steps, Austin, awaiting him feverishly, hastened to smooth the florid jocose mask over his features, and walked into the room, big hand extended, large bantering voice undisturbed by the tremor of a welcome which filled his heart and came near filling his eyes:

"So you've stuck the poor old Government at last, have you? Took 'em all in—forts, fleet, and the marine cavalry?"

"Sure thing," said Selwyn, laughing in the crushing grasp of the big fist. "How are you, Austin? Everybody's in the country, I suppose," glancing around at the linen-shrouded furniture. "How is Nina? And the kids? . . . Good business! . . . And Eileen?"

"She's all right," said Austin; "gad! she's really a superb specimen this summer. . . . You know she rather eased off last winter—got white around the gills and blue under the eyes. . . . Some heart trouble—we all thought it was you. Young girls have such notions sometimes, and I told Nina, but she sat on me. . . . Where's your luggage? Oh, is it all here?—enough, I mean, for us to catch a train for Silverside this afternoon."

"Has Nina any room for me?" asked Selwyn.

"Room! Certainly. I didn't tell her you were coming, because if you hadn't, the kids would have been horribly disappointed. She and Eileen are giving a shindy for Gladys—that's Gerald's new acquisition, you know. So if you don't mind butting into a baby-show we'll run down. It's only the younger bunch from Hitherwood House and Brookminster. What do you say, Phil?"

Selwyn said that he would go—hesitating before consenting. A curious feeling of age and grayness had suddenly come over him—a hint of fatigue, of consciousness that much of life lay behind him.

Yet in his face and in his bearing he could not have shown much of it, though at his deeply sun-burned temples the thick, close-cut hair was silvery; for Austin said with amused and at the same time fretful emphasis: "How the devil you keep the youth" in your face and figure I don't understand! I'm only forty-five—that's scarcely eight years older than you are! And look at my waistcoat! And look at my hair—I mean where the confounded ebb has left the tide-mark! Gad, I'd scarcely blame Eileen for thinking you qualified for a cradle-snatcher. . . . And, by the way, that Gladys girl is more of a woman than you'd believe. I observe that Gerald wears that peculiarly speak-easy-please expression which is a healthy sign that he's being managed right from the beginning."

"I had an idea she was all right," said Selwyn, smiling.

"Well, she is. People will probably say that she 'made' Gerald. However," added Austin modestly, "I shall never deny it—though you know what part I've had in the making and breaking of him, don't you?"

"Yes," replied Selwyn, without a smile.

Austin went to the telephone and called up his house at Silverside, saying that he'd be down that evening with a guest.

Nina got the message just as she had arranged her tables; but woman is born to sorrow and heiress to all the unlooked-for idiocies of man.

"Dear," she said to Eileen, the tears of uxorial vexation drying unshed in her pretty eyes, "Austin has thought fit to seize upon this moment to bring a man down to dinner. So if you are dressed would you kindly see that the tables are rearranged, and then telephone somebody to fill in— two girls, you know. The oldest Craig girl might do for one. Beg her mother to let her come."

Eileen was being laced, but she walked to the door of Nina's room, followed by her little Alsatian maid, who deftly continued her offices en route.

"Whom is Austin bringing?" she asked.

"He didn't say. Can't you think of a second girl to get? Isn't it vexing! Of course there's nobody left—nobody ever fills in in the country. . . . Do you know, I'll be driven into letting Drina sit up with us!—for sheer lack of material. I suppose the little imp will have a fit if I suggest it, and probably perish of indigestion to-morrow."

Eileen laughed. "Oh, Nina, do let Drina come this once! It can't hurt her—she'll look so quaint. The child's nearly fifteen, you know; do let me put up her hair. Boots will take her in."

334

"Well, you and Austin can administer the calomel to-morrow, then. . . . And do ring up Daisy Craig; tell her mother I'm desperate, and that she and Drina can occupy the same hospital to-morrow."

And so it happened that among the jolly youthful throng which clustered around the little candle-lighted tables in the dining-room at Silverside, Drina, in ecstasy, curly hair just above the nape of her slim white neck, and cheeks like pink fire, sat between Boots and a vacant chair reserved for her tardy father.

For Nina had waited as long as she dared; then Boots had been summoned to take in Drina and the youthful Craig girl; and, as there were to have been six at a table, at that particular table sat Boots decorously facing Eileen, with the two children on either hand and two empty chairs flanking Eileen.

A jolly informality made up for Austin's shortcoming; Gerald and his pretty bride were the centres of delighted curiosity from the Minster twins and the Innis girls and Evelyn Cardwell—all her intimates. And the younger Draymores, the Grays, Lawns, and Craigs were there in force—gay, noisy, unembarrassed young people who seemed scarcely younger or gayer than the young matron, their hostess.

As for Gladys, it was difficult to think of her as married; and to Boots Drina whispered blissfully: "I look almost as old; I know I do. After this I shall certainly make no end of a fuss if they don't let me dine with them. Besides, you want me to, don't you, Boots?"

"Of course I do."

"And—am I quite as entertaining to you as older girls, Boots, dear?"

"Far more entertaining," said that young man promptly. "In fact, I've about decided to cut out all the dinners where you're not invited. It's only three more years, anyway, before you're asked about, and if I omit three years of indigestible dinners I'll be in better shape to endure the deluge after you appear and make your bow."

"When I make my bow," murmured the child; "oh, Boots, I am in such a hurry to make it! It doesn't seem as if I *could* wait three more long, awful, disgusting years! . . . How does my hair look?"

"Adorable," he said, smiling across at Eileen, who had heard the question.

"Do you think my arms are very thin? Do you?" insisted Drina.

"Dreams of Grecian perfection," explained Boots. And, lowering his voice, "You ought not to eat *everything* they bring you; there'll be doings to-morrow if you do. Eileen is shaking her head."

"I don't care; people don't die of overeating. And I'll take their nasty old medicine—truly I will, Boots, if you'll come and give it to me."

The younger Craig maiden also appeared to be bent upon self-destruction; and Boots's eyes opened wider and wider in sheer amazement at the capacity of woman in embryo for rations sufficient to maintain a small garrison.

"There'll be a couple of reports," he said to himself with a shudder, "like Selwyn's Chaosite. And then there'll be no more Drina and Daisy—Hello!"—he broke off, astonished—"Well, upon my word of words! Phil Selwyn!—or I'm a broker!"

"Phil!" exclaimed Nina.. "Oh, Austin!—and you never told us—"

Austin, ruddy and bland, came up to make his excuses; a little whirlwind of excitement passed like a brisk breeze over the clustered tables as Selwyn followed; and a dozen impulsive bare arms were outstretched to greet him as he passed, returning the bright, eager salutations on every hand.

"Train was late as usual," observed Austin. "Philip and I don't mean to butt into this very grand function—Hello, Gerald! Hello, Gladys! . . . Where's our obscure corner below the salt, Nina? . . . Oh, over there—"

Selwyn had already caught sight of the table destined for him. A deeper colour crept across his bronzed face as he stepped forward, and his firm hand closed over the slim hand offered.

For a moment neither spoke; she could not; he dared not.

Then Drina caught his hands, and Eileen's loosened in his clasp and fell away as the child said distinctly, "I'll kiss you after dinner; it can't be done here, can it, Eileen?"

"You little monkey!" exclaimed her father, astonished; "what in the name of cruelty to kids are *you* doing here?"

"Mother let me," observed the child, reaching for a bonbon. "Daisy is here; you didn't speak to her."

"I'm past conversation," said Austin grimly, "and Daisy appears to be also. Are they to send an ambulance for you, Miss Craig?—or will you occupy the emergency ward upstairs?"

"Upstairs," said Miss Craig briefly. It was all she could utter. Besides, she was occupied with a pink cream-puff. Austin and Boots watched her with a dreadful fascination; but she seemed competent to manage it.

Selwyn, beside Eileen, had ventured on the formalities—his voice unsteady and not yet his own.

Her loveliness had been a memory; he had supposed he realised it to himself; but the superb, fresh beauty of the girl dazed him. There was a strange new radiancy, a living brightness to her that seemed almost unreal. Exquisitely unreal her voice, too, and the slightly bent head,

336

crowned with the splendour of her hair; and the slowly raised eyes, two deep blue miracles tinged with the hues of paradise.

"There's no use," sighed Drina, "I shall not be able to dance. Boots, there's to be a dance, you know; so I'll sit on the stairs with Daisy Craig; and you'll come to me occasionally, won't you?"

Miss Craig yawned frightfully and made a purely mechanical move toward an iced strawberry. Before she got it Nina gave the rising signal.

"Are you remaining to smoke?" asked Eileen as Selwyn took her to the doorway. "Because, if you are not—I'll wait for you."

"Where?" he asked.

"Anywhere. . . . Where shall I?"

Again the twin blue miracles were lifted to his; and deep in them he saw her young soul, waiting.

Around them was the gay confusion, adieux, and laughter of partners parted for the moment; Nina passed them with a smiling nod; Boots conducted Drina to a resting-place on the stairs; outside, the hall was thronged with the younger set, and already their partners were returning to the tables.

"Find me when you can get away," said Eileen, looking once more at Selwyn; "Nina is signalling me now."

Again, as of old, her outstretched hand—the little formality symbolising to him the importance of all that concerned them. He touched it.

"*A bientôt*," she said.

"On the lawn out there—farther out, in the starlight," he whispered—his voice broke—"my darling—"

She bent her head, passing slowly before him, turned, looked back, her answer in her eyes, her lips, in every limb, every line and contour of her, as she stood a moment, looking back.

Austin and Boots were talking volubly when he returned to the tables now veiled in a fine haze of aromatic smoke. Gerald stuck close to him, happy, excited, shy by turns. Others came up on every side—young, frank, confident fellows, nice in bearing, of good speech and manner.

And outside waited their pretty partners of the younger set, gossiping in hall, on stairs and veranda in garrulous bevies, all filmy silks and laces and bright-eyed expectancy.

The long windows were open to the veranda; Selwyn, with his arm through Gerald's, walked to the railing and looked out across the fragrant starlit waste. And very far away they heard the sea intoning the hymn of the four winds.

337

Then the elder man withdrew his arm and stood apart for a while. A little later he descended to the lawn, crossed it, and walked straight out into the waste.

The song of the sea was rising now. In the strange little forest below, deep among the trees, elfin lights broke out across the unseen Brier water, then vanished.

He halted to listen; he looked long and steadily into the darkness around him. Suddenly he saw her—a pale blur in the dusk.

"Eileen?"

"Is it you, Philip?"

She stood waiting as he came up through the purple gloom of the moorland, the stars' brilliancy silvering her—waiting—yielding in pallid silence to his arms, crushed in them, looking into his eyes, dumb, wordless.

Then slowly the pale sacrament changed as the wild-rose tint crept into her face; her arms clung to his shoulders, higher, tightened around his neck. And from her lips she gave into his keeping soul and body, guiltless as God gave it, to have and to hold beyond such incidents as death and the eternity that no man clings to save in the arms of such as she.

THE END